FADED NOTES

a mystery
by

TIMOTHY REYNOLDS

I0545439

cometcatcher
press

First Edition: 2025

Cover Image: iStock: Juanestey iStockphoto ID:184336158

Cover Design: Cometcatcher Press

Library and Archives Canada Cataloguing in Publication

Reynolds, Timothy G. M. 1960 -

Faded Notes

Mystery/Timothy G. M. Reynolds

ISBN: Paperback print: 978-1-7380328-5-3

ISBN: eBook: 978-1-7380328-6-0

    1. Fiction 2. Mystery I. Title II.

Title: Faded Notes

Cometcatcher Press

Calgary, Alberta, Canada.

For my mother, Ann, cancer conqueror.
For Sonja Gosteli, because she fought so hard, for so long,
and is now at peace.

For Teresa Swann,
and Tracy Storozuk,
who left their families much too soon.
Fuck cancer.

CHAPTER ONE

The wind off Westview, Washington's Payne Bay was cold and wet and the rumbling late-night trucks across the waterway on Bosun Island were loud, so Franco raised his voice, as much to be heard as to express his anger. His right hand rested on the .38 tucked in the belt holster in the small of his back, under his wind breaker. "You said you wanted to make a deal. I don't deal. What I *will* do, is kill everyone you love, like I promised. Every member of your family, every friend you have, even neighbours you've never met."

"I really wish you wouldn't. They've done nothing to you. *I've* done nothing to you." She was covered head-to-toe in an oversized dark green rain suit with a big hood, so Franco couldn't see the petite speaker's face in the shadows, but he didn't need to. It was a hated face he knew only too well.

"You know *exactly* what you've done. I'll take them out one at a time, leaving you for last so you know what it feels like to have no one left to love you, just before I gut you."

"I'm sorry to hear that, Franco." Her voice shook. "I truly am. I wish there was another way."

The big man didn't see her gun until the muzzle flashed twice from within the too-big sleeve. Fire ignited briefly in his chest before the darkness he'd brought to so many others took him, too.

oOo

ONE YEAR LATER.

Bobby Odini snapped a clove off the fresh bulb of garlic and set it in the middle of the bamboo cutting board on the kitchen island. He picked up his chef's knife and gestured toward his furry audience perched on the tall cat tree near the balcony door. "The not-so-secret secret to my crushed garlic, Vinnie, is two-fold. First, it's got to be hard, which means it's fresh. No old, soft garlic allowed in this house. Second, no salt or oil. Just the garlic." He sliced the clove into four pieces and crushed one with the flat of the blade. "But the real secret to my sauce is a teaspoon of shaved dark chocolate. Seventy per cent cocoa, no more, no less. I'll bet MJ never used chocolate in the sauce when you lived there. She always thought I was crazy. She was more a chili powder kinda girl."

The one-eared orange English Shorthair stretched and yawned, but kept watching, waiting for any tidbits thrown his way. Two old boys, they each knew their role in the reluctant relationship. The rescue cat listened, and the former bus driver fed, petted, administered medication, brushed, vacuumed, and wondered how the hell he'd outlived his daughter and inherited her fat cat.

"Of course, big guy, fresh tomatoes are vital. Fresh—"

The phone rang twice, quickly. The condo's concierge desk was calling. Bobby quickly wiped his hands on his black apron and pushed the speaker button on the phone's base. "Casa Odini. Talk to me."

"Hi. Mr. Odini. It's Tomasz in the lobby. There's a courier here with a package for you, sir."

"Is his truck blocking the driveway?"

"No sir."

"Then send him up, please, Tomasz."

"Yes sir."

Bobby hung up the phone and went back to the task at hand. He finished crushing the garlic, scooped it into one of the little glass dishes next to cutting board, then washed his hands more thoroughly. "Did you order something from Amazon, Puffball? Mouse-scented candles? A bionic ear to replace the frostbit one? I know *I* didn't order anything, so it *must* have been you."

Vinnie meowed his usual denial just as there was a knock on the condo door. Bobby strode over, spun the deadbolt, and opened it. The tall, dark young man in the courier company uniform looked familiar, but after driving for Westview Transit for thirty-five years, odds were good he'd had the young man on his bus at some point in time.

"Good morning, sir. I have a package for Robert Odini."

"That's me."

"It's a registered package, sir. If I could see a photo ID, please."

Bobby picked up his wallet from the entry table and flipped it open to his driver's license.

"Thank you, Mr. Odini." He handed Bobby a tablet and a stylus. "Sign on the line, please."

"Sure thing." Bobby signed, handed the tablet and stylus back, and was given a large envelope a little less than an inch thick. He turned it over to see the return address. It was from the lawyer who'd handled MJ's estate, who was now his lawyer, too.

"Have a good day, sir." The courier left.

"Yeah. Thanks." Distracted, Bobby closed the door, took the envelope over to the couch, and sat. With a heavy thump, Vinnie jumped off of the cat tree and padded his way over to hop up beside his human.

"I'm not so sure I want to open this, buddy. I thought we'd got everything taken care of in the month after Puppet died."

Vinnie meowed at the mention of his mistress' name and rested his chin on Bobby's lap.

"Yeah. Fuck cancer. You'll get no argument from me." He tore open the cardboard package and pulled out a manila envelope. A three inch-square sticky note with the law firm's logo was stuck to it. *Sorry about the delay in getting these to you, Mr. Odini. They accidentally got filed instead of sent off ASAP. Regards, G. Dewar.*

"Well. Now they've got me curious." He tipped the contents onto the coffee table in front of him. "What the hell could they—. Oh no. *A year later?*" It was a bundle of envelopes wrapped in an elastic band. The top one was addressed in his daughter's handwriting. *Dad. Open this one first.* An ice-cold fist gripped his gut and his hands shook.

"I'm going to need a drink." He gently placed the bundle back on the coffee table and went into the kitchen, where he covered the containers of ingredients sitting in dishes on the island. He saw Vinnie hop up on the coffee table and start sniffing the packet of envelopes. "Yeah, buddy. They're from your mama. Someone at the law firm screwed up. Gimme a minute and we'll take a look." He took a bottle of Stella Artois from the fridge, popped it open, and returned to the couch. Vinnie pawed gently at the bundle of envelopes, but leaped back to lie beside Bobby when he picked them up and carefully slid the elastic band off.

Bobby stared at the top envelope. *Dad. Open this one first.* MJ had always had the most concise handwriting, he thought. No, that wasn't entirely true. For the three years she fronted her own rock band in high school, she'd reverted to chicken scratch, but he suspected it was more to fit the image of a hard-ass post-grunge lead guitarist than any true rebellion on her part. He wondered what her fellow members of *SnarkPuppet* thought when she went off to Seaway College to study criminology. Like Vinnie, he gave the envelope a sniff, as if there would be a whiff of his daughter's scent a year after her death. It was probably his imagination, but he was sure there was. "Damn." He wiped an errant tear with the back of his hand.

"You'd think I'd have gotten used to this when her mother died." He sighed, took a breath, and slid the letter out of the envelope. It was just a single page of printer paper, not fancy stationary. He opened it, afraid. If he didn't read the letters, then it would be like a piece of his baby girl was still alive, waiting for him just around the corner. But if he *didn't* read them, then he would be missing out on what were probably some of his daughter's last words. There was no way he could just let them sit, unread, the words uncherished. The first one was just a short note. The handwriting was wobbly. The date at the top was two days before she died. He read on, his hand trembling slightly.

Daddy, I'm scared. I thought I was ready, but I'm not. This is my last note, though. My last letter to the only man I've ever truly loved. But I said all the mushy stuff in the letters before this one, which you'll get to in due time, in the proper order. I wanted you to read this one first because my new partner, Sam—the detective taking over for me—just left. He'd come by to show me a piece of evidence from the last case I worked. I'm not supposed to tell you this, but what can they do to me? Suspend my dead ass? Haha.

Anyway, the victim in the murder is a suspect in over a hundred contract killings in the Pacific Northwest over the last thirty-five years. He didn't exactly keep a diary, but he kept a ledger with dates, times, and cities listed. No names, no details, though. The thing that got my attention is that on the second page there's an entry I know. "February 6th, 1990. 2am. Banff." Yeah, I know you recognize it, too. That's wasn't just Mom's birthday, it was the date, time, and place where Auntie Marion was murdered. Dad... I think this piece-of-shit killer-for-hire, Franco Vetere, may have killed your sister thirty years ago. It doesn't make any sense, but at the same time it does, *because her killer was never caught.*

I'm sorry I won't be around to hunt down the bastard who hired Vetere, but talk to Sam Hernandez in Homicide. He's taken over the case. Show him this letter. Get him to look into it.

I'm so goddammed tired. I have to sign off. Talk to Sam—his card is in the envelope. And go back and read the letters in order. Please.

I love you with all my heart, Daddy. I'll give Mom your love when I see her.

Your bella Marionette.

Bobby slowly folded the letter up, pressed it hard to his heart, and wept.

o0o

When he took early retirement a week after his fifty-ninth birthday the previous year, Bobby quickly discovered the joy and value of afternoon naps. He was hardly old, and except for his worn-out hips and knees, and a bit of a pot belly, he was in pretty good shape for a sixty-year-old who'd spent more than half his life bouncing up and down in the driver's seat of a city bus. But when MJ got her diagnosis a month later and the inflammatory breast cancer progressed so damned fast, he was by her side as much as he could be, and it was exhausting. He discovered pretty quickly that he was no longer the young man he'd been when his wife had faced her own battle with the disease. Back then, with the help of his mother, he had worked, cared for Betty, and cared for six-year-old MJ. Naps were out of the question.

He slept on the couch, with Vinnie stretched out on his legs, purring. Once the tears started, the cat was right there with him. The orange beast was a mean-looking bastard, but he had a heart of gold, for a cat.

o0o

As it usually did, the nap recharged Bobby's internal battery and he woke up with a purpose. He also woke up with no feeling below his knees, his circulation cut off by Vinnie's fifteen pounds of hyperthyroid fat and fur. "Okay fur ball, up and at 'em." He gently but firmly pushed the cat until he reluctantly climbed off and wandered away with a short protest 'mrow'. "Yeah, well we have—" The blood flowed back into his legs and his calves and feet caught on fire. "*Goddammit*! Ow! Ow! Ow!" Swinging around to sit up, he put his feet flat on the floor but was afraid to stand up until the pain subsided. "Holy crap, cat! Are you trying to cripple me?" The sharp tingling continued, so he cringed and waited. He picked up the nearly full beer, but it had lost its chill long ago. "Screw it." He took a swig and swallowed with a grimace. "Never mind. Put the coffee on, Vinnie. The beer is dead."

Vinnie meowed at the sound of his name, and Bobby chuckled. Then he saw the stack of envelopes again. He kissed two fingertips and touched them to the stack. "We'll get to the bottom of this, Puppet." He shook the detective's card out of the envelope, and slipped it into his shirt pocket. "Let's finish up this sauce, get it put away, and we'll give the man a call.

o0o

"I'll see what I can do, Mr. Odini. Since your sister was an American citizen who died abroad, the State Department's Bureau of Consular Affairs would have handled communications and been kept up-to-date with regards to the RCMP investigation in Banff; but to be honest, the FBI is most likely to have copies of any and all reports. I'll get in touch with my contact at their main office here in town and see what he can dig up."

"I appreciate that, Detective. I know it's an old case, but if this connection is solid..."

"I understand. It's odd, but I can see where MJ was heading with it. If you don't hear from me one way or another in a week, give me a call and I'll see what other trees I can shake."

"Thanks. I don't suppose you could email me something about this guy, your victim?" Bobby already knew the answer, but if he didn't ask, he'd never know.

"I'm sorry. It's an ongoing investigation. To be honest, though, if you can pull up the Westview Times for the two weeks after Vetere's murder, you'll see they had just about all the personal details we have now."

"Good idea."

"Just do me a favor, though, and don't go asking around. Do your research online or in the library where they have digital files for the paper. This guy was connected to anyone and everyone, including the Curcio's. We're seeing threads leading to City Hall, the Teamsters, and even your very own American Federation of Transit Workers. If you start poking sleeping dragons with sticks, you're liable to get burned. Let me do the public legwork."

"Of course." Bobby knew how nasty contract negotiations could get, but a hit man?

"If you find you can't keep your hands off—and I understand why you might not—then quietly dig up whatever you can about your sister's life back then. Photos, letters, videos... anything that shows or mentions people other than family."

"Will do. I think our stepsister has a few boxes in storage."

"Excellent. I have a lot of work on my plate, but you're Family. If MJ was still alive, she'd be excavating the crap out of this and I'll do the same, whenever I can."

"Thank you, Detective."

"Call me Sam, sir."

"Thanks, Sam. And enough of the 'sir' crap. It's Bobby. Or Old Man Odini, which is what MJ's friends have called me for thirty-five years."

"Just so you know, we all miss her. A couple of the Ds here have been putting together the idea of a scholarship in her name."

"That's...that's wonderful. I think she'd love the idea." Maybe he should start one in her name for a musician.

"Me, too. I gotta go, Bobby. Give me a week, and don't poke the dragon."

"A week. No poking. Done. Thank you." He gave Sam his cell number and hung up.

Bobby fired off a text to his stepsister, Rachel, inquiring about Mar's boxes she'd mentioned a couple of years ago. The two girls had been really close for the five years his mother and Rachel's father—Alex Charleswood—were married, but that was thirty years ago. The marriage ended within a year of Mar's murder, when his mother just walked out. Alex had been winding up running the mayoral campaign for one of his land-development cronies and kept trying to parade her out at fundraisers as the sad but supportive wife. Not one to lose her temper, Sophie simply moved out while he was at some banquet, and had her lawyer file divorce papers the next day. She didn't take a cent from him in the divorce. She just wanted to be free and clear. Bobby wanted to send her an email, too, but she was 83 and he didn't want to bring up such a painful part of their pasts without some resolution to offer her. The questions he had for her could wait until there was a strong reason to ask them. His Mom wasn't weak, but why upset her if he didn't have to? Besides, she was on a cruise up the coast and probably too busy taking pictures to check her email.

He just couldn't get his head around the idea Mar's murder was in any way connected to someone in Westview. The police in Banff had investigated, but came up with so little they unofficially chalked it up to one of the hundreds of transients the resort towns of Banff, Lake Louise, and Jasper attracted. Mar had simply run into the wrong sicko at the wrong time—it's what they had all believed for thirty years.

His phone rang and Caller ID said it was the lawyer.

"Odini here."

"Mr. Odini? Grant Dewar with *Mitchell, Hiroko, & Toffelmeyer*. I'm just checking that you received the package okay."

"I did. Thank you. It was quite a surprise."

"I'm sure it was. I also wanted to apologize again for the delay in getting it to you."

"What can I say, Mr. Dewar? It's better late than never. To be honest, as much of a shock as it was, it's a special treat to get something from my daughter a year after. I'm going to read them slowly and savor them." He wanted to read them all in one sitting, but he also wanted them to never end, which of course they would, eventually.

"I don't blame you. I would feel the same way if they were letters from my brother, who died in Afghanistan. By the way, you may get a call from my boss, Mr. Mitchell—Chaz. He knew about the letters a year ago but lost track of them. When he heard they'd turned up and I'd couriered them over, he was livid. I suspect he wanted to deliver them personally, since he was the one your daughter had entrusted them to. He may call to apologize."

Bobby's phone beeped and Rachel's reply text popped up on the screen. *Come by anytime for key. Am home all day but storage place closes @ 5. Bring your kitty. Anaïs would love to have a visitor.* "Tell Mr. Mitchell it's all good. Or I can tell him when he calls. Mistakes happen, and it's not like someone tossed them into a shredder or something before I got them."

"True enough. Have a good day, sir. Thank you for being so understanding."

"Of course. You, too, Mr. Dewar." He hung up. It was just after two o'clock now, so he texted back that he was on his way, and would bring Vinnie.

"Excursion time, Vinnie." The cat's single *mrow* reply was followed by his thumping footsteps as he jogged out from behind the roll-top desk. "We both need fresh air." Having grown up with dogs, Bobby still hadn't gotten used to the idea of going out and leaving his animal behind. Vinnie didn't walk on a leash, but he was content to curl up in his chest carrier and call out to the world while Bobby did the walking. Vinnie sat by the front door while his servant got organized. Once Bobby had his wallet, phone, and keys installed in various pockets of his Westview Orcas windbreaker, he strapped the harness on the cat and hefted him up and into the carrier. The device was designed to hang in front of him, just like a baby carrier, but it had a clip to attach the harness, and a padded bottom instead of leg holes. With Vinnie secured in place, Bobby swung the carrier over his shoulder. They were only going as far as the Jeep in the underground garage.

Vinnie complained loudly that he wasn't being carried in the usual way. "Relax, buddy. It's a ten-minute drive, then you can get out and visit."

o0o

True to his word, Bobby pulled up in front of the Victorian-style townhome on West Mossland fifteen minutes later. He hoisted the carrier and went in through the private wrought iron gate. His petite, curvy, redheaded stepsister was waiting in the doorway as they came up the short walkway.

She laughed at the sight of Vinnie in his carrier. "You need to teach that fat boy to walk on a leash."

"Are you talking to the cat or to me, Ray?" They had a quick hug and cheek kiss, then Rachel stepped aside and Bobby entered. She shut the door behind them just as a long, slender tabby cat came strolling down the stairs.

"The cat. I've known you too long to think anyone could get you to walk on a leash."

He lowered the carrier and released Vinnie to greet Anaïs. "I'm not against a leash, just so long as there's a studded collar attached to it."

"I can't picture you as a sub, Bobby. You've always been a dom, in my mind." She led the way into the bright, stylish living room featuring windows across the entire west wall.

"I have no idea what you just said, Ray. Sub? Dom?" He sat where she motioned him to while she poured him a cup of coffee from the carafe on the low table. The two cats followed them in and both climbed up on the couch with him.

"Submissive, and dominant. When you mentioned the collar, I thought you knew about BDSM. Still drinking it black?"

"Yes, thanks. I'm an old square who wouldn't know a B from an M, let alone D or S." He accepted the offered cup. "I like what you've done with the place."

"My taste, my ex's cash infusion. Unlike your mom, I took my cheating ex for everything he had. Then again, she's always had more restraint and patience than I ever did."

"You're saying your dad cheated on my Mom?" This was sad news to him.

"Well, no one told me officially, but I always had a feeling back then he was seeing someone on the side. He had too many unexplained weekends away and cancelled dinners."

"All stuff I missed. I behaved like I wasn't even part of the family."

"You were already off and married by then."

"So long ago." The past held a lot of heartache for him, but that's why he was here today. "I appreciate you letting me get those boxes. Do you want them back?"

She thought about it for a moment. "No, thanks. If I haven't looked in them for ten years, then I won't miss anything they contain. Besides, I'll know where they are if I want to have a peek. So what's up? Why the interest now? Looking for something in particular?"

Bobby didn't think it could hurt to tell Rachel the truth. She was hardly the dragon Sam said not to poke. Then again, Bobby didn't know what he was going to find in those boxes. A half-truth would have to suffice. "No. Nothing in particular. I was just looking for some old photos to put up in the condo. I'm tired of the same pictures, and so wondered if Mar had any of the family in the early days."

"I know there are a couple of photo albums in there, so you may be in luck."

"Here's hoping." He raised his coffee mug in a toast, and sipped. "You and I have never talked about that trip to Banff. I guess I was giving you some time and distance from it."

"It's been thirty years, Bobby. A helluva lot of time and distance. What did you want to know? I'll tell you what I remember."

"Your memory is spotty?"

"It's got huge holes in it. You may or may not know that after Mar's murder, I was seriously screwed up. I was in and out of rehab for three years, for booze and coke."

"I remember you being pretty hammered at a few of the family functions, but I was kind of oblivious to other people's problems for a long time. I'm sorry."

"Hey, you didn't pour my drinks or cut my lines, so you have nothing to apologize for, B."

"Still..." He had no idea what to say. He and Rachel were closer now, but they hadn't always been, and when they did talk, they never really talked about the past, only what their current lives held. "How did Mar end up in Banff? She was supposed to be somewhere in Montana for the week, wasn't she?"

"In Whitefish, skiing for the week with some friends from school, she said. When that fell through, I talked her into coming to Canada with me when Sarah Chang got sick and cancelled on me. Dad represented the major investors in one of the new hotels they were building in Banff and it came with a condo for his exclusive use until the project was done. I was heading up there to snowboard and party the week away. Mar was only too happy to join me. Sure, she moped for a couple hours, and slept for a while, but by the time we hit Spokane, she was as psyched for fun as I was."

"She always did recover fast from disappointment."

"True enough. We ended up hanging out with three or four local staff. They're still up there, in Banff or the area."

That surprised him. "How do you know?"

"We keep in touch. We always have. At first it was letters or postcards to check up on each other after Mar's murder. I've been back a couple times. Then it became email, and now we just a have a private little Facebook group where we post memories or whatever's happening with us now. Those letters and Dad's patience got me through rehab. It was a pretty rough few years. A bunch of crap happened back then, all seeming to be one after another. Our folks split up, Dad had his first heart attack." She sipped her coffee and thought.

"How is your dad?" He hadn't really thought about Alex in some time.

"He's still out in Portway, but now he's in a senior's place. His memory is choppy and he thinks it's the nineties."

"I'm sorry. Tell him I say hi next time you're chatting with him, please."

"The phone confuses him, so I drive out to see him every couple weeks. Why don't you come with me one of these trips? He may or may not remember you, but he loves visitors."

"It would be nice. Thanks. Can I bring Vinnie? He loves the ocean."

She looked down at Vinnie, who was currently grooming Anaïs. "Definitely. I'm not sure how Anaïs would do. I may have to try it." Her slender, sculpted eyebrows scrunching together as she concentrated. "There was something else back then, when Mar died. Or maybe a couple of years later. Something big. I can't remember."

Bobby knew exactly what she was referring to. "Betty died."

"That's it! *Betty* died! Damn. Betty *died*. Cancer, wasn't it?"

"Breast cancer."

"Oh damn. And now MJ. I'm so sorry, Bobby." She put her coffee down, stood up, and walked over to him with her arms open. He stood and accepted the embrace. "I'm so so sorry, B."

"Me, too, Ray."

They held the hug for a while, neither caring if the other shed a tear or two. Eventually they released each other and sat back down. Rachel broke the silence first, while dabbing at her eyes with a cocktail napkin. "Did I tell you I'm a grandmother now?"

"I saw your post on Facebook. She's such a beauty. She's Tina and Treyvon's isn't she?"

"Yes. And she is the most beautiful baby in the whole wide world."

"Don't let your own kids hear you say that!"

"Are you kidding? All three of my kids were ugly-as-hell babies. They took after their fathers."

"Then they all blossomed and took after their mother."

"You're such a sweet talker. It's a good thing we're siblings." She winked at him.

"*Step* siblings."

"To hell with the 'step' part. Like it or not, you're my big brother. Maybe our folks were only together five years, but I always looked up to you and admired how you had your life together, and how you *kept* it together even when Betty died and you did the work of two parents."

"I just did what had to be done." And he did. "Mom helped out a lot. It also made a big difference that MJ was the most mature six-year-old on the planet. Some days I felt like she became the parent and I was the kid."

"Yeah. She grew up fast, that one did."

"Like she knew she wasn't going to get as much time as the rest of us and she had to get as much living done as she could in the time she was given."

Rachel nodded solemnly, and sipped her coffee. Bobby drank, too, needing a moment to push back the threatening tears. After a moment, he returned to the subject at hand. "Now that I'm retired, I have more than a little time on my hands, so maybe you can convince one or two of your friends to talk to me about what they remember about that night in Banff."

"Of course. I'll send them all messages. I can't make any promises, though. Thirty years is a long time, especially when some of us have done our best to erase the horror as best we can."

"Hey, anything will be a big help. It's not like I'm going to be able to solve it. I suppose I just want to hear about my kid sister's last days. I'm sorry, though. I should have done this years ago."

"You were busy with life, Bobby. Your wife was dying. Don't beat yourself up. What could you have done that the cops weren't already doing?"

"I never even went to Banff to see where she died. Mom has been, but I haven't."

"Not exactly the kind of trip you take a little girl on. 'Hey MJ! Wanna head up to Canada for the weekend to see where your auntie was stabbed and left behind a building?'"

Bobby flinched. "She probably would have loved it. I think that's one reason she became a cop, and then a detective. To solve her aunt's murder."

"That's sweet, but a little out of her jurisdiction."

"Two state lines and an international border? Just a little. But maybe it's time I took a trip up there."

"Maybe. It's a little morose, but I understand your need. Besides, Banff is gorgeous any time of the year."

"Well, we'll see. I've got a few things I'm involved with here for the time being." Like figuring out what the Westview connection to Mar's death was, he thought.

CHAPTER TWO

T he two of them sat and chatted about Rachel's children and her work for the television station for another half hour before she glanced at her watch and jumped up off the love seat. "Oh hell! The storage place closes in forty minutes. It's a fifteen or twenty minute drive at the best of times, and it's rush hour, so you and Vinnie better get the hell out of here."

At the sound of his name, Vinnie looked up from his place at Rachel's feet, where he'd moved after the hug. She bent down and picked him up. "Holy crap, Vinnie. Lay off the cannoli! You're heavier than *I* am."

"Probably." Bobby took Vinnie from Rachel and slipped him back into his carrier with only minimal struggle. "Good boy." He held Vinnie up toward Rachel. "Say goodbye to Aunty Ray."

"Later, Vinnie." She touched her nose to his and Vinnie purred. Anaïs rubbed up against Bobby's shin, so he bent down slowly for the two to say goodbye. When he stood back up, Rachel was a step closer. "Your turn, big brother." She leaned in and kissed him quickly on the cheek.

"Let's not wait so long before we have coffee again,Ray."

"Definitely." She took a key out of the pocket of her jeans and handed it to him. "No rush to bring it back. I can't foresee me needing into it in the immediate future. You can give it back when we do coffee. Deal?"

"Deal."

oOo

Bobby arrived at the self-storage place on Keel in plenty of time. Winston the attendant—according to his name tag—frowned as Bobby stepped into the office to ask for the location of number 72, but when Bobby explained that he just wanted to grab two labeled boxes and be out of there fast, the young man brightened up. He marked the location on a blurry, photocopied-too-often site map, handed it over to Bobby, and that was that.

The roll-up door stuck half way and when Bobby threw his weight into and pulled as hard as he could, he felt something pop in his left hip. "Damn. I know *that* sound." It took a moment, but eventually the pain stabbed right into his joint and he had to shift his weight to the other leg and lean on the still stuck door. His heavy-duty painkillers were at home, so he knew he was just going to have to grit his teeth and get on with it. "Suck it up, Buttercup. This is why you retired early."

He took two long breaths and did his best to ignore the pain. With ninety per cent of his weight on his good leg, he grabbed the handle at the bottom of the door and pushed down. The door moved freely down, so he heaved it up as hard and fast as he could. It hit the sticky spot, slowed a bit, and then kept on rolling up. Pain lanced through his hip and groin.

"Christ Almighty, that hurts!" The ceiling-mounted light came on automatically, revealing the 8x10x8 space to be one-third full of boxes, an old desk, a handful of lamps with and without shades, and a rack of hanging clothes still in their dry-cleaning plastic. His enthusiasm for the task drained right out of him. "Damn." He sat on a wooden crate marked *Ark of the Covenant*, with a note scribbled below reading *Joking! Grandma's dishes. Fragile. Valuable.* Bobby smiled. "Wise ass kids."

From his makeshift seat, he looked at the low stack of bankers' boxes along the back wall. They were all labeled with the name of someone in the family, including four with *Papa Charleswood* neatly printed on them. On the right side, one layer down from the top, were two boxes with Mar's name on them, just as Rachel had promised. Bobby hobbled over, moving two lamps and easing the clothes rack out of the way. He didn't immediately excavate his sister's last remaining belongings; he just placed a hand flat on her name as if he could bring her back to life just by willing it.

"What happened to you, little one? Who could have done such evil to such a sweet kid?"

No disembodied voice answered him, so he lifted one of the top boxes and placed it to the side, wincing from the pain shooting through the whole lower half of his body. The second box was lighter, so the pain was less pronounced. He took a breath, and steadied himself mostly on the one leg, before gripping the first of his sister's boxes by the handles and sliding it out. It was heavy, which was a relief to him. He felt like his sister deserved more than a paper-light collection of nothings to be her legacy. He gently put the box on top of the old desk, then retrieved the second one, which was only a shade lighter. Unable to resist, he lifted the lid of the second box to peer inside and see what was left of his sister's life.

The first thing he saw was a journal with a photo of a single carnation on the cover. He picked it up and flipped through it. He hated violating Mar's privacy without her there to tell him to "put it the hell back, Bobby!" but his search for answers outweighed his concern for her secrets. Nearly all the lined pages were packed full with the inner thoughts of his sister. As much as he yearned to, there was no way he had time to read any of it here.

"Just about done, mister? I gotta close up." Winston stood next to the little Jeep Compass, smiling, but still wanting to get out of there.

Bobby tucked the journal into the big inside pocket his windbreaker. "Yup. I have a problem, though. I'm having trouble lifting the boxes."

"No problem, sir. Which ones?"

"These two marked *Mar*." He closed the lid of the open box and tapped both of them with his palm. "I appreciate it, Winston. Getting old sucks."

Winston came into the locker and Bobby hopped out of his way and over to the Jeep where he opened the door to the back seat. Winston followed him with the first box. "My Grammy always says that getting old is better than the alternative." He slid the box onto the back seat, then retrieved the other one and put it in there, too. "That's everything?" He reached for the knotted rope hanging from the bottom of the rolled-up door.

"It is, thanks. Watch out for the door. It sticks, which is how I popped my hip again."

"Damn, man. Sorry about that, sir. I'll have them grease the rails first thing tomorrow." He gave the rope a good hard pull, grabbed the handle when it came within reach, and closed the storage locker up. He even locked the padlock and handed the fobbed key to Bobby.

"I appreciate that, Winston." Bobby pulled out his wallet, pulled out a ten, and handed it to the young man. "Thank you."

Winston hesitated only a moment before smiling widely and tucking the bill into his shirt pocket. "Thank you. I'm glad I could help."

"Can I give you a ride back to the entrance?"

"Nah. I gotta walk the aisles before I lock up. Would you mind pulling the gate shut until it latches, after you drive out? It'll keep the winos from sneaking in while I'm making my rounds."

"Will do."

oOo

By the time Bobby got home and carried Vinnie up to the condo, his hip hurt so badly he decided to leave the boxes in the Jeep until tomorrow. He was pretty sure Mar's journal would keep him busy enough tonight. As soon as the condo's door latched behind them, Bobby searched out his painkillers and took a double dose. "If we have to go out, Vinnie, *you'll* have to drive. I'm about to be very stoned and pain free."

The cat ignored him while it scratched in the litter box, so Bobby poured himself a glass of his homemade merlot and retired to the couch to wait until the drugs kicked in so he could stand long enough to make dinner. Two sips of wine in and he remembered the journal in his coat pocket. He levered himself up and limped over to the entry closet to get it. By the time he made it back to the couch, Vinnie was done his business and sitting in the spot Bobby had just vacated. "Move it over, fur ball."

Vinnie yawned, laid his chin on his folded paws, and closed his eyes.

"You're an asshole, Vinnie. I love you, buddy, but you're an asshole." He picked up his glass of wine, limped past the cat, and settled at the other end of the couch. "An asshole." He took a sip, placed the glass on the side table, and opened the journal. His phone vibrated and rang the James Bond theme from his back pocket. With a little effort and a lot of pain, he got to his phone only to discover it was only a reminder of his lunch tomorrow with a half-dozen of his fellow retired bus drivers. The second Thursday of every month, like clockwork, or a bus schedule, as the case may be. He pressed the button to stop the ringing, and put the phone down between himself and Vinnie.

He went back to the journal. The sight of his sister's handwriting thirty years later took his breath away. The two of them were ten years apart in age. There had been a baby brother three years after Bobby, but Angelo died of SIDS when he was only a couple of months old. The hurt of loss had been so bad it had taken his parents another six years to think about having another child. Mar arrived a year later. Bobby was as excited about having a baby sister as his parents were for having her. All three of them spoiled her rotten for the first year, then his father was killed when he had too many cocktails at an office function and drove his new Chevy Impala into a lamp post. After that, Mar was spoiled a lot less as everyone struggled to keep moving forward.

His mother had done her best to keep their home a happy place, despite the weight on her shoulders. Rather than becoming a wailing, grieving widow, she became Zen-like in her acceptance of the tragedies they'd been given, and found a balance in her heart that had always amazed Bobby. It was no surprise she was now eighty-three and still going strong, golfing, running errands for her friends, travelling when the mood struck her, like the cruise she was currently on. Whenever life served her crap, she simply nodded, and moved on. It was her stoic Scottish strength that Bobby did his best to emulate when Betty first got sick, then when Mar was murdered, and finally when Betty died. When his father died, his mom had lifted her chin and lived for her two remaining children, so it was the least Bobby could do for MJ. There were times when he wondered if their family weren't a magnet for death, or cursed, or something.

With all of that memory and emotion bubbling up as he opened Mar's journal, he couldn't help but howl with laughter when he read the first sentence in her peculiar left-handed script.

June 20. Sometimes Bobby is SUCH a dick!

Vinnie jumped up off the couch at the sudden outburst, then wandered into the kitchen with an irritated flick of his tail. Bobby kept reading.

I just got the birthday card he sent, and it's one of those pop-up ones. Instead of a waving puppy, though, it has fake boogers! It's disgusting!

He remembered the card! It said *You can pick your friends, and you can pick your nose, but you can't pick your friend's nose. Happy birthday to the pick of the bunch.* Or something like that. He wondered if it was somewhere in one of the boxes. He swiped at a tear with his sleeve, then took a gulp of wine. "Damn. I'd better eat before I can't get off the couch at all." Vinnie meowed piteously from the kitchen. "Yes, buddy, I'll feed you, too. And we both need our meds."

Not having the energy to make anything fancy, Bobby settled for a quick chef's salad with garlic bread on the side while Vinnie was happy chowing down on his homemade tuna special with his hyperthyroidism medication snuck in. Bobby took his Omegas and the pill for his high cholesterol, and then moved from the dining room table back to the couch and the journal. The place was too quiet, though. He could hear a hum of traffic on the street five floors below, but an uncomfortable hush seemed to have settled within the walls. "Siri, shuffle all James Taylor songs."

A female voice answered him from the speakers on either side of the fifty-inch LCD screen perched on the electric fireplace. "Playing all James Taylor songs, shuffled." J. T.'s cover version of *Up On The Roof* filled the place at a nice, comfortable volume.

"Man, I *love* technology."

The songs shuffled back and forth, filling the home with something other than pain. Bobby didn't read every single detail of his sister's life in her last seven or eight months, but instead skimmed it for things which stood out. Most of it was mundane stuff such as how her exams went, how bad her menstrual cramps were, and her emotional exhaustion with the rain of the last few weeks. More than once she pined for the beaches of Maui or even Southern California.

And then she mentioned a weekend of romance in a bed & breakfast on the Oregon coast. Bobby flipped back to the first page and skimmed it all again. This was the first she'd said anything about dating in—he checked the entry's date—four months of notes.

"This is odd, Vinnie. She just writes *A wonderful weekend together at the B&B in Seaside. He always makes me feel like we were meant to be together like this.* Nothing else. Like they've been a couple forever, but there's no other mention of him." Vinnie yawned and Bobby got the hint. "Yeah. It's late." He put the journal down on the coffee table, finished his wine, then limped his way back to the entry closet. The pain spiked with every step. He slid open the bi-fold door and reached into the back left corner. He didn't find what he wanted so he tried the other corner, and there it was, his old cane. It was nothing fancy. Just a wooden, drug store stick with a rubber base and a crook handle, but it would take some of the weight off. He gave it a try, liked the way it felt, then closed the door and made his way to the spare bedroom for the next stage of dealing with the pain.

Three-and-a-half decades of gripping steering wheels while bouncing up and down had stretched the rotator cuffs in both shoulders, irritated his sciatic nerve, and given his hips a mind of their own. Physiotherapy helped, as did chiropractic adjustment and massage therapy, but when it got this bad, the only thing that gave him some real relief was reversing gravity.

The inversion table in the middle of the room was the best $200 he'd ever spent on himself. All he had to do was lock his ankles in place, then lean back, and the stretcher-like platform pivoted until he was upside down. He hung the cane on the doorknob, stepped into the ankle straps, and tightened everything up. Inverting didn't repair the anterior tear to the labrum cartilage in his hip, but it did seem to relieve some of the pressure so he could sleep better, which is what he needed tonight. Between the wine and the drugs, he wasn't in much pain at the moment, but he knew what he had to do. He leaned back against the frame and lifted his arms over his head. Even that small shift in his weight tilted him back to about a seventy-degree angle. He grabbed the frame with his hands and pulled until he was truly vertical and hanging by his ankles.

After about a minute, Bobby felt things start to loosen up a bit. After two minutes there was actual relief. He closed his eyes and simply hung there, hearing his pulse coursing in his ears and praying to God he didn't die of a heart attack and not be found for weeks. But the last time he was checked his heart was in good shape and he expected it to still be when he had his annual medical in a few weeks. He tried to relax and just breathe. He had nowhere to go and nothing to do except loosen up, and eventually go to bed.

He heard Vinnie's purr before he felt the cat's coarse tongue lick his inverted forehead. "Thanks, buddy. Give me a couple of minutes and then we'll call it a night." Vinnie ignored the request and rubbed his chin right on Bobby's mouth. Spitting out orange fur, Bobby quickly brought his hands to his waist and the motion flipped him back upright. "Darned cat." He bent over slowly, letting his internal organs shift back into position, then he unstrapped his ankles and carefully stepped out of the rig. He felt a bit more solid, but he knew it wasn't permanent. Only surgery would be permanent, and he wasn't ready for that.

Ten minutes later he had the last of the fur out of his mouth and was changed into his t-shirt and sweat pants. "Okay, Skinny Boy, bedtime." He set the alarm for 8:00 AM, and turned out the light. A moment later he felt and heard Vinnie land on the duvet with his usual grunt, followed by a purr-of-contentment.

o0o

Bobby was up to relieve himself long before the alarm, but tumbled back into sleep as soon as he crawled back under the covers. He had some odd dream about him and Mar when they were kids, but when he finally responded to the beeping alarm, the dream slipped away with the night, forgotten.

Vinnie jumped off the bed with a double thump of heavy paws on carpet, and Bobby followed, slowly. He heard Vinnie scratching in his litter box, so he got his own day started with a shower and a shave.

By the time he was clean and dressed in khakis and his go-to plaid flannel shirt, plaintiff cat cries greeted him in the kitchen. Vinnie sat at his empty dish, both his lone ear and his tail twitching in irritation.

"We've been roommates for over a year and you still don't get that *my* shower trumps *your* breakfast." He scooped a large lump of food into Vinnie's dish and in return got a grunt of what he assumed was thanks. "You're welcome, buddy. Do I have your majesty's permission to make *myself* breakfast?" The cat ignored him, his fluffy face too busy chomping at the tuna delight. "Thank you."

Bobby was halfway through his egg whites, grilled chorizo, and veggies omelet when his cellphone rang. Caller ID said *Sam Hernandez*.

"Good morning, Sam. You've got some news already?"

"Hi Bobby. Yes. The Special Agent in Charge couriered over photocopies of the files. The reports of the Alberta Office of the Chief Medical Examiner are the bulk of it. There are also statements from the friends she was with earlier that night and a list of people the investigators interviewed. The RCMP were damned thorough, but there was almost no useful forensic evidence and no witnesses, which makes sense if he was a pro."

"I guess we shouldn't be surprised. If they could have solved it back then, they would have. Hopefully this new link will lead you somewhere."

"Let's hope so. You're welcome to swing by and take a look through the reports. I'll be in and out of the office all afternoon, but I have a couple case-review meetings this morning, so I'm here for the next few hours. I'm in the same location as MJ was, on Fifth Avenue."

"Perfect. Thank you. It's within walking distance, so I'll see you in about half an hour."

"I'll leave word at the front desk that I'm expecting you."

"Thanks, Sam."

o0o

It was a gorgeous, sunny spring day so the uphill walk along Bosun Avenue to Seneca Street warmed Bobby up quickly. He briefly considered driving or even taking a cab to Police Headquarters, but despite the pain yesterday, he felt up to the task today. He used his cane, though, just as a precaution. Since he planned to swing by the bodega on the way home, he left Vinnie to his own devices at the condo. Following Seneca downhill was easy, especially along the tree-lined north sidewalk. He often brought Vinnie down this way on their strolls, so the occasional local who knew the odd couple by sight waved but looked disappointed that the one-eared orange purr-machine wasn't with him.

He loved the mix of architecture in the area with the tall, red and buff brick eleven-story old apartment high-rise now a hotel and his favorite Italian restaurant on the northeast corner of Fifth and Lambeth Avenues contrasting with the modern all-glass-and-angles Watson Memorial Library dominating the southwest corner. Oddly enough, MJ was the one who really loved the older stuff, while *he* was into the way the modern ones seemed to be so visually fragile while solidly making whatever statement the architects were making. He didn't always understand what they were trying to achieve, but he liked the way their imaginations twisted. One thing and he and MJ agreed on, though, were the stained-glass windows of the domed Coastal Episcopalian Church. They weren't the magnificent windows they saw when they went to Florence for her sixteenth birthday to meet her Italian cousins, but the details were lovely.

Deep in thoughts of missing his little girl, he almost walked past Police Headquarters. In through the double grey metal doors, there were ten people in line for services at the front desk, so he texted Sam to tell him he was there. He didn't recognize either of the officers behind the armored smoked glass, so he sat. Since lunch with his fellow retirees at the diner on Stratford wasn't for another three hours, he wasn't in any big hurry. Of course, to actually have something new to look into thirty years after Mar's murder, he was a little antsy to get moving forward on it.

Rachel had promised him some news today about who of her friends up in Canada would be willing to talk with him, and he hoped they could give him some clues that would give him a place to start hunting here in town. Quietly, of course. Sam was right about poking the dragon or the bear or whatever. None of Bobby's family members were truly mob-made, but he had enough cousins who had skirted the questionable fringes of the city's Italian community to know *la Famiglia* got really protective when they felt threatened, and a cornered beast was a dangerous beast.

His phone beeped with a message and a quick squint at the screen told him Sam was on his way down. A minute later a fit, six-foot-tall, shaved-bald, goateed Latino in a simple light grey suit stepped off the elevator and greeted Bobby with a solid handshake and something of a sad look."Hi Bobby."

"Nice to meet you, Sam."

"Actually, we've met before, but it was at MJ's service, so I hardly expect you to remember one guy amongst hundreds of mourners."

All Bobby remembered of that day was watching his little girl's boxed body being lowered into the grave beside her mother. "You're right. It's all a blur. The Pope himself could have been there and I wouldn't have noticed. No one *ever* wants to bury their child."

"So true. My kids are thirteen and nine, and just the thought of losing either of them makes me see red." While they spoke, Sam quickly got Bobby signed in, walked him through the metal detector, and led him to the elevator. "Not that dealing with your sister's cold case is any happier. You've been dealt some crappy hands over the years. I don't know how you do it."

"Some days are easier than others, that's for sure." And some days were hell, Bobby thought. "But faith helps. I have a strong belief in Heaven and knowing they're all up there, waiting for me to someday join them, helps."

"You don't have to preach to this altar boy, Bobby. I have two cousins who are priests and an uncle who is a Bishop. Blessed Santa Maria gets me through the tough days, and there's no shortage of those in this business."

"That's what MJ used to say."

The elevator arrived at his floor and when the doors opened, the buzz of conversation Bobby caught a hint of was cut off fast and sharp. Sam motioned him to step off first, and the sight that greeted him nearly broke him. A voice called out from his left.

"Odini on the bridge! A-ten-*shun*!"

There were maybe a dozen men and women in the open-concept offices, and every one of them stood rigidly at attention and saluted smartly. Bobby couldn't have held back his tears if he'd wanted to. MJ had never married, never even dated seriously, and the force had been her adopted family since the day she started training. Bobby felt like his daughter was just given a 21-gun salute.

Sam stepped up behind him and whispered. "McHale is ex-Navy, Bobby. Sometimes he goes a little overboard."

Bobby managed a smile. "You'll hear no complaints from me. I think it's wonderful. I know how loved she was here." Detectives and support staff approached, one and two at a time, shaking his hand, welcoming him back, telling him how much they missed their teammate. There were four or five he knew quite well, and these ones he accepted hugs from. Sure, it had been a year since they'd lost their feisty Marionette, but Bobby knew some people fill the world so completely that their absence leaves a chasm the living sometimes struggle to cross.

He felt guilty as hell. When she was alive and healthy, MJ would have him walk down here to meet her for a quick coffee or just keep her company at the end of her shift before they went back to her condo for steaks, or his condo for her favorite *ragù alla Napoletana*. Since her death, Bobby hadn't had any reason to come near Police Headquarters, but he realized maybe some of these good people needed to talk to him as much as he needed to talk to them. He apologized, they smiled, one or two handed him their card and made him promise to call, for beers or coffee or whatever. They didn't care which. To them he was Old Man Odini, and he was family. His heart grew two sizes with the realization.

Sam led him over to a small conference room with a long table and two thick files sitting ominously at one end. He shut the door behind him and closed the blinds. "Only two others know why you're here, Bobby. Everyone else thinks it's just for a visit and to discuss the scholarship in MJ's name. Like I said before, I have no idea where this entry in a ledger is going to lead me, but now that a hired killer has been added to the mix, your sister's case is going from cold to hot pretty fast. There are finally one or two big investigations happening across the city I can't say anything more about, except that we in WPD are just support crew for the Feds running the show."

"But it's been a year since this guy, Vetere, was murdered."

"He was careful. He left no traceable connections to any murders except for the little ledger, and it's a miracle MJ caught that one date and place. It was her knowing the one entry led to a confirmed death that changed the focus of our investigation. Since then, we've been digging under every rock to find other strong connections. If your sister hadn't been killed in Banff, but instead here in town, even MJ might not have seen the link. I just wish she were here to do the digging herself. Her instinct for clues was rare, even amongst trained detectives."

Bobby sat, facing the files. "She also had an instinct for knowing what people needed to say, so she quite often just stopped talking and let them fill the silence."

"Exactly. She made silence so uncomfortable that confessions just *rolled* off their tongues." He took a deep breath and pushed one file toward Bobby. "See what you can find. Maybe between your relationship with the victim and my 'super-duper detection skills' as my youngest calls them, we can do what MJ isn't here to."

"We can only try."

Sam smiled. "There is no try. There is only do, or do not."

Bobby laughed. "Then we'll do, Master Yoda."

"Okay. Now, I have to get to another meeting." He told Bobby where they kept the coffee, and gave him a warning about leaving the room with the files out where they could be seen. "If I'm not back before you're done reading, just place both closed files on my desk and put my coffee mug on top. It's sort of our internal signal that they're off limits. We respect each other's space and trust there's a good reason for not wanting something disturbed."

"Will do. Thank you." Sam left him, closing the door behind him. Bobby knew what he had to do and prayed for the strength needed to open such an old wound.

He started with the file Sam had nudged at him, planning to go through it one page at a time. He got as far as the second line of the report where it listed the name of the decedent. *Marion Elizabeth Nancy Odini*. Named after Maid Marion, Elizabeth Taylor, and Nancy Sinatra... according to their mother. Age: 20. Twenty. *Twenty* damn years old and her life was ended by a knife behind a dumpster in a Canadian resort town. Bobby was torn between great sadness for Mar, fury at whoever killed her, and anger at himself for taking so damned long to face up to this and look closely at the murder.

"What kind of big brother doesn't tear down the world to find the bastard who killed his baby sister?" Of course, he knew the reason was exactly what Rachel said—he'd been dealing with Betty's illness and then death. He'd been trying to keep his chin up and a smile on his face for his daughter. Intellectually he knew those were valid reasons, but emotionally, there was no good reason. First to die was his baby brother, Angelo, then it was his alcoholic father, and finally his wife, and the little sister he'd sworn to always protect. The deaths added up, and he supposed he had just shutdown and closed the three doors with resounding thumps.

He had wrapped himself in the armor of going to work everyday, and raising his amazing little girl as best as he could without her just-as-amazing mother. With Mar's death, he'd done what his mother had needed him to, but he'd been on autopilot most of the time, going through the motions while he kept his heart strapped down and blanketed in Kevlar or steel or whatever. Now, thirty years later, he was sitting in a police station, finally doing what he should have done back then.

He blinked, he breathed, he gritted his teeth, and he turned the page. He turned *every* page, thoroughly digesting every detail. The problem was, although there were pages and pages of details, they were useless. There were details about how Mar was found, and who had seen her last, and where she had been in the hours prior to her death. There were photos of her crumpled body made surreal by the flash of the medical examiner's camera. There were lists of nearby businesses, and people who may have seen her and were interviewed in the aftermath. There were scribbled notes in margins for someone to ask someone else about a detail they had mentioned in passing. There were even alibi details for every family member and friend. Apparently, Rachel had been stoned out of her gourd, but the guy she had gone home with had vouched for her whereabouts, and her enthusiasm for their private activities.

Bobby wasn't sure how much trouble he'd get into if he was caught, but he took out his phone and snapped photos of the more coherent witness statements and the list of people the police had interviewed. One witness—Katherine Towne—thought she'd seen a short, stocky, dark-haired man following them from bar to bar, but no one else had seen him and the investigating officer hadn't been able to get anywhere with his queries. Bobby wondered if that man had been Franco Vetere. But Vetere was dead, so how could old reports tell him who had *hired* the killer, and why in God's name, had he targeted Mar? Could she have spoken to one of her friends in Banff about it? Who had his sister pissed off enough to want her dead? Bobby had to admit he really had no idea what he was looking for or what he hoped to gain by reading the reports. He wasn't a cop, and had no training whatsoever.

He kept reading, but none of the statements made by the people he actually knew personally stood out in any way, pointing a finger in one direction or another. There was mention of Mar maybe dating someone, but when the officers had questioned his mother, she had flatly denied it. According to Mrs. Sophie Charleswood, her daughter had most certainly *not* been seeing anyone. There had never been mention of a boyfriend in their conversations. *Ever.*

Reading that part over again, Bobby thought it odd. His mother had always let Mar date whomever and whenever she wanted. She'd never judged her daughter for anyone she might have brought home for dinner or drinks, or just to say hi before racing back out to some social event. And yet, here was Mom shutting down a conversation with the officer investigating the murder of her youngest child. It didn't fit with what he knew of his mother, either back then or now. He snapped a picture of the page, and read on. It wasn't much, but at least it was something he could ask Mom about. It wasn't a conversation he looked forward to, but he knew he was going to have to have it now that the can of worms was sitting in front of him.

CHAPTER THREE

Bobby spent another hour reading each and every word again, looking for more inconsistencies or incongruities, or whatever, but other than the fact his sister was murdered and no one really saw a damned thing, there was nothing outstanding in the reports. To his untrained eyes it appeared the officers had investigated every lead they had from every angle imaginable, and then had pretty much thrown their hands up in the air in frustration. There was even a note a couple years later that they should approach the team of the *Unsolved Mysteries* television show, but it appeared no one had followed through on it. The show was long gone, but maybe something like it existed and could be used. Of course, with a hired killer now being connected to the murder, he doubted Sam, his superiors, or the FBI would go for the idea of mass media coverage.

He was staring at the first page when there was a pair of taps on the door and Sam came in. "Anything?"

Bobby shook his head. "Nothing I'm sure you didn't already see. The one witness, Katherine, saw a man following them that night. Does the description fit Vetere?"

"Yes. To a tee. It was thirty years ago, but Vetere was still short and stocky and had a full head of thick black hair when he was fished out of Payne Bay."

"No surprise there, I guess. Other than my mother being oddly abrupt with the investigating officer when he asked about anyone Mar might have been dating, I found nothing to suggest someone here in Westview County wanted my sister dead. Could it have been a case of mistaken identity? Could he have been after someone else and made a mistake in the darkness behind the shops?"

"I hope not, because if Mar's murder was a mistake, without the killer to interrogate, we have no way of knowing who his actual target was. No, I'm going on the assumption he was after her. Otherwise, there would have been a second body when he realized his mistake."

"Unless he didn't know until he got back here."

"Maybe, but any pro worth his salt would have checked her purse to confirm her identity afterward. It's tough to get paid if you can't complete the contract."

The phrase punched Bobby in the gut. "That's really what it was, wasn't it? A contract. Someone wanted a happy, harmless, bright star snuffed out, and so Vetere did. No questions asked, paid in cash probably half up front and half on completion. A goddamned contract."

"It's been twisting *my* gut, too. Who the hell puts out a *contract* on a student on a ski vacation in Canada? All I can think of is that she saw something she shouldn't have, was in the wrong place at the wrong time. But none of her friends here *or* there could think of anything Mar could have witnessed."

"One thing has been eating at me—she wasn't even supposed to be in Banff that week. Like my stepsister told me yesterday and she first said in her statement thirty years ago, Mar was supposed to have gone to Whitefish, Montana. How the hell did Vetere know where she'd be when her own family didn't know until she called Mom from Rachel's dad's condo?"

Sam sat. "Going on the assumption she was the target all along, he must either have been following her, or someone close to her told him about her change of plans."

"Only Rachel and Mar herself knew."

"So, either Rachel told him, or he was following Mar."

Bobby balked at the idea that Rachel could have been involved. "He must have been following Mar. I can't think of a motive for Rachel wanting Mar dead, and back then, Rachel was so busy spending her money on coke and booze, that I doubt she could have afforded to hire a hit man, even if she knew where to find one."

"Agreed. He had to have followed her from here. All roads seem to lead back to Westview."

"Maybe so, but I have a feeling I need to go to Banff, not so much to investigate, but to finally see where my baby sister spent her last day."

"Sounds like a pilgrimage of a sort."

"That's exactly what it'll be. Better late than never, I suppose."

o0o

They chatted for a few more minutes, then Sam escorted Bobby back down to the lobby, where they shook hands, said goodbyes, and agreed to keep in touch. Sam reiterated his warning to Bobby about stirring things up, and Bobby agreed. As he stepped back out into the sunshine for the walk home, he really didn't feel like he was any further ahead than he had been before he subjected himself to the gory details of his sister's end. He checked the time and saw he had about an hour before lunch with the gang, which left him plenty of time to get home.

As he started off up Fifth his hip began to act up, so he decided the bodega could wait until after lunch when he had the Jeep and could buy all he needed without having to worry about carrying it all for blocks.

o0o

Vinnie went straight for his ankles when Bobby finally hobbled in the door, and the cat nearly earned a smack in the ass from the cane. "Christ Almighty, Vin! If you kill me, you'll end up in foster care, and you *know* how they treat ugly mugs like yours." The cat led him to the kitchen, where Bobby refilled the empty bowl with kibble. Without even a *mrow* of thanks or a grunt of acknowledgement, Vinnie dove his face in. Bobby shrugged and took himself to the couch. He set the countdown timer on his phone for fifteen minutes and closed his eyes for a power nap. Just before he nodded off, he considered cancelling lunch, but he had some questions the group might help with.

o0o

The waitress freshened the seven coffees on the table and left the old boys alone, as usual.

"Thanks, Danica." Greg raised his steaming mug in salute to her retreating back, then turned his attention to the conversation. He was the oldest of the group at seventy-three, but he'd only been retired for five years. "What I *don't* miss about the damned job is getting two sets of contradictory instructions from two different radio controllers."

"Especially when we get snow," Tony chimed in.

"'08 was the worst. That highway coach went clean through the barricade and almost down onto the I-4." Jasbir drove tour bus for ten years before he joined Westview Transit.

"The snow wasn't that bad." Rick shook his head. "'96 was pure hell, with a foot of snow on Boxing Day and then the crazy rains. Couldn't drive in the slush. My bus flooded and they practically needed a row boat to rescue us."

Bobby remembered Christmas of '96, too. MJ broke her arm snowboarding at Snowhaven Resort with friends and he'd had to drive out early to get her. "I miss hearing about lost and found items broadcast over the radio." It was often the best laugh of the day. "Like the purple thong, with the name 'Wendy' stitched in it."

"Or the wallet with $300 cash the week before Christmas."

"Or the four-year-old, back in '04. Got my picture in the paper for that one."

"At least it wasn't a kilo of cocaine like the one Junior found."

"Christ, if you're taking public transit, then you can't afford that much coke. And if you lose someone else's coke, you'd better be on the first Greyhound to Mexico."

"I don't miss being spat at. Little bastard teenagers."

"Teens? For me it was the crackheads."

"Crackheads, and pissed off grannies. They'd either spit at you or take a swing with their hand bag."

"Yeah, and God forbid you defend yourself. Lance shoved one cane-swinging granny back so he could escape her attack on the bus, and she fell down and broke her wrist. Didn't matter that all six witnesses were on Lance's side—he got a three-day-no-pay and had to take anger management. If it wasn't for the union, he'd have been fired for defending himself."

"He's dead, you know."

"Who?"

"Lance. Last week. Pneumonia."

"Dammit. I had coffee with him three weeks ago. He looked like crap, and he was bored stiff."

"Boredom is our big enemy." Boredom was why Bobby was signed up for two upcoming cooking classes.

"You gotta have a solid hobby *before* you retire. Fishing, bowling, woodworking... *something*."

"My hobby is the Honey-Do list Lucy posts on the fridge every Sunday evening."

"She's getting work done on the house and keeping you healthy at the same time."

"Walter got so bored he's driving part-time for the coroner."

"Wow. Bobby, how are you doing in the year since you lost Marionette?" Emile asked.

"Day by day, but better, thanks."

"Fuck cancer," one of them whispered, and the others responded in kind, keeping their voices low.

"Fuck cancer."

"Yeah, fuck the Big C."

"Cancer *and* Parkinson's." Jasbir's wife was in the late stages of the latter.

"Yeah. And Alzheimer's."

They went silent, each caught up in their own thoughts. Bobby decided there was no better time to change the subject. "Do you guys remember the contract negotiations that revolved around paid sick days?"

"Yeah." If any of them would remember, it would be Greg. "I was on the Executive all through it. A couple of the meetings got heated. Someone took a swing at the mayor and the cops got called."

"Who was local President back then? Sabbatini or Jones?" Bobby knew the answer, but played dumb to let the others lead the conversation.

"It was that prick, Sabbatini." Tony ran against Julius Sabbatini years ago and lost by only forty votes. "I swear he woulda put a horse's head in the mayor's bed if he coulda found a horse. He was as crooked as they came. Even the Teamsters were afraid of him."

Emile sipped his coffee slowly, then whispered just loud enough for them all to hear. "I heard from more than one source we got that sweet contract because Sabbatini found a few weak spots on the City's committee and twisted them into submission."

Bobby had heard the rumor, too. "But was there ever any proof?"

"None. For all I know, that asshole started the rumors himself. He liked to hint he was a 'made' man, but he was just a school yard bully from way back."

"I heard he had some young thing on the side for a few years. Some cheerleader straight outta high school, or a college girl."

Bobby hadn't heard *those* rumours. He had no idea if Mar had ever met Julius, but if she had, it might explain Bobby's own mother's reaction to the questions from the police. Julius was married and twice Mar's age, so Mom would have been more than a little pissed off.

"Why're you wondering about an old contract for, Bobby?"

He wasn't sure how much he should say. Then again, these six were hardly what Sam meant when he said don't poke dragons. "My sister was murdered back then, and some new evidence has come up. I was just trying to put the year into context."

"Damn, that's right. Up in Canada some place, wasn't it?"

"Banff."

"How are you doing with *that* resurfacing, Bobby?"

"I'm not sure, Jasbir. I've got a couple boxes of her old stuff out in the car I'm going to go through and see what turns up."

"What are you expecting to find?" Rick leaned in as he asked, his voice low and intense.

Had he just poked a beast? No way. Rick was the most harmless of the bunch. "I'm not sure. It'll probably all add up to nothing."

"Does the evidence point at Julius?"

"Not at all." Damn. Time to change the subject. "It's not a big deal. It was a pretty thin connection. So, anyone going to the union picnic next month?"

Conversation quickly turned to the picnic and the other upcoming events, but both Rick and Karl kept looking over at him as if they sensed there was more to his queries than he was letting on. He steered the topic as best as he could, getting them all distracted by mentioning his hip pain and how he wouldn't be in this year's three-legged race no matter *how* drunk he got. Once he mentioned pain, they all started in on everything that was wrong with their aging bodies and why it was all Westview Transit's fault.

o0o

Bobby leaned heavily on the grocery cart as he limped his way up and down the aisles of the bodega, gathering what he needed for lamb curry. He had most of the spices at home, but lacked the green chili, fresh onions, chocolate chips, and the actual lamb shoulder.

Once he told the bodega owner/butcher, Loc, exactly what he needed, he was sent off to pick up the other ingredients while the perfect shoulder was cut for him. Bobby and Loc occasionally swapped recipes, each trying to surprise the other with unlikely combinations that blended perfectly when cooked *just right*. A tiny Vietnamese refugee, Loc had the fastest hands with a knife Bobby had ever seen, and those hands often had a secret cut to teach the Italian regular customer.

Today, though, the bodega was busy. "Next time, Bobby-Oh, I'll show you my secret butterfly cut for steak on a grill."

"I know how to do a butterfly cut, Loc."

"Not the Loc-way, you do not, Mr. Bobby. Next time."

"Next time," he agreed with a grin.

Loc quickly wrapped and tied the cut on the block in front of him and called to his son at the counter in front of Bobby. "Jimmy! For Mr. Bobby!" While finishing up with the customer ahead of Bobby, Jimmy raised his left hand high and caught the perfectly thrown lamb without even looking.

"You two should get a stall at Lyric Bay Fish Market and put on your own show." Bobby stepped up to the counter and waited while Jimmy weighed and marked the shoulder.

"Not us, Mr. Bobby. We like our own little place. Busy here without tourists watching the show but not buying the product."

"Good point. Ciao, gentleman."

"Ciao, Bobby."

"Ciao for now, Mr. Bobby." Loc flipped two knives in the air, spun a full circle himself, and caught them cleanly when he came back around to face the front, just like Bobby had shown him how to do three years before. Bobby laughed, and went to the front cashier to pay for it all. The painkillers he'd taken after his power-nap were finally starting to kick in and he didn't feel so useless and old.

A light rain had come and gone while he was in the store, leaving the city glistening and smelling heavily of ozone, which never failed to cheer Bobby up. The cheer was drowned in a puddle when he arrived at the Jeep, though, and saw the driver-side rear window was smashed and Mar's boxes were missing. "What the *hell*?" He spun and searched for some sign of the asshole fleeing, but there was no one suspicious in the small parking lot. He walked around the SUV to see if there was any more damage, but everything else was fine. He put the groceries on the front passenger seat, sighed, and called Sam the detective.

"Hey Sam. Someone just broke into my vehicle and stole those two boxes of my sister's stuff." He listened. "I don't know. I hadn't had a chance to go through them, yet." Mar's journal was still at home, on his bedside table, but he wasn't about to mention it on the phone, out in the open. For all he knew, the thief was hiding two cars over and listening, or had somehow bugged his phone. "Yeah. I'll wait here for a uniform. I'm at Loc's Bodega. Thanks."

He disconnected the call, but rather than put the phone away, he photographed the entire scene, including the licenses of the cars on either side, and the locations of the security cameras mounted on the bodega, near the roofline. When he was done, he called Rachel, but it went straight to her voicemail. "Hey, Ray. It's Bobby. You don't by any chance remember what was in Mar's boxes, do you? Some asshole just broke into the Jeep and stole them. I'm waiting for the police to arrive. Give me a call when you can, please."

Expecting to be waiting for an hour or so for the police to show up, Bobby was pleasantly surprised when a cruiser pulled into the bodega's parking lot two minutes later with his lights flashing, blocking the driveway so no vehicles could get in or out. He wondered what Sam had called it in as. He met the young cop halfway.

"Mr. Odini?"

"That's me."

The officer extended his hand and Bobby shook it."Officer Marvin Gaye."

Bobby couldn't keep himself from chuckling. "Really?"

"Really. He's a distant relative, and my mother was a huge fan of his music. Your daughter used to give me grief, too, when we crossed paths. I'm sorry for your loss, sir."

"Thank you." He didn't know what else to say.

"What happened here? Detective Hernandez just said some evidence in a cold case was stolen and asked me to secure the scene until he could get here. "

"Really? It's just a couple of boxes."

"Maybe so, but someone must think there's something valuable enough in them to take a big risk stealing them in broad daylight."

"I guess." Bobby suspected he'd stirred things up and it was his own damned fault. Loc arrived. He stopped short of the police cruiser and the broken glass.

"Mr. Bobby! What happened? Are you okay?"

"I'm fine, Loc. Thanks. Someone broke into my car. Nothing serious."

"Nothing serious but needs police so fast? You were just in the store."

"Must be a slow crime day downtown."

"I guess. I'll go get the broom and clean up the mess. Don't want anyone getting flat tires."

Officer Gaye raised his hand to stop Loc. "Please don't, Mr. Dang. I'm afraid we have to leave it until a detective gets here."

"A police detective? In my parking lot?"

"There's nothing to be done about it, sir. In the meantime, are those security cameras functional?" He pointed up.

"Sure thing."

"Perfect. Please don't touch the equipment. Someone will come in and deal with it."

"Okay. Do you need me out here? Or can I go back in?"

"Please, go back in, sir. When we need you, we'll come get you." He turned to Bobby. "I'll be back in a minute, sir." He took out his phone and started photographing the license plates of all twenty or so vehicles in the full lot.

Not sure what else to do, Bobby took out his own phone and checked his email. Rachel had said she'd send him something as soon as she heard back from her friends in Banff, and sure enough, there was a note containing phone numbers and email addresses of three people whose names he recognized from the police reports. *Hey Bobby. I heard back from George, Katherine, and Tanis. George is happy to talk to you, Katherine doesn't remember much from back then, but says she'll do her best, and Tanis says no way she wants to talk. I've emailed you all of their contact info. Tanis might come around if you ask her yourself.* Well, thought Bobby, it's a start. He'd wait until he got home to give them each a call, but at least he had a direction in which to proceed. Right now, though, he just wanted to kneecap the asshole who stole his sister's stuff. He was less concerned about any evidence and just pissed off that what little he had left of Mar's life was now gone, probably to be burned in a bin or tossed in the river.

Sam arrived and Officer Gaye hustled to move his cruiser out of their way so Sam could get into the lot, which was too packed with curious looky-loos for anyone to move their vehicles.

The scene was secured, the people were spoken to, his statement was taken, and then Bobby and everyone else were allowed to leave.

o0o

As he parked the car in his stall beneath the condo complex, Bobby realized he was too tired to cook. He hauled the groceries up in the elevator, then stowed all of it while fending off Vinnie. He then called an auto glass shop and arranged to bring the Jeep by in the morning to get a new window put in. With that taken care of, he heated up some chicken soup and sat down with Mar's journal again. He hoped that somewhere in there was the clue they were looking for.

It wasn't. He didn't skim this time, but instead absorbed every private thought his sister had recorded thirty years before. It was all pretty mild. In fact, he thought, it was almost *too* mild. It was even boring. He knew for a fact Mar had done a little heavy partying back then, but there was no mention of even a dinner party, which made Bobby wonder if maybe there was a second journal, or Mar had simply not wanted to commit that part of her life to paper.

That's something he fully understood. He himself had never got into the habit of keeping a journal. He'd had to do it for a month in high school, but that was enough. More than once over the years he wondered if he should write down some of the crazier things that happened in the life of a bus driver, but he never got around to it. Some people found their art in words, he found his in saucepans and skillets.

Maybe Mar just didn't think her private life was anybody's business but her own. He always assumed anyone who kept a journal had to do so with the knowledge it would someday be read by others. He found a brief mention of a big, beautiful cabin cruiser in Payne Bay, but he couldn't tell from her words if she'd been on it in August when the entry was dated, or she had simply seen it from a distance and admired it. He just didn't know. He'd have to ask Rachel, or even his Mom, which would mean telling her at least a little of what was going on.

While he wondered if he had the energy to read one of MJ's letters, his phone rang. It was Rachel.

"Bobby! Oh my God! Are you all right? Did they hurt you?"

"Ray, I wasn't there, I was in the bodega. My message said they broke into the car and stole the boxes, not mugged me."

"I'm sorry. I was multitasking and may not exactly have been giving your message my full attention. My bad. They got the boxes, though?"

"Both of them."

"*Both*? But there were three boxes in the storage locker."

"I only saw two." A third box meant there may still be some answers to be found. This time he'd shut up and not poke anyone or anything by discussing it. It still freaked him out that one of his fellow retirees was maybe connected to Mar's murder.

"Dammit. There's another one in there somewhere. I can meet you there tomorrow to take a look if you want."

"Sure. I have to take the Compass in to get the smashed window replaced, but they promised to have it done by noon. How's one o'clock for you?"

"Perfect. Did you get my email about Tanis, George, and Katherine?"

"I did. I'll make the calls tonight."

"Let me know how it goes. If Tanis talks to you, I'll be amazed."

"Then let's hope George and Katherine will. I'll let you know what they say when I see you tomorrow at the storage facility, at one."

"One. See you there. Be safe, Big Brother."

"Of course. Besides, I've got the world's ugliest cat to protect me."

"Hey! Vinnie isn't ugly, he's just a little war-torn."

"And frost bit. He was in pretty rough shape when I found him cowering and bleeding in the bus garage and brought him to the vet."

"I thought MJ rescued him?"

"I found him, she gave him a home. A team effort."

"And now he's your bodyguard."

"Just so long as I only get attacked in the kitchen."

"Well, it's better than nothing. Go make those calls and I'll see you tomorrow."

"Will do."

o0o

Rachel was right about Tanis, though Bobby had expected her to hang up on him and was surprised she at least explained that she'd needed years of therapy to get her head back on straight after the murder. Her life had been screwed up enough *before* that weekend, but went to hell afterward. He told her he understood, thanked her for her time, and let her get back to her life.

He called Katherine next, but got her voicemail, so he tried George. Rachel said they'd married fifteen years ago and were both now general managers of small hotels in the mountain resort town. George picked up on the second ring.

"George Houtman." He sounded a little younger than Bobby, though not much.

"George? My name is Bob Odini. My stepsister Rachel said I could call you and gave me your number."

"Of course! Yes. Marion's brother."

"Exactly. Have you got a few minutes to talk about what you remember about that night?"

"No, I'm sorry, Bob. I can't."

"But Rachel said—"

"Not over the phone. Or online. I don't suppose you're going to be up this way any time soon?"

Go to Banff? He'd been wondering if it would be necessary. Apparently, it was. "I can be. It's a bit of a drive. Can you at least tell me if you remember much?"

"I remember everything quite clearly, and I'd really like for you to know about Marion's last days, but in person."

Before someone broke into his car to steal boxes of old stuff, Bobby would have thought George was being a bit paranoid, but not now. "I'm retired now, so I can be there by Sunday." It was maybe a ten-or twelve-hour drive and he could do it in one stretch, with a couple stops for food and bathroom breaks.

"Sunday is good. I'll comp you a room at my hotel, if that's okay. We don't fill up for another few weeks. How long would you like to stay? Would three nights be enough?"

Bobby was thinking a week up in the mountains would be a perfect break for him and Vinnie, but three free nights would be a good start. He could see how the visit went and adjust his plans once he got there. "Three should be fine, George. Thank you."

"It's the least I can do, Bob. My wife's hotel, The Wilson-Bow Inn, is packed full, so it'll have to be The Banff Starlight, which is just on the outskirts of town. We're off the beaten path, but not so far that you can't walk into the center of town."

"Sounds great. What's your policy on pets, though? I'll be bringing my cat."

"Pets are always welcome at The Starlight."

"Great. Then I'll see you all on Sunday. I'll aim to arrive around four."

"We go to church in the morning, so four is perfect. And don't make plans for dinner, because Katherine and our girls will insist you come over to the house."

"A home-cooked meal sounds wonderful, George. Thank you. I know I'm digging up old, dark memories, but I do appreciate your help."

"Of course, Bob." Bobby heard someone speaking in the room with George, but couldn't make out the words. "Sorry, Bob. I have to go. The General Manager's work never ends. Give me a call once you arrive and have checked in. I'll take care of your reservation as soon as I find out why my chef has run out of venison."

"Will do. Thank you. Good luck with the deer."

"Thanks. Just so long as I don't have to go out and kill one myself."

CHAPTER FOUR

B obby ruffled the fur on top of Vinnie's head. "Looks like we're going on a road trip buddy. When was the last time we two amigos got the hell out of Dodge? Too bad your driver's license has expired—it would be nice to not have to do all the driving."

As much as Bobby yearned to read at least one of MJ's letters, Mar's journal had sucked the emotional energy right out of him. Instead, he poured himself a glass of Casa Odini merlot, and retired to the couch to let Prime entertain him. He managed to get through two episodes of the late chef Anthony Bourdain's terrific *No Reservations* before calling it a night.

o0o

He dropped the Jeep off at the glass place just after 9:30, as requested. Mario the tech stared at the smashed window.

"You sure this isn't no crime scene?"

"It's all good to go. They cleared it, but if you want me to call the detective in charge, I can do that, just so you're approved to replace it."

Mario thought about it for a moment, then shook his head. "No. I'm good. Don't want to bug no detective over a broken window." He checked his watch. "We got three others to do before yours, so it'll be a while. You're welcome to hang out in the waiting area, but I gotta be honest and tell you the coffee *sucks.* There's a Starbucks two blocks east, and a Tully's across the street from that. I got your number on the form, so one of us will give you a call when we're done."

o0o

Bobby got the call just after 11:30 and was back, paid up, and on the road again by noon. Since he still had the key to Rachel's storage locker, he went straight there. If he could find Mar's last box of memories, he could save Rachel a trip out.

Winston greeted him like an old friend, asked him how his hip was, and offered to do any heavy lifting Bobby needed doing. "Each locker has a call button just inside the door and I'll be there in two minutes if you press it."

"I'm sure I'll be fine, thanks, Winston, but it's good to know you're here."

"Of course. That's why they pay me the big buck." They both chuckled at his word play.

o0o

Mar's third box wasn't in an obvious spot like the first two were, so Bobby had to do a little rearranging in the small space. There was no way he could move the desk, so he started with the lamps, moving them out into the laneway with the Jeep. The clothing rack was on wheels, so with a tug and a push, and by shoving the desk a whole three inches to the side, the rack joined the lamps. He checked the sky for signs of rain, but the few clouds were a long way off. There's no way he wanted to get caught up digging through the locker while it rained outside on Rachel's things.

Whoever had filled the locker had done so efficiently, to maximize the available space, but they hadn't given any thought to a future need to find something in particular. His own small locker in the basement of the condo complex had a list just inside the door detailing where each box was, and a summary of what each contained. Here the banker's boxers were stacked two deep, all across the back of the locker. Assuming the rows were all the same, Bobby estimated there were nearly fifty boxes.

"Damnation. If it were for anything else, I'd say screw it, but after thirty years, Mar, I'm going to figure this out, even if your box is on the bottom of the back row."

He started with the same two boxes of his stepfather's, moving them easily to the desk top. He grabbed a third one labeled *Papa Charleswood*, expecting the same reasonable weight, but it was as solid as a rock. "What the hell?" He considered ringing Winston, but his stubborn streak won and decided he could handle it himself. All he had to do was maybe take a few things out of the box, to make it manageable.

He lifted the lid, torn between rooting through boxes that didn't belong to him, and getting done what needed to be done. Just because he was retired didn't mean he needed to spend all day in here. The box was packed with textbooks whose gold-lettered, dark brown spines said they were about Washington State Real Estate Law. "Really Rachel? Obsolete law books? He grabbed one and slid it up and out, thinking he could lift the box if it had two less books in it. Two photos dropped out, landing on his feet. With effort, he bent down and carefully picked them up by their edges.

The first was a photo of Alex and Sophie—Bobby's mother—on vacation in what looked like Maui. They were laughing, each with an arm around the other, very much in love. His mom's left ring finger was still bare, so this photo was at least thirty-six years old, before they were even engaged. They looked so happy. Bobby used to wonder what had happened to them, but if what Rachel said was true and Alex was cheating on Mom, then Alex was lucky Sophie hadn't cut his nuts off while he slept. If it had been either of his father's sisters being cheated on, they would have.

He flipped over the second photo. It was of Rachel and Marion in a dark pub, with a small birthday cake with lit 1- and 8-shaped candles, sitting on the table in front of Mar, surrounded by a sea of shot glasses. The two of them were hammered, and he guessed it was Mar's eighteenth birthday, which meant she was drinking under age. He was hardly surprised. He was pretty sure his own relationship with alcohol started with a six-pack of Ranier's out back of the just-closed Orca Stadium. He couldn't have been much more than sixteen, and he was pretty sure he'd inherited his booze palette from his late father. For Mar to be drinking in a bar at eighteen was just par for the Odini course. If Bobby hadn't met Betty and scaled his drinking *way* back to match her only-occasional social drinks, he probably would have ended up in an early grave like his father.

He sat on the edge of the desk and leafed through the textbook, finding more than a dozen secreted photos. It was an odd place to store them, but they had obviously been important to Alex. Bobby had gotten along fine with his mother's second husband, but he hadn't really seen much of him except at family functions. Alex had always seemed to care about Mar and their mom, although cheating on his wife was a good sign all was not sunshine and roses.

Ten pages from the back of the book, Bobby's world stumbled and face-planted when he found a yellowed newspaper clipping and another photo. The clipping was a short one about Marion's murder, but it was the photo that rocked Bobby's foundation. It was his sister and Alex, standing in front of the Eiffel Tower, holding hands and gazing lovingly into each other's eyes. Alex *had* cheated on Bobby's mom—with her *daughter*.

Bobby remembered Mar's Paris trip. She had brought back MJ a real French beret for her sixth birthday. He knew it was *that* birthday because they'd given MJ a new bicycle with streamers on the handlebars and she rode around the neighborhood in her fancy new raspberry-red beret, saying to everyone she met, "Je m'appelle Marionette. Je suis très élégant." Marion was twenty, it was seven months before she was stabbed to death behind a dumpster. Betty's battle with breast cancer seemed to have taken a turn for the better and life was looking up, especially for Alex, apparently. Of course, there could be a totally innocent explanation for the photo, but Bobby was damned if he could think of one. He wasn't even sure who he should be mad at, because he didn't have any idea what Mom and Alex's relationship was like then, and he certainly didn't have a clue what happened between Mar and Alex. For all he knew, it was Mar who had done the seducing. The only way for him to know was to actually ask Alex, and he was pretty sure that was a bad idea. Besides, it's not like it had anything to do with Mar's murder. Did it? He put the textbook down and took the photo over to the Jeep, where he locked it in the glove compartment. There was no way he was going to tell anyone about it unless it became relevant to the case, but he also wasn't going to take a chance someone else would find it in the locker and destroy it or post it online. At least her older man wasn't the union thug, Julius Sabbatini.

He really needed a drink. This was going to take some time to process. Hell, he wasn't even sure how he was going to talk to Rachel or his mother without asking what they knew. What *was* clearer, though, was his mother's response when the police asked if Marion had been seeing anyone. There's absolutely no way she would humiliate herself by telling the world her just murdered daughter had been sleeping with her own husband.

Since there wasn't any booze at hand, Bobby went back to hunting for Marion's third box. Now that he knew what he knew, he could only imagine what the hell he'd find in the box. If there were a second journal, would she have said anything more about Alex than the one hint in the other one? Or would he find love letters between the two of them? And if there were details hidden amongst Mar's stuff, had Rachel already seen them, or had she just boxed the stuff up and kept it safe, out of respect for a stepsister she loved? Bobby's head was ready to explode with the implications. He wasn't a big fan of human drama. In all his years of driving buses, he'd done his best to just keep the dash fans roaring and drowning out the dramatic lives of his passengers. Once, when he was a rookie driver, he'd heard a male teen say to the girl whose hand he was holding, "Your mom is telling people my dad got her pregnant," and the girl responded with "Yeah. I know. I'm sorry." After that, Bobby tuned it *all* out and just drove the bus.

He still hadn't found the box when Rachel arrived ten minutes later. He didn't hear her drive up and nearly screamed when she spoke to him from three feet away.

"I'm guessing you're still looking."

He huffed, frustrated. "Yes."

"You should have waited for me. It's right there." She pointed at a box at the bottom of the front stack, two boxes over, and one down from where he was working. "Silly boy."

"It says *Accounting Class Notes*."

"It does, but that's Mar's writing, not mine." She squeezed past him, lifted off the box on top, and pointed at the lid. In big black letters it said. *Marion's*. She tried to pick it up. "I'd forgotten how heavy this is. Going to take two of us, at least from this angle." She shifted over and made room for him to get in beside her. It was snug. "I got this end, big brother, if you can reach in and grab the other."

"Probably." He leaned in and snaked his hand behind the box, feeling for the handhold. "Yup. Go." Between the two of them, they got it up and out, then Bobby straightened up and took it from Rachel.

"Are you sure?"

"Yup. Just give me a second to shuffle backwards." He took tiny steps back until he could place the box on another stack and open the lid. There was an old photo album on top, so he couldn't see everything else, but he recognized the album cover as one of his grandmother's. "This is her stuff."

"I know."

"You know what's in all of the boxes?" Had she seen the photo he now had hidden in the Jeep?

"Hell no. Just the ones of my murdered sister, because I'm the one who had to pack it up. Also, for the first ten years after her death, they were in my basement, and when I really missed her, I'd go down and root through them, trying to feel the connection again."

Bobby hadn't realized how close the two girls had become in five years. "I'm sorry."

"For what?"

"For not being there for you." He felt now like he'd missed out on something important over the years.

"I probably wouldn't have let get you close, anyway. I kept getting hurt by men, emotionally, physically, and mentally, so there were some pretty big walls up around me. Three weddings, three divorces. Even Dad eventually pissed me off, though I forgave him when Tina asked me to invite him to her high school graduation. We're all a little screwed up, but we're back to being whatever kind of family we can be."

"Do you ever hear from my Mom?"

"Of course. Cards on special occasions, occasionally a call. We never talk about Dad, but there's plenty of life going on to fill a conversation every so often."

"I have her over for dinner once a month or so. You should come."

"That would be nice. Or I could have you both over to my place. What's this weekend like?"

"Mom's actually on an Alaska cruise for the next week or so, and believe it or not, I'm driving up to Banff to meet with George and Katherine. George is happy to talk with me, but only in person." Standing in the middle of a big locker full of family memories, Bobby felt like maybe he needed to make more effort with regards to what family he had left, even if they hadn't technically been a family for decades. Something more than periodic coffee and occasional texts. "But when I get back, let's make time." He looked around at the mess. "First, let me put this box in the car, then we'll put this place back in order."

"Let's not. We'll bring the stuff back in from the laneway, but I think it's time I went through these boxes and did some sorting. I like your idea of putting up family photos. Maybe I can find some for Dad's room in Portway."

"Good idea." Bobby wondered if there were any more photos of Alex and Mar hidden between book pages, and how would Rachel react if she didn't already know they were there and found them.

o0o

They had to shove a few things around in order to get the lamps and the clothes rack back in, but they got it done. Bobby returned the key to Rachel with thanks and a hug. Despite the fact he was digging into a murder, he felt like part of him was finally healing, as he reconnected with his fractured past. He missed his little Marionette so much just thinking of her made him want to curl up in a blanket on the couch and not go anywhere for a while, but if she could reach down from Heaven, she would kick his ass and tell him to get his act together.

He had to make two trips from the garage to get everything from the box up to the condo, but there was no way in hell he was leaving anything in the Jeep overnight, even in the locked parking garage. Since only Rachel knew the box existed, he was going to keep his damned mouth shut, unless he found something Sam could use to actually solve the case. He didn't stash the photo of Mar and Alex away, but instead found a frame for it and hung it in his bedroom, with the rest of the family photos. As disturbing as the idea was that Alex had cheated with Marion, there was something good in the thought that she knew love in her short life.

He and Vinnie ate, then he retired to the couch with a mug of decaf and the first letter from MJ. "This is going to hurt like hell, buddy. Are we sure we want to do this? Then again, these are words from our little girl, so how could we *not* read them?" Vinnie climbed up next to Bobby and rested his lopsided, furry head in his master's lap as if he knew comfort was soon to be needed.

Hey Old Man Odini.

I just got home from dinner with you. I'm so sorry to deliver the news I did, but with you in my corner—as always—we're going to beat this. Fuck cancer!

I remember when you and Mom sat me down and told me she had it. I know I didn't completely understand what that meant in the beginning, but YOU did. And now I'm putting you through it all again. I'm sorry.

I wanted to write down a quick memory I have. It's a happy one I forgot to share at dinner. You and I were in Florence, strolling along, nibbling gelatos with the Italian cousins—Berto, Claudia, and Lucilla—and it started snowing these humongous, floaty snowflakes. Without a word to anyone, you whooped and started spinning around, catching snowflakes on your gelato, holding your cup up high in the air, so I skipped and danced with mine, too, and we spun and laughed and caught snowflakes in our gelatos like crazy people. Then all of a sudden, EVERYONE was doing it! The cousins, the really old couple that had been eating together on the bench, even the constable on the corner!

It was the perfect definition of my life with you. Relatives—mostly the Italian ones—have asked me for years why I never married, never found a buon uomo—*a good man—and settled down. My answer has always been the same...none of them want to catch snowflakes on their gelatos with me.*

We cried a lot at dinner tonight, Dad, and there are going to be oceans of tears to come, but they'll never wash away the snowflakes you and I have shared.

Let's be strong together. Odini & Odini, always.

Love and kisses,

Your little Marionette.

Bobby broke down. The ache in his heart was suddenly so great he thought he was going to burst. He thought the pain had faded in the year since he'd lost MJ, but obviously it hadn't. Her words, her handwriting, the memory of snowflakes in Florence... it all punched him in the gut, hard and without mercy. He folded the letter, kissed it, and gently placed it back on the table as if it were made of snowflakes. Upset by his master's emotions, Vinnie had stopped purring, but he was snuggled in tight, sharing whatever it was his human was going through. Bobby stroked his back, taking comfort in the softness of the orange fur, wondering how many nights MJ had sat with Vinnie and done the same thing. "Buddy, I have no idea what level of emotional pain you can feel, but I know you miss her, too. Life isn't fair, is it? How did we end up down here while the beautiful souls ascend? Do we still have work to do? Have I still got sacrifices to make, sins to atone for? Whatever the answer is, I'm glad she left you to me, along with her guitar, her firearm and her motorcycle. Her cat, her gun, her axe, her ride, and these letters... all I have left of my girl." He sighed, wiped his wet face, and closed his eyes, for a minute or two.

Eventually Bobby finished his coffee, gave Vinnie his medication and food, and got himself to bed, though not before a last look at the photo of Mar and Alex. He kissed a fingertip and touched it to the forehead of his smiling sister. "Goodnight, Mar. I'll find out who did this to you." He looked at Alex's face. "And if you had anything to do with it, old man, I'll gut you and serve up your liver with fava beans and a nice chianti."

o0o

Bobby's phone alarm woke him at 8:30 the next morning, but he couldn't remember why he'd set it until he squinted at the screen. *Ten jars, Creamy Tomato-Vodka Sauce. Noon.*

"Oh crap. That's today." Still wrapped up in some weird storage locker dream he was quickly forgetting, he sat up slowly. Vinnie stretched and threw himself across Bobby's legs. "Nice try, buddy, but I have work to do. I promised Stacey from the Cancer Society I'd donate ten jars of Odini's Secret Sauce for the Breast Cancer Silent Auction and Fundraiser tomorrow, and I completely forgot about it."

He had a quick shower and went through the refrigerator and pantry to see what he needed to buy. His stock was good, but he was out of vodka and whipping cream, was short four mason jars, and only fresh tomatoes would do. Nobody would ever accuse Bobby Odini of using canned tomatoes, crushed or not.

Halfway through berries and cream and eggs Pacifica with smoked salmon, an incoming text message from Stacey asked when she could pick the jars of sauce up. He texted back *How's Noon?* leaving out any mention of the fact he hadn't even started yet.The reply was quick. *Perfect! I'll come by then.*

"Time waits for no chef, Vinnie." He grabbed his windbreaker from the closet. "Guard the place for me." He stopped at that thought. He knew Vinnie was useless as a guard dog or cat, but he *did* have an alarm he never used. MJ had installed a small but sophisticated magnetic door sensor after he moved in, but he never activated it when he went out. He reached up and pressed the battery test button, pleased when the light went green. Gathering up his cloth grocery bags, he held the alarm button down for three seconds and as soon as it started beeping the ten-second countdown, he slipped out, shut and locked the door. If anyone entered and didn't insert the deactivation key within five seconds, the alarm would sound. It would also send a silent text message to his phone as soon as the door opened, just in case the intruder managed to disable the alarm within the time limit.

He considered hiding Mar's box and even MJ's letters, but if someone got further than the door, then there was really no place he could hide anything in the condo they wouldn't think of trying. No, the alarm would have to do. It was loud and obnoxious and would draw attention. On his way down to the garage he stopped by the front desk and told the concierge, Tomasz, that he was not expecting any company and would let him know when he returned. He also mentioned the alarm and if he got any calls about it going off, to call 9-1-1.

"Being paranoid, Mr. Odini? We have good security here."

"You have *excellent* security, Tomasz, but someone broke into my car yesterday and stole a bunch of valuable stuff. For a few days, yes, I'm going to be a little paranoid."

"Ok, sir. I'll be paranoid *with* you. Thanks for letting me know."

"Of course. Back soon."

o0o

As he drove, he didn't see anyone who might be following him, but then, he had zero training on eluding a 'tail'. He was a bus driver, not a spy. All he was trained to do was watch for assholes trying to pass him when he pulled out from bus stops, and keep enough distance around his vehicle so it went back to the garage with the same number of scratches it left with.

Loc had to dig through the storeroom to find enough mason jars of the size Bobby wanted, but he found a whole case. Bobby bought them all, knowing he could never have enough. He was stepping up to the cashier to pay for it all when his phone chimed. He checked the message. It was actually an intruder alert! "Someone is breaking into my condo!"

The cashier nodded, scanned and bagged the items in a blink, and sent him on his way with everything stacked on the case of jars. The Jeep was still parked unmolested in the lot, so he loaded it up and got back on the road. He considered calling 9-1-1 himself, but was sure Tomasz would be taking care of it. Besides, it was vaguely possible it was a false alarm and he'd feel stupid if he called out the police without even seeing what the situation was.

He was home, parked, and calling the elevator in record time, but the elevator took its sweet time arriving. When the doors finally slid open, Bobby limped in, and pressed his button. It felt like it took forever, but the elevator went straight to his floor and opened to pandemonium. His alarm was screaming at 105 decibels and the hallway had to be filled with everyone who lived within a three-block radius of the building, most of them with their hands over their ears. "Excuse me! Excuse me! Owner coming through with the key to shut the damned thing off." People seemed to hear him and make way for him. "So sorry. Sorry about that."

He got to the condo and found Tomasz standing guard, on his cellphone. "Mr. Odini!" the concierge shouted. "9-1-1 has me staying on the line. Told me not to go in. They'll be here soon."

"I appreciate that, Tomasz. I'll turn it off. I have to close the door." The sound was crazy. No wonder everyone was wondering what the hell was going on. Bobby slipped into the condo, placed his supplies down, then he whipped out the key and shoved it in the side of the sensor. The wailing stopped. The relief was immeasurable. He opened the door back up and apologized again to everyone. "I'm sorry folks. I've never actually had to use it before. I'll never use it again. Tomasz... how did a burglar get up here?"

"He must have slipped in while I was helping Mrs. Mendicott get her groceries out of the cab."

"Wonderful." Bobby was no longer impressed with the building's security.

As the crowd dispersed with grumbles, the elevator opened and two officers stepped out. One of them was Officer Gaye. He started to speak, but was cut off by a voice behind him. "There was two of them. Dressed like couriers, all in brown, but with black leather gloves." Mrs. Waisglass stood alone, dressed to go out. "I was just going down to check my mail. I stepped out into the hall at the same second they opened your door and set off that screaming mimi racket. Between the noise and me seeing them, they got spooked and ran like hell, down the stairs."

Officer Gaye joined what little was left of the gathering while his partner went straight for the stairwell. "Mr. Odini. Have you been inside?"

"Just to shut off the alarm."

"Good. Please everyone step away from the door while I check the interior of the apartment." He drew his weapon and entered the condo. Bobby could hear him using his radio to update someone as he cleared each room of the small unit. He was back quickly. "It's safe," he announced to Bobby. "Do you mind if I bring this lovely young lady in so I can get both your statements?"

"Of course. I'll make some coffee. Mrs. Waisglass...coffee or tea?"

His elderly neighbour followed them in, looking around, admiring or comparing, Bobby wasn't sure. "No thank you, Robert. Bernie and I are going out for lunch shortly. I don't want to spoil my appetite."

"Of course. Officer?"

"No, thank you, sir. I'll just get your statements and get out of your way. Ma'am? Mrs. Waisglass, you said they were both wearing gloves, but they didn't actually get into the apartment before the alarm went off?"

"That's right. Gloves. And then that wailing banshee. It was obnoxious, Robert, but it worked."

Officer Gaye nodded. "Gloves. Then there won't be any fingerprints. There may be video footage, so we'll check with the concierge when we leave."

While Mrs. Waisglass went over the details of what little she saw, the other officer returned. He took Bobby's statement and then they were gone, down to speak with Tomasz and look at the security videos. Mrs. Waisglass left when her husband Bernie arrived, looking disheveled.

"Where did you go, Marlene?"

"There was a break-in."

"What?"

"There was a break-in! Someone tried to burgle Robert!"

"What?"

"You idiot! You forgot your hearing aids, again."

"What?" She led Bernie back down the hall, throwing Bobby a little wave over her shoulder.

It wasn't until he closed the door and threw the deadbolt home with a definitive *thunk* of metal on metal that Bobby realized he hadn't seen Vinnie in all the confusion. From where he stood, he could see that the balcony door was closed, the couch was empty, and so was the cat tree.

"Vinnie! Where are you, buddy? It's all safe. Come on out!" He hoped the big goof was just hiding and hadn't run out into the hallway with the fake couriers. "C'mon buddy, I'm home. It's all good."

CHAPTER FIVE

H e thought he heard a faint *meow*, but he couldn't tell where it was coming from. "Vinnie! Talk to me, buddy!" He began a methodical search, moving clockwise around the condo, starting with the half-bathroom, then the main bedroom. Thinking his roomie might be cowering under the bed, he slowly lowered himself down onto all fours and looked. No cat. Another *meow* sounded, further away, so he abandoned his bedroom and checked the guest bedroom and closet. No Vinnie.

Back out in the living room he heard a closer *meow* coming from the direction of the kitchen, and sure enough, Vinnie was on top of the kitchen cabinets—the one place Bobby didn't think the big cat could get to.

"Vinnie, buddy. I'm here. It's okay." He reached up to him and Vinnie climbed down onto the refrigerator and into his rescuer's embrace. His purring started immediately. "I guess I can't expect you to guard the place if the alarm freaks you out. I should have given you earplugs and the Beretta. Do you know the combination for the gun vault in the closet?" He and Vinnie settled on the couch, Bobby stroking the cat's back, calming both of them.

After a few minutes, Bobby lifted Vinnie off his lap and placed him on his fleece blanket on the copilot seat of the couch. "I have a boatload of sauce to make, mister, so you chill out while I work." He picked up the groceries by the front door and took them to the kitchen."Hey Siri." He heard the answering beep. "Please shuffle the *Snark Puppet in the Kitchen* Playlist."

Siri's sweet female Australian voice answered him. "Here's the *Snark Puppet in the Kitchen* playlist, shuffled." A moment later, MJ and the boys filled the condo.

Vinnie *mrowed* and Bobby laughed. "Yeah, I know. You expected Sinatra and Deano. Sometimes this Italian boy needs some Frank to put rhythm in the kitchen, but today, it's Snark Puppet. Now let's make some culinary magic."

It took two glasses of wine and almost an hour of singing and shuffling along with four post-grunge teens for Bobby to make and bottle enough of his 'super-secret special' creamy tomato sauce for both the fundraiser and himself. It took him another ten minutes to print off his custom labels and stick them neatly to the bottles, signing each one personally. The front labels had the same simple *Casa Odini* logo he used on his homemade wines and the back ones had a list of ingredients for allergy alerts, but they didn't reveal proportions, nor which one of the ingredients he sautéed lightly before adding it, so he was hardly afraid anyone could replicate his recipe. He checked his watch—he had half an hour before Stacey arrived. He put on a pot of coffee, but left the re-corked bottle of wine on the counter. He was happy to sit and have either with her, if she had time. They'd met during MJ's treatments and had gone for coffee a handful of times in the past year. There were occasional sparks, but he still didn't know if she liked gelato.

He was zoned out, staring at the world beyond the balcony doors, when it occurred to him if they'd found whatever they wanted in Mar's boxes, they wouldn't have tried to break into the condo. Which meant either they're scared and desperate, or they knew exactly what they were looking for. Either way, they thought *he* had it, and he didn't even know what *it* was. He was pretty sure it wasn't the journal he'd already read a half-dozen times, so it had to be in the third box—the one stashed in the guest room. He had to find whatever it was and get it to Sam before they came back with reinforcements.

"What the hell did my sister do, Vinnie? I mean, *besides* fall in love with our stepfather?" He poured himself a strong coffee and went to get the box. Vinnie padded along behind him. Bobby considered spreading everything out on the dining room table, but Stacey was due there any minute. "The spare bed'll do. It's definitely big enough." He lifted the banker's box up onto the comforter, then realized it was MJ's favorite comforter, so he fetched a couple of clean sheets from the shelf in the closet and spread them out on the bed. "Let's add the journal, too, buddy." Vinnie hopped up on the bed and immediately settled in. Bobby sighed. "Don't worry. I'll get it, you lazy brat."

He fetched the journal from the coffee table, and placed it next to the box. Flipping the attached lid back, he once again saw the photo album. He lifted it up and out and put it next to the journal. "We'll empty the box first, then go through everything one at a time. We'll take pictures of it all, as back—" The kitchen phone rang twice. "Stacey!"

It took a quick hop-limp combo step, but he got to the phone before it stopped ringing. "Hello."

"Hey Mr. Odini. It's Tomasz. Miss Stacey is here to see you."

"Thank you, Tomasz. Send her up, please."

"Yes sir."

Bobby scooted Vinnie out of the guest bedroom and closed the door. A moment later there was a knock at the front door, but before answering it, Bobby checked to make sure the alarm was turned off.

There was no point in scaring the crap out of everyone again. He unlocked the door and opened it. Stacey was tall, fit, and looked great in her casual yoga pants and LOVE PINK sweatshirt. For a moment Bobby forgot why she was there, but was glad she was."Hey, you. Come on in." He stepped aside to let her in, then closed and locked the door behind her.

Before he could say another word, she leaned in and kissed him quickly on the lips. "That, Mr. Odini, is my way of saying 'thank you' for the generous donation to a wonderful cause."

He certainly liked the way she said thank you, and was tempted to ask if he got a thank you for each of the ten bottles of sauce. "The donation is my pleasure, Stacey." He led her to the kitchen island where the bottles sat ready to go in a box. "Ten bottles of Casa Odini's Special Secret Pasta Sauce. Hand-made with all fresh ingredients and no preservatives."

"Perfect! Thank you! I may end up buying them all myself."

"Why not keep one for yourself and bundle the other nine in groups of three, for three auction items?"

"Brilliant!" She picked up a bottle and examined the label. "This is wonderful. And you've signed them! I hope you'll be able to make the event. MJ's picture will be on display, along with so many others we've lost since last year."

"Of course, I will." He'd been having such a fun moment with Stacey that he forgot what the whole thing was all about. He took a deep breath.

Stacey noticed. "I know. You still miss her."

"Always will."

"Come." She grabbed his hand and led him to his own couch, but when she sat them both down, she kept a respectable distance. "Bobby, there are two types of emotional catastrophes in a person's life. The first tears a hole in their past, and the second tears a hole in their future. For example, the death of an elderly parent tears a hole in the past because of the memories of life with that person, while the death of a young child tears a hole in the future, for all of the things that will no longer happen. The death of an adult child gives the worst of both catastrophes, though. It rips a hole in the past, *and* a hole in the future, creating a place where footing is uncertain and handholds are few to be found." She squeezed his hand. "Have you been to counseling, like I suggested?"

"Actually, yes I have." He'd been twice. "But it was still too early and I wasn't ready, I guess. Instead, I've buried myself in cooking. I'm thinking of writing a cookbook."

"That's great! But it's avoidance. If you come tomorrow—and I really hope you do—I'll introduce you to a couple of survivors who just started a counseling group that's a little less rah rah rah and a bit more casual conversation. I'll let you decide. Agreed?"

He was certainly open to the idea. MJ and Betty would both want him to go and heal. "Agreed."

"Good!" She stood up. "Now I have to get my butt out the door with those bottles, or else I won't get everything done today that I have to do."

Bobby followed her to the kitchen and picked up the box of full mason jars. "Can I carry these down for you?"

"No. You're limping, but trying to hide it, which means your hip is acting up again. While I appreciate the offer, I can manage. Thank you." She took the box from him, and then leaned across it and kissed him with the kind of enthusiasm that is usually meant as a promise.

Bobby kissed her right back, then broke it off. "Careful. Don't want to drop the jars."

She laughed. "Of course not. But I strongly suggest we pick this up another time, when there aren't any jars in the way, and I don't have to fly out the door."

"I like the thought of that."

"Good. Now please unlock the door and let me out before...well, before *whatever*."

He unlocked and opened the door. "Go. Drive safely. I'll see you tomorrow."

"Yes, you will. Otherwise, I will hunt you down on Sunday."

He laughed. "I'll be out of the country by then. Vinnie and I are going away for a few days. But don't worry. I'll be there tomorrow. For MJ, her mother, and all the others."

Stacey's smile faltered. "I know you will. Thank you." She blew him a kiss and left. He watched her walk over to the elevator, allowing himself to admire the way her fitness regime made her yoga pants move. She turned and smiled at him until the elevator came, then she was gone.

Bobby locked himself and Vinnie in the condo again. The cat was watching him from the top of the big cat tree. "Yes, Vin, I'm a pig, staring at her ass. I'm sorry. After a kiss like that I'm not supposed to let my imagination wander?" Vinnie began grooming himself. "Fine. Judge me all you want. I'm going to go back to Mar's box while you lick yourself in full view of the neighborhood."

In addition to the photo album, Marion's box contained a vinyl CD travel case containing disks of Queen, Bon Jovi, Tears for Fears, Journey, Depeche Mode, and INXS; a Bon Jovi concert shirt with a small plastic sandwich bag attached containing a ticket to a concert in Portland; five shot glasses from towns in Northern California; a small plush Orcas Orville the baseball-playing Orca; a half dozen fantasy paperbacks; a faded and worn-thin American flag beach towel Bobby knew had been in the family since *he* was a kid; and, at the bottom of the box, a thick *Advanced Accounting* textbook.

He laid everything out on the bed, then got his cellphone and photographed each item, front, back, and sides. "I'll scan the photos in the album later, but what I really want to know is what's between the pages of this textbook." He quickly flipped the pages just to see if there were any secrets within it, and sure enough there were at least a dozen photos and pieces of paper. He took the book back out to the couch and sat. He was long past worrying about violating his late sister's privacy, but was he being an idiot, thinking he could figure out what the police couldn't? Didn't they have access to all this stuff, too, back then? They must have. His mother would have gladly turned over everything she had in order to find her daughter's killer.

Or would she? What if Marion had had a copy of the Paris photo in her belongings and Mom found it? Would she have turned it over to the police? Did she hate Alex enough to make him a suspect? Or maybe she herself suspected him. There was no such photo in the police files Bobby had seen, neither was there mention of interviewing Alex as a suspect. He had been questioned as a matter of course, but so had everyone else in the family, including himself. Bobby's mother couldn't have suspected Alex, if she even knew about the affair at all, but more and more it was looking like he'd have to sit down and have a chat with her about the deep past.

The first piece of paper in the textbook was a handout of accounting terminology, not some incriminating receipt or photo or even a cryptic phone number with a date and an explanation mark. As he leafed carefully through the book, he realized his sister had been better at keeping a secret than her lover had. Bobby was still a little pissed his stepfather had cheated on his mom, but the fact he kept that photo hidden and safe was a sign he had cared about Mar. Maybe he still did. The two men hadn't spoken since Rachel's daughter Tina's high school graduation, but it was a pleasant enough exchange. Maybe Alex would be willing to talk to Bobby, share some insights the police hadn't thought of, not being aware of the nature of Marion's murder. He would have to check with Rachel when he got back from Banff.

There was nothing secret or unusual stashed in the textbook. Not even a love letter. Except for the one photo, the two of them had been impressively careful. Any or all of the keepsakes in the box could have been cherished gifts from Alex, but only Mar herself knew what was cherished and why. He picked up the photo album.

Of all the items from the box, the album was the most obvious choice for incriminating evidence, but since he had no goddamned idea what he was looking for, he'd simply have to scan each and every one of the photos and hope Sam—the actual detective—could root out proof of something.

On his way from the guest room to the desk and his scanner-printer, Vinnie nearly tripped him, meowing loudly for his attention.

"What?"

Mrow.

"It must be hunger, because I just cleaned your litter box." He checked the time. "Damn. It's nearly three. Food. Both of us. Now." He booted up his computer, turned on the printer, put the album on the chair, and set about feeding the two of them.

Once both he and Vinnie were stuffed full, Bobby started the tedious process of scanning the photos. There had to be over two hundred snapshots in individual pockets, four per page, but his fear of the tedium vanished when he opened the album and looked at the first page. They were Marion's candid baby photos. In the first one was his mom and dad, her holding their little bundle and him holding a beer. His father sported a permed afro and a dark horseshoe mustache that grew down to either side of his chin. He looked like an Italian porn star version of artist Bob Ross. Bobby's laugh startled Vinnie, who wandered back to the cat tree. Bobby's mother, on the other hand, had long dyed blonde hair tied back. Sophie's smile completely eclipsed her husband Carlo's snide grin. She had never looked happier.

The second photo was none other than himself, age ten, holding his freshly hatched little sister. He was dressed in an open-collared lime green shirt with a paisley bandana/scarf thing around his neck held in place with a double gold ring. "Holy crap, I look like one of the Brady Bunch, or even a Partridge." The third photo was of the whole family taken with a tripod in the living room, while the fourth was Marion, sound asleep on her mother's chest. Bobby tugged the photos out of their pockets, placed them on the scanner, and pressed the start button.

While the machine did its thing, he flipped through the album. There were a surprising number of pictures of the two of them playing together or with one or both of their dogs. The Boston Terrier was Caesar, and the chocolate lab was Nova. They had both followed him around everywhere he went, as faithful as any dogs could ever be. When Marion was born, they adopted her as one of the pack, and were both extremely protective of her. He remembered one night when his father had had a few too many drinks and started screaming in frustrated rage at the Yankees/Red Sox game on television. Suddenly Nova positioned herself between him and the bassinet and growled menacingly until Carlo settled down and sat back in his chair. From that day forward, for the year until he died in the crash, his father never fed, petted, or walked Nova again, and Nova never seemed to mind a bit. She got all the love she needed from Bobby and his mom.

The scan popped up on his computer's monitor and Bobby did a quick save as *Marion-1*. He could separate them out and re-label them all later, but for the time being he just wanted to get them scanned and in the cloud. He continued, page-by-page, memory-by-memory. There were vacations he remembered, birthday parties he sort of did, and pictures of Mar with her friends he had no clue who they were. He watched his little sister grow up in still life before his eyes, as if she were a stranger he hardly knew. If he were honest with himself, he *didn't* really know her. The ten-year age gap meant he was in high school while she was skinning her knees and playing hopscotch in grade school. He didn't remember a lot of the details of the younger years, and once he moved out at nineteen, they hardly saw each other except for Sunday dinners with their mother.

He did okay, scanning, reminiscing, reliving, until he turned a page and saw a picture of him and Betty, at what must have been the dinner he brought her home to meet his family. It was June 13th. A Saturday. He didn't even need to think about it. He remembered. It was Mar's eleventh birthday dinner. She and Betty had hit it off so fast Bobby thought he'd suddenly become invisible. Marion was fascinated with Betty's waist-length auburn braid and green eyes. If Bobby ever had any doubts about who he would marry, his little sister never did. By dinner the next week she had collected half a dozen bridal magazines and spent an hour showing Betty all her ideas for her big brother's wedding. He protested vehemently, but was ignored. Secretly, he was pleased, because he'd fallen in love with Betty the first time he saw her waiting in line at the theatre to see Rocky Horror Picture Show, and didn't want to spend his life with anyone else.

Betty was only eighteen, and a year into her nursing diploma. After six months, her parents liked Bobby and could see the two of them were serious about each other, but they insisted she finish her diploma before they made any major life decisions. He proposed to her the morning of her graduation ceremony, so she walked across the stage in cap and gown with a sparkly engagement ring on her finger. When she wiggled her fingers mischievously, the entire hall fell silent, but after two heartbeats exploded in cheers, screams, whoops, and hollers. Bobby turned the page of the album and burst into tears. Marion had a photo of him and Betty that very day, with him holding his fiancée's diploma while she held up her hand to show off the ring. The two of them were grinning like Cheshire cats. Bobby had never seen the picture before. He had photos taken by others that day, but he'd never seen Marion's far superior version. He held it to his chest and let the tears come.

After Betty's death, he'd spent thirty years being strong and brave and solid, just to show MJ and the world he was fine and that life went on even when hearts got broken, but his heart hadn't broken, it had *shattered*. Or it had imploded, or been crushed. Whatever it was, he was a mess for about a month, then one morning he woke up to breakfast in bed, served by his six-year-old daughter who had recently watched her mother get sick and die before her very eyes. MJ, her eyes damp from tears of her own but her chin held up, looked at him over the tray of scrambled eggs, toast, and orange juice and simply said "It's just you and me, now, Daddy. Mommy said she wants me to grown up to kick ass and rule the world, and I need you to help me." Her breath caught. "I *really* need you to help me, Daddy. I...can't do it alone." That was the official beginning of Odini & Odini.

Bobby put the album on his desk and shuffled over to the couch. He propped the photo up on the coffee table where he could see it, and then he tipped over and curled up in a weepy ball. Vinnie came over and climbed on top of him, purring for them both.

When the emotional purge finally stopped, he was exhausted. His face wet with tears and snot, he rubbed Vinnie's head. "That was unexpected,

buddy. But what did I think would happen when I started digging into a
past where three of the five women I love are dead?" He sat up slowly and
Vinnie hopped down. There were no tissues in sight, so Bobby went to
the bathroom and got cleaned up. When he was done, he splashed cold
water on his face.

"Break time is over. Let's get this done." Before going back to the
computer, he poured himself a glass of water from the filtered jug in the
refrigerator.

The album waited for him, pages open like a lover from the past,
yearning to embrace him. "No. You're not going to suck me in. I can do
this." So, he did. He sat down, slid four more photos out, and got the
scanner going. Then another four. They were photos of his life, mixed
with his sister's. He forced himself past little Marionette's baby pictures.
He had those hanging on the walls here, so they weren't quite the shock
they could have been; finally, there was a photo of Alex, Rachel, and
Mom. Interspersed with shots of her own world with her friends, there
were a substantial number of photos of the new family, especially of Mar
with Rachel.

The eventual wedding group photo made him smile. His mother
had asked him to give her away, so there he was on the end, in a
rented tux, holding baby MJ on one arm and his other linked through
maid-of-honor Marion's. It had been a gorgeous, wonderful day. A
second photo, this time including Betty on his arm, gave him pause. He
took a shaky breath and pushed on.

The photos continued, jumping months at a time, probably because
by then Mar was a teen and left the camera at home more often than
not. There were a few party and family vacation pictures, then her high
school graduation popped up, and there was the whole family, again.

After that there seemed to be more and more pictures of strong, fit, active, charismatic Alex, usually caught on film when he wasn't looking. Whether she realized it or not when she put the album together, it showed her growing affection for their stepfather.

The mish-mash of life photos went on, including a series of Mar sunning and having fun with Rachel on board a large cabin cruiser. He remembered mention of Alex having a boat, but he'd never gotten around to visiting it with his own little family.

In the photos from that point forward, Marion started to mature before his eyes. Her make-up became subtler, her hairstyle less sorority-cute and more professional working woman, and her wardrobe moved away from t-shirts and short skirts into blouses and longer skirts, with heels instead of sneakers or flip-flops.

Bobby continued scanning, marveling at the transformation of a sister he hadn't really known in her last few years. More photos of her life on the boat came up, but Rachel was absent in these ones. He kept scanning. Some of them looked to be taken when Alex was conducting business and Mar was snapping away from a distance. He squinted at one shot of a group of men in golf shirts and slacks and recognized not just Alex and union local president Julius Sabbatini, but also Jake Brand, the candidate for mayor Alex was supporting back then. It's probably why Mar took so many photos. Brand had been a minor celebrity in the area, having sailed solo around the world at the age of twenty, pitched a season with the Orcas before a hiking accident destroyed his throwing arm's elbow, and then hosted his own nationally-syndicated sports talk radio show for four or five years. He'd lost that election, but now he was Washington State Senator Brand. He didn't recognize anyone else in the photo.

Marion seemed to be developing a fondness for older, successful men. Could this have been what got her in trouble? He scanned the photos and slid them back into their sleeves. Three pages later, he was done. The last photo was one of Alex and Rachel standing in front of a Christmas tree, waving at the photographer. He put the photo aside for Rachel, then went back through the album and picked half a dozen photos that would be perfect for his own walls. It was the sum of a life, in an album in a box hidden away for thirty years.

o0o

By the time he was done scanning the photos and letting memories long filed away now claw at his heart, Bobby needed food, a shower, and exercise—in that order. He settled for Ethiopian Kifto raw beef and peeled, shopped, cored, squeezed, and fried enough for two days. When he was done, the wonderful tang of the onions, cayenne, Berbere sauce, ginger, and beef filled the home, banishing the maudlin past with culinary present.

He fed Vinnie his tuna, and took his own plate and a glass of wine out to the tiny balcony. It was a cool night, but the hot, spiced meal kept him warm as he slowed down and gave his complete attention to his *al fresco* Zen repast. It was a wonderful dish he was taught to prepare by Desta and Iskanda, who owned a delightful little restaurant downtown. Between the sauce and the fresh ingredients, there was variety and spice galore in every mouthful. It cleansed his palate, his sinuses, and the blues that had been settling on him for the past few days.

A week ago, he'd been plodding along in his retirement, doing a little of this, a little of that, and now he was digging around in the roots of the family tree, finding secrets that had completely passed him by as he lived a life of oblivion on the bus or in the kitchen. The loss of Marionette in his day-to-day world had battered him like a frigid, biting perfect storm from Hell rolling in off the ocean, but he'd weathered it as best he could, for his own sake as well as for his daughter's memory. His digging, though, was shaking his foundation.

He realized now how complacent he'd become. More than three decades driving a bus, keeping life simple and straightforward, would do that, he supposed. He often wondered what it would be like to have a desk in an office on Third Avenue with a window overlooking the bay, but just the thought of wearing a suit and tie all day while selling one thing or forecasting another made him cringe. He'd loved working at street level, seeing the people day in and day out. He'd been a part of the pulse of the city, keeping it moving, functioning, *living*. Up in a glass tower he would have been merely an observer, but behind the wheel of a forty-foot, seventeen-ton, diesel-powered behemoth, he was a *participant*. He may have tuned out their day-to-day drama, but their laughs and smiles and waves were the spoons stirring the stew of his life.

Five stories up on his balcony, Bobby was *just* close enough to the street to be able to relax to the rhythm of its life, but high enough up that he had his sanctuary, his Kitchen of Solitude, as it were. At least until those two assholes had broken in. Whatever they wanted, he was determined to deny them—for Marion, for MJ, and even for Rachel, who had lost her sister and friend at the hands of a now-dead hit man.

The air was cooling quickly, so Bobby took his empty dishes inside, stepped into a hot shower to re-energize him and scrub away what memory remnants the Ethiopian beef hadn't. He'd been so caught up in the case that he and Vinnie hadn't gone for a walk together in a few days. Once Bobby was dressed, Vinnie padded around the condo behind him, seeming to suspect something was afoot. When Bobby pulled the cat chest-carrier out of the closet, Vinnie went into affection-mode, turning his purr up full blast while rubbing his scent all over his kind and wonderful human slave.

"Looks like someone agrees with my plan. Since I need a little exercise and you're useless as a guard cat, you might as well come with me. Let's go see if any of your friends are out at Wind Hill, then wander around from there."

oOo

He lasted almost an hour before his hip strongly suggested they make their way back home. It was a good walk, though, with relaxing random conversations as people stopped to greet the orange, one-eared beast hanging from Bobby's chest. Vinnie may have been ugly and intimidating, but he was one big, furry bundle of purring love for anyone who took time to scratch his head and take his chin-rubbed scent home with them.

It was dark by the time they greeted Tomasz' evening replacement. "All quiet tonight, Martin?"

"Yes sir, Mr. Odini. Very quiet. No one breaking in. I have watched cameras real close."

"Thank you. I appreciate it. We *all* do."

"Oh yes. Very scary. Never happen again, that's for sure." He flexed his scrawny bicep.

"I hope not. But you be safe. No being a hero, Martin. If you have trouble, call the cops."

"You betcha. Call the cops, then kick burglar asses."

"No, Martin. Call the cops, then stay safe. They may have guns. You're not Superman."

"Okay. I will stay safe. Goodnight, Mr. Odini. Goodnight, Mr. Vincent."

As Bobby limped onto the elevator, he prayed that in whatever storm was gathering, no one got hurt that didn't deserve it.

Upstairs he slipped out of the carrying rig, let Vinnie out of his harness, then went in and hung upside down again for a few minutes before taking his meds and feeding Vinnie his. He climbed into bed with his iPad, spent a total of ten minutes zipping through Facebook updates, and debated with himself whether he should send Sam an email telling him about the third box and the scanned photos. He didn't send it, though, because he simply didn't trust electronics and computers enough to risk it. He trusted Sam, but the detective still worked for the city and the city monitored emails sent and received on their equipment, so nothing was completely secure. He'd saved all of the photos to the cloud, so even if someone broke into the place and stole his computer *and* the photo album, he could retrieve the images. Of course, he had no idea if they had any value to the case, but so far, they were the best bet.

o0o

He was up at seven the next morning, knowing he had a lot to do before he and Vinnie left for Banff. Since they needed to be there by 4pm on Sunday and according to Google Maps it was just under a twelve-hour drive, he estimated they needed to depart just after midnight. It would give them time for a nice breakfast in Spokane, and if he got tired, he could pull over and nap at any of the truck rest stops on the I90 and still make it in plenty of time. The route straight north and mostly through Canada was supposed to be quicker, but he was familiar with the southern route at least as far as Coeur d'Alene, and that would make all the difference in the middle of the night.

He and Vinnie ate and then he hauled out his little weekender suitcase and packed the basics. He'd take his camera, too. The phone was fine for recording an event, but he'd never been to Banff National Park and his research showed stunning vistas, grand hotels, and wildlife galore. He didn't have any plans to go back after this one trip, so he might as well make the most of it. Vinnie's mini travel litter box was down in storage, so he'd have to pull that out, too. Stacey's Breast Cancer Silent Auction was from noon to four, which gave him plenty of time. He'd even have time for a long nap before they left. He wished he had a co-pilot for the drive, but given the nature of what he was looking into, it was probably best he did this trip alone.

Booting up his computer, he spent an hour editing the photo scans, isolating the ones he thought might interest Sam. He doubted anything would come of them. Even the ones taken on the boat by his besotted sister were of a man Alex was already publicly connected to. There were no secrets there, and if Marion had *heard* something she shouldn't have on the cruiser, she hadn't written it down anywhere, so it was lost when she was stabbed to death.

When he was finished, he called the detective. "Sam. It's Bobby Odini."

"Hey Bobby. What's up on a Saturday?"

Not even trusting the security of his own phone, Bobby lied. "I wanted to discuss the scholarship in MJ's name with you. Do you have time this morning to drop by my place for a few minutes? It's *important.*"

"Important?"

"Yeah. I just want to clarify a few things we were chatting about at Headquarters the other day, before we get the paperwork started."

"Oh. Of course." Sam seemed to clue in there was some hidden meaning in Bobby's cryptic call. "My kids have baseball practice at ten. I can swing by now. I'll pick up coffee. How do you take it?"

"Black, thanks. I'll see you shortly."

Bobby threw a load of laundry in the apartment-sized washer off the master bathroom, then slid open the balcony door to let in fresh air and banish the cat smell that couldn't be avoided no matter how well he scrubbed the place.

CHAPTER SIX

S am arrived fifteen minutes later, and Vinnie joined Bobby at the door to welcome him. "Fat Cat! Long time no see!" He bent down and ruffled Vinnie's head before stepping in and shaking Bobby's hand."Hey Bobby. I'm guessing this couldn't wait."

Bobby closed and secured the door behind them, and led Sam to the living room. "No. After those bastards smashed into my Jeep and then tried to break in here, I think it's best that anything I turn up would be safer with you." He accepted the Tully's cup. "Thank you." They sat, and Vinnie immediately climbed into Sam's lap.

"So, you've turned up something?"

"Yes and no. It turns out there was a third box of my sister's stuff in storage. Also, there was a journal I'd taken out of the first boxes, even though I left them in the car."

"A journal? That's great!"

"Not really. I've been over and over it and there's nothing about anything important. But you're welcome to take a look. In the third box, though, there was a photo album. I've scanned all the photos and was going to email them to you, but I just don't know who's monitoring either of our computers. They sure found out in a hurry I had those boxes. As I said at the bodega, one of my old transit buddies must be involved because no one knew about the boxes but them."

"It's hard to say. Do you have the album here? The scans would be great, but I'd like to see the original prints, if I can."

"Sure. It's right here." Bobby retrieved the album from his desk and flipped it open to the boat pictures. "These were taken by Marion on our stepfather's boat, *The Rachel*." He slipped the photos out of their sleeves and placed the mall on the coffee table in front of Sam.

"That's Senator Jake Brand, Bobby. Didn't he run for mayor back about the time this was taken?"

"He did. My stepfather, Alex Charleswood, ran the campaign. That's Julius Sabbatini, transit union local president, and next to him, in the green shirt, is Alex."

"Yeah, I recognize him, too. He's been a mover and shaker in this town for a lot of decades. Is he still alive?"

"He is, but he hasn't been well. I hope to talk to him when I get back from Banff next week."

"You're going all the way to Banff?"

"My stepsister, Rachel—Alex's daughter—is still in touch with the people who were there that night and two of them are willing to talk to me, but only in person. Also, I never went up there to see where Marion died, so it's well past time for that. I leave late tonight and should only begone a few days."

Sam tapped the photos with a finger. "This stocky, dark-haired guy looks familiar, but I can't quite place his face. I have no idea who anyone else in these shots are, but I know who might. If you have them scanned, do you mind if I take the originals? Our scanning gear is a bit more sophisticated than your average home machine."

"Of course. I'll get you the journal, too. As a matter of fact, come take a look at the contents of the box. I've got it all laid out." He picked up his coffee and led Sam into the guest room.

"This is all that's left of my sister's life."

Sam took five minutes to examine everything carefully. He even felt up the Orville the Orca. "Always check stuffed toys for hiding places. It's a favorite of people with secrets." He smiled, shook his head, and placed the moose back on the bed. "No secrets here."

Bobby handed him the journal. "Maybe you can see something in here I can't."

"Thank you. I'll get this back to you when I'm done."

"I appreciate it."

They returned to the living room. Bobby wrestled with his conscience. He wanted to protect Mar and Alex's secret, but not if doing so kept them from finding out who hired her killer. "How did the investigation into Vetere's murder go?"

"Like your sister's case, it's hung up. We've tied him to a dozen murders over the years, but the ledger suggests there were over a hundred contracts. We're still trying to connect them back to anyone in particular. The Feds may be getting further with the national and international stuff, but I'm not in the loop any more so I don't know how close they are to solving anything. All we know is that he had seventeen aliases, but Franco Vetere was the name he grew up with. He was fifty-six, no siblings, and his mother is dead. He had a few assault charges before he turned twenty-one, but nothing too serious. After twenty-one, his life is pretty thin. He paid his bills, filed tax returns, and generally stayed below the radar. He was damned good."

"He sounds like the kind of pro you send after a senator, not a college co-ed."

"Exactly. He couldn't have been cheap."

"How did they link him to the dozen murders? DNA or something?"

"A variety of things. Some DNA, some ballistics. The DNA is sketchy, though, because it isn't accurate at all."

"I thought DNA was foolproof."

"It's supposed to be, but someone in the lab screwed up the samples, and then his body was cremated."

"Screwed up, how?"

"He came up as a familial match for MJ, whose DNA and fingerprints are on file as part of the job. It doesn't make sense. We tied him to the murders in other ways, though. At least we don't have to go to trial and prove it in court."

"No, we just have to find out who hired him to kill my sister."

"We may never be able to prove it, Bobby."

"Well, someone is worried that we will. They're desperate enough to steal the boxes in broad daylight and then try to get in here." He re-packed the contents of the box and picked it up.

"Good point." He checked his watch. "I have to get going. Have a safe trip, and good luck."

"Thanks, Sam. I don't know what I expect to find, but I have to try. I'll give you a call when I get back."

"I appreciate it." He slipped the photos into the journal, placed it in the box Bobby held, then took the box from him. "And thank you for all of this. I'll take good care of it all."

"I know." He let Sam out, much to Vinnie's displeasure.

o0o

Bobby spent the remaining time before the fundraiser making sauces with the fresh ingredients in the refrigerator, just so they wouldn't go bad while he was gone. When he was done, the little chest freezer in his pantry was well stocked. He loaded and started the dishwasher, hand-washed each of his precious knives, sharpened them on the whetstone, then hung them on the magnetic strip on the wall.

With plenty of time to spare, he changed out of his jeans and tee into khakis and the *F*CK Cancer* polo shirt MJ had bought him. He loaded Vinnie up again, set the door alarm, and took the elevator down to the garage. He did a circle check of the Jeep, ensuring no one had broken any more windows or shoved nails into the tires. He didn't relish driving all the way to Canada with cardboard taped where glass should be, or riding on a skinny spare tire.

The vehicle was fine. He put Vinnie inside, then checked underneath for leaks. Old habits die hard. More than once over his decades of driving professionally spotting a leak early had prevented a disaster. The concrete was dry, and he couldn't see any Hollywood-style explosive devices with flashing red lights attached to the chassis. He stood up slowly, leaning on the Jeep for support. "Paranoia, thy name is Bobby."

As he drove to the Community Center six miles north, in Old Harvey District, he kept looking in his mirror for vehicles tailing him and wondered if this was what life was like all the time for cops like MJ—always wondering who was coming after them and when they would strike. He'd be a wreck, spooking at every unfamiliar face or vehicle. No wonder she carried her personal firearm even when she was off duty. She had made him get a Washington concealed carry permit when she got sick so he could take her personal weapon to the range and learn how to use it properly, but he wasn't quite ready to start carrying it loaded around the city. What he needed to do was get his mind off of the whole thing before he got to the fundraiser. He turned on the stereo and hit play on the CD player. He could hear the disk spinning up to speed, and a moment later Billy Joel's *Piano Man* filled the car. He sang along as he drove, ignoring the strange looks from other drivers who were probably not as surprised by the singing as they were by the fluffy orange feline in the carrier hanging off the passenger seat.

oOo

The community center parking lot was full when Bobby arrived a few minutes after noon, so he parked down the street and got Vinnie all set up in the carrier. They walked back to the center and followed the little tent signs directing them to the gymnasium. Even as they approached down the hallway, he could hear Stacey addressing everyone over the loudspeaker.

"Welcome everyone to the Third Annual Westview Eff Breast Cancer Silent Auction! I love you all and this afternoon we are going to raise hella funds!" Bobby walked through the double doors and into the softly lit gym. Stacey was at the microphone on stage in front of a six-piece band. "If you look to my left, you'll see TheBoard. On it are pictures of far too many women and a few men who lost their battles to one form of breast cancer or another in the last 18 months. Some of the battles were fought long and hard, and some were over so fast the surviving friends and family are still reeling at the loss. Next to The Board is our support group table. Introduce yourself to the wonderful staff and volunteers there, and remember to take their card, because they are there to help, *whenever* you need it."

Moving around the room, towards The Board and the stage, Bobby passed through a bright light and Stacey saw him.

"Bobby! Come on up, hon!" She waved to him. He waved back and the crowd parted to let him pass through. Normally he would have preferred to stay in the shadows and let others take the spotlight, but this was a special event, and he'd promised Stacey he would step up and do what needed to be done. Apparently, that meant going up on stage, where she welcomed him with a light hug so as to not crush Vinnie.

"Everyone, I'd like to introduce you to Bobby Odini. Almost thirty years ago, Bobby lost his wife Betty to metastatic breast cancer. He raised his daughter, Marionette, on his own, and did such an amazing job that she joined Westview Police Department and worked her way up to detective." The hundred or so people gathered applauded loudly. "A year ago, Detective Marionette MJ Odini was taken away from Bobby by inflammatory breast cancer."

The gymnasium fell into a pained hush. Someone called out "We love you, Bobby!" and it took real strength for him to not lose his composure right there in front of a hundred strangers.

Stacey kissed him on the cheek. "And with Bobby today is MJ's BFF, Vinnie, who has adopted Bobby and makes sure he's cared for now that MJ is gone. I met Bobby during MJ's treatments, and over the brief time poor MJ had from diagnosis to her final breath, I learned that Bobby—a retired bus driver with Westview Transit Commission—is an *amazing* chef. Over on Table 6 you will find three lots of Bobby's original, orgasmically tasty, Casa Odini Secret Pasta Sauce, made and bottled yesterday from only fresh ingredients. They are just a few of the wonderful items donated today. I'm going to let Bobby and Vinnie join you down there to see what they want to bid on and take home. Thanks, boys. See you in a bit." She blew Vinnie a kiss and winked at Bobby, who returned down the steps and back into the crowd. Stacey continued on to describe some of the many other donated auction items.

Bobby sort of heard the list while he made his way away from the stage, stopping frequently as people greeted him with "I'm so sorry for your loss" or "Thank you for the donation" or "He's such a handsome cat". He smiled and thanked each one. Although this event put both MJ and Betty's deaths front and center, he was starting to feel less alone than he had in a long time. Probably most of the people in the gym had lost someone to cancer of one kind or another. They'd had their hearts torn out, too, when they watched their loved one fade from the vibrancy of life to the shell that Death would claim. Their kind words weren't platitudes; they were an understanding acknowledgement of his anguish. He stopped and turned back to face the stage, looking around at the crowd. There were smiles and tears everywhere, sometimes on the same face.

Stacey finished her welcome speech with "Let the bidding begin!" She handed the microphone back to the band, and stepped down to hugs and air-kisses and handshakes. The band turned out to be a jazz combo and they added a perfect background to the event without overwhelming all of the conversations.

Bobby watched Stacey, then lost her in the crowd, so he and Vinnie made their way to the dozen or so tables holding the silent auction items. The selection was amazing! There were cases of wine, spa treatments, cupcake parties, and, to Bobby's complete astonishment, a *signed #26 Carlos Sanchez Westview Orcas 2015 season jersey* in a big frame. He looked down at the bid sheet. The minimum bid was $200. He added his name, phone number, and a $250 bid. "It's all for a good cause, Vinnie. I'm sure we can find room for it at home." Vinnie head-bumped Bobby's hand, so Bobby scratched the cat's head, and took comfort in the resultant purring. They continued around the room, amazed at the variety and value of the donated items. There was even a heli-skiing adventure worth over $1000. Bobby placed bids on a few items, just to get them started, but by the time he got to Table 6, the bids on his sauce in sets of three were already over $40, each. He smiled at the silliness, and wished MJ could be here to see what people were bidding for her old man's creamy tomato-vodka sauce.

After once around the gym, he'd placed ten bids, but he was only serious about half of them. There was a gift basket/bed of cat toys and treats; a gift basket of Gordon Ramsay Bread Street Stoneware; a wooden box of books by twenty West Coast science fiction and fantasy authors, including Steven Barnes, Tananarive Due, Terry Brooks, and Brian Herbert—all favorites of his; a framed satellite photo of Westview at night; and dinner for two up the Coast Tower. Over the next few hours, he would keep his eye on those five items, trying not to look too eager, but also watching who else was watching them. He and MJ had always had great fun making a game of silent auctions, whether it was for her school, the church, or just a local scout troop.

He was doubling back to check on the bids for the Sanchez jersey when Stacey caught up to him and linked her arm through his. "How are you two boys doing? Outbidding everyone on everything?"

Bobby squeezed her arm. "Just a few select items, including dinner up the Tower. Of course, if I win it, I'll need a date, because they won't let my chunky feline buddy up there."

"If that's an invitation, Mr. Odini, I accept. But what if you don't win the item?" She pouted melodramatically and Bobby had to fight the urge to kiss the pout away.

"Then we'll just have to go anyway."

"Deal. By the way, have you seen what's happening to the bidding on your sauces?"

"Yeah. It's crazy. They were up to $40 for three jars."

"$40? Bobby, there's a freaking bidding war going on. *Each* set is now over $150. That's $450 for nine jars of your pasta sauce. $50 *per jar*. I'm tempted to run home and bring back my jar."

He had no idea what to say. "My sauce is good, but $50 a jar? That's ridiculous."

"It's not about the sauce. It's about the cause. And it's about showing you they understand your loss and they are 100% in your corner."

"I'm just one of the dozens here who have lost someone."

"That's true. Would you like to show the others the same kind of support? I can walk you around and show you which items were donated by people who lost someone to cancer."

"Please. Yes." He would bid on them. It was the least he could do.

"First, let's go over to The Board, so I can show you the faces of the ones they lost." She guided him through the crowd, but it took them nearly five minutes to get there, as people stopped to say hello and scratch Vinnie's head. When they finally reached The Board, Bobby was blown away. There were over a hundred pictures. They were posted alphabetically, so he found MJ's quickly.

"So many."

"Last year there were over 40,000 deaths, nationwide. Just from breast cancer."

"Oh Christ." He stared at The Board, looking at each photo, reading each name to himself.

Stacey began pointing to photos, indicating which ones had items donated specifically in their memory, and which items they were. It turned out eight of the eleven items Bobby was bidding on were donated by someone like himself, who'd lost someone. He told Stacey as much. "You've bid on eleven things?"

"Sure. But just six, seriously, including the Sanchez jersey."

"Don't get your hopes up about that one. There's a certain oncologist here who has a signed Sanchez home run ball she personally caught, and she wants the jersey to complete the set. Her pockets are extremely deep."

He *had* had his hopes up, but it was all good. "I may give her a run for her money, but only for the cause. A retired bus driver can hardly win a bidding war with a determined doctor."

"Maybe not, but I'm sure you'll have fun trying."

"Of course."

"I'm going to let you wander on your own for a bit. I have to go make sure the food gets set out within the next ten minutes." She leaned in and kissed his cheek. "Stay out of trouble, Mister Odini."

"I suppose. If I have to."

"You do." She flitted off into the crowd, and Bobby shook his head in wonder. He hadn't dated seriously in... well, *since Betty*. At first, he hadn't hadtime, between work and raising MJ, and then he just hadn't really had much interest in it. There had been dates over the years, of course, but when it all came down to it, when he wanted the company of an intelligent, funny woman, he'd more often than not just called his daughter. He hadn't thought of his previous coffees with Stacey as dates, but maybe he should.

His phone buzzed in his pocket, so he stepped to one side to answer it. It was a text from Sam. *They found your courier/burglars up near Albatross Bay. Dead. Still trying to ID the bodies. Stay safe. Lock your doors. Maybe carry the gun, but not on your "road trip".*

"Dammit." He put his phone away. "One step forward, two steps back, buddy." He rubbed Vinnie's head, lost in thought. On one hand he was relieved that the two men wouldn't be breaking in again, but on the other, really *big* hand, whoever hired them wasn't screwing around. Whatever they had to lose, it was serious enough to kill for. He was *so* in over his head that for the first time in a long time, he was afraid for himself.

The lead singer of the band announced the food was ready and a buzz arose in the crowd as people drifted over to line up for the midday buffet. Bobby didn't have much of an appetite after Sam's text. He went back to the auction items, seeing where his bids stood in an attempt to distract himself.

Bidding on the basket of cat toys was heavy, but in one- and two-dollar increments, so he bumped it up ten. The stoneware only had one other bid, but she had outbid him by twenty-five dollars. It was worth over two-fifty, so he saw her twenty-five and raised her fifty. Bidding on the basket of books was slow, but the top bid was one of the donors Stacey told him about, so he left it alone. The satellite photo was already twice its retail value, so he skipped it, and finished by bumping his dinner bid up thirty dollars.

His own bids taken care of, he cut back to check on the Sanchez jersey. It was already up over $800, so Bobby tipped an imaginary hat to those battling for it and walked away. He wanted to check how his sauce was doing, but at the same time he was afraid to look. It was sauce. Just sauce. It wasn't worth fifty bucks a jar.

A man about his own age was at the bid sheet, so Bobby stood back and let him finish. The fella put the pen down and looked up at Bobby. "I lost my wife, too. We saved my daughter. God bless you, friend." He gave Vinnie a pat and Bobby's arm a squeeze.

Bobby favored the man with a half-smile. "I'm sorry for your loss, but congratulations for your daughter. I'm glad your story had a different ending than mine. Bless you both."

The man returned the smile and left Bobby alone at Table 6. Even from a few feet away, Bobby could see the organizers had added an extra bid sheet to each of the three sets of jars. He took a breath and stepped up to see where they stood with an hour to go on the bidding.

He blinked. He rubbed his eyes. He shook his head to clear it. Then the tears started. "Wow," he whispered. "He bid $300. A hundred a jar. That's...not possible."

"What's not possible, handsome?" Stacey came up behind him. She looked over his shoulder at the bid sheets. "Mother of God, Bobby! Three hundred...two hundred, and... two-ten!"

He was stunned. "I need some air."

"Want some company? I can't be gone long, but I can slip out for a couple minutes."

"Yes. Please." He needed out, and he needed to sit. Company would be good. Stacey's company would be *very* good. They slipped out a side door and sat on the first bench they came to.

Stacey found a tissue in one of her pockets and wiped away his tears. Then she kissed him, gently. "You okay?"

"I will be. It's a lot of money."

"It is, and it's for a wonderful cause."

"Can I ask you a favor?"

"Anything."

"When you announce the winning bids on the sauce, please add that I will round up the number of jars each gets to an even dozen. I'll add nine jars to each set. It's the least I can do for them."

"You would do that?"

"Without hesitation. It'll have to wait until I get back from Banff, though."

"Banff? As in *Canada*? That's *really* out of town. I thought you meant Seattle or someplace close. When are you going?"

He looked at his watch. "In about ten hours. Vinnie and I are driving up. I have some family business I have to take care of."

"I didn't know you had family in Canada."

"I don't. It's a long story, and I want to tell you, but how about over dinner when I get back."

"Of course. In the meantime, though, you need to eat something. I've been watching you and you didn't go near the buffet. It's quite the spread."

"Okay. In a minute. You get back inside and we old boys will join you shortly."

"You'd better." She kissed him on the top of his head and returned to her event.

Vinnie *mrowed* at him.

"You want down for a bit, buddy? Feel the grass between your toes? Sure. Let's do it." He unbuckled the carrier and placed it beside him on the bench. Before Vinnie had a chance to struggle, Bobby had him out of the device and on the end of his retractable leash. The cat leaped off the bench and strutted over to the grass, where he immediately collapsed and rolled over on his back.

"Feels good, doesn't it, big guy?"

Vinnie purred, swatted his own tail, and chatter-meowed in the sun, before finally lying on his back with his legs wide open and his belly exposed.

"You're just the picture of grace and class, Vin. I'll give you one minute before we go back in."

Vinnie wiggled, but stayed put.

"One. Minute."

Three minutes later, Bobby scooped the happy cat up and got him set up in the carrier again. "We have to check our bids. *I* want the stoneware, and *you* need those toys."

Inside, word of the bidding war for Bobby's sauce had spread and the place hummed with conversation. People smiled, waved, and made brief, passing remarks about Casa Odini kicking ass or some such, while Bobby followed Stacey's "orders" and went to the buffet. She was right. It was an amazing spread, not the usual generic buffet fare that made him cringe both as a cook and as a diner. There were ricotta crespelles, Mongolian-style beef tenderloin tips, grilled vegetable polenta, smoked salmon hash, and a dozen other items he wanted to sample. He filled his plate with a little of just about everything, plopped a heaping tablespoon of salmon hash on a side plate for Vinnie, and found a chair out of the way, from where he could watch the room.

Never one to fight over food with a cat, Bobby fed Vinnie first. The salmon was nearly inhaled, Vinnie was so hungry. "Well done, big guy." He looked at his watch—he still had time to eat and check his items before Stacey closed the bidding. At first Vinnie thought the forkfuls were for him, but after the first couple of gentle swats of his reaching paw, he got the message and let his master eat.

Unlike some culinary aficionados, Bobby didn't mind letting others cook for him, and he certainly wasn't a vocal critic when something was less than excellent, but this buffet was as tasty as it looked. Sweet and salty, spicy and cool, the balances were delicate and well thought out. It had been a long time since he'd actually enjoyed a meal on a paper plate on his lap in a gymnasium.

The music faded to silence. Bobby looked up at the stage, where Stacey was once again at the microphone. "Fifteen-minute warning, everyone. The bidding closes in fifteen minutes. Now, we're all friends and family here, so no pushing, shoving, dropkicking, or tazing. Table monitors please take your places. Shoot on sight." The gym abruptly went silent. Stacey laughed. "Gotcha! Play nice, have fun, and know you have all helped raise a lot of money today. Thank you all. Once everything closes, we'll do a quick tally and announce it." She turned the mic back over to the band and joined Bobby.

"How's the food, boys?"

"Best buffet I've had in years."

"Chef Peter will be glad to hear that."

"This is a Chef I-Have-My-Own-Cooking-Show Peter buffet?"

"It is. He lost his sister to cancer just before Christmas, and volunteered to help. He's here somewhere."

"Now I'm really impressed."

"Good! Let's go update our bids, and then I'll introduce you to the support team."

"Sure." He looked around at the gathering of people who knew pain like he did, and acknowledged to himself that maybe he needed a little help to finish healing.

When the event was all done, Bobby had won both the stoneware and the cat toys, though he suspected his competition backed off of the cat toys because they'd met Vinnie in person. His sauce hadn't gone up much higher, and when Stacey announced he was going to add nine more jars for the winners, the gym exploded in applause and cheers. He got the contact information for two of the winners so he could call them once their jars were ready.

A few minutes later, a man stepped out of the crowd and strolled up to Bobby, while drying his hands on a small towel tucked into his black apron. He was a little taller than Bobby's five-nine, his tight, salt-and-pepper afro was cut close to his very dark skin, and he had the unmistakable aura of a celebrity. He extended his hand and Bobby took it, knowing Chef Peter on sight.

"Peter Beebe, Bobby. I bought the third batch of your Casa Odini sauce."

Bobby was awed. "*You* bought *my* sauce, Chef?"

"Your list of ingredients was intriguing. I look forward to seeing how it all comes together. I'd like to make you an offer. Let me try the sauce over the next week, over different dishes, and if I like what I taste, I'll triple my donation to the fund in exchange for you showing me how you make it."

"I, um..." Bobby's words slipped away.

"If you're willing. I would also never mention the sauce without giving you credit, either as Robert Odini or Casa Odini, whichever you prefer."

"Um..."

The chef seemed to rethink his proposal. "No, I have a better idea. If I like it, I'll have you on the show and you can teach all of the Pacific Northwest how to make it. I'll pay you $5000 for your appearance, and donate $5000 to the fund. We can make it a big deal, focusing on Breast Cancer Awareness." He smiled, and Bobby almost giggled. "But first I have to try the sauce. What do you say?"

Bobby finally found his voice. "I say I'd be a fool to say no. But on one condition."

"Let's hear it."

"My fee goes to the fund as well."

"Seriously?"

"Seriously, Chef."

Peter shook his hand again. "Deal. And if your sauce sucks, we'll find another reason to have you on." He took a business card out of his wallet and wrote on the back of it before handing it to Bobby. "This is my card, and that's my personal cell number on the back. Give me a call after next weekend and I'll let you know what I've decided."

"Of course." Bobby tucked the card in his shirt pocket.

"Now please excuse me. I have to help my staff breakdown the buffet and load the truck. It was a pleasure meeting you, Bobby. I look forward to trying the sauce and I'll speak to you in a week or so."

"The pleasure is mine, Chef. Thank you."

Chef Peter half jogged over to the buffet and grabbed one end of a chafing dish a staff member was struggling with. Bobby wasn't sure if he wanted to laugh or cry. Laughter was his auto-response for anything exciting or cool, but the afternoon was so overwhelmingly full of emotion that tears were a possibility, too.

"You look like someone gave you a million dollars and then punched you in the face." Stacey brushed his cheek with the soft back of her pale hand. "I saw you chatting with Chef Peter."

Bobby told her about their exchange, but the words sounded so surreal coming out of his mouth. Stacey just stared at him, even more caught off guard than he was. He squeezed her hand. "You okay, Stacey?"

"I want to cry and scream and jump and dance and sit down so I don't fall down."

He laughed kindly. "Yeah. Me, too." People were carrying their bid-on-and-won items out to their vehicles, each passing by and thanking Stacey for all her hard work. She thanked each of them individually and gushed over their wins. Bobby took the opportunity to slip away and go pay for his new stoneware and Vinnie's basket of cat toys and treats. The basket of toys wasn't heavy, but the basket of stoneware needed two hands and no cat, so he got Vinnie set up with the toys in the Jeep before locking it up again and returning to the community center for the stoneware.

Stacey met him at the door. "There you are. Can I help?"

"I should be okay, thanks. I just didn't want to crush His Lordship with the stoneware. He's useless as a porter, so I've got him guarding the car. Do you need a hand with anything?"

"No, Mister Star of the Day, I don't. I have a dozen volunteers at my beck and call and you need to get home and have a nap before you drive off into the sunset."

"Technically, I'll be driving into the sun*rise*, and I'll only be gone a few days. I should be back before the end of the week."

"Good, because I want to take *you* up the Tower for dinner, to thank you for being my show pony today, and to celebrate your upcoming television appearance. Unless letting a lady buy you dinner violates some macho Italian male code."

"It probably does, but I'm hardly a stickler for following rules."

"Then go get your plates, and I'll get back to work. Will you text me before you leave, and then once you arrive, to let me know you both made it safely?"

"Of course." Somehow, in the course of a day, their relationship had evolved from casual coffee dates to something else entirely, and Bobby liked the idea. He leaned in and kissed Stacey, surprising her. She responded with just the right amount of enthusiasm and promise for two grown-ups in a public place surrounded by people they knew.

"Are you sure you don't want a co-pilot?"

"Thanks, but next trip, I promise." He wanted to tell her everything, but it could wait until he got back.

"Deal!" Someone called her name from the other side of the gym. She gave him another quick kiss and was gone.

Bobby picked up the twenty-pound basket of stoneware and carried it out to the Jeep, which was still in one piece, with Vinnie safe inside. "Alright, buddy, home again, home again, jiggety jig."

CHAPTER SEVEN

O n his way up to the condo with Vinnie and the toys, Bobby stopped at the concierge desk to make sure everything was quiet. He was tempted to tell Martin the two burglars were dead, but he figured it would be in the news soon enough.

"All okay, Mr. Odini. Not even a smoke detector going off. Just the way I like it."

"Thanks, Martin. Just so you know, I'm going out of town for a week. I can be reached on my cellphone in an emergency, but I am *not* expecting any company. No cleaners or contractors or deliveries or family staying over. And if anyone asks, tell them I'm home, but fighting the flu. No visitors, please."

"Got it. No one. Sick with flu."

"Exactly. Thank you." He pushed the elevator button. "Have a good evening, Martin."

"Will do, Mr. Odini. You, too."

Bobby got the load upstairs and shut off the little alarm within the time limit. His phone chirped with the notification he had entered the condo, but he ignored it and returned to the garage for the stoneware. It was a gorgeous grey set of sixteen pieces, and would nicely replace the old set he could now donate to a shelter or the Women's Center. He was still a little off balance from both the bidding war on his sauces and the surreal encounter with Chef Peter, and settled on a small glass of wine before his pre-trip nap. While he sipped, he checked the AAA app for the weather and road conditions for his route. It was all good. The alternative route north to British Columbia showed quite a bit of construction, confirming his decision to go east.

Stripped down to his boxers, he climbed into his bed for the last time for the better part of a week. Vinnie wasted no time hopping up with his usual *mrow-squawk* combo and claiming his side of the bed. Bobby didn't know about Vinnie, but *he* was asleep in under a minute.

oOo

The alarm went off at 10:30, which gave Bobby plenty of time for a shower and to finish off the rest of the Kifto beef. He and Vinnie both got their medications on schedule, and then he took a thermos full of Ethiopian dark roast, his suitcase, and the litter box down to the Jeep. At the last second, he grabbed MJ's letters. If they broke in again while he was gone, they could have anything they wanted, but he'd be damned if he'd let them take his daughter's final words to him. He thought about taking Mar's album, too, but since everything was scanned and uploaded to the cloud, it was unnecessary.

Once down in the garage, he grabbed both the plastic cat kennel and the travelling litter box out of his storage cage, and put it in the Compass along with everything else. Vinnie wouldn't be happy about it, but it might be best to have him contained when they crossed the border. He had no idea what the laws in Canada were with regards to driving with animals, but in some states loose pets were considered driving distractions. He had no desire to get a ticket, either at home or in Canada. Inside his passport folder was also Vinnie's vaccination records.

A few minutes after midnight, Bobby and Vinnie pulled out of the parking garage with the his phone hooked into the stereo's USB port and Bobby's *Faves* playlist keeping them company. They were soon on the highway heading east with Bob Seger's *Night Moves*. Bobby estimated five hours to Coeur d'Alene, where they'd make their first stop. He'd have to do the return trip during daylight, to make up for missing the mountains while travelling in the dark, though he and MJ had done their share of camping in the eastern part of the state. This would be the first time he'd been there without her. Maybe it was a good thing he was driving at night after all, he thought.

The night was warm, and as soon as they were away from the city lights, wildlife spottings increased. Deer and coyote were the most frequent, and Bobby had to keep vigilant to avoid collisions. He told Vinnie about each one, pointing them out as he passed, but Vinnie ignored him, preferring to do his co-piloting while asleep. Bobby loved to drive, so he didn't mind, singing heartily along to whatever the playlist presented.

He kept his speed to no more than five over the limit, and they reached Spokane in just under four hours. Not having travelled this late at night before, he was impressed with the steady flow of vehicles in both directions on the highway. For hours it seemed to be just him in his little Jeep Compass sandwiched between one long, fast-moving convoy of big rigs. The I-90 cut straight through the middle of Spokane and out the other side and they were in Coeur d'Alene in half an hour. Letting his GPS guide him, he took the off-ramp at 95 and swung around to the *Shari's Café & Pies* on West Ironwood. He gave Vinnie a small dish of kibble, and got out of the Jeep with a little effort. He stretched out the kinks with snaps, pops, and groans in the pre-dawn light, then went in for breakfast.

The country fried steak and eggs were as good as it looked on the menu, but the coffee was utilitarian and couldn't compare to the brew in his thermos back in the car. He ate quickly, thinking to get back on the road, but just as the bill arrived, a wave of exhaustion swept over him and he felt like someone had just cut his strings. It was all he could do to not yawn in the server's face when she handed him the bill. He paid cash, adding a generous tip, as usual, thanked her, and returned to the Jeep. He needed a nap, but they were parked too close to the restaurant's front door, so he drove it around to the east side and parked under a tree. He set his phone's countdown timer for an hour and reclined his seat back as far as it would go. Sleep found him fast.

The alarm woke Bobby slowly, but he felt wonderfully well-rested and raring to go. He got the two of them back on the I-90 quickly and found a place in the northbound convoy.

Ninety minutes later he pulled off in the town of Bonners Ferry—eight miles from the infamous Ruby Ridge, site of an eleven-day siege in the early nineties—and gassed up the Jeep. He also coaxed stubborn Vinnie into the travel kennel in the back seat, which he strapped down with the seatbelt. Vinnie's license tag was attached to his harness, and Bobby put his passport and Vinnie's paperwork on the passenger seat beside himself. Fortunately, Vinnie's rabies shot was only three weeks old. They weren't far from the border, but traffic got heavier as they approached, and what should have been a forty-minute drive, took ninety.

It wasn't his first time across the border, so as he pulled up to the booth's window, he had his passport and driver's license both ready, all of his windows rolled down, and his sunglasses replaced by his regular prescription glasses. Three minutes later he and Vinnie were in BritishColumbia, driving through the East Kootenay Mountains. Bobby was well aware his ease at crossing the border had a lot to do with his being an older, clean-cut, white male, and that many others were not that fortunate. Coming *into* Canada it wasn't as big of a deal, but when he returned home, it would make all the difference in the world, and that saddened him.

The convoy reformed on the other side of the border and after getting Vinnie out of the kennel and back into his copilot seat rig, Bobby found a position in the traffic flowing north on the two-lane blacktop. It was an unexciting route, with low mountains and a river on the west, and evergreens all around.

They reached Radium Hot Springs in three-and-a-half hours. He sighted a gas station up ahead and pulled in, both for a bathroom break and to let Vinnie feel the grass under his paws. After being in the driver's seat for so long, he was tempted to find the hot springs and go for a soak, but his research showed Banff had some hot springs as well, so he postponed the pleasure and got on with the journey after a few minutes. The Jeep's GPS directed him onto Highway 93 and claimed he had under two hours to go. Traffic thinned out a bit on 93, which was a relief.

Not far past town, the highway started to climb and the mountains crowded in. Gone was the wide valley he'd been in and now he was heading up into the snow-blanketed Rockies, he thought. He approached another entry booth and it turned out to be for Kootenay

National Park. He bought a pass good for five days in all National Parks, and continued on.

The highway was carved straight through the rock, with hundred-foot cliffs coming right up to the edge of the road in some spots. There were short stretches where there wasn't even a place to pull over if something went wrong. It quite effectively reflected how he was feeling about poking into Marion's murder. Two men were already dead and he really had no back-up if something went wrong while he was in another country meeting people he didn't know.

It took him a little over three hours to get to Banff because as the vistas got more rugged, he pulled over whenever he got a chance to snap a few photos. His trip might have the darkness of his sister's murder at its heart, but he couldn't help to be amazed at the harsh landscapes and wildlife around him. He spotted elk, deer, a black bear with two cubs on the other side of a river, and even a moose. None of them were in places where he could safely pull over to photograph, but it was fun to see them. MJ would have accused him of being 'such a tourist', but he was okay with that because it's exactly what he was.

He was also as sore as hell. Just after they cleared Radium Hot Springs, he pulled over at the first pullout where he popped a few of the safer painkillers he had with him and stretched out as many kinks as he could. Then, at most photo overlooks, he got out and stretched a bit more. Eventually the painkillers started to work, but by that time he was driving up the long, wide approach to the British Columbia/Alberta border at the Continental Divide, and was only half an hour from Banff.

o0o

The town of Banff was a quaint little place. It seemed to have one main street and few buildings taller than three or four stories. The architecture was a mixture of Swiss Alpine and Canadian limestone. The mountains rose up high around the town, cradling it in its river-crossed, conifer-carpeted, rocky palm. The speed limit dropped drastically, forcing him to slow the Jeep to a frustrating crawl. Once he reached the core of the town, though, the sheer volume of pedestrian traffic was justification for the slower speed. Back home on the coast it was spring, but Banff was still in full ski and snowboard mode and most people were dressed for it.

Sitting at a red light, he was surprised to see a full-size transit bus drive past. "Well damn. Seven thousand people and they have a transit system. What a great place to retire and still get to play driver."

He had a few hours before check-in at the hotel, so he decided to explore some of the more touristy parts of the town, starting with the Banff Springs Hotel, a Scottish baronial-style behemoth, according to the photos and tourist websites. The signs were straightforward, so he found himself driving toward a valley with a monstrous mountain on one side, sloping down like a massive tipped-over table. Houses on either side were a mix of mock-Swiss and modern wealth, and he got distracted enough he didn't notice the hotel until he cleared the traffic light at the Bow Falls turnoff and drove past the tall trees on the corner.

"Holy crap, Vinnie!" He'd seen grand hotels in New York, Chicago, and even in Europe, but there was something fictional about the twelve- or thirteen-story brown-and-green castle. Sitting alone on its high perch with the tree-covered mountains directly behind it gave it a whole different scale. It was both huge and minuscule, imposing and insignificant. It couldn't compare in size to the surrounding mountains, but yet, sitting by itself, it seemed to be holding its own in terms of

solidity and permanence. He saw a single parking spot on the other side
of the road and with a quick check for traffic around him, did a quick
U-turn and zipped into the spot before anyone else could claim it.

He got out, retrieved his camera from the bag in the backseat, and
took a handful of photos of the hotel. It was warmer than it looked
from the car, but there was still a bit of a bite to the air. The sky was a
painfully perfect blue, with the only two clouds puffy and white enough
to be dessert toppings. He spotted three horses on the far side of a snowy
soccer pitch and zoomed in, only to discover they were elk. Excited, he
snapped more photos.

Vinnie *mrowed* from his copilot's seat. Bobby lifted him out and let
him stretch on the damp sidewalk, on the end of his leash. "Smell that,
Vin? That's a *real* forest." He took another deep breath and marveled at
the distinctive tang of pine, cedar, and spruce.

Bobby and Vinnie wandered up the road and explored all of the cool
nooks and crannies of the grand railroad hotel for a couple hours before
returning to the Jeep. They made a quick stop at the Bow Falls, which
were more like frozen rapids than a Niagara-style drop. At four-fifteen,
Bobby pulled the Jeep into the circular drive of the Banff Starlight
Hotel. While he was in the process of checking in, a tall, fit, balding,
clean-shaven man about ten years his junior approached.

"Bobby? George Houtman. Welcome to Banff and the Starlight."
George extended his hand and Bobby shook it. It was warm and solid.

"Thank you, George." He looked around at the natural pine and
fieldstone lobby, with its towering fireplace and big, comfy chairs. "Quite
the place you've got here. It makes me want to curl up in front of the fire
with a good book and never leave."

"Thank you. We're quite proud of how the renovations turned out. As for the fireplace, your chalet has one, so you don't need to hang out in the lobby if you don't want to."

"You've got me in a chalet, with a fireplace?" He was moved by the generous gesture.

"And a Jacuzzi. I'm sure you could use a soak after the long drive. What time did you leave Westview?"

"Just after midnight. I took my time, and even had a nap in Coeur d'Alene."

"Good thinking." The front desk clerk handed Bobby his keycard and bid him enjoy his stay. George motioned to the driveway. "Can I show you to your chalet? It's just a short drive."

"Sure. I don't want to take you away from your boss duties, though." He walked back out to the Jeep.

"My staff hardly need me hovering. Sunday is my short day. Just a few hours in the afternoon, after church."

Bobby opened the passenger door for George, but forgot it was Vinnie's seat. "Oops. Do you mind the back seat, since it isn't far? This is Vinnie, my bodyguard and roommate."

George waved at the cat. "Hey Vinnie. The back seat is fine." As soon as the doors were closed, George's attitude did a complete about-face. "Okay, Bobby. Why are you here all of a sudden, after thirty years? Your sister was butchered and tossed down the service stairs, and this is the first we've heard from you."

Bobby was lost for words. Of course, these were all things he'd thought of himself over the decades and much more so, recently, but no one had ever called him on it until now, when this complete stranger threw it in his face. "I have reasons, but no excuse."

George leaned forward. "Reasons are good. Let's get you to your chalet and you can reason away."

"Really?"

"Yes. I'll give you a chance. If you give me reasons I accept, it's all good. If not, you have one night here on me, in Marion's honor, and then you're out. And if that's the case, you don't get to go anywhere near my wife and kids."

"Fair enough. Where to?" He just wanted a soak and a nap, but he owed George an explanation. He just hoped it would be enough. Sometimes it wasn't even enough for himself.

"Straight ahead. Right at the first turn, then park. Number 22."

Following the simple directions, Bobby wondered what he'd gotten himself into. George's anger was justifiable, but was there more to it? He felt like he was skiing in deep powder but wearing skinny Nordic skis—he had little control and was making almost negligible progress.

George gave him a hand by carrying his little suitcase while Bobby got Vinnie and his camera bag. He went back for the litter box, and once it was set up and the Jeep secured, the two men sat facing each other from couches across a low coffee table. The place was gorgeous, but Bobby would have to take time to explore and appreciate it later. In the meantime, he had an explanation or two to lay on the table. He started simply.

"Mar was just nineteen when my wife, Betty, was diagnosed with breast cancer." He took a long, slow breath, then laid out for George what his life had been like thirty years ago, and how, although he grieved his sister in his own way, he had buried himself in the day-to-day world of a single parent.

If the local police had held out any hope whatsoever that the case could be solved and the guilty party could be found and punished, then maybe

Bobby would have stepped up. Maybe. In less than a year, the entire focus of his life became the little girl who would now grow up without either her mother or her aunt. He'd been overwhelmed and stayed that way for a long time. He finished up by showing George the photo of MJ and Betty he carried in his wallet. "And last year I lost my daughter."

George held the photo with reverence. "I'm sorry. I understand. Forgive my anger, please."

"No." Bobby accepted the photo back. "I won't forgive it, because you're right and I was wrong."

"Okay. Then why have you finally come to Banff *now*?"

Bobby brought George up to speed, filling him in on all the details of the past week. He had to trust someone and it was unlikely an eighteen-year-old ski bum would have hired a Westview man to kill a girl he'd just met, so Bobby chose to trust the former ski bum who had become a family man and grown up to run a hotel.

o0o

George leaned back on the couch, stunned. "A hit man killed Marion? Followed her to Canada, then stabbed her in the dark, and went back to Westview?"

"That's the assumption we're going on."

"Crazy."

"Don't I know it."

"So, what do you hope to learn here, thirty years later?"

"Honestly? Nothing. If I'm lucky, maybe I'll find some closure."

"Closure is good."

"So they say. I probably would have let the whole thing go if they hadn't broken into the car and stolen Mar's stuff and then tried to break into my condo. If someone wants to keep a secret buried—a secret that got my sister *and* the two burglars killed—then I have to dig. Someone is scared and it's time I stepped up and made like the big brother I once was."

"About as good a reason as any." His phone vibrated so pulled it out of his pocket and looked at the screen. "Katherine suggests dinner at six because the girls have school tomorrow. Why don't you have a shower and get unpacked, and I'll finish up in the office and we'll go eat. Once the girls are in bed, I'll answer all your questions about Marion's last day, at least with regards to the time she was with us."

"You mean she wasn't always with you?"

"We didn't meet them until dinner, then we bounced around town, from bar to bar. We can go over all this at the house, after dinner. Deal?"

"Sounds good. Thank you."

"I'll come get you in half an hour." The two men stood, shook hands, and George left. Bobby locked and secured the door, did a quick walk around the two levels of the beautiful chalet, and then stripped and climbed into the shower. Vinnie followed along behind him until Bobby started the shower, and then the cat made himself scarce.

o0o

The chalet came equipped with a single-serving coffee maker and Bobby had just enough time after showering and getting dressed to make and drink a mug before George picked him up. Bobby was prepared to drive himself, but since he didn't know the town at all, George said it would be easier for him to bring Bobby back when the evening was done. As he pointed out, it wasn't like the town was big anyway. He could drop Bobby off and be back home in ten minutes.

oOo

Katherine was a dark blonde with hints of grey and her wide smile made her eyes crinkle in the corners. Dressed simply but strikingly in a soft brown sweater and beige slacks, she greeted them at the door, with two sets of giggles behind her. Their daughters—Jadyn and Catryn—were sparkling and energetic combinations of their parents. They all welcomed Bobby into their home, and when the girls asked how the grownups knew each other, Bobby simply said they were friends of his family. The girls accepted his answer and spent much of the meal peppering Bobby about what it was like living near the ocean and did he drive all the way and who did he drive up with and where *was* Vinnie and why couldn't Vinnie have come for dinner, too, and what was it like to be a bus driver.

Katherine and George tried to hush the girls and make them eat and leave their guest alone, but Bobby laughed. "Please. I'm happy to answer any and all of their questions. My daughter was just the same at their ages." The words were out of his mouth before he could stop them, and they were like a punch in his gut. He took a sip of his beer to hide the sudden emotion welling up in his eyes, but the girls latched onto the topic.

"You have a daughter? What's her name? Is she our age? Or is she old, like twenty?"

He steeled himself. He'd been through this before in the last year. It never seemed to get easier, though. "Her name was MJ, short for Marionette Jayne. She was thirty-five."

Jadyn caught on. "Was?"

"She got sick and died last year."

Bobby wasn't sure how much he should tell the girls, or what reaction to expect, but what he wasn't prepared for was Catryn getting out of her seat and coming over to hold his hand. He clenched his jaw and held his breath, determined not to embarrass himself in front of strangers, but when Jadyn joined her sister, squeezing his other hand, the tears flowed despite his resolve.

No one said anything. The eight- and six-year-old girls just held on, like he was a family member they'd known all their life and his pain was their pain. Eventually, he got himself under control and accepted the tissue Katherine handed him. He squeezed the girls' hands kindly, and whispered, "Bless you." Then he wiped his eyes and nose, feeling a little stupid. "Well, *that* was unexpected. Sorry." The girls each gave him a final squeeze and returned to their chairs.

George put a hand on his forearm. "In this house we never apologize for tears, only for making someone else cry unnecessarily."

Katherine handed him another tissue. "You miss your daughter. I'd be suspicious if you *didn't* cry."

Bobby smiled. "You all would have liked her. She was named after her Aunt Marion, and had both the same stubborn streak and goofy sense of humour. She was a police officer."

Jadyn dropped her fork. "MJ was a *cop?*"

"Not just a cop, she was a *detective*, and a really good one."

"I want to be a detective when I'm older. Did she solve cases and everything?"

"She did. She was the smartest one in the whole family." While they finished the meal, Bobby regaled them with some of the stories MJ had told him about dumb criminals in Westview County, and how she and the other detectives caught them.

oOo

After dinner they retired to the townhouse's family room with coffees, where Catryn and Jadyn told them all about their school day, the projects they were both working on, and gymnastics class. They even moved the coffee table to one side and demonstrated their back walkover skills. The adults duly applauded. To Bobby it all seemed so heart-achingly familiar, but he kept it together and stayed in the moment rather than tumbling back into the past.

At exactly 8:25, Katherine gave the girls a five-minute warning, and they settled down. Jadyn, showing surprising maturity, sat next to her mother and asked her how *her* day went. Katherine hugged her oldest and managed a grin. "I was with you sillies. My day was perfect, starting with breakfast, then church, then everything else we did."

"Almost perfect, Mom. Your knee is sore again. You were limping."
George looked up. "You were?"

"I twisted it shoveling the steps. I'll ice it once we put the girls to bed."

Jadyn disconnected from her mother's embrace and jumped up. "I'll get the ice pack. We can put ourselves to bed." She jogged up to the kitchen, and returned a moment later with a frozen gel-pack and a dishtowel. She wrapped the gel-pack in the towel, handed it to her mother, and then set up pillows in a pile. "C'mon, Mom. Elevate and ice." Her arms folded across her chest, she waited like a Nurse Major Domo, until Katherine turned and got her knee propped up and the gel-pack in place. When she was satisfied, Jadyn turned to her sister. "Okay, Cat. Bed time." The two of them each kissed their parents and went up to bed.

Bobby was impressed. "Wow. If she doesn't become a cop, she's got a career in medicine."

"They're both amazing that way," Katherine commented. "Catryn knows exactly the right moment to give a hug, and precisely when to back off and give you space. She's a natural empath. She can also see through *any* lie, no matter who is spinning it."

"MJ was like that. Maybe Catryn should get into law enforcement."

"Anything is possible at this stage. George and I encourage everything except bad or disrespectful behavior. We never know when some book or project or hobby could ignite a life-long passion. How did MJ get into policing? Was she little Miss Detective growing up?"

Bobby nearly spit his coffee out. "Oh hell no. She was always curious about how things worked and what people were thinking behind their words, but she was a Rock and Roller, all the way. When she was twelve, she asked for an 'axe' for Christmas. She explained it was slang for 'electric guitar', like I'd grown up in a cave with no connection to the outside world. I bought her a starter kit with a little amp and ten lessons, figuring she'd strum a little, get bored and take up volleyball, or cooking, like her old man."

"But she didn't, did she?" George surmised.

"She only needed five lessons before she had me buying her how-to videos. To prove she was serious, she played Jailhouse Rock for me. I was blown away and agreed immediately. I had only two rules—no guitar until homework was *all* done, at her usual A+ level, and two, wear headphones so her shift-working father and the whiny neighbors could get some sleep. She formed her first band a year later, but it fell apart within the month. There were two more tries before she put together the little quartet that became *SnarkPuppet*. They weren't old enough to drive, but they put together a demo tape and started getting little gigs at any post-grunge club that would book them, just so long as they had a parent along with them, to satisfy the liquor inspectors."

"They were good?" George looked like he wanted to buy guitars for both girls.

"I'm not a fan of grunge or post-grunge or loud anything, but these kids could *play*. They stuck together until they finished high school and two of them, Ethan and Cadence, were all set to buy a van and go touring. What they didn't know was MJ had different ideas. She loved the band, but like old folkie Harry Chapin sang, music was her life, it was not her livelihood. She'd always talked to me about going to medical school and curing cancer, but her biology marks weren't strong enough to get her into a good school. It wasn't for lack of effort, because she studied her butt off. When she figured out medical school wasn't going to happen, she decided to get into law enforcement, to maybe someday solve her aunt's murder."

"Wow. And she did, sort of."

"Sort of, but not quite. Which is why I'm here, I guess." He took a sip from his mug. "Katherine, as I explained to George earlier, the victim in MJ's last murder case was a professional hit man suspected of more murders than you or I could conceive of, and a certain Detective Marionette Odini noticed one of the entries in his Ledger of Death was the date and location of Marion's murder. It was too much of an aberration from the other entries for it to be a coincidence, so we've made the assumption this Franco Vetere was hired by someone to kill my sister. Now we know *who* killed her, we just don't know who hired him and why they wanted her dead."

CHAPTER EIGHT

"A hitman? Seriously? George?"

Her husband nodded. "It makes sense, actually. She wasn't robbed or raped. No one saw anything or anyone. That sure doesn't sound like some random stabbing or a stoned transient looking for a fix. There was a similar murder years before that—Lucie Turmel, a cab driver. They eventually caught her killer, Ryan Love, who worked at one of the hotels. They looked at him for Marion's, murder, too, but he was in prison by then."

Bobby turned to Katherine. "Your witness statement said you saw a man you thought was following you all from club to club that night."

"You read my statement?" She seemed surprised, but not angry.

"I've seen everything the police have. One of MJ's detective friends let me have a peek, since he's busy with other cases."

"Ah. Okay." She thought for a moment. "Yes, that sounds like what I told them. I was a little drunk, so I don't think they took me seriously."

Bobby pulled out his phone and found an older picture of Vetere he'd saved off the Internet. "This is from the late nineties. Does he look familiar?"

"There's no way I'd know him now, B—that's him! Holy crap! I remember the way his dark hair fell across his forehead and his cold eyes. He didn't look like he was there for fun at all. Scared the crap out of me when I turned around and saw him watching us. He slipped into the crowd on the dance floor and I only glimpsed him once more, a little later at another club. Platinum City, I think."

"Thank you. This is Vetere. You've pretty much confirmed what his ledger suggested. Of course, I have no idea what difference this makes. We still don't know who hired him." He leaned back in the couch, discouraged.

"It's a start, Bobby." George stood up. "I'll go tuck the girls in and when I come back down, we'll tell you all we remember about Marion's last day or so. It won't solve her murder, but maybe it'll give you some peace."

"Thank you." George left, and Bobby picked up the three coffee cups. "Do you mind if I get refills, Katherine? Dinner was so wonderful and I've been up for far too long."

"Of course. Please, for both of us."

George returned to the family room a moment after Bobby did and they all took a moment with their coffees. George broke the silence first. "We were in Melinda's Missteak, having our one really good meal of the week and celebrating Tanis' nineteenth birthday. In struts Rachel, all flaming red hair, tight white turtleneck, and a smoker's laugh Hollywood thinks is sexy. Half a step behind her and half-a-head taller, was Marion, in ski pants, furry boots, and her dark hair up in a braid of some kind."

"A French braid," Katherine added.

"Right. We found out later Rachel was five years older, but the first impression was almost Mother/Daughter, with Marion being the mother. She had a less frantic way about her, slower and more mature."

Bobby could picture the scene easily. "Rachel loved coke back then, so she was probably a little high."

Katherine smiled. "Oh, she was. I ran into her in the ladies' room and she offered me a toot. I declined, but instead of being insulted, she introduced herself and invited us to party with them, her daddy's treat.

I said I'd have to check with my friends, but it sounded like fun. I went into a stall and by the time I got back to the table, she had introduced herself to everyone there, taken a sip of my wine, and skipped back to Marion."

"We were slow eaters and they were famished, so our two tables finished at the same time and we found ourselves standing on the sidewalk together, wondering where to go next."

George took over. "It was Marion who led us across the street to the Sulphur Pools Lodge where they had some folk musician playing in the lounge. Rachel ordered a couple of bottles of wine and we drank and sang along for an hour or so before Tanis insisted we go dancing."

Katherine interrupted George. "Before that, though, Marion asked the waiter where the pay phones were and went off to make a collect call, she said. While she was gone, Rachel filled us in that her baby stepsister was nursing a wounded heart because her super-secret boyfriend had just broken up with her. She suspected Marion was off calling him, again. It was her third time since they'd arrived in town, she said. Sure enough, when your sister came back about ten minutes later, we could see she'd been crying. She'd fixed her make-up, but her eyes told the whole story."

"So, he *didn't* stand her up, he actually broke up with her." Bobby found that curious.

"Apparently." George went on. "She was one sad cookie, but she perked up a bit after her third tequila. We wandered over to the Cascade Inn on Banff Avenue, danced a little, shared a tray of draught with a couple of off-duty park wardens, then dragged our asses to Platinum City where the DJ was ten times better. After the Cascade, Marion switched to drinking pop and sobered up pretty quickly. Rachel, on the other hand, got so wasted she whipped out her car keys and invited everyone to jump in so she could drive the party to the condo. Marion grabbed the keys and refused to give them back, said she was going for a walk. Rachel was livid, but she could barely stand, so she didn't chase after Marion, just yelled after her "I'm going to kill you, you bitch!"

"She did *what*? That wasn't in your statements to the police."

"Of course not. Rachel was wasted, but she wasn't a killer. Why make her a suspect unnecessarily. Besides, she had an alibi for the murder."

"Did she stay angry for long?"

"No way. Five minutes later she was wondering where her beautiful baby sister was. It was like the outburst had never happened. Marion came back about an hour later and said she was calling it a night, that she was exhausted from the drive. She tried to get Rachel to come with her, but by that time Rachel was making out with the DJ she eventually went home with. We swapped phone numbers with Marion and made plans to see a movie at the Lux Theatre the next day. She hugged us all and left. It was the last time we saw her alive."

"Thank you for being there. It's a good thing Rachel has cleaned up her act or I'd kick her ass when I got back to Westview." He took a long sip of his cooling coffee. "What kind of stuff did Marion talk about? Do you remember?"

Katherine laughed kindly. "I've always been such a light-weight drinker, so once I started with the tequila, my memory blurs right out. George? Do you remember?"

"At first, she moped about her 'Honey', as she called him. I don't remember her ever saying his name. She was worried about some people he was working with back home. One man was famous, but there were also some criminals, or thugs, or someone she didn't like. It was incredulous to us kids, but she was so serious. That's why I didn't want to discuss any of this over the phone or in emails."

So maybe she didn't just take photos from a distance, Bobby thought. "Did she say anything about where she met these people, or what they talked about?"

"No. She was just worried about him."

"What did Rachel say about all this?"

"She thought Marion was exaggerating and said she was better off without the asshole anyway."

"It sounds like Rachel didn't even know the boyfriend."

"She didn't. She even teased Marion about making him up because no one in the family had ever met him or knew his name. To be honest, he did sound a bit fictitious. He sounded like a successful older businessman with shady dealings and no name."

Bobby was so close to telling them the truth, but couldn't. He still had no idea why someone had Marion killed, and he didn't want to put these wonderful people at risk with information that could still be dangerous. He was seriously going to have a long chat with Alex when he got back home, though. "It does sound a little fishy, that's for sure. Because of the ten-year difference in our ages, I really didn't know much about what Mar was up to back then. Thank you for being so candid. I'm impressed with how much you've managed to remember."

George laughed. "I didn't really have much of a choice. After Marion's murder I freaked out and went on a bit of a bender."

"A bit? Sweetie, you were drunk for a month. Your roommates covered for you by saying you'd caught some Asian flu from a busload of tourists."

"It was a long month. Katherine rescued me and made me get some therapy. We didn't actually start dating until I cleaned up my act and didn't reach for a bottle every time I thought about Marion's murder." He reached over and took his wife's hand. "We exchanged occasional letters and phone calls with Rachel, to make sure she was okay. As I'm sure you know, she was really messed up for a long time afterward—worse than I was. Because she let Mar go off on her own she really blamed herself for her death. She still does."

"I know. By the way, she doesn't know exactly why I'm here. Only Sam, the detective working the Vetere case knows. When I get back, I'll sit her down and tell her everything. There's no way she could have prevented a pro from killing Marion. In fact, he might have just killed them both if they'd been together." A thought occurred to him. "So why won't Tanis talk to me? You two have been open and honest, but she refuses."

"If George spent a month drunk, it was still nothing compared to what Tanis went through. She didn't discover your sister's body, but she *did* see it when she went to see what all the flashing lights were about behind the building. She spiraled down hard and fast. The sight of all that blood just broke her. She tried to take her own life a couple weeks later. Her parents rushed her home to Newfoundland and got her help. Eventually she got married and divorced, twice, and finally got so fed up with living in a town where everyone knew your entire family tree going back eight generations, she moved back to Banff about five years ago with her son. She married a local chiropractor and even though we each barbeque at each other's houses all the time, we have *never* spoken about that night since she moved back."

"Okay, then. I'll leave her alone; although, she's always welcome to contact me if she wants to."

"She won't, but it's nice of you to offer."

Bobby looked at his watch. "I have a feeling I'm out by one time zone, and it's later for you than it is for me."

"You're on Mountain Time right now, so one time zone off. Yes, it's late. I should get you back to the hotel. I'm in the office tomorrow at nine, so send me a text when you're up and if you want to do breakfast after I get in, we can meet in the restaurant. Or you can sleep in and order Room Service. Relax with Mr. Vinnie."

"Either one sounds like a good plan. Thank you." He stood, and George did likewise.

Katherine slowly turned and carefully stood, putting most of her weight on her good leg. "What do you have planned for tomorrow? Touristy things?"

"Some, yes. But I want to see where Marion died, and where she spent her last evening."

"Well, Melinda's Missteak has moved, but the Sulphur Pools Lodge is still there. The Cascade and Platinum City are long gone, too. The Zurich Tower Mall is still there, although the bookstore closed up years ago. I think it's just another clothing store now. If there's something this town needs like a hole in the head, it's another clothing store."

"Sounds like Westview and coffee shops." Bobby extended his hand to Katherine. "Thank you so very much for welcoming me into your home, for feeding me, and for letting me bring up the old darkness again, Katherine. You have two amazing daughters and I look forward to hearing about their adventures in the years to come."

She looked down at his offered hand. "Screw the handshake, Bobby. It's a hug or nothing." She opened her arms and shuffled into a brief but strong hug. "You're welcome, for all of it. And if you're in downtown tomorrow or Tuesday, look me up at the Wilson-Bow Inn and we can do lunch."

"I'd like that. Now, I need to get back to Vinnie and give him his meds before I pass out in a bed big enough for a family of six."

Vinnie was asleep on the rug on the hearth in front of the cold fireplace, and roused himself slowly and deliberately before wandering over to Bobby as his human took off his shoes and hung up his jacket.

"Hey Buddy. I'm back. Thanks for not tearing the place apart while I was gone." Bobby plunked himself in the closest chair and Vinnie hopped up to give him a sniff and rub his chin all over, re-establishing ownership. Bobby stayed put, scratching Vinnie's head and letting his vibrating purr relax him.

Eventually Bobby lifted Vinnie to the floor, pried himself out of the chair, and limped over to the chalet's kitchen where he'd stashed both the cat kibble and their medications. He doled out some of each while Vinnie paced, chatted at him, and head-butted his calves repeatedly. Bobby was wiped out and sore and the idea of a hot soak before bed really appealed to him. He made his way upstairs to the master bedroom, where the tub was conveniently located in one corner, overlooking a dark window that probably had a mountain view in daylight.

He started the tub, checked that the flow was nice and hot, then unpacked, putting his meager clothing selection into the dresser drawers. There was a long lump in the outside pocket of the soft-sided suitcase so he opened the zipper, confused.

"Oh, right. The letters." He looked over at the tub. It was filling slowly. "Plenty of time." He slipped the next letter out of the packet and took it over to the low chair next to the sliding balcony door.

Hey Daddio.

Five minutes after you left, I got an email from the oncologist's office with a crapload more information about what's next. Whatever happens, they want me to be well informed.

Speaking of informed, get your damned PSA tested. I know you hate the doctor sticking his lubricated finger up your ass and feeling for lumps, but do it anyway, please. Get the blood work done and make the appointment to be probed. Isn't it ironic—my name is Marionette, but you get to play meat puppet.

I know you're angry with the results of the CT and bone scans—I am, too. But the fact that it has spread is one we have to face and deal with.

Memory time. Do you remember when we went whale watching the first time. I was maybe ten or eleven. I still remember being blown away by how the huge pair, Ophelia and Leo, imposed themselves between the boat and their calf, Nerka. Well, you've been both my Leo and my Ophelia, protecting me while I frolicked and played, just speeding along, oblivious to life's risks. You gave me a safe place to just try shit, and I love you so very much for it.

I'd always expected to be your Ophelia, protecting and sheltering you. That's looking less and less likely now. I'm sorry.

I just sent you a text suggesting dinner at El Gaucho tomorrow. It's been almost a year since we ate there. Or we can go somewhere else. I don't care. I just want to hang out with you all I can.

Always.

Puppet-Gurl.

Through tears, Bobby read it twice more, cherishing each curving line that came from her pen, and the precise choice of words. He remembered the whales, and the vow he'd made to protect her always, but he'd failed.

o0o

The long soak in the steaming jet tub helped banish both his aches and pains from driving, and the blues from thinking about loss and family. He dozed off a couple times and eventually dragged himself out, dried off, and almost literally crawled into the king-sized bed. He heard Vinnie scratching in the litter box wherever he'd left it, and a moment later felt the cat's weight thump on the bed beside him, but he was asleep before any purring started.

oOo

Bobby woke with the sun at 6:30, although his watch still said 5:30. He took a moment to change the time. Vinnie stretched beside him, but stayed put. "Best night's sleep in a while, eh, big guy? Might as well get some more. If we can't sleep in, it's not much of a vacation. On second thought, if I'm retired, can I be on vacation? Isn't it *all* one long vacation?" It took him less than two minutes to fall back to sleep, but it was ruined twenty minutes later when his phone peeped at him with an incoming message. He tried to ignore it, but it was persistently irritating. It was a message from Stacey.

"Damn. I forgot to text her when I left *and* when I arrived. She's not going to be happy." He texted back an apology and a quick note that the evening went well and Vinnie said hi. He promised to call her later, and asked what time would be best. Then he muted the phone and went back to sleep.

oOo

When Bobby finally decided to start the day an hour later, he had two text messages and a voicemail. The first text was from Stacey, saying if he called before noon, he might be forgiven for forgetting to let her know he was safe. *Might*. The second text was from Sam.

Bobby, you've poked a dragon. The photo your sister took on the boat thirty years ago is probably what got her killed. In addition to Brand, Charleswood, and Sabbatini, we've identified Pablo Santacruz, a leader of the Cali cartel until his death in 2003. We're still trying to ID the other two men. I shared this photo with the feds and they practically pissed themselves. We're still digging. Be safe. Maybe consider spending retirement up there in Canada.

"Oh, Mar, what did you get yourself into? What am *I* getting myself into?"

He listened to the voicemail. It was from his fellow transit retiree, Karl, oddly enough. "Hey Bobby. Give me a call when you get this, chief. I need to talk to you about something we started in on at lunch. I dropped by your place but your doorman said you were sick as hell and not taking visitors. Get better. Gimme a call."

Bobby held the phone out in front of him, staring at it, dumbfounded. "What the *hell* is that all about? And why did you go to my home, Karl?" He was starting to get a better picture of who might have stolen the boxes, and how it was connected to the attempted break-in at the condo, but it still didn't make sense. Or maybe it did, when he connected the dots of Karl's message to those of Sam's text. Was Sabbatini the common link they were looking for? Bobby sure as hell wasn't calling Karl from Banff. The old man could wait until he got back home and tell him face to face what he wanted.

After he was dressed and had his first coffee in him, he called Stacey, but got her voicemail. He hated leaving messages but thought he'd better leave *something*. "Hey Stacey. Just Bobby calling. Sorry I missed you. Talk to you soon." He next texted George to say he was going to avail himself of room service before wandering into town, but if he was still around later when Bobby got back, maybe they could grab coffee. He then ordered a huge breakfast with a loaded omelet, hash browns, toast, orange juice, and a side plate of bacon. His cholesterol levels didn't like bacon, but when in Canada, do as Canadians do, he supposed.

He switched his phone to Wi-Fi and logged on to the internet with the hotel guest password posted on a card on the desk. He had no idea where anything was in the town, so he looked up the locations George and Katherine had told him about, and marked them on a map he then screen-captured to his phone. He also looked up Katherine's Wilson-Bow Inn. He would have to eat lunch at some point, so he would take her up on the offer. By the time he was shaved and dressed for a day in the mountains at a cool elevation of 4600 feet above sea level, breakfast was knocking at the door.

o0o

Since he wasn't going to be able to take Vinnie into whichever restaurant he ended up at, Bobby left his roomie to lie in the sun and pretend to guard the chalet. He drove to the town center, found a spot in a tucked-away parking structure, and joined the foot traffic on shop-lined Banff Avenue. The variety of retail outlets was amazing, from the expected t-shirt/postcard/placemat-filled souvenir shops to outdoor shops supplying serious or casual gear for anyone not wanting to hide inside when outside was so much more interesting.

The air was cool and crisp, and periodically he caught the scent of fudge wafting past, smothering the whiffs of people strolling and vaping. He finally passed the source of the wonderful olfactory assault and stood with a small crowd watching the *Fudgetown* fudge master work her product over on a big butcher's block table in the front window of the shop. She wielded her wooden paddle deftly, and Bobby was impressed enough to go in to try a couple of their samples. His taste buds fell instantly in love and made him buy a selection of slabs, including the sour cherry bark, Vanilla caramel fudge, and almond amaretto fudge. He just hoped he could get it all back to the hotel without gorging himself. He had a hunch he would be back for more before he left town.

Expensive fudge goodies clutched tight in his hands, he got back on task. According to the map, the Zurich Tower Village Mall was still a few blocks away. He needed to see where his little sister had been butchered, and the other shops could all wait. He'd put it off for so long and now he was minutes away and he wasn't sure if he felt relieved or ready to throw up. His stomach twisted and turned, his pulse raced, and he felt a little warmer than the weather would explain. But he'd seen the crime scene photos, which captured the horror only too well, so the scene without his sister really shouldn't be so bad. Or so he hoped.

A few minutes later he stood across the street, staring at the three-story Swiss-look Mall, with it's clock tower on the right and two long balconies, one above the other. Five flags danced from poles jutting out of the upper balcony and tourists strolled past on the wide pedestrian way, all oblivious to the heartbreak so near to them.

"It's taken me thirty years. I'm ashamed," he mumbled to himself. "Let's do this. It won't find who hired your killer, Mar, but I need to see it."

He waited for traffic to thin, then crossed the street. His hip was acting up and he stumbled a little when he crossed the median, but nothing was going to stop him now. In through the front entrance, he made his way through the shoppers and to the sunshine-lit rear exit. He went out the back and up the steps to the parking and loading area. It was an odd design, on two levels with two separate sets of steps down, one ending at a service door, and the other with a long ramp up, for dollies, carts, strollers, and wheelchairs, he supposed. It was on this narrow ramp running parallel to the building where Mar was found.

It didn't take him long at all to find the spot, and when he did, it was unreal. Bright sunlight, and a wave of laughing chatter from a pair of young men vaping nearby washed away his expectations of horror. He stood and stared, wondering if the dark stains on the pavement held any remnants of Mar's blood. There's no way they could, after all this time, but he still stared.

"You okay, dude?" The vapers approached, tucking their devices in their pockets. They both wore name tags, each from a different one of the mall's shops.

"My sister died here."

"Damn. Sorry to hear that. Wait... was that way back in the nineties?"

Bobby turned and squinted at the young man. "Uh. Yes."

"No way, dude. You're Marion's brother, Bobby." The kid couldn't have been older than twenty, twenty-five, tops. There was noway he could have met Mar, even if he'd been born and raised in Banff.

"How do you know our names?"

"Here, man." He pointed up about eight feet, just below the windows of the pizza place. There was a weathered little plaque, screwed to the wall. Bobby followed him over, had to squint to read it.

In this spot the world lost a beautiful soul to darkness. Marion Elizabeth Nancy Odini of Westview, WA was murdered here. She died alone. Read this and say a prayer, for no one should die alone like that. Rest in peace, Little Sister. Rachel and Bobby.

Bobby lost it. He crumbled, was caught by the young men, and eased to a sitting position. "Oh snap, dude! You *are* Bobby. We're so sorry." A bottle of water was handed to Bobby and he drank, but he couldn't take his eyes off the plaque.

"When...?"

"When? Hell, the plaque has been there forever. It's a bit of a legend for the locals. She wasn't the first or last to be murdered in Banff, but because they never caught the bastard, people wander past and say a word or have a moment of silence. Every February 6th there are flowers all over the place. She was just a kid, like us. I heard the building owners tried to take it down and the uproar was *insane*."

Bobby handed back the water bottle and held out a hand for a lift up. "Thanks. Our sister never told me she'd done this. I'm blown away." He looked to the two young men. "Just so you know, they've finally got some leads and have reopened the case back in Westview."

They lit up. "Are you *kidding*? That's amazing! Have they charged anybody?"

"No. The guy they think killed her was himself murdered last year."

"Karma is a bitch, man! Serves him right. I hope he suffered."

"So do I, guys. So do I."

The kid pulled a business card out of his vest pocket. "I'm Chad. I have a ski-tuning business on the side. Can you email me everything you can about the case. This news needs to be *celebrated*."

Bobby accepted the card. "Sure, Chad. I'm only in town for a few days, but when I get back to Westview I'll round up what information I can." He looked back up at the plaque. "Pass the word that I really appreciate everyone keeping my sister in their hearts and prayers. I'm truly stunned. Thank you."

"No problem, Bobby. Anyway, we gotta get back to work. It was nice to meet you. Sorry it had to be here, like this."

"Yeah. Me, too." He shook their hands and let them return to work. He took a dozen pictures of the plaque and the location, both wide shots and zoomed in. He was pretty sure his mother was going to be as touched by the situation as he was. "And Rachel... you couldn't tell me about this? Hell, even George and Katherine didn't. Good old Bobby—the last to be in the freaking loop."

He stood for a few minutes longer, finding an odd peace in finally being there. Eventually he kissed the fingertips of his right hand and touched them to the stained asphalt. "I know you're not here, Mar. This is just the place where your earthly life ended. I'm sorry you didn't get more time with us, but I know you're up there with Betty and MJ, so me missing you is just me being selfish. I may have taken half my lifetime to get here, but that doesn't mean I haven't missed you every day of those years. Now excuse me while I go catch the bastard who hired Vetere."

Bobby left that spot, a little calmer but so much more determined. The idea someone had been hired to murder Marion hadn't been much more than an abstract thought until he saw not just where she died, but what the spot had become to people who had never even met her and yet cared about what had been done to her. He consulted the map on his phone and cut back through the mall to the front doors, waving to Chad and his buddy when they looked up from their shops.

Since the two dance clubs were long gone, Bobby decided to swing by Katherine's hotel and set up a lunch time with her, then continue over to hotel where Marion had made her phone call.

He stepped up to the rustic little hotel's front desk. "I'm here to see Katherine Towne-Houtman, please."

The young Asian clerk smiled pleasantly. "Of course, sir. Can I tell her who is here?"

"Bobby Odini."

"Thank you Mr. Odini." She picked up the phone and dialed a three-digit number. "Hi Ms. Houtman. It's Sarah at the Desk. There's a Mr. Odini here to see you. Of course. I'll send him right back. Thank you." She hung up and pointed to a simple door marked *Executive Offices & Sales* to the left of the Front Desk. "If you go through that door, Mr. Odini, and down the hall to the end, Ms. Houtman's office is the last one."

"Thank you, Sarah." He followed her directions, passing three offices of sales managers before reaching the desk of an administrative assistant at the end. The young man sitting behind it got up and opened the door of the office behind him as Bobby approached. "Mr. Odini. Please go straight in, sir."

"Thank you."

"Bobby!" The door closed behind them and Katherine came around her big desk slowly to give him a hug. If he'd thought she was striking in her casual sweater and slacks at home, she was even more so in her dove-grey pinstripe jacket and skirt. He welcomed the hug and returned it.

"Katherine. You didn't tell me about the memorial plaque."

She returned to her chair and motioned Bobby to sit. "It's still there? Good Lord. I thought it was taken down years ago. There was some screaming match in the local paper about it and a protest, but I forgot about it completely. It's not an area I go to very often. I'm sorry. It must have been quite a shock."

"That's the understatement of the day. But it was okay. A couple of the local lads explained it all to me. It's quite touching. Rachel never told me about it, either."

"That doesn't surprise me. She was still battling her demons when she came back and put it up. She was drunk when she arrived and stayed that way until she left. She might not even remember doing it. For the first few years George and I checked up on it, made sure no one vandalized it, but people showed a lot of respect for it. On the anniversary of her death, we used to put flowers there."

"They still do, apparently."

"I'm glad. I'll have to take the girls by to see it. Now that they've met you, they'll have a touchstone for understanding what it means."

"Thank you. So, I came by to see if you're still available for lunch."

"I'd love to." She looked at her watch. "I have a short meeting in fifteen minutes, and a presentation at 11:30. It won't last longer than forty-five minutes, so how's 12:30?"

"That's fine. I'm just going to go see the place where you listened to music and Mar made her phone call, then check out a few of the shops."

"Okay. Well, the new Melinda's Missteak is a bit heavy for me for lunch. How do you feel about Mexican?"

He hadn't had Mexican since MJ died. "I love it. It's been a while."

"Then we'll eat here. We have a terrific little spot. My treat."

"Don't be silly. It's *my* treat."

"Nice try, but it's *my* hotel. I can expense it, just so long as I can get your full and professional opinion as a visiting chef."

"Ha! I'm not a chef. There's no Red Seal on my resume."

"Bobby, just shut up and accept my invitation. Let this lady buy you lunch."

"Well, since you put it that way, Katherine, I'll let you get back to work and then see you in the lobby at 12:30." He smiled and stood, and so did she.

"Good. I look forward to it."

"Me, too." He let himself out, cut through the gift shop to the street, and oriented himself to finding where the hotel in question. He was all turned around and had to consult the photo of the map on his phone.

Five minutes later he stood on the sidewalk outside where Melinda's Missteak once stood, not quite sure why he needed to see the place. It had nothing to do with her death, other than being part of her last night."Maybe all I need is to see where they all met." He looked, shrugged, and, turning around, saw the long, low Sulphur Pools Lodge across the street where George or Katherine had said they listened to a musician and where Mar made her collect call from.

He crossed Lynx Street, walked down the block to the main entrance, and in through the sliding glass front doors. He stopped, looked around, thought it would be a nice place to stay if he came back to Banff. He saw the sign for the washrooms and decided it was as good a time as any for a quick trip in. He did what he had to do, and left. He wasn't sure what he hoped to gain by seeing the place. Everything that really interested him was in the past, where he couldn't go. Back out on the street he snapped a few pictures of the hotel, the street, and the building that used to be where Mar had her last meal. He noticed six big trees on the lawn in front of the hotel, facing the building across the street, so he supposed Vetere had watched them from there. Or maybe he'd sat in a parked vehicle. Bobby had no idea. He'd never done surveillance, so he didn't know which was the most effective way to watch someone.

There were big planters around a couple of the trees that would have made good makeshift benches, but if it was winter, would he have sat there in the cold the whole time they ate? Being parked, though, would limit his options because if he was parked facing the wrong way when they exited the restaurant, he would have to do a three-or-four-point turn on the narrow street, and that would draw some attention. On foot, Vetere would have had much more flexibility, maybe with a vehicle nearby, should he need it. Bobby looked at the photo on his phone again and saw he was only a block from the river that cut through the town, so he walked in that direction, gathering his thoughts.

He knew the trip to Banff was more about closure than it was about solving the murder, but he'd still hoped to learn more than the fact that Alex had broken up with her *before* that weekend, and she was concerned about the people he was hanging around with and associating with. With the photo from the boat showing Brand, Santacruz, and Sabbatini with Alex and others, it was no surprise now that Mar had been worried; Bobby just wished she'd been more worried about her own safety than about Alex's. If Santacruz had ordered the hit, then it was too late to do anything about it—he was dead. If Brand had ordered it, then there was someone with a lot to protect. Sabbatini didn't have as much at risk, but he, too, was still alive and had at least his reputation to protect.

Bobby couldn't imagine Alex ordering the hit, because he truly believed the man had loved his sister. Of course, Alex had also loved Bobby's mother, so maybe he was capable of ordering a murder. Whoever was guilty, they were connected enough to know Bobby had those boxes in his car, and to steal them. They were also in Westview, where they could react quickly. And they were not only able to hire fake couriers to break into his home, but were quite capable of killing them when they screwed up. It didn't sound like Alex, but either Brand or Sabbatini could have pulled it off. Now he just had to prove it.

CHAPTER NINE

B obby found an empty bench by the river and sat, looking out, watching the water roll slowly past with floats of ice from the spring thaw, and letting it carry away his feelings of confusion and inadequacy for the task. He needed to get himself organized, needed to start taking intentional steps forward rather than just dancing around semi-randomly, hoping to step on something important. He knew he was on to something because of the theft and the break-in, but he also knew Sam, the WPD, and the local FBI Field Office were on the case, too, and they were better equipped than he ever could be. But were they even trying to solve Mar's murder, or were they just trying to tie Vetere's work to as many deep pockets and criminal enterprises as they could?

He had read that the Bow River in front of him came from one main glacier—The Bow—and at least five more, which meant the water came not only from snow melt and natural springs, but from ice frozen for thousands or even millions of years. If he drank out of it now, it would be a taste of the past, with ancient microbes and mammoth crap. Now that he was dipping into Marion's past, he felt like he was stirring up political microbes and the mammoth crap of corruption that would do him serious harm if he drank too deeply.

Sitting in the sun by the river, thinking thoughts a little more complex than usual, Bobby nibbled on each of the fudges he'd bought, both to see if he'd got his money's worth, and to determine which one to stock up on while he was in town. He also wanted to take some back for Rachel, his mother, and Stacey. Hell, even Sam would probably like some. Of course, he could get T-shirts, but that was more complicated than the gesture was worth. He decided the vanilla caramel was the most fun on the palate and twisted off another piece before leaving the bench and the river behind. It was almost time for lunch with Katherine.

o0o

"So, what are your plans, Bobby?" Katherine regarded him over her cup of green tea while she sipped.

"Plans? Now that I've seen all there is to see with regards to Mar's death, probably a little shopping, a nap back at the chalet to make sure Vinnie doesn't feel neglected, then dinner back here in the core. I was thinking of the place with their own distillery."

"Good choice. The best gin *ever*. And the food is terrific, too."

"Tomorrow, I think Vinnie and I will drive up to Lake Louise. The pictures I've seen are impressive."

"Not as impressive as it is in person. George and I worked up there for years. There are a lot of beautiful places on the planet, but few as striking as Lake Louise with the grand hotel right at the shore. Make sure you wander through the Chateau while you're there. Unlike the dark, moody, Scottish-inspired Banff Springs Hotel, Chateau Lake Louise is bright and airy and so much more inviting. They're both owned by Fairmont Hotels & Resorts, but two grand siblings couldn't be more different."

"Then I'll do that. Thank you."

"But don't eat there. The food is wonderful, especially in the Wine Bar, but the locals go to the much simpler Peyto Bill's in the Youth

Hostel/Alpine Club down in the village. Of course there are other choices. The Post Hotel is part of the *Chateaux et Relais* chain, and worth every one of its five stars. The Station Restaurant is excellent, too, and a real treat for railway buffs.

"Wow! You really know the area."

"George was in Sales at the Chateau, and I was in Front Office. It was our jobs to know. It still is, really."

"Makes sense. For thirty-five years I drove people around Westview County, and knowing about various famous menus, or if the Orcas, Osprey, Riptides, or Cascades were in town could make all the difference to a tourist's visit."

"Exactly." She lowered her voice. "Now, what about the *case*? Marion's murder? Are you going to keep digging?"

Bobby put down his fork. "Do I have a choice? What was once unsolvable might now be solvable."

"True, but some people will do anything to protect a secret, especially if it threatens their power, their influence. You said two men have been killed, in addition to your sister. Digging could get *you* killed, too. Is it worth it? It won't bring Marion back, and everyone has moved on, so there's no burning need for closure for any of us."

"There *wasn't* a need, for me, but now that finding the truth is a possibility, I want to see it through. The detective, Sam, is doing all the heavy lifting, so to speak. I'm just trying to gather what facts I can for him."

"Then do it quietly, please."

"That's what Sam said."

"He's right." She swapped her tea for her burrito. "With a hired killer thrown into the mix, you're asking for trouble, even thirty years later."

"Don't I know it." He resumed eating.

They changed the subject and chatted about Catryn and Jadyn, then about how much Westview had changed over the years, what the drive up was like, and other options for a route back home. Eventually Katherine had to return to work, so they finished up.

"Thank you for lunch, Katherine. It wasn't necessary."

"Sure it was. I love to share our services, and besides, it keeps my staff on their toes when they see me out and about, not hiding in my office like some general managers do. George works much the same way, although he has quite a different property than we do here."

"You've both got wonderful hotels. The whole town seems geared to giving the visitors the best experience possible. No wonder it's such a popular destination."

"It's also a great place to raise a family. It's not cheap, by any means, but the fresh air, the natural activities, the low crime rate... we just love it."

"I can see that. Now let me get out of your hair so you don't have to work late to make up for the time I've taken you away from the job."

"Fair enough. Give us a call when you get back from Lake Louise tomorrow. We'd love to have you over again before you head home."

"Of course. That would be nice."

o0o

Bobby wandered up and down Banff Avenue for another two hours, shopping as he went until he had three pounds of expensive fudge, two Banff sweatshirts for himself, a book of local history recommended by the one-legged clerk in the small bookstore he discovered on one of the side streets, and a small wooden carving of a black bear basking in the sun.

His treasures in hand, he returned to the Jeep, then joined the slow flow of traffic leaving town. He turned into the Starlight Hotel just before the town limits.

Vinnie was as excited to see him as a fat, lazy cat could be. He chattered up a storm while Bobby rubbed his belly and head. "I know you've been napping all day, buddy, but now it's *my* turn, and of course you're welcome to join me." He stored the fudge in the refrigerator, then limped straight upstairs. When he finally climbed into bed, he promptly fell asleep without setting the alarm.

o0o

It was dark out when Bobby woke, and before he rolled out of bed he knew his hip was unhappy. He put his weight on it carefully. It held, but he was going to need the heavy-duty painkillers. He found those, took one extra for good measure, then hobbled downstairs to feed Vinnie. Part of him really wanted to dine out, but his energy level was low, so he ordered room service, again. If he'd been at home, he would have made dinner, then retired to his big chair and spent the evening reading, but he forgot to bring a book. Then he remembered the book he'd bought about the local Banff history and was relieved he could stick to his usual routine, except for letting someone else cook. He enjoyed routine, was a creature of habit. It helped him get through the half-empty days that now made up his life.

He ordered the house specialty bison burger, a Caesar salad, and the apple crumble for dessert, and a half-liter of the house red wine.While he waited for them, he called Stacey. She answered on the second ring.

"Mister Bobby Odini. We finally get to chat."

"I'm sorry I forgot to text you, Stacey."

"It's okay. I know you have a lot on your mind."

"Yes, but I also have *you* on my mind."

"Really?" She sounded surprised.

"Of course. I'd much rather be here enjoying the incredible scenery with you than doing what I'm doing."

"You never did tell me why you're there. You just said 'family business'."

"It is, but it's pretty morbid. I know I promised to fill you in over dinner when I got home—which I still will—but the gist of it is that thirty years ago my kid sister was murdered here in Banff, and I'm here on a pilgrimage of sorts."

"Oh my God, Bobby! You should have told me!"

"I wanted to, but it all came up so suddenly I was still trying to get my head around it and didn't know how to explain it. I also know you would have insisted on keeping me company—"

"Damn right I would have!"

"—but this is one trip I needed to do alone."

"I get it, I do. Next time. Will there be a next time?"

"I think so, yes. The area is beautiful, the air so crisp it practically crackles, and the people are wonderful. They even leave flowers at the place Marion died, on the anniversary of her death."

"Amazing!"

"It is, isn't it? Tomorrow we're off to Lake Louise for the day, just me and Vinnie."

"Oh, you'll love it! Now I really wish I was with you."

"You've been there before?"

"As a teen. Family trip, one August. If you ever want to go back, I'm calling 'shotgun' right now. I so want to see it again, as an adult this time."

"Deal. We can talk about it at dinner."

"And one or two other things, I think."

Oh crap. Was this all moving faster than he could control? "Sure. Of course."

There was a knock on the chalet's front door. "Room Service!"

"Speaking of dinner, Room Service has arrived." He walked to the door. "I'll give you a call tomorrow evening, when we get back from Louise."

"You'd better. Have a good dinner, and a good day tomorrow, Mr. Odini."

"Thanks, Ms. Mitchell. You, too."

He answered the door and stepped aside to let the waiter in with the tray.

oOo

The bison burger was just what Bobby needed after the long day of walking in the past. It had a richer flavor than beef and he could think of one or two things he'd do a little differently with respect to seasoning, but even picky Vinnie liked the little piece he was given. The salad was a little bland, but Bobby liked his Caesar salad to have a bit more kick than most people, so it was all good. He took the book and the last of the wine over to the big chair, and planted himself there. Vinnie climbed up and sat on the back of the chair, well aware of the routine his human followed. He purred while Bobby read.

Three pages in, Bobby just wasn't feeling the need to learn about Banff right at the moment. A thought had been tickling the back of his mind for a while now, so he searched out his phone, switched it over to hotel Wi-Fi again, and opened the browser. Before returning to the chair, he also raided the chalet's desk for a note pad and pen.

Based on the photo he'd given Sam, he had four names to start working with. Sabbatini, Brand, Charleswood, and Santacruz. Hopefully Sam would be able to get the name of the fifth man whose face was visible in the shot; but the sixth one, facing away from Mar when she snapped the photo, would likely never be identified. Bobby started with the easiest name, Jake Brand. He quickly found the Washington State Legislature webpage with the list of all forty-nine senators. Brand was sixth on the list, right after Democratic Senator Alf Bittner. Brand's office was in the James A. Williams Building. Bobby wrote the address down on the pad, along with the office phone number and the three committees Brand served on: Transportation, Law & Justice, and Ways & Means. There was even a list of bills Brand sponsored, either as the Primary or the Secondary. The list was long, and nothing stood out at the moment, so Bobby just scribbled *Check out sponsored bills* on his notepad.

He Googled Brand's home address and the first link to come up was the senator's page on the Washington State Democrats site. It added his Westview address, the name and number of his Legislative Assistant, Michelle, and his Communications Specialist, Garret. Bobby wrote it all down. There was no home address, so he tried the White Pages website and sure enough, found Brand's landline number and home address. He added both to the list.

While he was on the White Pages site, he entered 'Julius Sabbatini' in the search field. After a moment, Sabbatini's information came up. Bobby wrote it on the pad. He then tried Alex Charleswood, just in case, but nothing came up. He suspected whatever number Alex had it was probably listed in Rachel's name, as his caregiver. He looked at the information he had. It was a good start. He had a hunch, and entered Franco Vetere. Nothing came up under Franco, but there were six other

Veteres listed. Bobby jotted down each of their names. He certainly wasn't going to be knocking on the doors of the family of a dead hit man, but at least he had the information.

When he was done, he bundled Vinnie up, grabbed his jacket and boots, and went for a walk. The night was cold and clear and the area around the chalets was lit in such a way that the sky wasn't lost to the parking lot. He didn't wander too far, though. The front desk clerk had warned him about roaming elk being frequently encountered, but coyotes and bears were also common this far from the center of town, he'd added. They stayed in the light and didn't run into any wild beasts, though Bobby was sure he could hear coyotes howling back and forth in the meadows behind the hotel. Since neither he nor Vinnie were equipped to fight off a pack of coyotes, he sauntered back to the chalet, frequently checking back over his shoulder.

Despite the nap earlier, he was exhausted. He blamed it on the thin air, not his age, and when they were both ready for bed, he and Vinnie were quick to sleep.

o0o

After starting the day with an early shower, Bobby texted George to see if he was available for breakfast. The answer came back quickly and the two met in the hotel's restaurant ten minutes later. The conversation was much the same as the one at lunch the day before with Katherine. George even recommended lunch at Peyto Bill's as well. He added that if Bobby had the time, it was worth the drive into nearby British Columbia to the Natural Bridge and Emerald Lake.

Halfway through their post-meal coffee, George was called away, so Bobby finished up and tried to pay for their meal, only to find George had already charged it to his own account. Bobby left a hefty cash tip and made his way back to the chalet. The day was cloudy and cold, and the weather app predicted snow flurries in town, but called for clear skies in Lake Louise, almost thirty-five miles away.

He checked his phone for any messages from Sam, but there wasn't one. He loaded the Jeep with the camera bag, cane, litter box, Vinnie's water and kibble, and then, finally, Vinnie in his copilot's seat rig. Once they got onto the Trans Canada Highway, traffic was moderately heavy, but moved pretty much at the speed limit of ninety kilometers per hour. Twenty minutes later he pulled over at the halfway point to get a few pictures of the striking, aptly named Castle Mountain, and then was quickly back on the road.

The highway followed the wide valley carved by the Bow River, with the snow-covered Rockies dominating both sides. The turn-off to Lake Louise gave him a choice of right, to the ski hill, or left, to the Lake. It had been a long time since he'd strapped on skis, so left it was. After passing a small shopping area, the road wound its way up the side of the valley, four kilometers. When it leveled off and straightened out, he caught a glimpse of massive five-hundred-room Chateau Lake Louise off to the right, just as the road forked to the left, to the public parking. He'd read the lake was at an elevation of just over a mile above sea level, and even this late in April the snow was piled high on either side of the road.

Even though it was still frozen, Lake Louise didn't disappoint. The view was as stunning as Katherine had said it was, and the nine-story Chateau Lake Louise on the eastern shore was just like her sister in Banff—both dominating and dwarfed. Being the tourist he was, Bobby snapped pictures, marveled at the mountain to the west with the towering cliff face and hanging glacier, let Vinnie bask in the attention from the tourists passing by, and just soaked it all up. A wide, snow-plowed pathway followed the north shore of the lake, looking like it went all the way to the other end, but two minutes along it, his phone chimed with a message.

He stepped to one side of the footpath. The text was from Rachel. *Bobby! There was fire @ storage place in the middle of the night! 6 units completely destroyed, including mine!12 more bad damage. Everything was destroyed! When are u coming home?!*

"Oh crap!" He continued walking, selecting the option to call the person who sent the text. Rachel picked up immediately.

"Bobby!"

"What the hell happened, Ray?"

"It's a goddamned mess, B! The police and fire departments won't tell me anything, but from what I can gather, the six units were random, with no relation to each other and in different parts of the compound."

"I'm sorry. Was anyone hurt?" He was worried Winston might have tried to stop whoever it was.

"No. It was after they'd closed up. The call came in about three in the morning."

"How the hell did they torch the units through the big metal doors?"

"They cut the locks."

"What about sprinklers in the units?"

"None. The place predates some 2009 building code law, they said."

"And the cops are thinking it was vandals? They sound pretty damned organized and determined to be vandals. Did they use any kind of accelerants?"

"It smelled like gasoline, so I guess yes. I just got back from there. They wouldn't let me into the unit because it isn't safe, yet, but I was allowed to stand back and look. Two days ago I told Dad I'd bring him his boxes, so he could pick a few things for his room. Now I can't! He's going to be heartbroken."

"You talked to him recently? How's he doing, generally speaking?"

"Good, I guess. He's usually lucid, but sometimes he's still lost in the past."

"Damn."

"How's your trip going? When are you coming back?"

"You didn't tell me about the plaque you put up for Marion."

"I...did I put up a plaque?"

"You did. I took a picture. I'll send it to you. No worries. Katherine and George said you did it while you were still in full party mode."

"Sounds like me. How are they?"

"They're great. We can do lunch when I get back and I'll tell you all about the visit. Right now Vinnie and I are walking along the shore of Lake Louise and I'm pretty sure my roaming charges are going to be insane. I just wanted to check to make sure you were okay."

"I am, thanks. Pissed off, more than anything. Just because I hadn't looked in the unit for ten years doesn't mean I didn't want to keep the junk. First *you* lose two boxes to thieves, and then this. All that's left is the third box you took. I hope you have it locked up safe and sound."

"Definitely." He wasn't about to tell *anyone* it was with Sam.

"Thank Christ. Okay. You go, enjoy your trip. Give Mr. Vinnie a snuggle for me. I'll see you when you get back. I'm supposed to go out to see Dad on Thursday, with the boxes of his stuff. I'll still go, but he's going to be pissed."

"I don't blame him, but *you* didn't burn it all up, someone else did."

"I know, but *still*. Don't worry about me. Go."

"See you later in a few days."

"You betcha."

He tucked the phone back in his pocket, and kept walking. "Vinnie, things are getting real. Stolen boxes, dead would-be burglars, arson... I'm thinking more and more that carrying MJ's firearm might actually be smart. Or, when we get home, we'll barricade the condo door and live like hermits."

Vinnie mrowed.

"Okay. We'll do it *after* we figure out who the hell started all this way back when. What a goddamned mess."

The stream of pedestrians thinned out a bit as people turned back, so he kept going. It wasn't much further anyway. Two very pretty Asian ladies asked if they could pet Vinnie, and who was he to deny Vinnie love from complete strangers. The ladies giggled and petted and took pictures, but Bobby stopped noticing. Breathing became a bit more difficult, and he started to perspire. As soon as the ladies thanked him and moved on, he found a bench and sat. Either he was getting old or Vinnie was getting fatter, because the harness was feeling heavier than usual. He tried to loosen the strap around his chest, but he tweaked a muscle and a pain radiated through his arm.

It was obvious his body was missing his own bed and regularly hanging in the inversion table, because his back and neck complained the chest rig was twisting things up. He checked the time. It was lunchtime and his blood sugar was likely a little off, too. Even as close as they were to the end of the lake, he decided they'd better get back and get some food in their bellies. He sat and enjoyed the view of the mountains across the flat white expanse of the frozen lake for a few more minutes, and then started back.

They stopped a couple more times at benches as they came upon them, but eventually Bobby felt better and was looking forward to getting Vinnie off his chest and seeing what the fare of the cafe was like.

He always said the only way to find the best eateries was to follow the locals. Back at the Jeep he gently unhooked Vinnie's rig and let the big fella out to make use of the litter box, while he himself eagerly drained the half-full bottle of water in the console's cup holder. "Oh Christ, that's better." Vinnie finished up quickly, so Bobby got him back in his rig and sealed the litter box back in its big plastic bag.

Peyto Bill's Café was a tiny place with a handful of tables on the first floor of the perfect movie set ski resort log cabin. The building was solid wood everything, vaulted ceilings, stone fireplaces... Bobby was impressed. It had to be one of the nicest youth hostels he'd ever seen, though admittedly he'd only seen a handful of them, back when he was a teen. The menu was simple and solid, and, still battling a bit of nausea he opted for the clubhouse sandwich. It was hard to go wrong with a clubhouse. He bypassed coffee and opted for ginger ale, thinking he might have a touch of indigestion.

oOo

An hour-and-a-half later he released Vinnie out of his carrier and into their little chalet at the Starlight. The club sandwich had been perfect, but afterward Bobby was still feeling the effects of the elevation, so he'd driven straight back to Banff. His back was still sore and his hip had once again joined the bitch-and-whine party, so he'd filled the hot tub and had a long hot soak before climbing into the bed for a nap. He was disappointed he'd not seen the inside of the Chateau, or gone to see the Natural Bridge and Emerald Lake George had recommended, but it sounded like Stacey was going to twist his arm to return to the area soon and he'd much rather see it all in her company than alone. Before conking out, he texted both Stacey and Katherine to let them know he was back in Banff and having a short nap.

Katherine texted back so quickly he was still mostly awake when the phone chimed. *Word has spread in town that you're here & an impromptu celebration is happening at the Lois Trono Gazebo in Central Park in the town center. If you're up for it, why not come over for dinner and then we'll all walk over together? Dinner at six, celebration at eight. The girls really want to see you again before you leave for home. George and I do, too. :)*

Bobby smiled. He had mixed feelings about going back out when he was so tired now, but he still had time for a two-hour nap and that should be plenty to recharge his battery. He texted back that it sounded like a great plan, and he'd see them at six. He realized he didn't actually know their address, so he sent another text asking for it. George replied he would be leaving the office then, too, so he'd be happy to drive. Bobby gladly accepted, and put the phone on the bedside table. He fell asleep just as Vinnie curled up next to him.

CHAPTER TEN

The alarm woke Bobby from a bizarre dream where he was standing on a beach, fishing, but everything he caught and reeled in was a burned remnant from Rachel's storage unit. There were accounting textbooks, clothes in plastic wrap, and lamps without shades. Just as the alarm began its chiming and started reeling *him* out of sleep, he thought the end of his line had snagged something big, heavy, pale, and bloated. He woke without ever knowing what it was, but he was a little off-balance for a few minutes as he stood at the sink and splashed cold water on his face.

Vinnie rubbed up against his leg and mrowed. "Yup. Give me a second buddy, and then we'll take care of your food. I have to go back out this evening, so you're on your own again." Vinnie purred and rubbed and led Bobby downstairs to the kitchen. His master filled his bowl with kibble, put out a plate of tuna special, then poured himself a big glass of water—he was going to avoid coffee and alcohol until he got back home—put on his boots and coat, and went out to the deck, where the sun was doing its best to end the day on a warm note.

He had one more night in Banff, and had to be checked out by noon Wednesday. He asked himself if he'd achieved what he wanted? He also wondered *what* he really wanted. Was it closure, like Katherine said they didn't need? Was it the kick in the ass he needed to start digging and dissecting Mar's life and death? How far was he willing to dig, though?

He'd discovered the affair, which led to understanding the photo on the boat better, which then gave him a list of possible suspects. Or maybe *none* of them were involved and it was something else that got his sister killed. He had to think like MJ would have, and look at *all* sides, consider *all* possibilities. Just because there was a union boss, a wanted drug king, a real estate developer, and a future senator all on a boat together at the same time, didn't mean anyone but Alex knew Mar was there, or that she took pictures for any reason other than a school girl celebrity crush. She'd probably had no idea who anyone was, other than her lover and Brand.

Bobby suspected just putting the four men together in the same place and time was enough to get her hurt, but was it worth one of them hiring a pro to follow her to another country and cut her up? It sounded like something the Colombian would do, but from what he'd read of Santacruz, he would also have cut the throats of everyone on the boat himself, and disappeared into the night. The photo was taken in summer—judging by the golf shirts and shorts the men were wearing—and Mar wasn't murdered until February. What had happened in that time to suddenly make her a risk to someone? Had anyone else died around then that was connected to the boat? What about the captain and crew? Or the fifth and sixth men in the photo?

His phone's alarm went off with his fifteen-minute warning. He went back inside, brushed his teeth and shaved quickly, then put his camera bag by the door, along with his winter hat and gloves, his cane, and two slabs of fudge for Jadyn and Catryn. He topped up Vinnie's kibble bowl, turned on the recently-discovered radio in the kitchen to keep the cat company, and was in his coat just as George pulled up in front of the chalet. He grabbed everything he needed, double-checked the key card was in his shirt pocket, and joined George.

"Hey Bobby. How was the road trip?" He drove while they caught up.

"It was good, thanks. The elevation is knocking me for a loop, so I didn't get as much done as I'd hoped, but it was worth it to see it all in person. No wonder you and Katherine stayed up there for so long. If I was a kid again I'd apply tomorrow."

"That's how I ended up out here. I came out for a vacation, giving myself a week to find a job, or head back home. I got a job at the Banff Springs Hotel the day before I was due to fly back home. I met Katherine in Hotel Orientation two days later."

"You've been together a long time."

"Not exactly. We've *known* each other for ages, but we didn't start dating until we both ended up in Lake Louise, after the rough stretch I told you about."

"Love in the Rockies."

"Exactly! We have quite a few friends who met here in Banff or up in Lake Louise and are still together. Life here forms a bond that's pretty damned strong, even when things aren't perfect."

"I know what you mean. For Betty and me it was the ocean. Whenever we had trouble, we drove to the coast, parked, and sat on a beach, looking out at the Pacific, letting the great peaceful sea put everything into perspective. It's hard to feel that what car you buy, or where you spend holidays are relevant and important when faced with tides rolling in and out without any input from you."

George laughed. "That's how I feel about the mountains. Katherine and I have never been able to stay mad at each other when we force ourselves to drive out to Calgary and back. The city lies in the foothills and the mountains are a distant line of rock from there, but on the drive back here, the mountains grow and grow as we get closer, and we finally get home feeling like everything happens for a reason, and God's plan is progressing as it's supposed to."

"Be faithful in small things, for it is in them that your strength lies."

"Yes. Who said that?"

"Mother Theresa."

"A wise lady."

"Most of the time. But she definitely had her dark side."

"As do we all, I suppose."

They arrived at the townhouse and Bobby was barely in the door when Jadyn and Catryn charged up, all giggles and laughs. He decided right there and then of all the things he'd miss about Banff, he'd miss these two the most. He was now even more determined to bring Stacey up to meet them. The girls ran off and Katherine stepped in for a hug. She then took his coat, gloves, and hat, and hung them up. George led him to the couches.

"How was your day, Bobby?"

"Lake Louise was wonderful, but I got a message part way through the day that I'm still trying to process. Rachel sent me a text saying vandals set six of the storage units on fire, including hers. The fire destroyed everything. Ray is pretty upset. I called and spoke with her and fortunately no one was hurt."

"That's horrible! Do you think it's related to what you're digging into?"

Jadyn came down from the kitchen with a dishcloth over her arm bent like a waiter. "Pardon me for interrupting, madame and messieurs, but may I take your drink orders?" They could hear Catryn giggling from the kitchen.

Katherine smiled. "Yes, please. I would like a very dry Manhattan with a twist of lemon."

"I have no idea what a Man-whatever is, Mom."

"Then how about my fresh café on the counter next to the sink, s'il vous plait."

"Café it is, madame."

"Messieurs? Daddy? Uncle Bobby?"

George seemed to think about it for a moment. "I'll have a Grasshopper, please. In a glass."

"Une wheat ale coming up. Uncle B?"

Bobby hoped the flush of joy he felt at once again being called 'Uncle Bobby' by a child didn't show on his face. It felt really good. "I'll have a glass of the house tap water, please."

"*Oui monsieur. Une l'eau glacée.*" She jogged off to fill their orders.

"I hope that means water."

"Yes. Ice water. She has a French test later this week and I've suggested she practice as much as she can."

"Well, it's close enough to Italian and Spanish I might actually understand some of it."

"If you speak either of those languages, I'd love to see her reaction."

"You got it."

Jadyn returned with a tray with the three drinks on it, and Catryn followed behind her with what Bobby assumed were their own glasses of water. Jadyn served her mother first.

"*Merci mademoiselle,*" Katherine thanked her.

"*Avec plaisir, madame.*" She then handed Bobby his water.

"*Grazie mille, signorina. Apprezzo il tuo eccellente servizio.*"

Jadyn stopped cold, her mouth open. Confused, she looked at her mother, then at her father, neither of whom could help her. "*Avec plaisir, monsieur?*"

"*Perfecto, signorina*!" Bobby winked at her. "That was the perfect response, Jadyn. What I said was Italian for 'Thank you very much, miss. I appreciate your excellent service.'"

"That was Italian? *So* cool! Mom, I want to learn Italian!"

"Okay. But do you know where they speak Italian?"

"Um, French is from Quebec, so Italian must be from Ontario."

George and Katherine howled. Bobby didn't know the province of Ontario at all, but he guessed it was like an American saying that Italian was from 'New York'.

George accepted his beer from Jadyn. "Honey, you don't know how right you are. Actually, Italian originates from the country of Italy, which is in..."

"Europe."

"And is right next to..."

"Um, France?"

"Which is where what language *originates*?"

"France? Um, French."

"Exactly. But your idea about Ontario was interesting. Toronto has the fourth or fifth largest Italian population in the world, outside of Italy. In North America, I think only New York has more."

"Wow." She took her glass of water from Catryn and sat next to Bobby. "Are you from Italy, Uncle Bobby?"

He smiled, and clinked his glass with hers in a toast. "*I'm* not, Jadyn, but my family is. I have a lot of cousins over there. My father and two of his sisters came to the west coast from New York, where they grew up with their parents, who came from Florence, Italy, which is in the middle of the country, closer to the north than the south."

"Cool!"

Catryn sat on her father's lap, but her attention was on Bobby. "Say something else in Italy."

"Please," George admonished her.

"Please, Uncle Bobby."

"Something else in Italian? Like what?"

"I don't know. How about "I can't go to school tomorrow because I was up all night eating cake with my family."

"Really?"

"Yes, please. Just for fun."

"Okay." He thought about it for a moment, then gave her his best translation. *"Non posso andare a scuola domani perché sono stato sveglio tutta la notte amangiare dolci con la mia famiglia."*

Catryn stared at him and Jadyn laughed. "That sounded like a spell from Harry Potter!"

Katherine congratulated her. "Well done, Jadyn! What Bobby spoke was Italian and Hermione's spells are in Latin, and they're not the same, but they're from the same part of the world."

"Then I want to learn Latin, Mom."

"Italian would be a better choice, Honey. There's no such thing as real magic spells, and no one speaks Latin in every day conversation any more. Pass your French test this week, get all the way through junior high and high school with some fluency in French, and then we'll look into Italian for you. One language at a time. It's less confusing." A timer in the kitchen chimed. "Casserole is ready. It still has to cool off for a few minutes, so Catryn, would you please get the salad out of the refrigerator while Jadyn sets the table."

"Yes, Mom."

"Oui, Mama."

The two went off to their tasks, and Katherine followed them, presumably to get the casserole out of the oven. Bobby looked at George.

"You've got them well-trained. MJ was pretty good, but by the time she was Jadyn's age, we butted heads occasionally."

"Our girls are well-trained, but they're on their best behavior for two reasons. One, you're here, and they really like you. And two, I gather Katherine told them they could only come to the celebration if they behaved. They're not badly behaved as a rule, but they're children and every now and then they forget who's really in charge of the house."

"Katherine?"

"Exactly. It sure as hell isn't *me*."

o0o

Dinner was wonderful, and Bobby found himself wishing he lived close enough to have the family over to his place to return the favor. The condo could use the sound of little girls' laughter to chase away some of the emotional cobwebs. Hell, *he* could use that sound in his life again on a more regular basis. Watching old videos of MJ wasn't nearly as healthy as hanging out with living children. He shook off the maudlin thoughts and put an idea out there as George put the fruit-filled dessert Jell-O on the table. "I'm not sure what you folks do for your vacations, but if you ever want to come down Westview way, I'd love to host you and show you my town. I have a spare room for the adults and air mattresses for the girls, if you don't mind a big, fat, one-eared, orange cat climbing on top of you when you go to sleep."

Jadyn was the first to respond. "That would be amazing fun! Where is Westview?"

"It's in Washington State, which is south of British Columbia. Almost straight down the road from Vancouver, south of Seattle. I live about two hours from the ocean." He had a flash thought of Mar on the boat with those men, but this was neither the time nor the place to get sidetracked.

"We've been to Vancouver!"

"Well, Westview is three-and-a-half hours straight south from Vancouver."

George nodded. "That sounds like fun, Bobby. Thank you. We much prefer to take the girls somewhere real than to a Disney-style destination, though those can be fun, too."

Katherine began to dole out Jell-O. "George and I have been there a few times for business, but we've never taken the girls. I think they'd like it, especially if we can time it with an Orcas game. Catryn and George are hardcore baseball fans."

"Really? The Blue Jays I assume."

"Of course!" Catryn chimed in. "O-kay! Blue Jays! Lets! Play! Ball!"

They all laughed. Bobby tried to remember the Orcas' schedule. "The Blue Jays come to town at least once a season, so I'll look into it. I have season's tickets. MJ and I hardly ever missed a game. Nowadays I tend to go with one or another retired bus driver, or I give them to our condo concierge, to take his son." He accepted the Jell-O, then let Jadyn slop a huge dollop of whipped cream on top. "Whatever you decide, the invitation is open. If you're serious about catching a game at Arden Field, give me as much warning as you can and I'll arrange enough tickets for everyone." He ate. It was simple, yet delicious. A wonderful palate cleanser after the very nice chicken casserole.

"Thank you, Bobby. I like the idea of road trips. We try to expose the girls to the world from the ground, where they can meet other people and see how others live, even if it's still in our part of the world. We were thinking of Maui near to Christmas, but we can probably find a week before then, in summer. *Should* find a week in summer. It's our busiest season, absolutely crazy around here, but a good manager should never be without a team that can't take over in an emergency. A week away would be a good test. George?"

Her husband was quiet. "Sure. I might be able to arrange it. Our owners aren't quite as flexible as Katherine's, but I think I can get away with a week, if I prepare everyone for it." He took a bite of dessert, chewed, swallowed, thought a moment, and smiled. "*Yes*. Let's see what we can come up with."

"I don't mean to put pressure on you two. If summer doesn't work, there's always fall. If you love sports, football season starts in October, and the Orcas are still playing then. Or just whenever you can. There's more to Westview than sports."

"True. Since we'd drive, though, we'd have to come before the snows hit. There are a lot of mountains between here and there."

"That's for sure. I have a feeling I'll be back here before fall, too."

"Really?" Jadyn nearly jumped out of her seat.

"My friend, Stacey, wants to come up. She was here when she was about your age, Jadyn, but she hasn't been back since."

Catryn leaned in close and pointed her dessert-full spoon at him. "Is Stacey your girlfriend, Uncle Bobby?" She ate the mouthful, but kept her eyes on him.

A strange feeling swept over Bobby. He realized he'd never had this conversation with MJ because he didn't really date while she was alive. He never had much desire to do the 'relationship thing' as she called it. "No. Not yet. Maybe soon. We're having dinner when I get back and I think Stacey is going to suggest we take it to the next level."

"The next level?"

Oops. He forgot he was talking to kids. "Go from just friends to boyfriend/girlfriend."

"Ah. Then you tell her she has to come meet us before you get married."

"Catryn!" Katherine was apoplectic.

"What, Mom? That's what grownups do. They get married. Even Aunty Cheryl got married, and we thought she would *never* get married."

Katherine chuckled. "True. We didn't. But Bobby and Stacey are just friends right now, and there's a lot of life to be lived between 'just friends' and 'getting married'." She looked up at George for help, but he smiled and put his hands up in surrender. "Oh, thanks for the support, mister."

"What? My girls won't have to worry because they won'tbe dating until they're over thirty."

"Oh, good luck with *that* one, my friend." Bobby knew this argument only too well. "I said the same thing about MJ. She had her first escorted date at thirteen and first unescorted date at fifteen. She was playing bar gigs with her band back then, too. She was always much more mature than her friends the same age. She had one football-playing boyfriend who grabbed her hard by the arm, twisted it, and told her to choose her music or him. When he regained consciousness, it was with a broken nose and a very sore groin. The band played a gig in Tacoma the same night and opened with a brand new song about a dude with a glass jaw and no need for athletic support, if you know what I mean. So, like I said, good luck, George. The best you can do is to teach the girls how to make solid, intelligent decisions, and how to see who their real friends are. I think you're well on track now. They'll drive you crazy, but there's no better kind of crazy and I miss her so much my heart nearly explodes once a day. I wouldn't trade the pain I feel now for the joy I had for thirty-five years."

All four of his hosts reached across the table and took one of his hands. After a moment, Katherine let go and stood up. "On that note, let's get cleaned up, dressed for outside, and walk over to the gazebo. The girls wrapped candles in tinfoil for each of us. Word spread pretty fast, Bobby. Most of my staff who aren't working are planning on going."

"Wow. I guess we'd better get going, then. I'm sorry Rachel can't be here. After the day she had, she could use the break. Then again, the event revolves around the darkest time in her life, so maybe it wouldn't fix her day. I'll take pictures, though, to share with her when I get home."

The temperature had dropped quite a bit by the time the five of them stepped outside, and Bobby was glad he'd brought his gloves, hat, and was wearing one of his new sweatshirts. He didn't think he owned a pair of long underwear, and it's not something one really needed in Westview, so the wind cut cold through his jeans. After the long day he'd had, it didn't take long before he had to put some weight on the cane, but it wasn't too bad.

One thing he noticed about Banff was how many people liked to go out and walk in the evening. Back home, temperatures like this would keep people inside, but here it was just another April evening. At first he thought it was just the magic hour for everyone to get out and walk their dog, but after a few blocks Bobby realized there was a steady line of people in front and behind them and they were all heading in the same direction. He may have underestimated what they were walking into.

Jadyn and Catryn danced and skipped around them as they walked, or ran up to greet friends and neighbors, and Bobby just let their joy infect him in all the good ways, which is why he didn't notice the crowd until they crossed the pedestrian bridge over the Bow River and arrived at a park. He stopped in his tracks and people flowed around him. In a town of over seven thousand people, it looked like at least half of them were out tonight, for *his* sister. Jadyn saw he'd stopped and came back to him.

"Are you okay, Uncle Bobby?"

"This is a lot of people."

"It sure is. Almost as many as when the Prime Minister came to visit." She gave his coat sleeve a gentle tug and he let her pull him toward the eight-sided, thirty-foot-wide, raised gazebo. They joined Katherine and Catryn, and Jadyn let go of him, though she stayed right at his side. George was nowhere to be seen. Bobby looked around at everyone. It was like a ski-gear-wearing United Nations. He heard snippets of half a dozen languages and at least a dozen different accents around him. He'd never been in such a small place with such a diverse make-up. He powered up his camera and began taking pictures. Sunset was still maybe an hour away, but dusk was settling fast.

George returned to them. "This way." He took Catryn and Katherine by the hand and Jadyn took Bobby's sleeve again, as if she'd taken responsibility for keeping him close. She was so much like MJ that Bobby had to blink away the past before he tripped over his own feet. George led them up to the stage where Bobby recognized Chad, one of his vaping friends from the day before.

"Dude! Bobby! You made it! No one knew how to reach you!"

"Hey Chad. Is this all your doing?" He looked around them at the amazing crowd.

"Yeah, sort of. I told my girl you were in town and she said we needed to light the place up, for Marion. We put the word out on every platform that the case was reopened, and like every other news in this town, word spread like wildfire." He looked at the time on his phone. "Eight o'clock.

It's time. No pressure, Bobby, but can we call you up on stage? Maybe say a few words? Would you be okay with that?"

Would he? This was the second time in four days where he'd been up on stage, which was amazing for a man who stayed as far away from the limelight as he could his entire life. The stage had been MJ's thing. "Sure. That'd be cool."

"Sweet!" Chad climbed up the steps to join a handful of people already there. He spoke with a pretty brunette, gave her a quick kiss, and approached the microphone. He tapped it twice to make sure it was on, then quietly spoke. "It's time." Surprisingly, the gathered masses hushed right up. "In this place," he started, and the crowd joined him, speaking in unison. "The world lost a beautiful soul to darkness. Marion Elizabeth Nancy Odini of Westview, Washington, was murdered here. She died alone. Read this and say a prayer, for no one should die alone like that. Rest in peace, Little Sister. Rachel and Bobby." He reached back and took his girlfriend's hand, bringing her to the mic with him. They held hands and raised their free hands. "A moment of silence for Marion."

There was nearly complete silence. A few young children could be heard, but they weren't an irritant to Bobby, rather a reminder life goes on. The minute was over quickly. Chad looked out over the crowd. "Thank you all for coming. Some of you know what it's all about, some of you just heard we were celebrating something and you thought you'd tag along and see what it's all about. That's cool. It's *all* cool. We all know the plaque. We all know what happened over there." He pointed in the direction of the nearby Zurich Tower Mall. "By now many of you know there's news." The crowd erupted in a roar. Bobby could even see police officers cheering nearby. "But this isn't my news to share when we have none other than *Bobby Odini* himself here with us. Dudes and dudettes, ladies and gentlemen, visitors to Banff and residents alike, please welcome Marion's big brother, Bobby Odini."

If he thought the roar a moment ago had been loud, the welcome this mountain resort town gave him as he climbed up the steps was deafening. Catryn and a number of other children clapped their hands over their ears, it was so loud. He took a deep breath and did his best to keep his tears at bay. It's not that he was afraid of embarrassing himself, he was afraid they'd freeze right on his face.

He stepped up and accepted a hug from each of Chad and his girlfriend. Facing the microphone and the crowd, he waved. He'd already decided to not tell the entire story, but to give them all a few facts to give them some reward for their loyalty and love to Marion's memory. "Thank you, Banff." The cheer subsided. "Thank you, Banff. To say I'm overwhelmed, blown away, shocked you're all here, would be a huge understatement. Let me start with an apology. I am so very sorry I haven't been here before, to see where my sister spent her last day. Banff was just a town I associated with death and heartbreak, and I really had no need to see the spot where Marion lay crumpled, bleeding, and alone." Emotional gasps came from the crowd.

"Sorry, but that's what happened to her, and that's what I thought of the town. It's still what happened to her, but it's no longer what I think of Banff. I have met wonderful people, made amazing friends, and can't think of a better place for my sister to have been visiting for her last day. Back in Westview, I was recently able to review all of the files from the investigation." He looked around and found a half dozen officers on the perimeter of the crowd. "And I just want to thank the Banff RCMP for the thorough job they did investigating my sister's brutal murder. Please take a moment to acknowledge the men and women who not only handled the case back then, but who do their best keeping us all safe day in and day out." He applauded the officers, facing each of them one at a time as he did, and the crowd joined in. The officers each saluted him in turn and he nodded back.

"Some of you over the years have probably thought they dropped the ball and Marion's killer should eventually have been caught like Ryan Love eventually was after he murdered the cab driver, Luci decades ago. What no one could have known is that Marion's killer wasn't still in Banff. He wasn't even in Canada. After he killed her, we suspect he returned to Westview, where they think he was based." Murmurs of shock rippled through the crowd. "That's right. We don't know yet *why* Marion was murdered, but new evidence has given the Westview police a reason to reopen the case at their end."

Someone yelled out. "Have they caught him?"

"The investigation has taken on a whole new life back in Washington and I don't want to compromise it in any way. But I've seen the evidence and it looks good. It's the first real break in thirty years and I'm confident they'll soon have answers for all of us."

Another cheer ripped through the crisp mountain air, and he let it go on as long as it needed to. This was a bit of closure. This was what this faithful town had been praying for, for thirty years. "Amen, brother!"

Bobby crossed himself and nodded in the direction of the shout. "Amen." He reached down to Jadyn, and pointed to his candle she'd been holding for him. She smiled and handed it up. "I know we don't all share the same faith. Marion and I were raised Roman Catholic, but I'll bet every variation of faith and belief is probably represented here tonight, including those of you who don't believe in a Higher Power. That's okay, because we're all here because we believe in one thing. *Love*. You've placed flowers for my sister in that dark place every year for thirty years, out of love for someone you never met. You're here now because your love in the darkness needs closure, or at least Hope, so light can once again shine.

"I'm going to give the microphone back to Chad and ask him to lead everyone in the Lord's Prayer, or a blessing, or a poem, or a song. Whatever he chooses is good with me, and I know it will be good with you, because it's for Marion, and it's for other loved ones lost, and loved ones we can't bear the thought of losing. It's for the children, and our hope they live to know a world where they don't have to be afraid of dying behind a dumpster or in an alley. And it's for my daughter, Detective Marionette Odini, who died last year of cancer, and was still trying to solve her aunt's murder while lying on her own death bed. *Love.*" To loud gasps and shouts of "Love!", he stepped back and let Chad move up.

While the young man asked everyone to take out candles if they had them, or lighters, or even just the flashlights on their phones, Bobby motioned for Catryn, Jadyn, Katherine, and George to join him on stage to one side. Katherine took out a lighter and lit Bobby's candle. He in turn lit each of the girls' with his, and the girls lit their parents. Very shortly, the ten or so people on the gazebo stage had their candles lit, and Bobby turned back to the gathered crowd.

The sun was nearly gone, but the park was illuminated by thousands of wondrous, flickering flames and cellphone screens. Occasional flashes went off as people tried to capture the moment in photos, and Bobby remembered the camera around his own neck. He raised it up and took a few pictures. He wasn't happy with the quick previews he saw on the screen, so he let the camera hang again and took out his phone. He took a few pictures with it and the results were much better. He couldn't get the entire scene in one photo, so he switched to panorama mode and slowly panned the phone from left to right. At the microphone, Chad and his girlfriend started to sing, a capella, and it took Bobby a moment to focus and recognize the song. It was Ben E.King's classic, *Stand By Me*. He had expected Leonard Cohen's *Hallelujah*, or *Somewhere Over the Rainbow*, or *Amazing Grace*, but as he listened to the surprisingly pure voices, the lyrics made perfect sense.

He added his voice to the thousands already singing, and didn't fight back the tears. This was for his baby sister, and it was a long time coming. He held his tin-foil-handled candle up. This was truly the vigil his sister deserved, and in his heart he was singing, too, for his daughter, his wife, and even his baby brother.

o0o

When they got back to the townhouse, Bobby gave Jadyn and Catryn their slabs of fudge, then sat on the couch while Katherine and George got the girls ready for bed. His only regret was that he hadn't recorded the event for Rachel to see. It really would have warmed her heart.

Teeth must have been brushed, faces washed, and little monkeys changed into the pajamas in record time, because a sudden thundering of footsteps snapped Bobby out of his reverie when the sisters came roaring down the stairs to give him big hugs.

"Thank you for the fudge, Uncle Bobby! Come back soon! Bring your girlfriend, and Vinnie! Have a safe trip home!" They each gave him a final squeeze and fled back upstairs to bed. A few moments later Katherine and George came downstairs and Bobby stood up.

George put his coat back on and grabbed his keys, while Katherine gave Bobby a warm, honest hug. "You, sir, have made quite the impression on our daughters."

"And on *us*," George added.

"*And* on us. I'll be honest and say that thirty years after Marion's death, I didn't think there was any closure to be had. Yes, I know catching whoever did it would close that door, but I hadn't realized what was missing until we had it tonight. You came to Banff to ask some questions and finally see the place for yourself, Bobby, but you started the healing of an entire town. There may be a plaque and people may put out flowers every year, but none of that dispelled the cloud we didn't even know was hanging over us. In a town this small, it doesn't take much imagination to think 'it could happen to me or to my daughter'."

"Or my wife." George put his arm around Katherine and kissed the top of her head. "Katherine said it perfectly. You've helped heal our town somewhat. I know a couple of the RCMP constables spoke to you afterward, but what you didn't see was that there were some off-duty officers there. If you get a chance tomorrow, before you leave town, maybe swing by their detachment and tell them the details you didn't tell the people tonight. I think they'd appreciate it. I'm pretty sure a case like this eats away at them."

"An excellent idea. Thank you, George. I honestly hadn't thought about it. I hadn't even planned to mention them until I saw them standing with everyone else, not as crowd control like they so often do back home, but as men and women who live and raise families in the town, too. In them, I saw MJ."

Katherine squeezed his arm. "Your daughter would have been really proud of you tonight."

"As I am of her, every single day. She was the hero, I'm just the dad."

"Not tonight. Tonight you were hero to an entire town."

"Thank you. But I'm a tired hero. George, I can call a cab if you're too tired."

"Don't try that crap on me, Bobby. I'm not too tired. Let's get you back to the Starlight."

"Okay." Bobby turned to Katherine again, stepped in and took both of her hands in his. "You four are part of my family now. When the girls called me Uncle Bobby, I nearly lost it. I have two step-nieces and a step-nephew, but they're grown and I don't see them too often. Thank you for everything, but mostly, thank you for being with Marion in her last hours. I'm glad she got to know you, even if it was too brief."

Katherine wiped away a tear. "And you're part of *our* family, Bobby. One way or another, we'll see you soon. And as for the last, I'm so very glad we got to spend time with Marion that night. Even in those few hours, I could see she was a shining star with a huge heart. Give Rachel hugs for us, please. And if I don't get a chance to speak with you before you leave tomorrow—I'm in and out of meetings all day—have a safe trip home."

"Will do. Thank you."

CHAPTER ELEVEN

While he drove Bobby back to the Starlight, George added his own thanks and expressed how much he appreciated the respect Bobby had shown Jadyn and Catryn, treating them not as little children to be tolerated, but as miniature adults who have something to contribute. He added that, as a father of daughters he was scared shitless, but meeting and getting to know Bobby took away some of his fear.

"George, it's the hardest damned job on the planet, and you're doing great. When you have a son, you have to worry about *one* pecker running around town, but when you have daughters, you have to worry about *every* pecker running around town. In a world that still has places where women are second class citizens, where #MeToo has changed things but not soon enough or fast enough, you will spend the next forty years living on the edge of your chair, worried for your little girls, if you're lucky. But you will also find just about every moment of joy in your life has one or both of them at the center of it. Cherish those moments. And as I said to Katherine, if you need me, call. I have no idea what I can do to help, just being an old bus driver, but even if it's to vent frustration about raising daughters, call."

"I will. Thank you. And maybe we can get you to Skype the girl's every so often. They'd love to hear from you, as we all would."

"I like that idea. MJ and I used to Skype. There was something reassuring about seeing her face while we chatted. If you think raising a daughter is tough on your heart, her being a cop makes it doubly so."

"I don't doubt that at all."

George dropped Bobby off with a big hug like the family members they seemed to have become. Vinnie met him at the chalet's door, vocal and hungry and impatient, so Bobby fed him immediately. He got them both their medications, then was done. Exhausted. He probably should have sent Sam a text about the fire, but he couldn't focus. He wanted a full night's sleep before their long *long* day tomorrow, so telling Sam could wait until at least the morning. He checked his phone for messages and saw a simple heart emoji from Stacey. He sent back a smiley face.

o0o

Bobby was asleep by ten-thirty and slept right through his first alarm at eight, finally being roused by his back-up alarm at nine-thirty. Or it might have been hungry Vinnie sitting on him that woke him, but either way, he felt rested and clear-headed and ready togo. The day's plan was simple. There were so many things he wanted to explore in the area that he decided to wait on all of them until he returned, either with Stacey or alone, however it worked out. The one thing he did have to do before leaving town was visit the Royal Canadian Mounted Police detachment. He Googled the address and got directions to it.

He packed everything up, double-checked under the furniture for any 'surprises' Vinnie may have left, or toys he may have hidden. When he was sure it was all clean, he texted Sam to suggest he look into the fires at the storage company, then texted Katherine that he was checking out soon and would be on the road shortly. He thanked her again for everything and hoped to see them soon.

He texted George to ask if he had time for breakfast, but when he didn't get a reply after a few minutes, he walked over to the hotel's main building and had a quick breakfast alone. Back at the chalet, he packed everything into the Jeep, including his copilot, then drove over to the main building to check out. As promised by George, the room had been taken care of. Fortunately the meals he'd charged to the room were still on the account, so he was able to pay for those. He didn't mind paying his own way, but he supposed the hospitality industry worked a little differently, especially at management level where they could easily discount or write off things at will.

He thanked the staff, sent a final thank you note to George, and got back in the Jeep. Ten minutes later he parked in the little lot adjacent to the RCMP detachment and went in through the front doors. A constable sat behind a glass reception window, entering data on his computer. "I'll be with you in a moment, sir."

"Thank you."

After a moment, the constable looked up and did a perfect double-take. "Mr. Odini! Welcome, sir. I'll get the Sergeant." He picked up his landline and made a quick, hushed call. "Sergeant Ducharme will be out shortly, sir. I was at the event last night at Central Park. Thank you for sharing your news in person. Your sister's case is one we read about in training, to remind us we can't always catch the bad guys."

"There's a bit more to the story that I didn't share with the public. That's why I'm here now."

An unmarked door to one side of the reception desk opened and out strode a tall, broad, greying career cop with short cropped hair, age and worry lines, and a big smile. "Mr. Odini." He extended his hand

and Bobby shook it. The grip was steel, but not aggressive in any way. "Sergeant André Ducharme. I just got back into town this morning and my team told me all about last night. What can I do for you, sir?"

Bobby wondered if he was stepping on toes by speaking out of turn and not clearing it with Sam, but maybe he could give them the basics. "Well, I wanted to again thank your people for everything that was done in the investigation. I realize no one who worked on it back then would still be around, but maybe you know someone who could use the good news."

"As a matter of fact, I do. My uncle was the lead investigator, and though he's retired back home in Quebec City, he would be very much interested in this news. It was the one case that haunted him. He'll be glad it has been reopened. The FBI called a few days ago to ask some fresh questions. I hope they have better luck finding the killer now in Westview than we did here."

"That's the thing, though. Everything I'm telling you is unofficial, unconfirmed, and likely classified in some way, so I'll probably get my ass kicked when I get back home for saying anything at all. The man some of us are sure murdered my sister was a professional hit man. His body was found floating in a Westview-area bay last year, shot twice in the chest. What isn't known is who hired him to kill my sister, and why. The killer was Westview-based and is assumed to have followed her up here from back home. So, yes, some of us are pretty sure we know who killed my sister, but—"

"But he was only the weapon, not the hand that aimed it. I understand. Do you have any idea who else might have been involved?"

"I have a hunch, but Detective Sam Hernandez of the WPD can answer any questions you might have. My understanding is that because of the nature of what this guy did for a living there is a massive multi-agency investigation going on, so you may not be able to get anything out of them until they're finished. I'm sorry I can't give you more. I'm as keen to get answers as you are, maybe even more so."

"My uncle will be happy with even this small news. Even if it's only a theory right now, it explains so much that drove him crazy. The profile of the killing didn't fit the evidence, and now we know why." He took a card out of his shirt pocket and handed it to Bobby. "Thank you. I will get in touch specifically with your Detective Hernandez. As soon as I have confirmation this dead man was the killer, we'll gladly take your sister's case out of the Cold Case file. I don't expect there is anything I can do for you, but if you're back in the area again, please drop by. I was told your late daughter was a detective, so it makes you a member of the law enforcement family, and you're always welcome here."

"Thank you, Sergeant. It's a family I'm proud to be associated with, even if just as her father."

"I'm sorry for your loss. I have three daughters and a son, and my nightmare is outliving any of them."

"The same as any parent. Now, I'll let you get back to your day, and I'll get started on the trip home. With breaks, it's a little over twelve hours."

"Then have a safe drive, sir."

They shook hands again, and the constable at the desk repeated his thanks before Bobby took his leave and returned to the Jeep. After fueling up and grabbing two large bottles of water and a sandwich at the Shell station down the street, Bobby got back out on to the highway a little before noon. Maybe the trip hadn't done much for solving the actual case, but it had taken a weight off his shoulders he hadn't realized was there. As he left Banff in his rearview mirror, he felt like it was a journey well worth the time and effort. They settled in at highway speed and Vinnie ducked his head down into his bag and fell asleep. Bobby drove on.

oOo

The drive was steady and fun and the predicted snow held off. He followed the same route back, and at fifteen minutes after midnight he and Vinnie curled up in their own bed back home in Westview with MJ's letters safe and secure under the second pillow. He texted both Stacey and Sam to let them know he was back, then he muted his cellphone and gave in to exhaustion.

oOo

As nice as the clean, crisp air, the huge bed, and the lack of traffic sounds in Banff were, Bobby swore he had the best sleep of his life back in his own bed. He hadn't set any alarms, he'd closed the drapes to keep the sun from forcing him awake when it rose, and Vinnie had enough kibble in his bowl to keep him happy for a few extra hours. The one thing Bobby hadn't counted on was his landline, and at ten minutes after eleven it screamed at him and dragged him away from that best sleep.

"What the hell? I thought I muted you. Son of a bitch." He pulled himself up into a sitting position and answered it, mostly to just stop the ringing. "Hello."

"Uncle Bob?"

Bobby was sure he was still dreaming, because the only person with his number who called him 'Uncle Bob' was... "Tina?"

"Oh thank Christ! Yes. It's me. There's been an accident. Mom and Grandpa. On the 105 near North Cove."

Bobby broke free of the haze of sleep, threw back the covers, and got out of bed. "Are they okay?"

"The police wouldn't say over the phone. They airlifted them to Westview Medical Center. Treyvon is up in Redmond all day in meetings with Microsoft and I can't reach him. I'm trying to get a babysitter, but I can't find one and I don't know what to do and Mom's dying and I can't go to her."

"I'm on my way, Tina. I'm ten minutes from there. Call them and give them my name. I've got her. I'm going. Is Alex—your grandpa—there, too?"

"Yes."

"Okay. I'm on my way. Get there when you can." They exchanged cell numbers, then he called Sam. He wasn't exactly sure why, but he couldn't call MJ and this was all too much at once. "Sam? Bobby."

"Hey Bobby. How was the trip?"

"It was great and I'll tell you all about it, but right now my stepsister and stepfather have been in an accident and are in Westview Medical. This isn't something I'd normally bother you with, but since someone torched Rachel's storage unit, I'm wondering if, you know..."

"And you think this is connected to what we've been talking about?"

"Yes. I'm on my way to the hospital now. I have no details other than they're both alive and it happened out on the 105, south of North Cove."

"Okay. I'll see what I can find out from WSP, talk with the state troopers who responded. I'll call or see you at the hospital as soon as I can."

"Thanks."

o0o

Bobby didn't bother with a shower, though he did multi-task by toasting and eating a bagel while he dressed. Twenty-five minutes after Tina's call, he was standing at the inquiry desk at Westview's Emergency and Trauma Center.

"I'm looking for two patients, please. They arrived by chopper a little while ago. A vehicular accident out on the coast. Rachel and Alex Charleswood."

"Please spell the last name, sir." The clerk typed while Bobby spelled it out slowly. "Thank you. Yes. They're here. Are you a family member?"

"Yes. It's my s...sister and... father. My name is Bobby Odini."

"Okay, Mr. Odini. Please have a seat over there and someone will come out to get you as soon as they can." He pointed to a group of seats near the sliding glass doors labeled *NO ADMITTANCE*.

"Can you tell me how they are?"

"I'm sorry, sir, even if I had the information, I'm not qualified to discuss it. I'm just a clerk."

"I understand. I'll go sit. Thank you." He went where he was directed, mumbling quietly, "I *despise* hospitals." He sat, picked up a random magazine from the table, and tried to read. This was the part he hated the most. The waiting. They'd made him wait when MJ broke her arm at the skateboard park, and they'd made him wait again when she took on a PCP-influenced thief with a knife when she was a rookie cop. She'd received a few minor cuts but ended up needing her Taser *and* her baton to put the guy down. She'd saved two lives and earned a rep on the force for being fearless and furious. When she had told him about it, Bobby said it sounded a lot like a certain song about a glass-jawed boy some band used to play in clubs around town. She'd smiled up at him and admitted quietly, "I *may* have been humming that in the heat of the moment."

He texted Tina that he was there but hadn't seen anyone, yet. She texted back she was waiting for the babysitter to arrive. A moment later the barrier doors slid open and a stocky young doctor stepped through. He looked around at the two dozen or so people and settled on Bobby.

"Mr. Odini?"

Bobby stood. "Yes."

The doctor extended his hand and Bobby shook it. "Dr. Antony. Come with me, please." He led Bobby into the inner sanctum of the ER. He talked as they walked. "Your father, Alex, is good. He has a fractured wrist, but it's a clean break and will heal well, even at his age. He is extremely confused, but his Medic Alert bracelet told us why. We have him sedated, for his own safety. It was either that or strap him down so he doesn't wander off. He has a few contusions from the airbags, so don't be shocked.

"Your sister, Rachel, wasn't as lucky. She has two fractured ribs, fractured left foot, ruptured spleen, severe whiplash, and some swelling in her spinal cord. The most serious injury though was to her head. She's in a medically-induced coma to allow her brain to rest and hopefully reduce the swelling. Her skull didn't fracture, but she has a serious concussion. The initial tests are promising, but with head injuries like this we prefer to err on the side of caution." He arrived at a curtained-off bed and drew back the curtain. A nurse stood next to a badly bruised, wrinkled old man with a cast on one arm.

It took Bobby a moment to realize the old man was Alex. It wasn't the bruises that threw him off, but the fact Alex had aged so much since he last saw him. The big, handsome man who won both his mother's and his sister's hearts was still there, but the muscle tone was gone, as was most of his now white hair. Bobby did some quick math in his head. Alex was eighty-three, the same age as Bobby's mother who didn't look nearly as old as this man in the hospital bed.

The nurse looked up. "He's sleeping, and probably will be for another hour or so."

The doctor thanked her and guided Bobby further into the ER. "Your sister has just come out of surgery, where we repaired her ruptured spleen and set her fractures."

"Do you know what happened? I just heard there was an accident."

"I don't know. Sorry."

"Thank you." They arrived at a room.

Even knowing the extent of Rachel's injuries, Bobby was not expecting what he saw. She was unrecognizable with tubes, wires, casts, braces, bruises, and bandages. "Holy...!"

"Yes, she looks bad, but it's early still. The swelling will go down eventually and although the bruises will get worse, they will fade after time."

Bobby had a sudden twisted thought. " She's never going to believe she was this bad." He snapped a picture of her.

"I'm not sure that's such—"

"She's a stubborn woman. She'll get frustrated with the speed of her recovery. She wants everything *right now*. This picture will remind her that no matter how bad she thinks it is, it was definitely worse today."

"That actually sounds reasonable." He left Bobby.

He took two more photos; almost ashamed he was capturing Rachel at her worst, but he was serious when he said he would use them to encourage her. Looking at her like this, he suspected her recovery was going to be long and slow. He was dying to know the details of the accident. Hopefully, Sam came through with those soon.

oOo

He must have dozed off in the chair because he was startled by a hand on his shoulder, giving him a light shake.

"Uncle Bob. You were snoring."

Blinking off the doze, Bobby stood up to greet his niece. He'd seen photos of Tina recently, and except for her almost-white blonde hair, she was definitely her mother's daughter—short, curvy, and usually sparkling, but not today. "Tina, sweetie." They hugged, holding it for a long time. He remembered their last hug quite clearly. It was at MJ's funeral, except back then Tina had been pregnant. He was ashamed it had been that long. They lived in the same damned city, but it seemed that only tragedy brought them together. He vowed now to himself to change that. His trip to Banff had reinforced the importance of family for him.

Eventually they released the hug. Tina looked at her mother. "Is she as bad as she looks?"

"Almost." He told her what he remembered of the litany of her mother's injuries and why Rachel was in the medically-induced coma.

Tina gently put her fingertips on her mother's left arm and whispered, "We're here for you, Mom, and we'll take care of Grandpa."

Bobby sat back down. "What about Alex? Even if they keep him overnight for observation, if all he's got is a broken wrist, they'll be discharging him tomorrow."

"I know. I called the Home but they won't have anyone available to come get him until Sunday."

Since he knew there was nothing he could do for Rachel while she was unconscious, and he was itching to talk with Alex, this would be a perfect opportunity. "I'll drive him back. Just so long as someone is here with your mom."

"Trey and I will be here as much as we can, Nicole is flying in from San Fran, and Sandy says he'll be here by tomorrow, at the latest. I'll give them the keys to Mom's place and let them sort it out from there."

"You've got it all figured out. You're a queen of organization, just like your mom."

"I have to keep my mind busy or I'll snap, thinking about her like this. Will she be okay?"

If the news were bad, Bobby would have taken her out into the hallway, but he was optimistic. "The doctor sounds pretty confident that once all the swelling goes down, she'll be fine. The next day or two are crucial, but your mom's a fighter."

"Do you know what the hell happened? Mom's actually a pretty good driver. She and my dad used to drive rally on weekends."

"I haven't a clue. I have a cop friend looking into it. Why don't you sit here with your mom, and I'll go check on Alex, just in case he wakes up."

"Okay. Thanks, Uncle Bob."

"You betcha."

Bobby returned to Alex's bedside and pulled up the one chair. He didn't know much about medicine, but he knew a steady pulse and a healthy blood pressure when he saw them on the monitor. Considering what he'd just been through, Alex looked okay. "What the hell happened out there old man? And what was going on out on that damned boat? What did you get my sister into?"

"Hmmm?" Alex sounded like he was talking, not snoring.

"Alex?"

"Mmm..."

"Are you awake?"

"Mmmm. Who's there?" He opened his eyes and looked around. Bobby stood up so he could be seen.

"It's me, Bobby."

"Bobby? What are you doing here?"

"You were in an accident?"

"I was? Is your mom okay?"

"You weren't with Mom."

"Ah. Is Marion okay?"

Oh no, Bobby thought. "You were with Rachel."

"Rachel? Is my little girl okay?"

"No, she's pretty banged up."

"Banged up? She was *shot*."

"No, you were in a car accident, out on the coast. You're in Westview now. At Westview Medical."

"She was shot. I saw the muzzle flash."

Holy shit. His stepfather was too far gone. Bobby would never get the information he needed if Alex couldn't think straight. "You were driving down the 105."

"I know where the hell we were, Bobby. We were near North Cove, on our way to lunch. I was staring out the window. Just as we passed Larkin Road, I saw a flash about twenty yards off the road in the bushes on the right. Someone shot us."

Bobby had no idea what to say. Alex was confused, but at the same time, he wasn't. "Then what?"

"Um..." Alex looked like he was trying to grasp at a memory. "I remember the flash, and a bang, but I think that was the tire. We swerved, hit the shoulder, and I think we flipped."

"Okay, I'll take your word for it." He pulled out his phone and dialed Sam.

"You bloody well better believe me. I was there and you weren't."

"Good point, Alex." Sam answered. "Sam, it's Bobby. My stepdad is awake and remembers someone taking a shot at them just past Larkin Road. Any chance you could mention that to your state trooper friends and see what they can find out there?"

"Shot at? Really? Yeah, I'll let them know. If someone tried to kill them, they might try again. I'll have a couple uniforms sent over. I'll get back to you in a bit."

"Thanks."

Bobby figured it was now or never for the questions he had for his stepfather. "I've got them looking for the shooter, Alex."

"I heard. Thank you for believing me. Is Marion going to be coming to see me?"

Bobby bit back his first reply and decided to play along. "Maybe. So, Alex, when was the last time you were out on your boat, the *Rachel*?"

"Goddamned, kid. A month or two ago, at least."

"Marion really likes it out there on the water. She was showing me some of her pictures."

"She sure does. She wants me to teach her to pilot it."

"She'd be a natural. She really likes it when you have guests. She said you have some of the coolest people visit. Real celebrities."

"Yeah, occasionally. No really big names."

"Oh, come on. Jake Brand is pretty big."

"He's middling. Besides, he's not a celebrity, he's a friend. I just hope we can get him elected and kick that useless incumbent asshole out. Jake'll be a great mayor, though I think he's aiming too low. With his reputation, he should be in Olympia, or even in D.C."

"I agree. I think Marion has a bit of a celebrity crush on him, though. She was telling me about the time he was on board for a meeting."

"A meeting? Oh yah. *That* thing." His voice got quiet. "She told you about that? That's not good, Bobby. Pablo didn't know she was below decks. If he had, he'd have thrown her overboard. That bastard scares the living daylights out of me."

"Then why was he there? It's *your* boat."

"As a favor to Jake. His sister-in-law's husband is Colombian and put the two of them together. Pablo never comes to the States, but Jake was putting something together, something to finance his campaign and give Santacruz a foot in the door for shipping his product."

"You were dealing cocaine, Alex?"

"Hell no! I was just hosting the goddamned meeting. I didn't even know who Jake was coming on board until I got a call from that little prick of an assistant. Said Jake needed to sail out into international waters to meet someone—and he was bringing along that wannabe mob asshole from the transit union."

"Sabbatini?"

"That's the one. Arrogant union prick. Strutted around on the deck like the meeting was *his* damned idea. When Santacruz pulled alongside, I almost crapped myself. I hope to God I never see *him* and his goons again."

"Why was Sabbatini there? He's not exactly a mover or shaker of anything."

"His brother is local president of the dock workers but was out of the country, so Jake let Sabbatini stand in."

"Who else was there? Your crew?"

"No. I gave them the weekend off. I took her out myself. The fewer people involved, the better. I thought it was just some slightly shady strategy meeting Jake wanted to have, so I didn't see any harm in Marion coming along. She stayed below deck the entire time, like I told her to."

The facts were pretty close to Bobby's theory, but he still had no ideawho had put the hit on Marion. "So no one knew she was there except you?"

"I don't think so. The seas were a bit rough and both Jake and one of the others—a bodyguard, I think—had to use the head, but Marion was in our cabin."

One of them must have seen her, Bobby realized. Both Brand and Santacruz had the kind of power and money to put out a contract on a college kid. "Did they ever meet again, Brand and Santacruz?"

"Not so far. He left two suitcases with ten million in them, to help with the campaign and to grease some wheels for future considerations, but Jake hasn't heard from Santacruz in over a month."

Actually, Alex, it's been a lot longer than that, Bobby thought to himself. If his stepfather thought Marion was still alive, he wasn't sure how he would take it if Bobby told him the truth, so he kept it to himself. He was trying to decide what next to ask Alex when the old man started mumbling to himself.

"They'll never know she was there. I had everything destroyed. Nothing left. No one knows about Marion. Can't let them find her. Burned it all up. Gone. Burned. Stupid idea, keeping crap like that in her storage locker. Gone now. Still got my connections. Still got my—Bobby! When did you get here?"

Bobby was stunned. He didn't know if Alex had just admitted to having Rachel's storage unit torched, or whether he was referring to something else. Alex was definitely confused, but there was clarity in there, too. Had he underestimated this old man? Maybe he could trick him into saying more. "I'm glad you did, Alex. Good thinking."

"What was?"

"That fire in Rachel's storage unit. Brilliant. Make it look like vandalism. Don't want anyone to find out about Marion."

"Make it look random. That's what I told him. Burn number 72, and a random selection of others."

"He did a great job. Cops don't have a clue. Marion is protected."

"Of course she is. Can't let anyone find out, especially your mother. It'll break her heart. I love her, too, you know. I love them both. I can't explain it. Your Mom is wonderful. Smart, spunky, funny. Marion, though, makes me feel thirty again. Like when I first started my own business and the world was in my hand. Going to break your mother's heart when I leave her. I don't want to, but it can't be helped."

"Can't be helped Alex. Love is love." He had no idea what he was saying. He was just going along with whatever Alex said. He knew it was time to look into Brand and Sabbatini before someone else got killed. If Alex had the storage unit torched, who the hell was taking shots at them on the highway? Or was the old fella just imagining it?

The curtain was pulled back by a nurse and a uniformed police officer stepped up behind her.

"Mr. Odini? Officer Wayne Leibov. Detective Hernandez sent me. There's an officer with your sister as well."

"Thank you. This is my stepfather, Alex Charleswood. Alex, this officer is here to protect you, since someone took a shot at you."

"About goddamned time. Bobby, can you go find out when Marion is going to be by?"

"Sure, Alex. I'll go check on Rachel, too."

He addressed the officer. "You know where I'll be. Please don't let him leave."

"Yes sir. Detective Hernandez said he'd be here shortly to ask him some questions, so your stepfather isn't going anywhere, yet."

"Perfect. Alex, I'll be back. Stay put. Don't give the nurses any trouble or I'll have the officer shoot you with his Taser."

Alex actually laughed. "Piss off, Bobby. You're not as funny as you think you are. I have no idea how your wife puts up with you. I hope to hell that daughter of yours has her mother's sense of humor. Now go find Marion and let me sleep. I'm old, you know."

Alex hadn't meant any harm by the comments, but they shot straight through Bobby's heart. He suddenly needed air. He limped out through reception and onto the sidewalk. He dropped onto a bench, drained. That's where he was when Sam walked up.

CHAPTER TWELVE

"You look like crap, Bobby." He sat down.

"Been a long week."

"No doubt. How's everyone doing?"

"Rachel, not so good. She's busted up and in a medically-induced coma for the swelling on her brain. They had to repair her ruptured spleen and set a bunch of bones. She's lucky to be alive."

"And your stepfather?"

"A broken wrist."

"That's good news."

"That's just half of it. You know the fires in the storage place? He claims he had them set to destroy evidence Marion was on the boat that day. He's still trying to protect her."

"And you trust his story? Didn't you say he had memory problems? "

"He seemed pretty lucid. Told me all about why they were all on the boat. I guess if the troopers find any proof of a shooter from today's accident, it'll lend some credence to his stories. He's a little messed up on what year it is, though. He thinks Marion, Betty, and MJ are all still alive. Hell, he still thinks Pablo Santacruz is a threat."

"At least we know Santacruz's one person who *didn't* pull the trigger today, if one was indeed pulled."

"I'm still at a loss who it could be. I was sure the fire was set by them, but if it really was Alex, then why is someone trying to kill him and Rachel?"

"Let's just see what the troopers find."

"Okay." He stood. "I'd better get back in and relieve Tina, Rachel's oldest daughter. Thanks for sending the protection, by the way. I think Alex is enjoying the attention just a bit. At least I know he won't be able to leave the hospital."

"Not until I get a chance to question him. It'd be nice if he would give up the name of his arson-for-hire, but I'll be happy with his thoughts on who would take a shot at him and your stepsister." He followed Bobby back into the Emergency unit. "Just so you know, the feds want to talk to both you and Alex about the photo."

"Okay, but Alex thinks it was destroyed in the storage unit."

"Doesn't matter. It lit a fire under them like I've never seen. If they can get a State Senator for colluding with the head of a Colombian cartel thirty years ago, they're not going to back off. I expect the DEA is going to want a turn, too. Santacruz may be dead, but if they can find evidence Brand got where he is because of Santacruz's influence, they'll take him down. His voting record in the senate has shown him to be unfriendly to law enforcement, to say the least. Your transit union buddy, Sabbatini, is going to be under a magnifying glass for a while, too."

"Are you sure you should be telling me all this?"

"I shouldn't, but your own efforts are giving them leads they've been missing. I guess I'm hoping if you know they're taking it all seriously, you'll stop digging and putting yourself in danger."

"Do you think this accident was my fault?" Sam had a good point.

"Indirectly, yes. You dug. You were careful, but somewhere along the line you poked when you shouldn't have. You might not have realized it, but you did. Do me a favor and stop. The dragon is awake and seriously pissed off."

"Done."

"Thank you. Now go check on your stepsister while I have word with her father."

"Yes sir."

o0o

Tina was showing Bobby the dozens of baby pictures she had on her phone when Sam found them.

"Sam, you gotta see this kid. She's gorgeous. By the way, this is Tina, Rachel's oldest. Tina, this is Detective Sam Hernandez. He was a friend of MJ's." He held Tina's phone up to Sam.

"She *is* gorgeous! What's her name?"

"Lydia Rosa, for my grandmother, and for Rosa Parks."

"Beautiful name. Bobby, can I speak with you out in the hall for a moment?"

"Sure."

Out in the corridor, Sam closed the door behind them. "Alex was right. There was a bullet hole in the front right tire and they found a flattened area of grass just about where he described it." He ran his hand through his thick hair. "I'm going to try and get the feds to spring for protective custody, but your stepfather is going to have to talk. So far, he's keeping his mouth shut. It doesn't help half the time he thinks it's the nineties and he's still managing Brand's mayoral campaign. He also thinks he's protecting people who don't need it. I'm pretty sure no matter what he admits to being part of no DA is going to press charges. The best we can hope for is that he leads us in a solid direction."

"I asked him about the others in the photo, but he wasn't much help. From what I gather, Brand had some assistant with him that day, but I don't know if he's the face we see, the face we don't, or out of the shot completely."

"Maybe not, but it's one more person we can look for. We're going to find him, Bobby. For you, for MJ, and for Marion."

"I know. Thanks."

"We're obviously getting close. Someone is feeling threatened enough to be taking shots in broad daylight. Do me a favor and email me a list of everyone you've spoken with about this, even the people up in Canada. Someone knows something and they might not even realize it."

"Of course. I'll sit down tonight and put a list together."

"Thank you. I've got to go. Another case was dropped on my desk this morning. I'll call SAC Stevenson over at the FBI, so you should hear from him pretty quickly."

"Feel free to give him my number. Chances are I'll either be here or at home, and I'll help however I can."

"I know. Just stop stirring things up."

"That, too."

Bobby rejoined Tina. "Sorry."

"I heard a little of what you were talking about. You don't think this was an accident?"

"No. Your Grandpa saw someone fire a shot at them."

"A hunter, maybe? An accident?"

"Probably not. It's complicated, and although I know you'd understand it if I laid it out for you, people are getting hurt and I don't want you to become a target."

"Hurt? Worse than Mom?"

"Hurt, as in dead. It has to do with a cold case. I *will* fill you in, but not until it's safe to do so. To underline what I'm telling you, the FBI will be coming by to speak with me and Alex."

"You're serious? The Feebs?"

"Yeah. Or the DEA. I'm not sure about the ATF. I don't think the CIA are involved."

"You're joking, aren't you?"

"Only a little. Do me a favor and keep all this to yourself. Don't tell your siblings and maybe not even Treyvon, if you can help it. Let's just tell them they're looking into the possibility of a random shooter like the one in Virginia years ago, and your mom and grandpa were lucky they survived. What is it they say? Prayers and positive thoughts?"

"And some damn good medical help, I hope."

"The best. I'll make sure of it. " His phone rang. It was Karl the retiree. "Excuse me while I take this." He left the room and walked down the hall a few steps, now that he knew Tina could hear through the door. "Karl. What's up? Sorry I didn't get back to you."

"No problem, Bobby. I hope you're feeling better. I was just hoping we could sit down and chat about something connected to our conversation the other day."

"Which part of the conversation?"

"The part about Sabbatini and the Local."

Damn. If Karl was connected to the whole mess, he needed to be careful. "Sure. How about the diner, in twenty minutes?" He figured it best to make it a public place where they were both known.

"Sounds good. I'll see you there. I appreciate it. It's important."

"Of course, Karl." When he disconnected the call, he texted Sam to let him know who and where he was meeting, as well as why he suspected Karl had called. Sam texted back telling him to be careful, and not to go anywhere with Karl. He also suggested using his phone to record the conversation, or, if he felt more comfortable, he could call Sam just before he got there and leave the line open so Sam could hear, for safety reasons. Bobby texted back that the second idea was better, since a recording could be erased.

Twenty minutes later he was sitting in a booth with a view of the street outside, but not right at the windows. If someone out there was using a rifle to take out witnesses, he wasn't going to make it easy for them. His phone sat on the table, with Sam on the other end, listening illegally. Karl walked in two minutes late, and he wasn't alone. Silhouetted by the bright sunlight behind them, Bobby couldn't see who the big man with Karl was until they reached the booth. He laughed and stood to shake the man's hand.

"Donal! Good to see you again! It's been a few years. Are you still with Transit?" Karl and his son sat in the booth, and Bobby poured them each a cup from the carafe of coffee he'd ordered.

"Hey Mr. Odini. Yeah, still driving. It's why we're here. Didn't Dad tell you?"

Karl added four sugars to his coffee. "It's a big favor to ask. I wanted to be respectful and do it in person. You don't do this stuff over the phone. Kids, I swear."

"Dad, I'm forty-one."

"Then think like it."

Bobby was confused. "What's this go to do with Julius Sabbatini, guys?"

Donal leaned in and Karl leaned back, letting his son take the lead. "Since his three terms as Local President back in the nineties, the city hasn't taken the union seriously in any of the contract negotiations, and they ran roughshod over us last time. I want to fix things and the only way to do it is from the top."

"You're running for President?" He was impressed. Donal was smarter than his old man and would probably be damned good at the job. Bobby had known Donal for years and had seen him look at more than one problem from both sides before making a decision.

"I'm submitting my forms tomorrow."

"That's great! How can this old retiree help? Hand out flyers?"

"Actually, I was hoping you'd speak at my fundraising barbeque at the community center in two weeks."

"Really?"

"Please. You've only been gone a year, so most of the senior drivers know you, and you're well respected. You've always been fair and level-headed, and you won that Westview Magazine Community Service Award a few years back."

"It was twelve years ago, and I'm pretty sure no one remembers it."

"They will when we remind them. Dad's always in my corner, but they'll figure he has to be, since he's my dad. You've known me since forever, but you're not family and you're not known for just jumping in for any old cause."

Bobby didn't have to think too hard about it. "Sure. Done. Tell me when and where, and what kind of stuff you want me to say."

"Great! Thanks, Bobby! I'll email you everything."

"Perfect. Now that that's settled, I have some questions for your old man here." Sam was going to be furious, but this was his chance. "Just between the three of us... Sabbatini."

"What about him?"

"What's your opinion of him?"

"He's a has-been. Been retired three years and has spent the entire time drunk, from what I hear."

"Is he dangerous?"

"You mean, is he a 'made' man? No. Like we said the other day, he always wanted people to think he was, but the closest he got to being made was having two cousins that were. He's no more mob than you are. But it doesn't mean he's not dangerous. He's ex-Brinks and he's got a temper that's probably what kept him from being accepted by his cousins, etcetera."

"How so?"

"You heard about his wife, Alice?"

"No."

"Really? I thought everyone knew. Anyway, you know Alice was a supervisor with WTC."

"I knew that much, yeah."

"Well, she stepped out on Julius with one of the young women on the Transit Police Force and Julius *snapped*. Took a putter and beat the crap out of both Alice's truck and the Transit Cop's SUV while they were having a little rendezvous at the Best Western in Bellingham. He tried to take the putter to the two of them, but the cop was no pushover and disarmed him while just wearing panties. Nearly broke his arm doing it."

"How could I not have heard this?"

"You didn't like to hang around the break rooms or the garages listening to rumours and other crap."

Karl was right. He hated that crap. "Bunch of little old hens, I swear. Easiest job in the city and half the operators just whine like they have PhDs and are being disrespected."

"So why are you asking about Sabbatini?"

This was no time for the truth. "A friend of mine met him through some dating app and although I had an opinion, I promised her I'd get a second one."

"Tell her to lose his number and to change hers, if he has it. He's a loaded cannon just waiting for his fuse to be lit. Always has been. No wonder Alice did what she did."

"Thanks. That's pretty much what I told my friend, too. I only knew Julius by reputation, but you had a lot more contact through your bowling league."

"You can also tell her the bastard cheats at ten-pin."

"Will do." He had to get back to the hospital, just in case the FBI showed up looking for him. Even saying it in his head sounded bizarre. "Okay guys. I gotta go. Donal, send me the information and I'll be happy to help out. Do me a favor and don't tell anyone I asked about Sabbatini. He'll figure out it was her and I don't want her to get hurt if he's so far gone."

Karl and Donal stood and Bobby joined them. Donal shook his hand. "Thank you. I'll have it to you tonight or tomorrow. And neither Dad nor I will say anything to anyone. Sabbatini's name did *not* come up today. Nope. Not at all. Right, Dad?"

"Sabba-who?"

"Exactly."

oOo

Bobby was right about the FBI. He was back in Rachel's room for ten minutes when a Special Agent Wong stepped in and introduced himself.

"Can we talk, Mr. Odini?"

Bobby nodded at Rachel. "I'd rather not in front of my stepsister. Her daughter has just gone to the bathroom and for fresh coffee. She should be back shortly."

"I understand. How is your stepsister doing?"

"She's in rough shape. Medically-induced coma for the swelling on her brain. Though I guess it's a good thing he shot the tire and not her or her father."

"I suspect he wanted it to look like an accident."

"If my stepdad hadn't seen the muzzle flash, it probably would have been written off that way."

"Damn lucky."

Tina returned, and had company. SA Wong slipped out quietly, and Bobby assumed he was waiting in the hall for him. It took him a minute to realize who the young woman was. "Nicole? I almost didn't recognize you. Wow."

"Thanks, Uncle Bob. Give credit to Weight Watchers, a boob reduction, hair extensions, and three weeks in Mazatlan for the tan." She gave him a big hug.

Bobby knew she and Tina were only half-sisters, but they didn't look like they shared even a single strand of DNA. "You looked great before, but *this* is a real transformation. Congratulations!"

"Thanks, Unc." Nicole had been so intent on showing off her new self to her uncle she hadn't yet looked at her mother. When she did, she fainted. Bobby and Tina caught her and got her into a chair.

"Damnation! I'll get a doctor, Tina."

"Don't bother. She does this. It's like a switch in her head. I think she started fake-fainting as a kid to get attention, and eventually it became real. It's only serious if she hits her head on something on the way down. Give her a few minutes and she'll come round. Seeing Mom like this is enough of a shock for anyone, let alone Knocked-out Nicole. Go chat with Agent Mulder out there. We're okay."

"Is he that obvious?"

"All he needs are the sunglasses and Scully at his side. We'd better keep Nicole away from him. When she's conscious, she has a thing for both men in suits and men in law enforcement."

"I'll keep that in mind. Call me if you need anything."

"Will do."

Bobby joined SA Wong in the corridor, who was speaking with the WPD officer on guard. "Sorry about that."

"Is everything okay?"

"One of my nieces fainted but the other one has it all under control, she says."

"If you say so. Normally I would ask you to come down to our office to chat, but I understand it's important for you to be here. Do you mind if we talk in my car? It's as secure as we can get right now."

"Sure."

"This way." The agent led Bobby outside and to the inevitable dark blue sedan parked next to a police cruiser in the Police Only Parking not far from the entrance. Once they were inside, the agent turned on the car's stereo, then bumped the volume up high. A gentle hum came from the speakers, but no music. Wong smiled. "It's a CD. Playing a subsonic mess to foul any listening attempts."

"Seriously? Someone tapping an FBI conversation?"

"Sadly, yes. So, tell me what's up. Your own words."

"Well, thirty years ago my sister, Marion, took a photo on a boat, and six months later was found stabbed to death behind a building in Canada. Last week I got a letter from my late detective daughter connecting Marion's death to a contract killer found floating in Payne

Bay. Shortly after, I took some boxes of Marion's out of storage, to pass on to Detective Sam Hernandez."

SA Wong wrote while Bobby remembered. When it was all told, Bobby even included his conversation with Karl and Donal as Sam listened. The agent looked at his notebook for a moment. "Amazing. One single photo has given us a titanium-strength link to a case we've been working on for years. You say there was ten million in cash in those suitcases?"

"That's what Alex said."

"Do we have a date for when the photo was taken, when the meeting happened?"

"Marion was murdered thirty years ago, so probably the previous summer."

"Do you have the original print? There's a code printed on the back of most lab-machine-generated prints, which includes the date it was processed and printed. It won't be perfect, but it'll narrow it down for us."

"Or I could ask Alex."

"Do you think he'd tell you? He shut right up when I showed him my ID."

"It can't hurt to try."

"True enough. By the way, the big breakthrough for us came last year, when your daughter recognized the entry in Vetere's ledger. I'm sorry for your loss. I met her once, at a profiling training class, but didn't know her well."

"Thank you. I guess I'm pushing so hard on this case because she can't."

"I understand. As I reckon it, things started to heat up when the courier delivered those letters from your daughter. You say they were at the lawyer's for a year before someone sent them over?"

"Yes. MJ entrusted them to her lawyer, the senior partner, last name of Mitchell."

"Chaz Mitchell?"

"He's the one. The fella I spoke with—Grant Dewar—said the letters had been misfiled and recently found again."

"That's not good. *Mitchell, Hiroko, & Toffelmeyer* is a top-notch firm. For a year those letters are untouched, and then they get found and the crap hits the fan? We need to find out who had their hands on them and why they didn't just destroy them. You didn't even know they existed, so they could have been shredded and none of this would have happened and their secret would have stayed hidden. Putting together a chain of custody would be a big help, but we'll never get a warrant to get around lawyer-client privilege. It's too flimsy a connection for a judge to go along."

"Can't the client ask? They handled MJ's estate but they're also handling mine when the time comes. MJ hooked me up with them at the end."

"Technically, yes, but why would you? It would raise alarm bells all over the place. There are two dead burglars and a sniper in the mix."

"I can at least ask. Dewar said Mitchell was furious about the mix up, so I'll bet it's something the staff are aware of. I'll call from right here and ask Dewar what happened to them."

"It would be an innocent enough question. Go ahead." He turned off the CD player. "But don't put it on speakerphone or they'll be suspicious. Just lean this way."

Bobby opened his phone's contact list, found the law office number, and called. He held the phone in his left hand, far enough away from his ear that both he and SA Wong could hear everything.

"*Mitchell, Hiroko, & Toffelmeyer*. Denise speaking. How may I direct your call?"

"Hi Denise. My name is Robert Odini. I'm a client and was speaking with Grant Dewar about something last week. I had a few follow-up questions for him, if he's in."

"Thank you, Mr. Odini. I'll put you through." The phone rang twice and was picked up by a deep-voiced male that didn't sound like the Dewar Bobby had spoken with.

"Grant Dewar's office. This is his associate, Jackson Coyne."

"Hi Jackson. My name is Robert Odini. I'm a client of the firm and wanted to speak with Mr. Dewar about a parcel he sent to me last week."

"Actually, Mr. Odini, *I* sent you the letters. Or I took care of packing them up and getting them to the courier on Mr. Dewar's orders. How can I help you?"

"Well, I was wondering what happened to delay them so long, to be honest. It was a little upsetting to get letters from my dead daughter a year late."

"Yes sir. I understand it would be. Unfortunately, I can't discuss it over the phone. Mr. Dewar is in court all day, but I do know the answers to your questions. If you don't mind coming down to the office I'll gladly explain the mix up in person."

Bobby looked at the Special Agent, who considered the situation, then nodded. "Sure, Jackson. I can come down. Are you sure you can't just tell me over the phone?"

"It would be unprofessional of me to discuss any business of a client's with someone I've never met, just because he says he's the client and his caller ID says he's the client, sir. I hope you understand it's for *your* protection. Once I establish you are who you say you are, I will gladly answer any and all questions you have, and what I can't answer, I will find the answers for."

"You just gave me the perfect response, Jackson." He could hear the young man audibly sigh on the other end of the line. "Ethics and privacy are the reason I do business with your firm. I can be there in fifteen minutes."

"I will meet you in the lobby myself, sir. See you soon."

"Okay." He disconnected the call.

Wong looked at Bobby and raised one black eyebrow. "Nicely done. You're a natural. I'm only letting you do this because it's a law firm and no one would be stupid enough to hurt you there. That said, would you be willing to record your visit?"

"On video?"

"No. Just audio. I have a pen with a built-in audio recorder. In the State of Washington both parties must consent to the recording of a conversation, so I won't be able to listen to it. I'd like a recording so you can listen to it yourself to make certain you remember everything when you get back here. It's a slippery slope and I couldn't get a warrant from hearsay, but just from you relaying the conversation with accuracy we might get something we can work with, to give us a direction to start looking."

"I couldn't possibly remember everything I hear in there, so a recording would be a good idea."

"Thank you. Let's get you equipped with the pen, and I'll drive you over. Do you want to text your niece to tell her you'll be off property for a bit? We don't want her worrying. She has enough of that already."

"Good thinking."

Bobby sent the text while the agent went to his trunk and came back with a small aluminum case containing an assortment of electronic toys. They got Bobby set up and tested the pen with his phone then they drove the ten minutes to within a block of the office on 2nd Avenue. Bobby got out there and walked the rest of the way. He was met in the lobby by a tall, stylish young man in his mid twenties with a well-groomed full beard and one of the hairstyles Bobby'd heard referred to as a 'fade', with more hair on top than on the sides. He looked more like a male model than an associate at a law firm.

"Jackson? Robert Odini."

"It's a pleasure to meet you, Mr. Odini. I'm sorry neither Mr. Dewar nor Mr. Mitchell are able to meet with you." He shook Bobby's hand and Bobby noticed the strangest watch he'd ever seen on the young man's wrist. While everyone else seemed to be wearing FitBits or Apple Watches, this piece looked to be as retro as it gets.

"Your watch... I've never seen anything like it."

The associate smiled and showed Bobby the watch. The body was black and shaped a bit like a baseball home plate with cylinders and numbers like some WWII decoding machine. "I'd be surprised if you had. Only fifty were made. It's a Hublot LaFerrari."

"Fascinating. It looks like spy gear."

"It's meant to look like a car engine."

"Incredible. I can't even tell what time it is." There were five sets of numbers in different places in the clockworks.

"It takes some getting used to, but now I don't even think about it."

"Only fifty were made? Where on earth would you even buy one?"

"Only at auction, I suppose. It was a gift from a relative when I graduated from law school." He slid his sleeve back down over the timepiece, led them to the elevators, and smoothly changed the topic of conversation. "You had some questions, sir?"

"I'm sure the simple questions I have don't need a boss to answer them."

"No sir, you probably don't. Pretty much anyone in the firm can answer questions about your package because Mr. Mitchell was livid when he found out what had happened."

They had the elevator to themselves. "I hate to ask this, sir, but could I please see some photo ID, just so I can say I confirmed your identity before we had any discussion related to firm business?"

Bobby was expecting this and had his wallet ready. "Not a problem, Jackson." He took his license out of the wallet and handed it to the young man.

"A commercial driver's license?"

"Yes. I drove for the WTC for thirty-five years."

"Wow. My uncle drives for them. David Coyne."

"I know Dave. I haven't seen him in ages, but we worked the same part of town for a while. Tell him I say hi, please."

"I would, but then I'd have to admit how I met you, and that would get me in trouble."

Bobby laughed kindly. "I understand. In your business, ethics is everything."

"Exactly. If a client can't trust us to guard their interests, then we're no good to anyone."

They arrived at the sixth floor and Jackson led them down a photo-filled hallway to a small conference room. "Can I get you a coffee, sir?"

"Thank you. Black, please."

"Certainly. I'll be back in a moment."

Two minutes later the associate was back with a steaming mug, leading Bobby to assume it was from a single-serving machine."Thanks. Now, the letters. What the hell happened to them for a year?"

Jackson sat on the same side of the table, but turned his chair to face Bobby. "As I understand it, sir, the evening before your daughter passed away, she gave the letters to her lawyer, Mr. Mitchell, and asked they be passed to you after her funeral. Mr. Mitchell brought the letters back to the office with the full intention of doing exactly as your daughter requested. He put the letters on his desk then got called away to an urgent meeting with another client. When he returned to the office, the packet of letters was gone. He later discovered his secretary had picked them up with his mail, then they got sorted and filed, but they were filed in the wrong place. She had gone home for the weekend.

"Back then, we had a Chapter 7 bankruptcy client and because your daughter's name nearly matched that client's company name, the letters meant to go to you a week hence, were filed away in a box marked *CLOSED*. Since we have to hold on to the files for years, we have what we call 'cold storage' for those boxes. Two weeks ago the former owner of that bankrupt company passed away, and his ex-wife is contesting his will. In order to confirm the information she was giving us, Mr. Dewar had me pull the file box from the cold storage. I found the letters from your daughter, showed them to him, and on his orders, had them couriered over to you immediately. He went right up to Mr. Mitchell to inform him of the situation. What happened after is a matter of in-house politics, and the details are not appropriate for a discussion with a client."

"Wow. Sounds like simple mistake that anybody could have made."

"Maybe so, but here at *Mitchell, Hiroko, & Toffelmeyer,* we take pride in *not* making simple mistakes that anybody else could make."

"That's admirable. Just to be clear, and close the matter, the letters went from my daughter to Mr. Mitchell himself, then his secretary filed them in a wrong box, and the box sat untouched for a year until you retrieved it from the firm's 'cold storage' place?"

"Yes sir. Except that the secretary, Shannon, may have delegated the filing to one of the associates, just to show them the procedure."

"'May have'? So there's no way to know without speaking to Shannon. Is she here today?"

"Um, no sir. She's on maternity leave. Are you looking for someone specific to blame?"

"Blame? Oh no. I'm just trying to get it all straight in my head. But you know what? I have the letters, it was an honest mistake, and no harm no foul. As I said to Mr. Dewar on the phone, it was actually a bit of a treat to read my daughter's words so long after she wrote them."

"Then it's all good?"

"Yes, Mr. Coyne. I'm not going to sue the firm. It was a clerical error, nothing malicious or costly."

"Thank you, sir."

"No, thank *you*. You're the one who recognized the letters were in the wrong place and rectified the problem as soon as you identified it. Well done."

"It was my pleasure, sir. Now, can I escort you out?"

"Of course. You have files to clean up or corporations to save, or whatever it is legal associates do." He smiled at Jackson to show he was just being a smart ass.

They walked out into the hall of photos again and one of them caught Bobby's attention. "Wow. Senator Brand is one of your clients?"

"The Senator? No sir. But that *is* Mr. Mitchell with him. They've known each other since they went to Stanford together, though Senator

Brand was a few years ahead of Mr. Mitchell. Mr. Mitchell even worked on the Senator's unsuccessful mayoral campaign. They still golf together at Mythic Point at least once a month."

Bobby nearly crapped himself. He now had a damned good idea who Brand's assistant was on the boat! He forced a smile and moved on toward the elevators. "I just hope I can be that active when I'm their age."

"As do I, sir."

CHAPTER THIRTEEN

J ackson Coyne escorted Bobby down to the lobby and they parted
with handshakes and Bobby's thanks. He walked out the doors and
turned right instead of left, walking away from where SA Wong dropped
him off. With the revelation bouncing around in his head, he wanted
to make sure no one followed him from the building. He'd gone half a
block when SA Wong pulled up beside him and stopped. Bobby got in
and they drove off in silence. After they took a couple turns, they pulled
over. SA Wong handed Bobby a set of headphones, then plugged them
into the based of the pen.

"Give a listen to refresh your memory, and then tell me what
happened."

Bobby put the headphones on and listened. When he was done, he
turned on the CD player, handed the pen back to the Special Agent, and
repeated the visit, nearly word for word.

"Chaz Mitchell was on the boat with Santacruz?" SA Wong raised an
eyebrow. This was obviously not information he was expecting.

"I'm pretty sure." He handed the spy gear back.

The agent nodded. "I think you're right. It sounds like no one cared
enough about the letters to even look closely at whose name was on
them—except for Mitchell. He may have had time to read at least the first
one before he got called away, and when they vanished he didn't make
much of a stink because he didn't want to draw too much attention to

them, just in case someone else got the idea to look for and read them."
He shook Bobby's hand. "This is going to blow my boss' mind, and add
a layer to our investigation we didn't quite foresee. Thank you. I'll speak
with Detective Hernandez. The police protection your stepsister and
stepfather have now should be sufficient, but we need to get someone for
you, too. We'll get it all figured out fast and let you know. Whether it's
WPD or FBI, we'll take care of it. Now, please go be with your family. I'll
say a prayer for your sister's speedy recovery. One last thing. Please don't
say a word to anyone about any of this. Except maybe the Detective."

"Of course not. I'm glad I could help."

"So am I."

They shook hands again and Bobby went back into the hospital. He
went straight to Alex's room to see how he was doing.

Alex was watching the news on the flat screen, tears streaming down
his face.

Bobby put a hand on Alex's arm to comfort him. "What's wrong,
buddy?"

"It's not the nineties."

"Nope."

"The place I live in specializes in memory problems. They don't let us
watch the news. Screws with the head. It's been over thirty years?"

"Yes sir."

"And Marion's dead?"

"Yup."

"Sometimes I remember bits and pieces. Your mom left me."

"She did."

"Smart lady. I never meant to hurt her."

"I think she knows that." He poured two cups of water from the
pitcher on the table and handed one to Alex.

Alex took a sip. "Does she know about me and Marion?"

"I honestly don't know. I just found out myself. Alex, do you remember when the meeting was on the boat?"

"That's why Marion was killed. I'm sure of it. Someone must have spotted her and couldn't risk her talking."

"That's how it looks, yeah. But why did it take months for them to do it?"

"I don't know, but it had to be Santacruz."

"Maybe, but he died in 2003, so who is trying to kill you now?"

"2003? Then it wasn't him."

"When was the meeting, Alex?"

"Labor Day Weekend."

Perfect! "The money Santacruz brought. Who got it?"

"That phony crap?"

"Phony?"

"Phony. Fake. Counterfeit. Jake gave Mitchell a million to start up his firm, and gave me a hundred grand as thanks for making *The Rachel* available and to help with some city inspectors I needed to pay off. As soon as I actually got my hands on it later that night I could tell it was fake, though. The paper didn't feel right. I told Jake, and he told me he knew and for me to shut the hell up."

Bobby wished he still had the spy pen. What he *did* still have was his phone. Sitting next to Alex, he slyly took it out and began a fresh voice memo recording. "So the whole ten million was counterfeit and Brand knew. Did Santacruz know he knew?"

"I don't think so. I'm sure that slick bastard thought he'd pulled one over on us."

"What did you do with your hundred grand?"

"I burned it and found another way to pay off the inspectors. Except for a single Ben Franklin I have in a frame in my room. I tell people it was the first hundred I made in real estate."

"Wow. Since someone shot at you, I have to ask, who knew you were going to be on *that* road at *that* time?"

"Everybody at the home, because Rachel had to sign me out and give them an itinerary."

"That's a lot of people to know. I'm guessing you didn't start the storage unit fires yourself, but had someone do them for you. Who?"

"The fires? What fires?"

Damn! He was gone again. "Rachel's storage unit was set on fire and everything inside it was destroyed, Alex."

"Good. No photos, no risk. I can't let them find out about Marion or they'll hurt her."

Bobby slumped in the chair. Alex was mixing the past and the present, again. "Who did you call, Alex?"

"The usual guy. The Private Investigator my lawyer uses on the sly. For the right amount of cash, he'll do anything. But he owed me a favor. Now we're even."

"Have you got a name?"

"Neil Gillett. He's in the book. Tell him I referred you. What kind of job do you need done? Steal a bus? Knee-cap a strike scab?"

"Uh, no. I just want to make sure no one saw him at the storage place. I don't want it tracing back to you or Rachel."

"Or Marion."

"Especially not Marion."

"Good boy." He turned the television off with the remote. "I'm going to have a nap now. You go chat with Gillett." He rolled over on his side and started snoring almost immediately.

Out in the hall, Bobby informed the officer Alex was napping, and that he'd be back shortly. He didn't think it mattered to the cop, but he felt like he had to tell someone. He left the hospital and went out to the parking lot so he could walk while he talked. He called Special Agent Wong.

"Mr. Odini. What's up? Did you get the date of the meeting?"

Bobby gave him the date.

"Thank you."

"There's more. That ten million Santacruz 'gifted' to Brand was counterfeit."

"How the hell do you know *that*?"

"Alex said the paper was wrong. He was given a hundred thousand of it, but claims he burned all but a single hundred. He also said that Brand knew."

"He remembers a lot. That's great."

"He *did* remember. Now he's confused again."

"Damn. So where is that hundred?"

"In a frame at the home where he lives. By the way, the fire bug was a PI named Neil Gillett."

"Gillett? You're kidding, right?"

"No. That's who he said. Said his lawyer uses him for miscellaneous stuff and he'll do anything for a price."

"Including shooting out a tire to cause an accident on a country road."

"*What?*"

"Washington State Patrol just picked him up. Once they knew there was a shooter, they canvassed the area, found a security feed that captured his license plate when he parked on a side road, and they managed to pick him up at his place in Piolino. Still had the unlicensed hunting rifle in the trunk of his car. Okay. I have to call the WSP and get access to him. If we can get him to give up who hired him to take the shot this morning, then we'll be one step closer to knowing who sent two courier burglars to your condo and then killed them for failing to get what they came for. If you're not at the hospital, get back there, where there's protection. Someone with the stones and cash to get Gillett to pull a trigger will probably have other resources they can draw on to shut you up."

"But I don't know anything. I'm not a threat."

"You don't think so? You've been stirring the pot for a week. They'll cut your throat and toss you in an incinerator just out of spite. This kind of organized criminal is capable of anything. Remember, he may have hired someone to kill your twenty-year-old sister and make it look like a random attack. He has no scruples about hiding his tracks, eliminating loose ends and people who piss him off."

Bobby knew the agent was right. "Okay. I'm going back inside." He started back to the ICU.

"Thank you."

Bobby sat in a corner of the Emergency Room waiting area with his back to a wall, facing the doors. He sent a text to Stacey, telling her there'd been an accident, he was okay, but he was at the hospital with his stepsister who was in rough shape. He closed the text with a promise of a quiet dinner, soon.

As much as he wanted to spend time with Stacey, cooking, relaxing, maybe as much dancing as he could handle, he couldn't bear the thought of her becoming a casualty in this mess he'd fallen into. Until this storm blew over, Bobby knew his head wasn't exactly in a place conducive to nurturing a relationship. He sent the message, and then called Sam.

"Bobby, when you poke a dragon, you sure use a big stick."

"Sorry, Sam."

"So the troopers have a suspect in custody for the shooting?"

"He's more than that, Sam. I just got off the phone with our friend from Quantico. I'm still at the hospital if you want to swing by."

"Definitely."

"I'm going to go up and relieve Tina and her sister and make sure they get something to eat, then do the same myself. Just text me when you get here and I'll let you know where I am."

"Don't stray too far from the officers."

"I'll stay in the hospital and make sure the girls do, too."

"Good."

oOo

Tina and Nicole were famished, so Bobby gave them a couple of twenties and told them to go eat, but to stay on site. They whined and said they wanted real food and not hospital crap. He pointed at Rachel. "Someone tried to kill your mother and grandfather on their way to lunch. Stay in the hospital."

Nicole pouted, but asked with a gleam in her eye. "Can we take Officer So-Damned-Cute with us?"

"You can ask but since he's been assigned to protect your mom, I'm pretty sure he'll decline."

"I think I *will* ask. A girl has to try."

"Fine, but go and eat. I'll stay with your Mom, and then go when you get back."

Tina looked at the twenties in her hand. "Can we bring you anything back, Uncle Bob?"

"No, thanks. I can wait."

They left. He heard Nicole speak briefly to the officer on duty, and smiled when the man declined the offer. Bobby suspected Nicole wasn't going to give up so easily.

Two minutes later the officer opened the door and admitted a state trooper in the distinctive blue uniform.

"Mr. Odini. Washington State Patrol Detective Ron Renshaw. I'd like to ask Alex Charleswood some questions about the incident this morning and it was suggested I not only speak with you first but have you sit in, due to his health and memory issues. Do you have some time?" He nodded toward Rachel. "I understand you wanting to stay close. I'll try to make it as brief as I can."

"I'm actually covering for my nieces in here while they eat. When I left Alex he was having a nap. He's not especially fond of law enforcement right now."

"That's why I was hoping you could sit in."

Bobby knew Alex wouldn't talk, so they might as well give it a go before Sam arrived. He was starting to have trouble sorting out who was investigating what. "Sure. As brief as we can, please."

"Thank you."

oOo

The chat was even briefer than they had hoped because although Alex was awake, he turned his back to the State Patrol detective and told him to go screw himself. Bobby shrugged and returned to Rachel's room with the detective. They sat, spoke softly, and Bobby repeated everything Alex had told him that felt relevant, from how Alex knew Gillett, to who knew he was on his way down that road to lunch.

The detective took notes and asked questions to clarify various points. He admitted the more information they had to link Gillett to the fires, the easier it would be to get him to give up whoever hired him for the shooting. He gave Bobby his card and got Bobby's cell number, just in case he had further questions.

Ten minutes after Renshaw left, Sam arrived. A few minutes later, Tina and Nicole came back, so Bobby offered to buy Sam a coffee if he'd join him while he got something to eat. Sam quickly agreed.

Bobby didn't realize just how hungry he was until he finished his soup and sandwich and considered going back for a plate of lasagna. Sam decided coffee wasn't enough and opted for a big bowl of mushroom soup.

"So now we're looking at ten million in counterfeit, a state senator looking *very* dirty, and a prominent lawyer being added into the mix, too." Sam spoke softly. "What about Sabbatini? Do you think he's the type to hire a killer to keep a secret?"

"No. He sounds like a hands-on man. He would have done it himself, and it probably wouldn't have been as neat and tidy. He's too disorganized."

"So, we've narrowed it down to someone at the law firm," Sam concluded.

"Probably Mitchell. He was there on the boat with Santacruz for that meeting, he had access to the cash, bogus or not, he has a lot to hide, and if he found out Alex recklessly had the fires set, he might consider him a loose end after all these years. Is there a chance some of the counterfeit cash is still around? What if he doesn't know it's bad? Alex said he told Brand, but Brand told him to shut up."

Sam nodded. "We need to recheck the belongings of Vetere and Gillett, on the off chance the bills are in still in use. Mitchell is smart, so he probably wouldn't throw around excess cash and draw attention to himself. I doubt if he has any of it left after thirty years, but if he's at all like your stepfather, he might just have kept a souvenir. They need Gillett to roll over on Mitchell, and then search warrants will be forthcoming for the FBI and State Troopers. We still have no connection between Vetere's murder and Mitchell, so WPD has no part in it. Even your sister's cold case is really just a single link in the larger chain. Who are you suspecting? Brand?"

"I don't think so. But I've never even met the senator, so I don't know if he's capable of putting a hit out on his best friend's young lover."

"He doesn't have a reputation for angry outbursts and has no record for anything other than a few parking tickets. Our problem here is that all our evidence against both Brand and Mitchell is circumstantial: a pair of photos taken on a boat somewhere, and the word of a man suffering from dementia. Even *if* they find the bill your stepfather claims to have, and *if* it's counterfeit, and *if* we're lucky and it has Brand's fingerprints on it, without more bills in Brand's possession, there's nothing to go on. Really, the most we have here is a few more leads with which to crack open a few more closets, looking for thirty-year-old skeletons."

"Well, when you put it *that* way." Bobby knew Sam was right. He had watched enough cop shows to understand the concept of circumstantial evidence and hearsay. "All of this counterfeit cash and corrupt politics stuff is interesting, but all I really want out of it is to find who ordered my sister dead. What about Vetere's personal belongings?"

"It's all locked up in evidence, where we can get at it as we need it."

"And the ledger is the only hint he was a hired killer?"

"Not at all. We now have surveillance photos and video of him over the last twenty or so years, showing him in the vicinities of various murders at the times they happened, but nothing of him actually *committing* the crimes. He'd been pulled in for questioning at least a dozen times over the years, but there were never any reliable witnesses nor a speck of forensic evidence to link him directly to any of the crimes. We're sure he has other bank accounts, but we have no idea where they are, yet. Our cyber team has taken apart his life, but he was extremely low tech. He lived nearly completely off the grid. I've never seen anything like it, not in this age of electronic connectedness."

"Do you have any clue who killed him?"

"Nothing solid. He would have made so many enemies that nearly every person of power in the state would want him dead, either because of what he did *to* them or what he did *for* them. I'm amazed someone got close enough to that soulless paranoid to pull the trigger. There was gunshot residue on his shirt, so it was most likely someone he trusted, or at least someone he would never suspect, like a teenaged barista he sees every day."

"With that many enemies, his killer may not even have any connection to Marion's murder. I'm sort of back to step one."

"*You* aren't back to anything, Bobby. Step away, keep your family safe. Keep *yourself* safe, and let the Feds solve it. Especially now that we've identified the two who broke into your place. One was a known criminal, but the other was a retired bus driver. Do you know a Rick Plested?"

"Rick? Seriously? I have lunch with him once a month, along with a few other retirees. He broke in, and he's one of the two you found in Albatross Bay? Damn. I mean, that explains a lot, but Rick was a good man. A little secretive and odd, but a good man. He's been on the fringes of my social circle for years now." Something occurred to him. "Is it possible he's been keeping an eye on me?"

"It is. It's too much of a coincidence to assume there's no connection. Maybe after your sister was killed, they wanted to make sure she hadn't said anything to you. At least they didn't just kill you, MJ, and your mother outright."

"Rick? I can't get my head around it. I'm furious that he broke into the condo, but I'm crushed that he's dead. He's divorced, but has three kids and five grandkids."

He took a long sip of his cooling coffee before asking a question he wasn't sure Sam would answer honestly. "Do you think the Feds give a damn about Marion's murder? I think if they can solve it while taking down Mitchell, Sabbatini, and possibly Brand, they'll see it as a bonus, but that's not their goal."

"Maybe. But don't forget whatever crimes they do pin on anyone, murder carries the most weight. If they *can* prove murder, they will."

"But with Vetere dead, the odds are slim."

Sam sighed. "You're right. If it were *my* investigation, I'd be concentrating on the ten million. Even thirty years ago it would have been hard to hide. Sadly, even with a photo of these men meeting with Santacruz, if it was in international waters, there's little they can charge them with. But it does give them places they can look, as I said before. These kinds of investigations take years, Bobby."

"Unless someone makes too much noise."

"The next bullet may be for you, not a tire. Have you not seen the movie, *The Hobbit*? My kids love it, but when the dragon wakes up and goes on the rampage..."

"I did see it. Loved the book as a kid, too."

"Then don't be such a Bilbo, Bobby."

"Special Agent Wong thinks they should put out a press release saying they're investigating the two murdered courier-slash-burglars and have taken into custody all the related evidence dating back thirty years, just to take the focus off the family and keep us safe."

"That's an interesting idea. Of course, since your stepfather was actually there on the boat, they might try to get to him again. Sadly, from what you've said about his memory, there isn't a prosecutor in the state that would put him on the stand. Every single piece of evidence they or we get from him has to be verified through other sources."

"Someone is scared, though. If it's not Mitchell or Brand, it has to be someone in one of their organizations."

"Could your stepfather have enough enemies that this might not be related to your sister's murder at all? Are we just assuming that everything's connected, when it's not?"

"He was a developer in this city for decades. I'm betting he *has* made a few enemies. Not connected? It's possible. What do we have so far, Sam? I get the letter from MJ, which the law firm and you know about. I mention the new evidence to my retired buddies, including Rick, and then my Jeep is broken into and the boxes stolen. They don't get whatever the hell they're looking for and Rick and the other guy try to get into my condo. They fail and get killed for it. It gets quiet for a few days, then the fire that Alex set to destroy evidence that may or may not have been in the storage unit, followed by Gillett shooting them off the road."

"Sounds about right."

"One at a time, then. The letters and the new evidence: the law firm, you, or Rick. Rick is dead, and I'm going to go out on a limb and remove you from the suspects list." He winked and Sam smiled back.

"Gee. Thanks."

"At the law firm we have the lawyer Grant Dewar, the associate Jackson Coyne, and Senior Partner Chaz Mitchell. If it were Coyne, he could just have destroyed the letters when he found them and no one would have been any wiser, unless he didn't know what was in them. If it were Dewar, he could have destroyed the letters, too, but Coyne knew about them, so it would have been risky."

"Yes, but if Dewar knew about the top letter mentioning Vetere and your sister, he could simply have removed it before having Coyne send the rest to you. He could have tossed them into a courier envelope, sealed it, and told Coyne to send it off ASAP. But he didn't. The only ones who handled the letters *before* they were misplaced but not after they were found again, were Mitchell and the secretary out on maternity leave. A breast-feeding, stay-at-home Mom is hardly the profile of someone calling on a pair of break-and-enter experts and then killing them when they failed to get what she wanted. It's possible, but unlikely."

"That really only leaves Mitchell, at the law firm. Coyne is too young to have been around when the letters first arrived. My hope is that Gillett was hired by whoever hired the fake couriers and he takes whatever deal the state offers him."

"If he's handy and popular with off-book wet work, then the Feds may offer him all sorts of things in order to get him to talk. I hope for his sake he wasn't hired by whoever killed Vetere, because then he won't be safe no matter where they put him."

"Wonderful. What would MJ have been doing right about now when things got this twisted up?"

"MJ? She'd be at the range, taking out her frustration on paper targets. She was a helluva shot."

"That actually sounds like a good idea."

"I know you have a permit for her Beretta. Are you carrying it, like I suggested?"

"No. I have no serious training."

"I'm not a fan of civilians carrying firearms, but maybe you should at least load it and keep handy when you're at home, in case someone else breaks in."

"That, I'm comfortable with." Bobby looked at his watch. "It's late. You should get home to your family, and I'll go up and see how everyone is doing."

"Good idea. I might get home in time to tuck the kids in. That would be rare."

"Then do it and cherish it, Sam. I know with my shift work there were a couple years when my Mom came and babysat MJ for me three out of five nights a week. It was hell. It was lost time I wish I could get back."

"No doubt. Go check on your nieces and I'll talk to you tomorrow. You know how to reach me if anything comes up that can't wait."

"I do, but let's just pray for a quiet night."

"Agreed."

They took their trays, garbage, and recycling to the drop-off area, then Sam left and Bobby went first to check on Alex.

"I want to go home, Bobby."

"I know. But you're staying at least tonight, for observation."

"I'm fine. I broke my wrist."

"Sorry. Doctor's orders."

"The doctor is an ass-hat."

"Maybe so, but you're staying."

"I'm *bored*, Bobby!"

"Okay. I'll see if I can get you Netflix or DisneyPlus. I'll also talk to the girls to see if one of them can come and hang out with you. I think they're so scared to leave Rachel's side they forget you're here."

"That'd be nice. What's Netflix?"

"Uh, think TV with fewer commercials."

"Then get me that. Commercials have ruined television."

"Will do." He left Alex and went to Rachel's room. Both girls were asleep in their chairs, but Tina roused herself when he entered the room.

"Uncle Bob. Where were you?"

"Sorry. Detective Hernandez and I had a lot to catch upon."

"Is everything okay?"

"Not yet, but we hope it will be, soon. The good news is State Patrol has a suspect in custody for shooting out your mom's tire and causing all this."

"So it really wasn't an accident?"

"Nope. It's why there will be an officer outside all night, to keep your mom safe. There's one with your grandfather, too. Speaking of which, do you think one of you could go down and hang out with him for awhile? He's bored. I'll see about getting him Netflix, which'll help, but he's going stir crazy. Maybe show him pictures of his great-granddaughter."

"I can do it. I have to get home, soon, though. Treyvon is home, but Lydia is fussy before bed. You know that Grandpa may not have a clue who I am."

"That's fine. Just go along with whatever he says. You know the drill. His condition isn't new to you."

"I know. I guess I'm just tired and worried."

"Me, too. That's why I'm heading home. Have you got everything arranged with Nicole at your mom's place?"

"All set. She'll catch a cab to the house tonight. Sandy said he's going to rent a car when he arrives tomorrow, which will give them both some mobility."

"Any word on your mom?"

"A doctor was by a little while ago to check on her and said everything looked good. They'll run some tests tomorrow morning and give her 'something something medical jargon something'. I have no idea what he said."

He laughed. "Okay. I'll come back first thing, to be here when they do the tests. Also, if they release your grandfather I'll drive him back to Westport. I guess we'll play it all by ear."

"Okay." She hugged her uncle then gently shook her sister awake to explain where she was going.

Bobby left the two of them to talk. He stopped at the nurse's station to arrange for Netflix for both rooms and gave them his credit card to charge it all to. Rachel may not have been able to watch it, but whoever was sitting with her deserved to have something to entertain them other than their phones and the beeping of her monitors.

oOo

At home, Bobby lay down on the couch and closed his eyes for a moment. Vinnie quietly joined him, snuggling in beside him. He slept for at least an hour before the cat decided he'd waited long enough and needed to be fed. Once Vinnie was happily crunching his kibble, Bobby made a decision. He went to the closet in the master bedroom, got down on his hands and knees, reached beneath a pair of folded old blankets, and grabbed hold of the portable gun vault hidden there. He crawled back out of the closet and stood up slowly, the fifteen-pound, 8"x12" vault tucked under one arm while the other hand used the doorframe to brace himself.

He placed the vault on the bed and retrieved the stack of letters under the pillow. With the letters on top of the little vault, he returned to the couch, putting the load on the coffee table. Vinnie sauntered in from the kitchen and joined him as he closed the blinds. "Okay, big guy. Time to get serious about protection." Putting the letters to one side, Bobby placed the four fingers of his right hand on the biometric sensor pads of the case. He held them still, and a moment later there was a click and the case popped open. He could have used the key to unlock it as well, but the key was in the bedside table drawer and his fingertips were right there.

There, on its foam bed, lay the black steel Beretta handgun with custom ceramic gold accents he'd bought his daughter the day she graduated from the academy. If he remembered correctly, it was a PX4 Storm. He picked it up and remembered its weight. MJ had taken him to the range and taught him to use it. She had covered everything from loading it to dismantling and cleaning it. It hadn't been fired since the last time they'd cleaned it and placed it in the vault, though. He picked up one of the three magazines, opened one of the two boxes of hollow point bullets, and loaded the magazine. He then snapped it into place in the gun's grip, keeping his finger far away from the trigger. He checked the safety was on, and placed it back in the vault.

"There. Step one, done. I'll find the holster later." He pulled a slip of paper out of the pocket in the top of the vault. "I suppose I should actually have my permit in my wallet if I'm thinking of carrying this damned thing around." He stared down at the deadly black and gold beauty sitting so innocuously in the vault. "I'm not so sure about this, Vinnie. I seriously have no idea if I'm going to be able to point this at another person when the time comes. Ask me to pilot a forty-foot diesel beast of a bus through a construction zone, or make a soufflé so light it dances on your plate, but aiming this at an intruder's center mass and pulling the trigger... I just don't know." He sighed. "I suppose it's better to have it and not need it than to need it and not have it. We've lost enough people over the years. We have what it takes to defend ourselves, so I guess it behooves us to do so. Once we get your claws sharpened, we'll both be ready for another home invasion." Glancing up toward the ceiling, he half-smiled. "There you go, MJ—Old Man Odini is ready for war."

Vinnie stepped across to the coffee table and sniffed the vault and its contents, then leaped back over to the couch and curled up.

"Not impressed? I don't blame you. How about we take a look at the next letter, instead." The cat yawned long and slow. "Fine. I'll read it to myself, then." Bobby carefully slid the envelope from the top of the pile, leaned back, and withdrew the letter.

Hey Papa Rock!

You just dropped me off after we saw Cheap Trick at the casino. It was a great show, but I must be getting old because my ears are still ringing and they're not even a loud band.

I love sharing music with you! Do you know what my all-time favorite music memory is? Yes, it was a Snark Puppet gig, but it wasn't our first one, or even our biggest one. It was the night we lost the final riff-off in the Battle of the Bands at Club Re-Hab on 4th.

The MC announced the winner then let Snark Puppet play an exit song before the winners—our friends in 'Doofus'—played out the rest of the night. I was up on stage in my lime green, way-too-big Lacoste golf shirt, shredded jeans, fluffy pink tutu, and combat boots, and you were standing back at the bar in an identical tutu over cargo shorts, with the very first

Snark Puppet t-shirt. You had that horrid porn star moustache, and you were still a long way from going grey.

Lester started the beat and I joined in with a blatant rip-off of the opening riff to Aerosmith's Walk This Way, *and in the two-beat silence before I kicked into our own* Lick My Hightops, Jerkface, *you screamed out "That's my Snark Puppet! Go, Baby Girl, go!" at the top of your lungs. The place went nuts! Halfway through the song, the dudes from Doofus joined us on stage and we blew the doors off the place. We ended up playing side-by-side all night long with these twenty-year-old rockers, like we were their equals.*

I hope you know I've never been insulted by you calling me 'Baby Girl', because you let me define what that meant, and you never ever let me feel like my definition of being a girl was wrong. You even went to bat for me with Grandma and told her to stop buying dresses for me, and start buying clothes with me. It was a turning point for me and Grandma. She finally understood what you and I had, and came along for the ride.

I start chemo tomorrow, so I'm glad we had tonight, while I still have the energy to dance with you.

Just so you know, the music of my heart is accompanied by the sound of your voice, singing me to sleep.

Love you.

Always and forever, Daddio.

Your one and only Baby Girl.

xoxo

Oddly enough, it was Bobby's *second* favorite music memory. His favorite was that Cheap Trick concert a little over a year ago, because it was the last time his little rock star was able to get out and enjoy live music. That night at Club Re-Hab, though, was a close second. He was so damned proud of those kids. They played their hearts out and when they lost to the young men of *Doofus*, they didn't cry or pout or complain that they were robbed, they just ramped it up to eleven and showed the entire place what losing with grace was all about. Four kids with braces, zits, and homework to be done by Monday morning. They lost the competition, but they won the night.

CHAPTER FOURTEEN

In the condo, back in the present, Bobby slept well, after the fresh flood of tears drained him even further than he thought he could go.

When he woke with the sun, he had a feeling something was wrong, something small was off center. While he fixed breakfast for the two of them, then showered off the stress sweat and hospital stink, he fretted. He knew it wasn't the letters—he'd returned the packet to its place under the other pillow. And it wasn't the gun, because the safety was on and it was locked in the little vault, which now sat on the shelf of his bedside table, where he could reach it if he needed it.

Halfway through putting his travel clothes into the stacked washing machine at the back of the walk-in pantry, he clued in. It was too quiet. Considering all the crap going on, no one had texted or called him since late yesterday. He searched out the phone on the charger and discovered the problem. When he'd gone for dinner with Sam, he'd put the phone on mute and forgotten to take it off. He now had a handful of messages including three from Stacey, one from Donal asking if he'd received the email the young political hopeful had sent, and one from Sam, checking up on him.

Stacey's messages got more and more concerned, so he called her.

"*Mister* Odini..."

"Hi. I seem to be apologizing a lot lately. A week ago, my world was quiet and boring, and now people are dying and the crap is hitting the fan."

"Oh my God! Your sister died? I'm so sorry!"

"No no no! Sorry. I meant..." He stopped himself. He almost did it again. But he had to tell her something. "Rachel is in a medically-induced coma because of a brain injury, but her dad only has a broken wrist. Rachel's daughters are both here and her son is arriving some time today." He considered telling her about Gillett, but kept it simple. "The State Patrol are investigating the accident to find out what the cause was. Rachel can't tell them and Alex has memory problems. I'm sorry I didn't call."

"Hon, you had greater priorities than calming me down. You do what you have to do and every so often I'll send you a text to check upon you, if that's okay. When everyone is out of danger, we'll find time for ourselves, if you want."

"Trust me, Stacey, I want." And he did.

"Me, too." He could almost hear her smiling through the phone. "Now get yourself back to the hospital and make sure your sister is okay. Once she is, you can tell me all about it."

"Thank you. I will."

"I know."

o0o

Bobby found the leather belt holster for the Beretta in a shoe box marked *MJ* on the top shelf of his closet, then opened the vault and stared at the loaded weapon for a full minute before closing the vault up again and sliding it under the bed. He shrugged at Vinnie. "In all honesty, I can't imagine a scenario in the hospital in which me firing off a few rounds in self-defence is a good idea." He dug around in the shoe box and came up with MJ's retractable baton in its own holster, and her Taser projectile stun gun. He had no training in hand-to-hand combat, so the baton was almost useless, but the stun gun was another matter. MJ had shown him her 'toy' when she first got it, and even given him a lesson on how to use it, just in case he wanted to get one for himself, to carry on the bus. He'd pointed out that transit operators weren't allowed to be armed and when he named some of his more thick-skulled union brothers whom she knew, including Rick, ironically enough, she agreed. But they'd had the lesson and so he was familiar with it.

He checked the charge to make sure it was full, then slipped it back into its holster and clipped the holster to his belt. It was a fraction of the size and weight of the Beretta, and the chances of collateral damage were pretty slim with a stun gun. He filled Vinnie's bowl with kibble, put on his nylon Mariner's windbreaker to cover the weapon on his belt, and left for the hospital.

Just as he locked up the Jeep in the hospital parking lot, his phone rang.

"Sam! I'm just arriving at the hospital."

"Perfect! I'll be there in about fifteen minutes. I have some good news you're going to like."

"Good news is always welcome. I'll be in one of the two rooms. Alex is probably being kicked out of here today, so I'll check on him first."

"See you soon."

He could hear Alex from down the hall. A WPD officer stood sentry at the door, but was doing his best to ignore the shouting.

"I don't give a flying fart what the doctor says. I'm fine. I'm going home. Someone go tell Rachel I need a lift. For some reason I can't find my car keys. Which one of you bitches took my car keys?"

By the time he arrived at the room and stepped into the small space, Bobby was furious. He understood Alex was sick and bored and old, but none of that was an excuse for speaking like he was to the hospital staff. Two nurses stood at the foot of his bed, flush with anger and frustration themselves. Bobby nodded to them and went straight for Alex with both verbal guns blazing.

"Sit your ass down in bed, Alex. If I ever hear you talk to these ladies or any others like that again I'll have the doctor give you an enema every hour."

"But...!"

"The only butt is the one where your head is. Now sit back and be nice while I look into when you are being released, because when you're that disrespectful, I'm sure the staff want you out of here as much as you do. *Capisce?*"

"Bobby?" Alex leaned back into the pillows, his voice soft, cowed by Bobby's words. The nurses slipped out, whispering their thanks to Bobby as they did.

"Yes, Alex. It's me." He put a hand on Alex's arm to comfort him. "You're in Westview Medical Center. You and Rachel were in a car accident, and Rachel is in a coma. Now, I will look into getting you back to Westport, or you can stay here for observation and be close to your daughter for when she wakes up."

"My baby girl is hurt?"

"Badly. She's broken into pieces and has a head injury. As soon as Tina or Nicole get here, I'll send one of them down. Sandy is even coming in today, too."

"Sandy?" He looked a little confused.

"Your grandson. He's named Alexander, after you, but he goes by Sandy."

"Oh. Okay. Good name. Good kid?"

"He is. Are you relaxed now?"

"Yes, Bob."

"Good. Have you eaten?"

"No."

"I'll look into that, too."

"Thank you, Bob."

"Of course, Alex. It's what we do for family."

"I know. Will Marion be coming by today?"

Bobby sighed. "No, I don't think so. We'll talk about it later, okay?"

"Okay. Have you seen the remote?"

"It's on the table to your right."

Alex looked to his right and saw the remote. "Of course it is. Thank you."

"I'm going to check on your breakfast, and on Rachel, then I'll be back. Will you behave?"

"Yes." He picked up the remote and forgot Bobby was even in the room.

Out in the hall, Bobby apologized to the staff, but they laughed it off as part of the job.

"Maybe, ladies, but it shouldn't be. I told him I'd check on breakfast. I'd also like to know what the doctor has in mind for him, whether he's staying or I'm taking him home."

One of the nurses reached over the station's counter and picked up a file. "His breakfast should be along shortly, and the doctor is due in about half an hour. I don't see any discharge order, so there will be an assessment before the decision is made."

"Of course. Makes sense. How's my stepsister, Rachel?"

"I checked on her half an hour ago and there was no change. Her vitals are steady and strong. She's scheduled for a CT scan this morning to check how much the swelling has come down. If necessary, she'll have an MRI, too."

"Thank you." He left them to their work and went to see Rachel for himself.

He was shocked by how dark her bruises had become since last night. "You look like hell, kid." He took another picture of her. A quick text to Tina to let her know he was here, and then Bobby turned on the TV, and stopped. He really had no idea what Rachel liked to watch. She gave him the impression of being a *Real Wives of Beverly Hills* fan, but he just didn't see that being conducive to *anyone's* state of mind. He found a comedy special. Maybe hearing laughter would be just what she needed.

Tina texted back she was picking Nicole up and going for breakfast, before getting Sandy at the airport. She expected the three of them to be there within two hours, at the latest, if it was okay with him. He texted back it was fine and he'd see them when he saw them.

Sam arrived a few minutes later with a cardboard tray holding two take-out coffees. He handed one to Bobby. "Here you go. I gave the boys theirs already." He tugged the second cup out of the tray and sat in the other chair. "How is she?"

"No visible changes, other than her bruises darkening up. She looks like she went three rounds with Ronda Rousey."

"I noticed."

"They're doing a CAT scan in a bit, and maybe an MRI if necessary."

"Then I guess you need some good news."

"Always."

"My friend at the Bureau says Gillett is rolling over on Chaz Mitchell for hiring him to do the shooting. I don't know what kind of deal they offered him, but he took it."

Bobby was pleased. "That's good to hear. I don't suppose Gillett knows anything about Vetere and Marion?"

"I have no idea, but I kind of doubt it. He would have been in middle school when your sister was murdered and I can't imagine Mitchell bragging about it to anyone, least of all someone who would do *anything* for cash."

"What about Vetere's belongings? Can I take a look at them?"

"The Bureau now has all of his stuff, and even if they didn't, I can't just let a civilian rummage through evidence."

"Damn."

"I do have photos of everything we took out of his house, though. I guess it couldn't hurt to let you see them. What do you think you'll see that we didn't?"

"I have no idea, Sam. I'm grasping at straws."

"He wasn't a trophy keeper, Bobby. His personal belongings barely filled two boxes. I went through his place up in Albatross Point four or five times, looking for something, anything that would help us solve *his* murder, and saw nothing out of place."

"Vetere lived in Albatross Point?"

"Yes. Owned an old house on a quiet street. Why?"

"Because I grew up in Albatross Point. On 46th Avenue."

Sam nearly dropped his coffee. "Are you kidding me? *He* lived on 46th Avenue. South West. You might have been neighbors."

"I doubt it. Mom sold the place when she married Alex, and when she left him she bought the condo she's still in. She sold the house to a developer who was going to tear it down and put in a nice in-fill, but the last time I drove past, nothing had been done with it. It was neatly kept up, but nothing had been changed. That was about five years ago. I have some pretty mixed feelings about life at 32-32. Dad died while we lived there, and—" Sam was staring at him, his mouth moving, but no words were coming out. "Sam? Are you okay? Don't stroke out on me!"

Sam carefully and deliberately placed his coffee down on the table next to Rachel's bed. His hands shook. "Bobby, are seriously saying you lived at 3232 46th Avenue SW, in Albatross Point?"

"Yeah. Don't tell me Vetere lived across the street."

"Oh no. He lived in *your* goddamned house."

Bobby's grip on his coffee loosened and if not for Sam's quick reflexes, he would have dropped it. Bobby's heart pounded so loudly he thought his head was going to explode. Sam said nothing, and Bobby was grateful for the time to process it all. The detective looked like he was doing his own processing.

At some point laughter started to drown out his pounding heart and Bobby couldn't figure out why Sam would be laughing. It took a moment before he realized *he* was the one laughing. Well, of course he was laughing. There was nothing left to do *but* laugh.

Sam picked up his coffee and took a sip, the shaking of his hands having settled to a mild tremor. "I'm glad you see the humor in this Bobby. My abuela always said there was no such thing as coincidences. There was a reason why Vetere bought the house you grew up in and I'm not sure we're going to like it."

Bobby reached out and took back his own coffee. "I don't give a crap why he bought the house, Sam, because I know where his trophies are."

"What?"

"We need to go to the house. Now. I have a hunch. A really big, mind-blowing hunch. Do you have the keys to the place?"

"No. The Feds have them."

"They're going to want to be there for this, so give them a call and have them meet us there."

"You're serious?"

"As serious as I can be when I'm so excited I could wet myself."

"Okay." He took out his phone and dialed. It was answered quickly. "SAC Stevenson, it's Detective Sam Hernandez with WPD. I'm here at Westview Medical with Bobby Odini and we just figured out that not only did Franco Vetere live in the house Bobby grew up in in Albatross Point, but Bobby thinks he knows where Vetere hid his trophies or whatever. Can you get the keys to the place and meet us there in twenty minutes? Thirty? Sure. We'll see you there in thirty."

Twenty-five minutes later Sam pulled up in front of 3232 46th Avenue SW. It was a narrow, pale blue, one story bungalow with a few shrubs up front and three steps up to the front door. He and Bobby got out of the car, but stayed with it. Bobby stared at the place, memories flooding back. "It doesn't look like much from here."

"No, it doesn't. I was surprised to see how deep it is. It takes up the whole lot."

"Yeah. It's a good thing there's a playground out behind it, because we sure as hell didn't have a backyard."

"And the beach is only a few blocks away."

"We weren't allowed to go there without a parent, and since Mom was always working and Dad was always too drunk to move when he was home, we didn't see much of the beach." He thought about it for a minute. "No, that's not true. *I* didn't see much of the beach when I was a little kid, but Dad died not long after Marion was born, so Mom started making time to take us when she could. Dad's life insurance allowed her to pay off the mortgage and get rid of one job, so we might not have had Dad around, but life was actually more relaxing."

A dark Ford Taurus pulled in behind them and both Special Agents Stevenson and Wong got out, each with a large flashlight in hand. Sam opened his trunk and took out two more, one each for he and Bobby. He then handed them each a pair of latex gloves and a pair of disposable shoe covers. The four men shook hands, then Stevenson turned and stared at the house. "We've turned this place upside down. *I* have turned this place upside down."

Sam nodded. "Me, too."

The Special Agent in Charge pulled a set of keys from his jacket pocket and started up the front walk. "You really grew up here, Mr. Odini?" He put on his gloves and booties and unlocked the door.

"I did."

"So a professional killer murders a young woman, and then, years later, buys the house she grew up in? It just doesn't jive with me. I've seen some strange stuff, investigating killers all around the country, but nothing quite like this. There's something we're missing here. Some piece of Vetere's puzzle we're just not seeing." He swung open the storm door, unlocked the front door, and led them inside.

The three law enforcers went first and Bobby was just fine with that because when he got to the threshold of 32-32, he had trouble taking the next step. A force field of memory halted his step. Sam looked back at him. "You okay?"

His chest felt tight and he started to sweat a bit, but he pushed back, refusing to let panic win. "I'm good. It's been a while."

"No problem. Take a moment. We'll just make sure the place is clear." The three of them left Bobby and spread out to search the house, each with their flashlight and firearm leading the way.

Reaching under his jacket, Bobby drew the stun gun, turned it on, and eventually followed their example. The place smelled empty. There was a little mold and mildew, but no human smells. No aftershave or cooking residue or anything that would indicate anyone had been in the house in months. He looked around, scanning the place with the flashlight. The furniture was different. It wasn't the cheap matching set from Sears he remembered, but rather a mix-and-match of various pieces typical of every bachelor pad he'd ever been in.

The agents and detective returned. "All clear," Sam confirmed. "What are we looking for, Bobby? What didn't we see before?"

Bobby gestured with his flashlight. "Downstairs. It's in the basement. The workshop off of the laundry room. Or it *was*."

SA Wong took the lead, his boss went second, followed by Sam, and then Bobby. A flood of memories caught up with Bobby as he descended the steps. He recognized the scars on the plaster from when he banged into it with his bike on the first day of spring when he was nine. He smelled the cool dampness that had always permeated the basement, even in the middle of winter with the furnace blasting away. He smiled. Sure, there had been some ugly times, but there were some great memories here, too.

The four of them wound their way across the rec room and into the laundry room. Bobby noticed there was a dart board just like the one he'd practiced on for hours. Too, although the furniture was different, it seemed to be laid out the same as he remembered it. It shouldn't have been. Something was off about the whole place.

In the large laundry room, the other three moved aside and let Bobby enter the workshop. There was a loud metallic clunk behind him and the lights came on. He looked back and Agent Wong stood next to the breakers. "I thought this would make it easier."

Bobby turned off his flashlight, and the others followed suit. "I'm surprised there's electricity after a year of it sitting vacant."

SAC Stevenson explained. "We've got an application in the courts to keep this place for the Bureau. We assume he bought it with the proceeds of his murder-for-hire work, so it belongs to the government now. He has no family or dependents to challenge us, so we keep the bills paid until the decision is made."

"It'd make a great safe house." He flicked the light switch just inside the workshop doorway and lit the space up. It was just as he remembered it, except his father's tools weren't hanging on the black-marker-tool-outlined spots on the pegboard above the workbench. He handed his flashlight to Sam, and grabbed one end of the workbench. He lifted it just an inch off the floor, but a click could be heard behind the bench. He lowered the bench back to the floor, then grabbed the edge of the pegboard with both hands and pushed it. It didn't budge. He pulled on it and it moved an inch until it clicked again. "Sorry. Forgot a step. It's been a few decades." He tried pushing again, and this time the pegboard and the one-inch-thick plywood it was mounted on rolled cleanly out of the way, revealing a ten-inch-deep, four-by-eight space behind it.

"Jesus H. Christ..." Sam said what they were all thinking.

Bobby smiled and held up his arm like he was presenting a prize package on the Price is Right. "Gentlemen, where my father used to hide his alcohol and his porn, I give you the personal souvenir and trophy collection of one Franco Vetere."

The entire space was cubbyhole after cubbyhole, each housing something, and each labeled with a neat, typewritten label. Bobby reached out for a little globe in one of the cubbyholes and SAC Stevenson shouted, "Don't touch a thing!" He pulled his cell phone out of his suit jacket pocket. "Everybody out, now. I'm calling in Forensics. I don't want to risk tainting anything in here. Not a hair, not a fleck of dry skin. Let's go." He dialed a number. "Fisk? SAC Stevenson. I need a full collection team to 3232 46th Avenue SW, in Albatross Point. It's Christmas."

Bobby took a final moment to look around the rec room. When his father died after crashing his car into a tree in a drunken haze, Bobby secluded himself downstairs in front of the console TV, refusing to go to school or socialize or even talk to his mother or baby Mar. Then one day his mother came down and sat beside him on the couch. She put an arm around his shoulders and hugged him. She whispered the words that would break him out of his funk and change his life forever.

"Your father was a drunken asshole who used to slap me around after you went to sleep. As far as I'm concerned, he got what he deserved in that fiery wreck. It's time to stop mourning a man who doesn't deserve it, and promise ourselves to never become like the beast he was."

Sixty-year-old Bobby wiped a single tear and started upstairs. As soon as she was back in town, he was going to call his mother and have a long, loving chat.

While the two agents waited for their forensics team to arrive, Sam drove Bobby back to the hospital. On the way, Bobby remembered something. "I forgot to tell you to expect a call from the Banff RCMP. I kind of gave them your name, if they wanted more information on Marion's murder. I didn't tell them a lot."

"He called. I didn't have much for him, though I might, soon."

"Will the Bureau share what they find?"

"To a certain extent, yes. Not stuff key to any of their ongoing investigations outside of Westview County, but stuff related specifically to Vetere's murder, probably. They owe me—*you*, actually. They owe you *huge*."

"I'm just trying to figure out who ordered my baby sister killed."

"With luck, your answer will come out of the treasure trove in the basement."

"I'm still confused why the hell Vetere owned the place. Could Alex have pointed him in that direction? Did Alex even *know* him, like we think Mitchell did?"

"An interesting question. Let me know what he tells you."

"Ha! After I caught him giving the nurses a hard time, I'll be lucky if he has more than two words for me." They arrived at the hospital. "But it can't hurt to ask. Maybe he'll forget I snapped at him."

"Maybe. Anyway, go. I'll let you know if I hear anything from the Bureau. Keep carrying your stun gun, though. This is a long way from being over."

"That's what I'm afraid of."

oOo

Tina was back in her chair in her mother's room, but Rachel's bed—and Rachel with it—was gone, which explained why there was no officer at the door.

"Hey, Unc. They've taken her for the CAT scan." Bobby could tell from her puffy, red eyes she'd been crying. He sat down in the other chair and took her hands in his own.

"This is the hardest part. The waiting. Once we hand our loved one over to the professionals, there's not a damned thing we can do, Tina. We're powerless. They can succeed or fail, but it's without our help and it drives us crazy. You want to scream and cry and run up and down the hallways pulling your hair out."

"Exactly. I don't know how you did it, *twice*."

"Cancer is a whole different game than this. Here you have a chance modern medicine and time will simply result in healing. With cancer, especially MJ's type of breast cancer, modern medicine is a crap shoot, and time is your enemy."

"A crap shoot? They cure cancer every day."

"They do. And they don't. One of my aunts had Non-Hodgkins Lymphoma and got into a drug trial. It worked, she was healed, but do you know what the active ingredient in the cure was?"

"Cannabis oil?" She snickered.

"I wish. Chinese hamster ovaries. How the hell did someone discover Chinese hamster ovaries would do the trick? Why not Vietnamese hamster ovaries? Or guinea pig ovaries? A crap shoot."

"Wow."

"But what's wrong with your mom is blood and bone and swelling. It's not cellular, the way cancer is. She has hope. You asked me how I went through it twice? Well, they were twenty-nine years apart, which helped, but it only helped a little. My problem is I'm still going through it. I miss my wife, Betty, every day, but I miss MJ every single second of every single minute. We aren't supposed to bury our children, they're supposed to bury us."

Tina responded by squeezing her uncle's hands, then raising them to her mouth and gently kissing them. They sat there in silence, not wiping away any stray tears, or speculating aloud what was taking so long, just holding hands and giving the other what comfort they could.

Eventually Bobby stood, squeezed and released Tina's hands, kissed the top of her head, and gave her a half smile. "I'd better go check on Nicole. Your grandfather was being a bit of a jerk earlier, so hopefully he isn't taking his frustration out on her."

"Thank you. I'll give Trey a call and see how Lydia is doing. I can't believe I've been away from her this long."

"I know. Enjoy her while you can. Tomorrow she'll be singing lead in her own band, next week she'll be going to college, and by the end of the month she'll be an all-star detective."

"Oh God. Now I *really* want to hug her." She laughed. "Go check on the kids. Sandy is in with Nicole. Maybe between the two of them they can get him to behave."

"I should have left them my stun gun."

"Probably." She picked up her phone, and Bobby left her to her call.

The officer sitting outside Alex's room looked familiar. He stood as Bobby approached, and extended his hand. Bobby shook it. "Hey Mr. Odini! Leon Perlmutter. I was in MJ's class at the academy."

Of course! "Leon! You're the Bruce Lee specialist, teaching the rest of the class your hybrid Jeet Kune Do moves. You turned MJ from a badass into a lethal weapon. Who'd you piss off to get hospital duty?"

"When I heard it was MJ's family, I volunteered. She would have done the same for me."

"Yes, she would have." He nodded toward the closed door. "Has he been behaving?"

"Definitely. I heard he made a bit of a ruckus before I got here."

"He did, but it didn't last long. He's just tired and bored."

"It's been quiet for a while now."

"Good. Let's hope his grandchildren didn't hold a pillow down on his face to shut him up."

Leon's eyes went wide and he stepped into the room before Bobby could say he was just joking. He followed the officer in, and the two of them found Alex playing blackjack with his two youngest grandchildren. When he saw all was safe and quiet, Leon returned to his post, shaking his head and smiling as he passed Bobby.

Sandy stood up and stepped over to Bobby, opening his arms for a hug. The young man was half a head taller than Bobby. "Uncle Bob! Thank you so much for keeping an eye on Mom and Grandpa."

"My pleasure, Sandy."

"I hear you've got Staties, the Feds, *and* a homicide detective at your beck and call."

Alex chuckled. "Bobby has been kicking ass and taking no prisoners, haven't you, son?"

"Well, not quite. It's just an old case of MJ's we were looking into and it kind of blew up."

"Cool. Did you solve it?"

"Some of it. There are still some crazy pieces of the puzzle that don't fit, which is why I want to chat with your grandfather."

"Do you want us to leave?"

"Not at all. Are you okay chatting in front of the kids, Alex?"

"Sure, Bobby. No problem." He placed his cards face down on the table.

"Okay then." Bobby pulled up the last chair. "Alex, you were right, you were shot at."

"I know. You told me."

"It was Chaz Mitchell who hired Gillett, and Gillett has made a deal with the Feds."

"Like I said he would."

"You did. But why would your own lawyer want you dead?"

"Not a clue. I called, told him I got rid of the evidence, and we were all safe."

"Did he know what evidence you were talking about?"

"He did sound a little confused. I explained it to him."

"What did he say?"

"You sure you want me to say in front of the kids?"

"I think Nicole and Sandy can handle it."

"Okay. He said 'You stupid old bastard! I can't believe you're only telling me now there are photos! You're too much of a bloody risk, Charleswood!' Then he hung up on me. What an asshole."

"He is. Now we have an idea why he did what he did yesterday. It also gives some clue about thirty years ago." If Mitchell was willing to kill a client over photos that were supposed to be destroyed, then sending a hit man after Marion would have simple for him. "Alex, do you know the name Franco Vetere?"

Alex looked away from Bobby, his eyes lowered.

"Alex?"

"Yes."

"Really?" He was only playing a hunch, but hadn't actually expected Alex to say 'yes'.

"Yes."

"Do you know him from Mitchell?"

"Mitchell? No."

Really? "Then how do you know him?"

"I know his mother."

"*What?*" That didn't make any sense. "Did you know he was living in our old house on 46th Avenue?"

"He is? Yes, I think I know he is."

"He *was*. He's dead. Was murdered last year."

"No!" Without another sound, Alex rolled over on his side, away from Bobby, and with the thin hospital blanket crammed to his face, he wept. Bobby had no idea what reaction he expected, but this sure as hell wasn't it.

CHAPTER FIFTEEN

"Alex. *Alex.* I'm sorry. I didn't know the news would upset you." He touched Alex's shoulder but the old man flinched and pulled away. Bobby had wanted answers so badly he'd forgotten he was dealing with an eighty-five-year-old man with the early stages of dementia. He moved back from the bed, to give Alex space. To Sandy and Nicole he said, "I'm sorry, kids."

They looked as confused as he was. Nicole looked at her grandfather and then at her younger brother. "I guess this answers the question the doctors had about who was going to drive Grandpa back to Westport today. We weren't sure if you wanted to do it or if we could."

"They're releasing him today?"

"He only has a broken wrist. There's no reason to keep him and run up the bill. The home is expecting him."

"Okay. I guess I had expected to drive him back but although I think it's a good idea for you two to do it, you're not going to be driving." He pulled open the door a crack. "Officer Perlmutter?"

Leon stepped into the room. "Yes sir?"

"Leon, they're releasing Mr. Charleswood today. What are your orders with regards to his safety?"

"I was told to stick with him here, but if he was being sent back home, I was to drive him and personally escort him into the building, handing him off to the facility's security."

"Really? *Their* security?" That didn't sound like much protection.

"Their security chief is a retired State Trooper whose parents are in the facility, and most of his team are off-duty troopers."

"I guess they don't get many escapees."

"I wouldn't think so, sir."

"Since you're to take him home, do you mind if his grandchildren come with you? Will you be returning to the city after you drop him off?"

"I will, and I certainly don't mind. Company is always good, especially for long road trips."

Bobby looked at Sandy and Nicole. "Are you two okay with that? I'll feel much better with you in a cruiser with an armed and trained police officer."

Nicole blanched. "Mom and Grandpa are in here because someone shot at them? Then hell yes, I vote for a cruiser."

Bobby suspected she was also going to volunteer to ride shotgun and keep Leon company up front. "Sandy?"

"I'm with Nic on this one, Uncle Bob. Are you serious about a sniper?"

"I am. He's been caught. The guy who hired him is next. You'll be fine." He smiled, but part of him still fretted over the unanswered questions and he was worried about what Chaz Mitchell might do. Until the bastard was actually arrested, they were all at risk. Alex was still sobbing, so Bobby left the three of them alone, returning to the hall with Leon. "You're sure you're okay with them coming along?"

"Of course, sir. It's an excuse to go to the coast while on the payroll. I'll keep them all safe, and we'll get some fresh sea air."

"Thank you."

"My pleasure, sir."

"Now, I'd better see if my stepsister is back from her CT scan."

He walked the short distance to Rachel's unprotected room, but stopped and sat in the officer's chair next to the door. He took a moment to send a text to his mother to suggest Sunday dinner, after she got home from her cruise. He then sent a text to Stacey telling her Alex was being taken home by his grandchildren, but they were still waiting for an update on Rachel. He also asked if he could cook dinner for her tomorrow, Saturday. What he didn't say was how much he needed to get back into his kitchen to find his balance again, and it was always more fun to cook *for* or even *with* someone else. He stood, stretched the kinks out of his back, hips, and shoulders, smiling at a passing nurse who nodded, smiled back, and seemed to understand exactly what his body felt.

Inside the room, Tina was coo-cooing at her phone. "Uncle Bob! Meet Lydia!" She looked at her phone and Bobby realized she was on a video call. "Lydi, baby, this is your Great-Uncle Bob." She turned the phone to Bobby and he squinted at the screen.

"Hi Lydia! Hey Trey!" Lydia was being held up by her father, his dark hands a perfect compliment to his daughter's beautiful light brown skin.

"Hi Uncle Bob. Isn't she beautiful? I can't believe we made her!"

"She's absolutely gorgeous. You done good. One evening you and I are going to have to sit down over scotch and steaks to talk about raising a daughter. *You*, my friend, are in for the adventure of a lifetime."

"Thanks. I can use all the advice you've got. How long are you keeping my wife there?"

"No longer than I have to. We're still waiting on her mom. Once we know what the situation is, she can plan what's next. I don't need her here, but it's nice to have her with me. Nic and Sandy are riding along with the officer taking Alex back to Westport, and I've been assured he'll be safe there. How was your meeting at Microsoft?"

"You know about that? It was top secret."

"There are no secrets in this family, especially when someone's wife is so damned proud of him. Besides, she only told *me*. It's not like she posted in on Instagram." Bobby looked at Tina. "You didn't, did you?"

"Ha ha. No."

"Good. So, Trey, how did it go?"

"We knocked it out of the park. They loved the presentation, think our proposal is solid, and gave us an assignment to show what we can do in real time. We meet again next week. Fingers crossed."

"Done. Toes, too. Trey, it's been great chatting, but I'm going to go and get your wife and me some coffee while you break it to your future rocket scientist she's not going to be able to date until she's at least twenty-five."

"And not a day sooner. We'll do those steaks and scotches soon, Uncle Bob. It's been too long."

"Soon, Trey." He handed the phone back to Tina. "How do you want your coffee?"

"Two and two, please."

"Done." Again, he left the two of them talk. As he stepped into the hall, two orderlies approached with Rachel in her bed and the WPD officer in tow. "What's the word?"

"The doctor asked us to tell you she'll be along in about ten minutes. After they have had a chance to review the scan, sir."

"Okay. I'm going for coffee. Do you fellas want one? My treat."

"Thank you, sir, but we had our break while they were doing the scan."

"Fair enough. Officer?"

"Thank you, Mr. Odini. A large, black, caffeinated kick would be perfect."

"Back shortly."

While he was waiting to place his order in the hospital's own Starbuck's, his phone buzzed in his pocket. It was Stacey. Dinner would be wonderful. She asked him to call her later to sort out details and maybe just chat for a bit. He replied he'd give her a call when he got home and could relax and chat, though he wasn't sure how much chatting energy he'd have.

Back at Rachel's room he and Tina sat impatiently, waiting for the doctor to arrive. The ten minutes turned into twenty, and then thirty-five. Bobby was ready to go for a walk to get some air when the door swung open and a doctor he didn't recognize entered.

"Mr. Odini? Mrs. Pearson?"

"Yes?" Bobby stood. Whatever the news was, he didn't want to be sitting.

"Good news. The swelling is going down. We're going to keep Rachel in the coma for at least another seventy-two hours. There's no harm to come from a coma that's a bit long, but there can be serious harm done if we bring her out too soon. I've scheduled her for an MRI tomorrow, when the first opening is. Although there's no way she's going to be awake in the next couple of days, she's in no immediate danger, either. Her vitals are all good and strong and she has no medical history of heart trouble, so it's just a matter of confirming the results tomorrow with the MRI, and then slowly bringing her out of the coma when it's safe to do so. What I'm saying is, you can go home, see your families, eat homemade food, get some sleep tonight, whatever you like. It's up to you. The immediate danger has passed. Now we have to be patient—no pun intended."

Tina put a hand gently on her mother's unresponsive arm. "Seventy-two hours? That long?"

"It's really not long, for this situation. With some patients it can be months before their bodies heal themselves enough to be allowed to wake up."

"Okay. If you say so."

The doctor smiled, kindly. "I do. But please feel free to Google it. Most people do, as soon as I leave the room. Just know my decision is based on your mother's specific injuries, not an average of all cases or some random case I read about on WebMD. Now, I have to see a few other patients, but if you have questions, just see a nurse at the desk and she or he will find me."

Bobby nodded. "Thank you, doctor. We appreciate everything you're doing for Rachel. Will you inform the officer outside of the decision, or do we have to?"

"I'll let him know on my way out, and he can communicate with his superiors for further orders."

"Thank you."

The doctor left.

"So, Tina, what are you going to do?"

"I'm going to sit a bit longer, I think. I'll go home for dinner then maybe Trey can come for a few hours tonight. He can bring his laptop and get some work done without having a fussy baby to distract him."

"Ah, but that's the best kind of distraction."

"I know, but I want to cuddle my girl, and feed her. My breasts are so full they're going to burst."

"Then that's a good plan."

"How about you?"

"My breasts are fine, but I'm going to make sure everything is in order for your grandfather's release, then I'm going home. I'm still recovering from my whirlwind drive up to Canada and back."

"Yeah, that was kind of nuts."

"It was. So, you're good?"

"I am."

"Okay. You've got both my numbers. If anything comes up, call. And when this is all over, I'll do a better job of keeping in touch. It shouldn't take someone trying to kill your grandfather for us to behave like a family."

"No, it shouldn't."

He hugged her, kissed Rachel softly on one cheek, and left to check on Alex.

His worry was unfounded, because Sandy and Nicole had taken care of everything and were just waiting for a wheelchair to arrive with which to evacuate their grandfather. Bobby gave them an update on their mother's condition, repeated to them much of what he'd said to Nicole, and left. He was ready for one helluva long nap.

oOo

His nap had to wait, though. A letter from the condo board was in his mailbox with his few bills. It was a simple request to call one of the senior members of the Board to discuss the recent break-in attempt and his unauthorized secondary-market alarm. He stepped back into the elevator and called the president herself.

"Mrs. Engleham. Robert Odini. I got your request to call and just want to assure you and the Board my alarm will never disturb my neighbors again."

"Hello Robert. Thank you, but how can you be sure?"

"Well, the two men who pretended to be couriers, snuck past the concierge, and tried to break in to my condo are both dead. And I promise to never use the alarm again."

"Dead?" Her voice was barely above a whisper. His blunt statement had the desired effect.

"Murdered. And the man responsible is about to be arrested, so it's all safe and back to normal."

"Oh."

"Do you need me to get it in writing from an investigating officer, or is this conversation sufficient? I'm happy to do whatever you want, to make the Board happy."

"The two men weren't killed...?"

"Here? No. I never saw them again." He arrived at his condo, and after confirming the deadbolt was still in place, he unlocked it, opened it a crack and looked up out of reflex, to make sure he hadn't set the alarm and forgotten about it. He hadn't, so he entered, attacked immediately by Vinnie.

"Then this conversation should be enough, Robert. And just to clarify, we weren't concerned about your alarm, actually, just what might have brought those men into our building. In fact, I've had a few requests from our fellow residents to find out what kind of alarm it was. It was quite effective."

"I'd be glad to email you the information if you like."

"That would be lovely. Thank you. Have a good day. Thank you for getting back to me so quickly. We like having you and Vinnie here, Robert."

"And I like living here, Mrs. Engleham."

He fed Vinnie then whipped up a quick veal piccata for himself, before sitting at the dining room table. The cat tried to climb up, but Bobby pulled out the chair next to him and sat Vinnie on it. "Here. Relax, buddy. We'll go for a walk after dinner. It's not supposed to rain until later." Bobby ate slowly, savoring each bite, willing himself to relax and let the stress of the last few days go, washing each mouthful of veal down with sips of the Casa Odini merlot. It wasn't a perfect match, but the bottle was open and the veal didn't seem to mind.

When he was done eating, he and Vinnie strolled through the neighborhood, choosing chats with friends over distance covered. It was nice to get back out and feel the pulse of the community again. The scents of the loam and flowers and impending rain helped clear his head. They were only half a block from home when the drizzle started. He pulled the flap of Vinnie's carrier over the cat's head and limped home.

After a hot shower, he remembered the clothes in the washer and threw them in the dryer, then he loaded the dishwasher. Eventually he climbed into bed, waited for Vinnie to hop up and settle in, then retrieved the next of MJ's letters.

Hey Dad-Dad.

What a goddamned long day this was. Thank you so much for bringing Grandma with you. The look on her face when she saw me broke my heart, though. She's always been the strong pillar of the family, but I don't think she's ready to bury her granddaughter. Do me a huge favor, and get her ready, please.

Today's double mastectomy probably isn't going to save me, though it should buy me some more time. Then again, with a few prayers and lighting a candle or two, who knows what miracles can happen. I'm so glad you were both here when I woke up, but I'm even happier you aren't here right now to see my tears. They took my breasts, Daddy. They scrubbed up, knocked me out, and cut off my boobs. Even though they were killing me, to say I feel so much less a woman now is so great an understatement it makes me nauseous.

It's that loss of womanhood today that brings back the night I became a woman. I wanted to remember it with you while you were here, but I don't know if Grandma knows the story, and I certainly didn't want to embarrass you with one of my most cherished memories.

We were up in Canada, on Vancouver Island, near Mackenzie Beach, down the road from Tofino. We were camping at the Bella-Somethingerother Campground. I was twelve. It was a hot August night. Earlier in the night we had walked along the beach in our bare feet, splashing in the surf, marveling at the bright green sparks made by the plankton when we disturbed them. I grabbed your hands and made you dance/splash with me, pretending we were angels among the stars, waltzing at the end of time.

For dinner we had fresh crab and grilled salmon, caught that afternoon by the cool guy with the dreadlocks down by the pier. Afterward we sat around the neighbor's campfire, listening to two guitars and a banjo and singing along even when we didn't know the language the song was in. You got everyone singing "Volare" in Italian, and I taught them the song about eating up my baby bumblebee. It was all rowdy and hilarious and wonderful, of course.

Then, around 2am, I woke up to find blood in my pajamas. I was having my first period. I was shocked. We learned all about it in school, but a textbook isn't the same thing as reality. I must have let out a scream because you were awake in an instant.

You asked what was wrong, probably thinking we'd been attacked by bears or wolves, but when I cried and said I was having my period, you didn't even blink, you said "Roger! I'll be right back!" like you'd done this a *million times before! You crawled out of the tent in your t-shirt, sweatpants, and sandals, and ran off to the ladies' bathroom. I heard you scream in frustration and shout "What the hell?! I haven't got any change!" The bathroom door slammed and the next thing I knew you were standing in the middle of the campground, in the dead of a moonless night, under a canopy of stars, screaming "Has anybody got any tampons! My little girl is going to bleed to death!"*

I was mortified! But at the same time, I was so happy to have you as my Daddy, doing whatever you had to for me, no matter how it made you look. Thankfully, three ladies came to my rescue with pads.

The next morning you were the talk of the entire campground, with the men awed by your ballsy fearlessness and the women more than a little turned on by a single-dad coming to his daughter's rescue. A group of women campers took me aside and in at least six different accents I was given the facts of womanhood as learned around the world for tens of thousands of years. No girl ever had a more memorable first period. Thank you, Old Man. By remembering that day, that I'm getting through this day.

I love you, Dad. Never doubt it for a minute.

Now, since it's been a long goddamned day and I'm sore and still a little groggy, I'm going to get some sleep and dream about the tits I used to have.

All my Love,

MJ

Bobby sure as hell did remember that night. He'd been scared to death he was going to screw it all up and give his little girl emotional scars she would never recover from. What he didn't tell her that night—or anytime since—was that after she fell asleep again he lay in his own sleeping bag and sobbed. He had never missed Betty so much as he did that night. *She* should have been there to help their daughter, instead of MJ's clumsy, terrified father standing in the woods screaming for a tampon like a crazy man.

With thoughts of his lost 'girls' in his mind, Bobby stumbled into sleep.

o0o

His sleep was restless, but seemed to recharge his batteries just fine. He took a quick trip to the hospital to check in on Rachel and make sure one of her children was with her, then spent much of the rest of the day cleaning the condo, brushing Vinnie, raiding the bodega for everything he was going to need for dinner with Stacey, and finally, stealing a quick nap before she arrived.

o0o

Stacey slid her hand along Bobby's arm and teased the thick graying hair on his chest. "Good morning, Handsome."

Bobby had been awake for nearly half an hour, but hadn't wanted to disturb Stacey. She'd fallen asleep with one leg draped over his, snuggled in so close he could feel her wonderful breath on his neck. "Happy Sunday, Beautiful. How did you sleep?"

"Wonderfully. How's your hip?"

"Hip? What hip?"

She kissed him deeply.

CHAPTER SIXTEEN

"So, what are your plans for the day, mister? Your mother is due at four, but that still leaves you the morning and a chunk of the afternoon."

"Leaves *us*. I'm not kicking you out just yet." He really hoped she'd stay right up until his mother arrived. He hadn't felt this alive in a long time.

"Then how about I cook us breakfast and maybe we can go for a walk in the rain?"

"That sounds really nice. You don't have to cook, though. You're a guest here."

"Maybe, but after the magic you made with the manicotti, and then the magic we made together once the lights were out, I certainly don't mind doing my share of the work. Or is there a rule about no one else playing in Chef Odini's kitchen?"

He chuckled. "No rule. As long as you're having fun, it doesn't matter to me who cooks."

"Then let me dazzle you with my world famous Omelet de Stacey I'm going to invent on the spot. Of course, should you feel the urge to help, even a little bit, I won't deny you." She slipped her hands around his waist and kissed him. When he threaded his fingers in her long hair, she moaned and pulled away. "Food. We need *food*. Believe me when I say I could spend the entire day satisfying that *other* appetite, but there's something about being in the kitchen with you that makes me feel goose-bumpy all over."

"Goose-bumpy?"

"Yeah. You have a problem with my word choice?"

"Not in the least." He took her hand, intertwining his fingers with her, and led her to his kitchen.

o0o

"How's your trout, Mom? You've probably been spoiled from all the seafood on the cruise ship's buffet." She had been a bit late arriving, so Bobby had served dinner as soon as his mother was settled in with a glass of wine.

Sophie Charleswood swallowed her tiny mouthful and smiled. "It's poached to perfection, Bobby, as always. A meal is as much about the company as the food, and you're much better company than retired dentists and their spouses from Miami."

"Thank you." He ate, too. "Mom, a whole lot of stuff has come up I'd like to talk to you about."

"Okay. What's up?"

"How about we start with who you sold the house on 46th to. Who was the developer that was going to tear it down?"

"I sold it to Alex, and he was never going to tear it down. I lied." She said it calmly between mouthfuls, like she was commenting on the wine.

"Why did Alex want it? It's hardly a downtown office tower."

"For Franco."

Bobby felt a sudden tightness in his chest. "Alex gave our house to Franco Vetere?" Whatever direction he had expected this conversation to go, *this* wasn't it.

"Yes. How do you know that name?"

"No wonder he was so upset when I told him Franco was dead."

His mother stopped the fork mid-lift. "When did you see Alex?"

"This morning. He and Rachel were in a car accident. Alex has a broken wrist, but Rachel is in pretty bad shape. They have her in a medically-induced coma while the swelling on her brain goes down."

She nearly slammed her wine glass down on the table. "Good Christ, Bobby, why didn't you call me?"

"I haven't really had time, Mom. I got back from Banff late Wednesday and the accident happened Thursday morning. Between the hospital and the police, I've been trying to juggle a few balls. I'm sorry."

"You went to Banff? It's about damned time."

"I know. They had a wonderful candlelight vigil for Marion. Did you know Rachel put a plaque up where Mar died?"

"Yes. I'm glad it's still there. But back to the accident. What happened with Rachel and Alex?"

"Um, someone shot out their tire when they were on their way to lunch. They were trying to kill Alex."

His mother laughed. "They were trying to kill *Alex*? Who was?"

"His lawyer, actually."

"Chaz Mitchell tried to kill Alex?"

"You know Mitchell?"

"I wish I didn't, but, yes. I've known him for years, since he was a nobody fresh out of Stanford. What did Alex do to piss off Chaz?"

"He hired someone to torch Rachel's storage locker, trying to destroy evidence of something he and Mitchell were involved in back in the nineties."

"Oops. That would definitely get Chaz wound up."

"Do you know about *all* of it?"

"I have no idea what they were doing back then, but Chaz hates not being in control, and Alex, in his confused state, did something he damn well should've known not to do."

"So you've kept in touch with Alex over the years?"

"Of course, Bobby. I still love him."

A question niggled at his mind. "When exactly did you meet Alex, Mom?"

"Two years after you were born."

"*What?*" That didn't fit the timeframe he knew at all.

"I guess I owe you an explanation. The truth, as it were."

"There's a truth I don't know?"

"Oh yes."

"And you've kept it from me, why?"

"I didn't want you to hate me. You're all I have left."

"Mom, don't be silly! Why on earth would I hate you?"

She held up her empty wine glass. "How about you top us up and I'll tell us the whole story, so you can decide for yourself?"

Bobby filled both their glasses from the bottle on the kitchen counter, but left the bottle on the table where they could reach it.

Sophie took a sip. "This is lovely." She looked at the label of the bottle between them. "It's your own? You truly have a gift, Bobby."

"Thanks, Mom. Now, what in God's name is the truth that would make me hate you?"

"Your father was a bastard and a cheating, high-functioning alcoholic with a nasty temper. His drinking and whoring around after you were born pushed me so far away that when I met Alex at a cocktail party your father's company was throwing for clients, I fell head over heels for him."

"You cheated on Dad with Alex?"

"Yes. I know I should be ashamed of it, but I'm not. Alex treated me like an equal, like a human being and not like some domestic slave. Unfortunately, I got pregnant. I would have left your father in an instant, but Alex was still married to Rachel's mother, and he actually loved her. He loved us both, as odd as it sounds."

"Not so odd." Bobby thought of Alex loving both mother and daughter, years later.

"I had the baby. Your brother, Angelo."

"Angelo was Alex's kid, not Dad's? Holy crap, Mom."

"Angelo Michael Francis."

"How did Alex react when Angelo died?"

"Um..."

"*Mom?*"

"Somehow your father knew Angelo wasn't his son, and one night he stumbled home from another whore in another bar and went into your brother's room. I was so used to his coming in drunk at all hours I didn't wakeup until I heard your brother cry out, then stop, abruptly. He was only two months old and a mother is fine-tuned to hear her baby, day and night. I rushed in to Angelo's room to find your father holding a pillow over your brother's face."

"*Dad* killedAngelo? Jesus Chr—!"

"He *tried*. I grabbed the carousel music box on the dresser and smashed your father in the back of the head as hard as I could. Twice. He barely noticed the first hit, but I put everything I had into the second one, and he dropped like a stone. I scooped up your brother. He was breathing, but was having trouble. I wrapped him in a blanket, grabbed the car keys and my purse, and rushed him to the hospital." Tears trickled down her face and Bobby handed her a linen napkin.

"It's okay, Mom. You tried your best to save him."

"That's the thing, Bobby. I *did* save him. Angelo didn't die. But I knew if I brought him back into that house, your father would eventually try again, and I would probably end up killing him with his own gun."

"Dad had a gun? Why didn't I know *any* of this?"

"It was your grandfather's from World War I. It was hidden in his workshop, with his liquor and his magazines."

"So, Angelo didn't die that night, but instead died of SIDS later on."

"No. *That* was the night. After the doctor got Angelo stabilized, the nurse sat and listened to my story. At first I tried to lie and say it was an accident, but she saw right through me. I ended up telling her the whole truth, from the affair to your father and the pillow. She nodded calmly, not judging me at all. Finally, she made me an offer. She offered to take Angelo and raise him, keep him safe and away from your father."

"You gave my brother *away*?" He was gutted by this! It was so outrageous that he wondered if his mother was suffering from dementia, too.

"I didn't know what else to do! No one would have believed my story! Your father played high school football with the Chief of Police and at least two judges. Remember this was the early sixties, when a wife was expected to be barefoot, pregnant, and *silent*." She took another long sip. "By the time I came home *without* Angelo, your father had crawled into the bathroom and passed out in the tub, bleeding all over the place. I cleaned up the mess, then climbed into bed and wept. Your father woke up, couldn't remember a damned thing, and when I told him your brother had died peacefully in his sleep, he accepted that, and the story was born. Your father sobered up for a while, but it was years before I would let him even hug me in private. We put on a good show for friends and family, though if I thought I could have got away with it, I'd have gutted him in his sleep."

"Was Marion Alex's, too?"Was so much of what he knew as his childhood a lie?

"Oh Jesus, no. Alex and I didn't sleep together again until after his divorce was finalized. Marion was your father's daughter, from the *one*time I let him near me again, on our twelfth anniversary."

Bobby suddenly put the pieces together. "Mom, Franco Vetere was *Angelo*?"

"Yes. When I moved in with Alex, he bought the old house for Franco-slash-Angelo and his 'mother'."

Bobby felt flush and nauseous. He needed air, now. He got up from the table and shuffled over to the balcony doors. It was still raining outside, but the balcony was mostly dry. He dropped into his big Adirondack chair, numb.

A few minutes later, his mother came out and stood behind him, out of the rain. "Are you okay, Bobby? I know it's a lot to absorb."

He wasn't sure he could tell his mother the truth, now. He could barely handle it himself. "Mom, how did *you* know Franco died last year?"

"I saw an article in the paper about a man found in Payne Bay and I recognized his name. I went to his funeral. No one else was there. His 'mother' died a few years ago."

"Mom, do you have any clue whatFranco did for a living?"

"I did after the police told the press. I'm sorry, but I'm not surprised. I loved your brother, but when your father tried to suffocate him, he likely did some brain damage, and Franco grew up one very disturbed boy. We kept tabs on him from a distance, but it was heartbreaking. He was always in fights at school, and didn't care whether he won or lost, just so long as he got to hurt someone. By the time he was sixteen, he'd been arrested twice for assault with a weapon of some sort. I started putting more and more distance between him and us. Whoever he had become, he was no longer the beautiful little baby Alex and I had made."

"Mom, do you want to know *why* I went to Banff?"

"Of course. But come inside where it's warm and dry. I'm freezing out here and you're going to catch a cold."

They went in, and Bobby made coffee while he talked. He made sure his mother was sitting comfortably on the couch. Vinnie climbed up beside her. "Mom, on her death bed MJ sort of solved Marion's murder. It was linked to a case she was working on. Marion wasn't killed by some random ski bum druggie, she was murdered by a professional killer hired to do it."

"That's ridiculous, Bobby. Who would want your sweet sister dead?"

"That's what I wondered, so I started digging into it. I went up to Banff to see where she died, and to speak with a couple of the people who were with her that night."

"And they told you an assassin had stabbed Marion and left her behind a dumpster?" Her sarcasm was thick.

"No. They didn't know exactly *who* did it, but they did see someone following her, someone who we believe followed Mar there from Westview, to keep her from talking about something she saw and photographed while out on Alex's boat."

"So who was it? Who killed ourMarion?"

"Mom, I'm pretty sure Chaz Mitchell hired Franco Vetere to kill Marion."

To her credit, his mother didn't scream or have a heart attack or a stroke. She didn't even faint. She simply let out a soft peep, put her hand to her mouth, and cried. Bobby put down the coffee mugs and moved over to his mother. He held her, she held him, and they both mourned the accumulated losses neither could ever have handled alone.

oOo

Bobby billeted his mother in the guest room, and the next morning they went to her condo so she could get a fresh change of clothes. They then visited Rachel in the hospital, chatted quietly with Sandy and Nicole for quite a while, went back to Bobby's condo to fetch Vinnie, and the three of them drove out to Westport. While his mother visited with Alex—for the first time in ten years, she said—Bobby and his one-eared cat took a walk along the sea wall.

They were sitting on a bench, watching the gulls dip and dive into the surf when Bobby's phone rang. "Sam! I was going to call you. You're not going to believe how screwed up my family is."

"Oh sure I will. Did you know his real name isn't Franco Vetere?"

"Angelo Michael Francis Odini."

"How the hell did you...?"

"I'm with my mother. We had a *very* long chat. We're here in Westport now. She's visiting with Alex, who was Angelo's father. But how did *you* know?"

"SAC Stevenson called to tell me they found a birth certificate in with all of the trophies from the house and they believe it's his. He recognized the last name. I gotta say this solves one big puzzle."

"Which one?"

"Why MJ's DNA was a familial match with our murder victim, Vetere."

"Because he *was* family."

"Exactly."

"They're still going through the gold mine of evidence, but I wanted to let you know they're going to bring in Chaz Mitchell for attempted murder, for hiring Gillett. Well done, Citizen Odini. Your daughter would be proud of your sleuthing."

"I'm just a stubborn old Italian going-grey-hound who wouldn't let go of the bone."

"What's Italian for 'The Man Who Pokes Dragons'?"

"Um... *L'uomo che colpisce i draghi*, I think."

"That's who you are. Like I said, MJ would be proud of you."

"Thanks, Sam. That means a lot."

oOo

Bobby returned to the retirement home to join his mother and Alex in the lounge, sitting in the wingback chair opposite the sofa the two of them sat on. "Hey you two."

Alex favored him with a huge smile. "Hey kiddo. Thank you for bringing Sophie by. It's been too long between visits."

"Then I'll make sure she comes to see you as often as you both want."

"Just be careful driving out. There are snipers in them there woods." He winked at Bobby.

"Not anymore. Gillett has been caught and rolled over on Chaz Mitchell. I just heard from my detective friend."

Neither of the two looked shocked or upset at the news. "Chaz *did* do it? I hope he dies in prison."

"Mom!"

"What? He was an asshole who tried to kill Alex, almost killed Rachel, and killed your sister."

"We'll probably never know that for sure, but I agree." His phone buzzed with a text message. It was from Chef Peter. *Bobby, I loved the sauce! Let's do this thing! Are you available next Tuesday to tape the episode in front of a live studio audience? If you are, just text me a list of the ingredients and I'll have them ready. We tape at 11am but if you come in at 9:30 we can go over everything with my producer. I'll even have a couple of giant checks made up for the donations. Once you confirm, I'll have my assistant text you all the piddly little details like the address. Ciao, Chef.*

"Bobby, are you okay?"

"Um..." He was speechless.

"Your jaw is dragging. Is everything okay? It's not Rachel is it?" His mother clutched Alex's hand tightly and fear crept into her eyes.

"Rachel? Um, no. It's a text from Chef Peter, the TV chef. He loves my spaghetti sauce and is going to have me on the show to teach the world how to make it. I'm, uh..."

"That's great! *Chef* Odini."

oOo

Two days later Bobby was doing his 'shift' with now-conscious Rachel but sleeping when his phone buzzed in his pocket. He stepped out into the hall so as to not wake the patient. "Hey Sam. What's up?"

"Are you still at the hospital, Bobby?"

"Yup."

"I'm on my way. Stay put, please."

"Of course." He gave Sam the new room number, then returned to Rachel's bedside.

"Everything okay, Bobby?"

"Sorry I woke you. It was that detective I told you about. He's on his way over. Something seems to have him in a knot."

"Oh? Is he cute? Can you prop me up and get me some water, please. And maybe my hairbrush." Although no longer in the medically-induced coma, Rachel was nearly immobile, with casts, wrappings, bandages, and even sutures from where they cut her open to repair her ruptured spleen.

"Sure." Bobby used the bed controls to raise the top half of the bed in small increments until Rachel stopped him.

"That's good, thanks." She held out her right hand and Bobby placed a plastic tumbler of ice water into it. It took Rachel a moment to get the bendy-straw to swing around to where her mouth could grab it, then she drank like she hadn't had water in days rather than just an hour.

"Sam is happily married, Ray. With two kids. He was a friend of MJ's."

"Married. Damn."

"Now I know where Nicole gets her taste in men from."

"Both of my daughters have excellent taste in men. Nic just happens to share my predilection for men in uniform."

Bobby refilled Rachel's cup, then filled one for himself and sat down. He thought the feeling of tightness in his chest would go away once he left the high altitude mountains last week, but no such luck.

"You okay, big brother?"

"Yeah. Just tired."

"Then go home. I don't need a babysitter."

"Sam will be here in a few minutes."

"So chat with Sam, and *then* go home. Thanks to you I have Netflix and I'm thinking of binge-watching Sponge Bob."

"Ha! Then they'll *know* you're brain damaged and extend your stay indefinitely."

"Like hell they will. But you're trying to change the subject."

"Um, no. You brought up Netflix. I'm just sitting here, chillaxing."

"'Chillaxing'? Where the did you pick up that monstrosity of a word?"

"From your son-in-law. Trey caught me dozing off a couple days ago and said I was 'mastering the art of chillaxing'."

"Trey is twenty-eight. *He* can chillax. You're sixty and I'm fifty-five. We haven't chillaxed since Bush *Senior* was president."

"Speak for yourself. It works for me. I'm retired, so I'm allowed to kick back, flop down, or chillax whenever I want."

"Fine. Chillax all the hell you want, but you need to see a doctor about your shortness of breath. I've already lost one brother, I'm not about to lose another."

"I'm getting my blood work done tomorrow and my physical is scheduled for next Wednesday. And Franco-slash-Angelo might have been *our* brother, but we only found out this week, so we can hardly say we lost someone neither of us actually knew. Besides, he was a psychopathic hit man who took the life of the sister we *did* know, so..."

"Still—"

"I know. The brain's 'what if' game. What if—"There was a knock at the door. "Come in."

Sam entered, stalling Bobby's train of thought. "Sorry to interrupt." He turned to Rachel. "Ms. Charleswood, it's nice to see you awake. How are you feeling?"

"Broken and betrayed, Sam. Broken by the accident, and betrayed by my brother for not telling me how gorgeous you are."

The detective blushed and raised an eyebrow at Bobby."Yup. She's Nicole's Mom. No DNA test needed."

Bobby laughed and gave Rachel's good arm a gentle squeeze."We'll be back in a bit, Ray. Want a coffee?"

"Please. Two sugars, because apparently I'm not sweet enough for a certain detective."

"*Married* detective, sis."

"Yeah, yeah. Poe-tay-toe, poe-tah-toe."

Out in the corridor, Sam redirected Bobby toward the exit to the street. They walked as he spoke. "Chaz Mitchell is dead. Took the easy way out. Troopers arrived at his condo with an arrest warrant but there was no answer. While the security person was letting them in, Chaz decided to test gravity with a belly flop from his tenth-floor balcony and landed on the sidewalk next to the cruiser.

Bobby was both shocked and relieved. "Wow. I guess he didn't have much faith in his own law firm to get him off."

"That was *my* thought. His half-written suicide note was typed on his laptop."

"He may have planned to email it to someone. Dammit. With Mitchell gone, so is the truth."

"Yes and no. The suicide letter claimed responsibility for Marion's murder and hinted at two others that he felt guilty for. I'm trying to narrow down who he was referring to, though it's probably your old coworker and his accomplice. We'll keep digging, but him hiring Vetere makes sense. If he was on that boat and wanted to protect Brand or himself, killing your sister would have been necessary. I just can't figure out why he took so long to do it."

"Back then it might have taken him that long to find someone like Vetere to do the job. From what I can gather, he wasn't the mover and shaker he is now. Was now. I would think that hiring a killer takes care and secrecy."

"Not to mention money."

"But he had the counterfeit stuff, Sam."

"True. We'll keep digging, of course."

"Does this mean that Alex and Rachel are safe?"

"I guess so. Gillett took the shot and claims Mitchell hired him, so I expect my superiors will be pulling Rachel's protection immediately. To be honest, I don't think she was ever at risk. Alex is the one with ties back to that day on the boat."

"If you say so." He checked his watch. "I should get Rachel that coffee. Thanks for keeping me in the loop, Sam."

"Bobby, if you weren't in the loop we wouldn't have most of the evidence we have. You've got a knack for investigating."

"Hardly, Sam. I'm happy to leave the dragon poking up to you while I retreat to my kitchen and investigate nothing more deadly than spice combinations and wine-making."

"Speaking of spice combinations, what happened with Chef Peter?"

Bobby smiled big. "He loved my sauce."

"And...?"

"We're taping the episode in the studio next Tuesday."

"That's great, Bobby! You're going to be famous—I mean for something other than being related to a dead hit man."

"Yeah, I think I'll downplay *that* part of my life when I'm on camera."

"Good plan."

CHAPTER SEVENTEEN

The trip home was a quick drive in the rain, with a brief stop at the bodega to pick up a few fresh items for dinner with Stacey. At home, Vinnie begged so loudly and sadly that Bobby fed his furry roommate before he even put the groceries away.

"Your favorite lap is coming over this evening, Vinnie, so be on your best behavior, please. That projectile hairball from the top of your cat tree last time was impressive, but a little off-putting in the middle of dinner. You know that Stacey doesn't replace your mama. She and I have a completely different kind of relationship. No one could replace MJ, as *your* mama, or as *my* daughter."

His chonky, one-eared, orange roommate ignored him, so Bobby put the groceries away, and heated up a bowl of soup. Because of the blood work he was having done in the morning, he had to fast after ten tonight, so he couldn't afford to skip a meal. Also, with Stacey coming for dinner and hopefully staying the night, he needed to keep his strength up. He set the alarm and lay down on the couch for a much-needed nap. This was beginning to be a lifestyle he wasn't impressed with.

o0o

Stacey licked the last of the tiramisu off her fork, got up from the table, walked around to Bobby and kissed him. "You, Bobby Odini, are the only man I've ever met who could reach a girl's heart through her taste buds. Wow, wow, and *wow*." She stood behind him and massaged his shoulders while kissing the top of his head.

"You liked it? I thought you could tell that dessert was store-bought."

"It was *not*!" She released his shoulders and began clearing the table. "You lie like a rug. The only way that was store-bought is if you opened a store to sell your own desserts, and then bought one of your own masterpieces."

He followed her into the kitchen, stepping up behind her at the sink and wrapping his arms around her waist. "You caught me. It's my grandmother's recipe." He kissed the back of her neck and she wiggled back into him, pressing her body against his.

"I hope your grandmother isn't looking down and seeing the affect her dessert is having on me. I have this urge to take you right here on the kitchen floor, Mr. Odini. No mercy, no holds barred."

"Ha! I *dare* you!"

o0o

Both dressed in baggy sweat pants and comfortable hoodies, Bobby and Stacey sat on the condo's little balcony, sipping caffeine-free green tea and watching the late April rain wash Westview clean. Bobby was exhausted, in all the best ways.

"So, Mister, what would you be doing now if I weren't here to distract you?"

"Honestly?"

"Of course."

"I'd be right where we are now, reading a book, or if I was up to it, reading one of MJ's letters."

"You haven't read them all already? How many are there?"

"Six. No, I've only read five."

"Ah. You're torn between wanting to read her last words and never wanting them to end, aren't you?"

"Of course, though the first letter she had me read was her last."

"But you have another one? Do you want to read it tonight?"

"Yes...and no. They usually hit me pretty hard, and I don't want to kill the romantic mood."

"I don't think the mood is going to budge. If you'd like to read a letter, do so."

"Really?"

"Of course."

"Would you like to read the first five? There's nothing in them I can't share with you. They're just letters from a daughter to her father."

"You'd share those with me?" She looked truly surprised.

"Only if you want to. No pressure."

"I would be honored. I didn't know MJ for long, but she touched my heart."

"Let's get out of the chill and back to the couch." He stood and offered his hand, helping her up from her low chair. "You get settled and I'll get the letters." He slid open the door, using his socked foot to keep Vinnie from squeezing past him and out onto the balcony.

Stacey put their mugs on the coffee table and curled up under the blanket on the couch. Rebuffed from his escape attempt, the feline master of the house climbed up with her and settled on her lap. "Thank you, Vincent."

Returning from the bedroom, Bobby handed Stacey the second of MJ's cherished letters, the one about catching snowflakes in gelato, then he settled down next to her with the final unread letter. They each unfolded their treasures and got lost in MJ's words.

Hey Signor Papà!

Have I told you lately how much I love you, Old Man? Especially today when you offered to take me wig shopping! Unlike some women, losing my hair from the chemo isn't a big deal, though I suppose that wanting to shave it all off for the band when I was fourteen could have set me up for it. I'm glad I can finally see what a perfect skull I have! I would so have rocked the bald thing in my Snark Puppet *days, and you probably would have taken the razor in hand and shaved it for me.*

That's another thing I love so much about you, Daddy-Oh. Your willingness to do whatever my crazy mind cooked up, just for shits and giggles. You taught me to never fear. Do you remember that time we went to the Lyric Bay Fish Market and all of a sudden I decided that I wanted to learn to throw fish like the fishmongers? We bought a half dozen fish of different sizes and spent the afternoon in the backyard throwing them at each other. By the time supper rolled around, we were bruised, stinky, and cut to hell from the fins and scales.

I thought we were done with it, but the next day you had us back out there using shoes instead of fish, until we got semi-coordinated at it. Day three, we were back at it with the fish. You hadn't had a whole week off in six months and you spent the entire damned time trying to catch and throw fish with me because I thought it was cool. After those seven days we were experts at getting the stink out and bandaging cuts, but we still couldn't catch those slippery things worth a crap. You eventually showed me how you could juggle three chef's knives and stick one in a tomato I threw in the air, but the fish were beyond us.

Your vacation weeks were always the best times of my life, even when I was in school during them. You always made me feel like there was nothing you wanted to do more than spend them with me, and I damn sure never ever wanted to do anything but spend them with you.

Dad, I want you to promise me one thing. After I'm gone, promise me that you'll take a vacation. Take a little time to mourn, and then go somewhere. I don't care if you take a hooker to Hawaii, just do something more than hang out in the diner with that bunch of dried up, retired bus drivers. Promise me. Go ahead. Say it. I'll hear you. I'll always hear you, Dad of my Heart.

Always and forever.

Your salmon-throwing, perch-catching, bad-ass-bald,

Snark Puppet. xoxo

As he immersed himself completely in his daughter's words, Bobby tuned out Stacey beside him, laughing and crying as he read. He lovingly folded the wonderful letter up, gave it a tear-wet kiss, and placed it reverently on the coffee table. Only then did he look over to Stacey for her reaction to the gelato letter. "So, what do you thi—".

With Vinnie curled up on her lap, Stacey sobbed. Bobby had expected an emotional response, but... he slipped the letter out of her hands, put it with the other one, and then pulled Stacey into his arms. Vinnie found the angle awkward and jumped down, which then enabled Stacey to lie across Bobby's lap and sob away. He let her. He knew full well how deeply MJ's letters touched the soul, and his own tears started up again when he thought back to that first letter and the memory of the gelatos.

With one hand he stroked her still damp hair, while Stacey clutched his other hand tightly. He didn't check the time, nor did he care. Heartbreak didn't follow a clock. After a while, Stacey pulled his hand to her mouth and kissed his knuckles one at a time, then she carefully rose to sit beside him again. "Sorry about that. You told me that they were

heavy duty, but I had no idea a simple letter could reach that part of me."
She wiped her tears with her sleeve. "When I was a twenty-five-year-old
newlywed nurse, Harry and I decided to have a baby. I was only just
starting my career in medicine, but Harry was so keen to become a father
that it was an easy decision to make.

"Everything was going so well, then in the sixteenth week my cervix
began to dilate—it's called an Incompetent Cervix—and I had a
miscarriage. Normally, even a second trimester miscarriage isn't the end
of hope for a woman, but it was for me, and, so it turned out, for Harry,
too. He was so set on being a dad that when I lost our son due to no fault
of our own, Harry took it hard. When the doctor broke the news that
I was out of the baby-making game for good, that smashed our young
marriage into a thousand pieces. Harry asked me for a divorce on my
twenty-sixth birthday, and I agreed without hesitation. Reading your
letter from MJ was a punch in my gut, a reminder of the wonderful
experience of parenthood I almost had, but in the end was denied. Thank
you so much for sharing that with me." She put her arms around Bobby's
neck and pulled him in to nestle cheek-to-cheek, tears mingling with
tears.

After a while he remembered his conversation with Sam. "Sam called
this morning. His wife, Theresa, wants to have us over dinner some
time."

"That would be lovely. But are *you* ready? To be seen as a couple?"

Bobby chuckled. "I'm fine with it. As a matter of fact, one of MJ's last
wishes was for me to take a hooker to Hawaii. I'd rather take a nurse to
dinner, though."

"A hooker to Hawaii?"

"It was her way of saying 'Go on vacation, *Dad*, and I don't care who
you go with.'"

"In one of her letters?"

"The one I read tonight. Did you want to have a go at the next one?"

"I'm not sure I could handle it, Hon. Like you, I think I'll space them out, if that's okay."

"It's been working for me so far."

"Good. Change of subject. What time is your blood work tomorrow?"

"Ten."

"And what are they testing for?"

"It's my annual tune-up, so diabetes, liver function, cholesterol, PSA—all the fun stuff, including something to do with a witch in my poop."

"That's 'fecal occult blood', goofball."

"Like I said, a witch in my poop. What time is your flight to Spokane tomorrow?"

"Ten-twenty. I still haven't packed, yet, though."

"Well then, you'll need to get up early if you're going to get home in time to pack."

"Are you suggesting that we make sure we're in bed early?"

"It crossed my mind."

"I like how you think, Chef Odini."

oOo

Bobby dropped Stacey off at the airport, arrived early at the lab to have his blood taken, then went straight back to home to break the fast required by the lab. Halfway through his Denver sandwich the phone rang. Vinnie climbed up onto his lap as he answered the call.

"Sam. What's up?" With his free hand he stroked Vinnie's head, comforted by the purrmachine.

"Hey Bobby. I wanted to let you know that I think we have video of Mitchell's killer. He's wearing a hat and a disposable mask, but it's a start. The recording shows him coming into the building through the lobby, but leaving through an emergency exit near the loading dock where the tower has its garbage bins."

"So, you're treating it as a murder now?"

"Yes. We're pretty sure Mitchell's death wasn't a suicide. I'm just wrapping up some paperwork from a raid this morning, and will swing by to show you the footage when I'm done."

"Sounds good. I'm going to close my eyes for a bit but will let the fellas at the desk downstairs to let you up and in." They ended the call, Bobby called the concierge, and then stretched out on the couch. Vinnie hopped down until he resettled, then climbed back up and lay by his feet.

o0o

Bobby didn't wake when Vinnie climbed down to use the litter box, nor when his ginger bodyguard resumed his position, but he was drawn up and out of slumber completely when he heard the thump of the front door's deadbolt being shot back into place. He sat up and shook off the doze as Sam stepped out of the hall.

"Sorry to interrupt your nap."

"Not a problem, Sam." He levered himself up and off the couch, then shuffled to the kitchen. "Coffee will have me fixed up and alert in no time. Can I fix you one?"

"Definitely." He followed Bobby and sat at the kitchen island while Bobby fussed with the mugs and kettle. He took his phone out of his pocket. "I'm sure we'll figure out who this clown is eventually, but his hat and mask are a simple but effective disguise."

"And it's now a murder case?"

"It is. There was a bruise on Mitchell's left hip at the height of the balcony railing, but that's hardly conclusive. It's the fact that he landed so close to the building that has us treating it as a murder. If he'd jumped, he would have got at least a little distance from the building, but if he was pushed, he would likely have flipped over the railing and dropped straight down. There were no bruises on his chest or back to indicate that he'd been pushed, but it was raining at the time and one of the cushions on the sofa was damp, so I suspect it was used to pad the impact of a shove."

"I would never have thought to do that, but I'm also not a killer."

"Of course not. It was likely a professional job, rather than a crime of passion. The lab is checking the pillow for DNA, but I suspect that anyone that smart would have worn gloves."

"The police were at the door knocking, with security and their warrant. Why didn't they see the killer?"

"Best guess is he slipped out when they rushed to the edge of the balcony to look down on the body after the officer on the street radioed them. I have both the video from the elevator and the lobby cameras. The building's owner tried to stonewall us, citing the privacy of her 'socially elite' residents." He made air quotes around 'socially elite'. "We finally got a subpoena for the footage, despite the suicide note and Mitchell's reputation in the courts for making fools of prosecutors *and* judges. I'm pretty sure there's a long list of both who aren't shedding any tears for him."

"Who do you think is behind it all? I can't imagine Brand ordering it. He could explain the thirty-year-old photo away pretty easily and I doubt it would harm his reputation much. He just got re-elected, so he's got another four years to make us all forget about it a three-decades-old indiscretion." Bobby wasn't much for puzzles, but the whole situation stank. "Should I be worried, Sam?"

Sam leaned back and thought before replying. "Possibly. I'm not sure you should start carrying your gun, though. More harm could come from that than good. For what it's worth, here's the threat." He held the phone up for Bobby to see exactly what Sam had said it was... a white man wearing a nondescript, dark colored baseball cap and a light blue disposable mask nodded at the female security officer at the desk, strolled to the elevators, and tapped a pass key to the pad above the buttons.

Bobby spooned ground coffee into the large French press, the air filling with the delightful aroma of Arabica beans roasted with hazelnut filled the air. "Did you talk to the woman who was manning the desk? It looks like she knew him, passing him right through. And he has a key card, so he might have been a resident."

"I did speak with her. She doesn't know his name, but she's seen him enter with Mitchell."

"So, the victim and the killer knew each other. Those key cards are usually registered. Who was that one registered to?"

"Mitchell. He has four registered to his name and we found all of them in his condo." Sam smiled. "You're asking all the same questions I asked. Have you considered getting your license and doing some PI work? It's pretty obvious where MJ got her curiosity and observation genes from."

"From her mother, Sam. You can hardly call me curious when it took me three shameful decades before I looked into my own sister's murder."

"You were busy raising your amazing daughter."

"That's the excuse I've been telling myself for too long. I mean, sure, I closed down when Betty died so I could concentrate on MJ, but I've been doing that my whole damned life. First it was when my little brother was supposed to have died. Mom says I didn't even cry, I just curled up on her lap and sucked my thumb. Then when my bastard father died, the relief in the house was palpable and not even Marion cried for him. When *her* life was cut short, I tried to comfort Mom, but Betty was sick and it was all I could do to lift my chin halfway and face the world every morning. I'd lost my brother and my father, and was losing my wife. Dealing with Marion's murder was beyond me. I took that pain, walled it up, and locked it away from my heart. When Betty died, I lost the key to that lock. If I hadn't had MJ to care for, I probably would have sat down on a beach somewhere and simply let the tide roll in and take me away, I was that numb and defeated.

"Although MJ made sure I lived and loved my life, I know now how much I'd blocked myself from mourning. When my little girl left, too, I was already programmed to just put one foot in front of the other and keep moving forward. It wasn't until those letters arrived that I could really feel my own pulse again. Life has thrown crap at me over and over, but raising my little Marionette gave me the strength to turn my back on that walled-up heart..." He trailed off, thinking he was just repeating himself. He busied himself with making the coffee.

"Whatever you did to deal with or even ignore your grief, it didn't make you any less human. You couldn't have been, Bobby, and still have raised such an amazing young woman. There's no way you could have truly walled up your heart and given her the wonderful but short life she had. You were a goddamned superman. My abuela used to say that too many tears for the past will drown your present and wash away your future. The fact that you *didn't* lose yourself into a mourning morass is amazing. My sister lost my brother-in-law and she was a mess for over a year. My mother had to move in and look after her grandkids. We all deal with grief differently. When my mother died, I took her ashes on the Trans-Atlantic cruise she'd always wanted to take and I sprinkled them into the ocean near where the Titanic went down. That was her wish. Obviously, I didn't know your wife, Betty, but would she have wanted you to grieve her and ignore MJ? For that matter, as horrible as your sister's death was wouldn't she have wished you to stay strong and keep going? You were the man of the family. *Two* families. You don't need to keep your emotions walled up. Knock the bricks down. It's time."

Something in what Sam said tweaked Bobby's recent memory. "Time?"

"Yes."

"No. I mean, yes. Time. Run the video again, please."

Sam did, in silence, and Bobby was grateful for it. He needed to think. There was something about the man in the video. He watched it again, but couldn't be certain. "Can you enlarge it, or zoom in on part of the image? I can't with my videos."

"I can. It's a special app for law enforcement." He paused the recording, pinched his fingers on the screen to zoom in, then turned the screen back around to Bobby.

"No, not his face. His left arm. The one with the key card. As he's holding it up for the guard."

Sam adjusted the view, and held the phone up to Bobby again. Bobby grabbed his reading glasses from the counter, next to his own phone. He squinted at the frozen image, squinting despite the glasses. Bingo! "The watch. It's rare. A Ferrari something-er-other. Only fifty of them were made and it just so happens that one of the associates at Chaz Mitchell's firm owns one of them. Jackson Coyne."

CHAPTER EIGHTEEN

Bobby started the video again, then paused it when he saw what he needed to. "He has it tucked up under the mask, but he can't completely hide his beard. That's Coyne. I'm sure of it."

Sam returned to his chair and watched the video again, zooming and pausing and replaying as he needed to. "That *is* a damned strange looking watch. It might even be enough to get a warrant to search this Coyne's home. It definitely gives us a direction to look, which we didn't have ten minutes ago. Good eyes, Bobby. On the way home I'll call in and have a couple of uniforms pick him up. At this hour he should still be at work." He visibly relaxed and sipped his coffee. The identification of Coyne was like a pressure release valve being opened, and the two of them concentrated on their mugs for a few minutes. Vinnie strolled over to his cat tree and climbed to the top, where he lay down, facing out the window.

Bobby soon got restless and took a fresh lemon loaf out of the fridge. "This coffee is good, but it needs loaf. Can I cut you a piece?" He smiled and flipped his chef knife in a double back-flip and caught it easily.

"Thanks. That would be nice. I should probably make that call to pick up Coyne, though." He took out his phone again but a knock at the condo door stalled him.

"Package for Robert Odini."

Bobby, the big knife in one hand and a bread-and-butter plate in the other, looked at Sam, then glanced toward the front door. "Would you mind getting that?"

"Sure." Sam disappeared around the corner, down the short hall to the door. Bobby heard Sam throw the deadbolt open, but instead of a greeting from the delivery guy, there were three soft pops and the thump of something soft but heavy dropping to the floor. A second later the door closed and the bolt was thrown.

Plate and knife still in hand, Bobby looked toward the hallway just as Jackson Coyne stepped into view, a hoody covering his head, a mask covering his face, and a gun equipped with a homemade silencer made from a soup can pointed at Bobby's chest. Bobby froze, his heart hammering in his chest, threatening to explode.

"Mr. Odini. Good to see you again, sir. You've been a busy, busy man, poking around and making my life extremely difficult." Coyne glanced at Bobby's hands and raised an eyebrow. "Put the knife down on the counter, *Bobby*."

Vinnie chose that moment to jump down off the cat tree to investigate the new person in the room and his motion caught Coyne's attention for a fraction of a second. Bobby did the only thing he could. He awkwardly threw the plate with his left hand over Coyne's head. The man didn't even flinch, but he did lift his chin to watch the plate soar over, and that's just what Bobby needed him to do. He threw the ten-inch chef's knife with a practiced backhand and it sunk into Coyne's throat, just above his Adam's apple. Though stunned, Coyne managed to raise the gun again.

Stunned but not stupid, Bobby dropped to the floor behind the island. He was trapped. The four shots that rang out were much louder this time, but none of them struck him.

Coyne groaned, Vinnie meowed in protest, and Bobby crawled around the island, ready to tackle the killer and do whatever it took to save the cat. But Coyne lay face up on the ceramic tile, motionless, blood leaking from at least three bullet holes and from around the knife still sticking out of his throat. Sam leaned on the wall, smoking weapon in hand and three tightly placed holes in his crisp white shirt. There was no blood, though. Bobby kicked the gun from Coyne's hand, then froze. It was *his* gun. The Beretta with the gold accents. He bent over and picked it up, turning it over in his hands, examining it, confused.

The detective reached out and took the gun from him before looking him up and down. "Are you shot? Did he hit you?"

A little light-headed, Bobby looked himself up and down. "No." He pointed at the Beretta. "That's *my* gun. MJ's gun. But it's locked in the safe." He shuffled to the bedroom, retrieved the safe, and returned to the kitchen where he placed it on the counter. His hand shaking, he placed his fingers on the biometric sensor pads and opened it as quickly as he could. The padded imprint where the gun always lay was empty, and one of the three magazines was missing.

Sam placed the Beretta on the counter, awkwardly holstered his own weapon, and took out his phone. Bobby heard Sam call the shooting in, but he didn't catch any of the details as he dropped onto the couch. The blood pounded in his ears and he couldn't tell if it was because he's just thrown a knife into a man's throat, or because another person he cared about had almost been killed, but with *his* gun. His hands shook. He looked for Vinnie, but he was nowhere to be seen. Sam's four gunshots still echoed in Bobby's ears, so he expected Vinnie was wisely hiding somewhere. He sat, numb and in shock, and barely aware there was a body on the floor behind him. Eventually there was another knock at the door. He looked up and winced as Sam opened it, this time revealing two uniformed officers—one man and one woman—and a man in a suit. Sam greeted them and motioned them in.

"Bobby, why don't you take your coffee into your bedroom while we deal with this?"

Bobby nodded and did as Sam suggested, taking his cellphone, too. He closed the door most of the way but left it ajar, needing to be able to hear at least the hum of low conversation out in the living room. He sat on the edge of the bed, part of his mind pacing a circle trying to get around the idea that he'd come so close to dying right there in his own home, while another, calmer part of his mind nodded and agreed that of course Jackson Coyne was behind it all. He couldn't be sure, but he suspected there also had to be a connection leading to Senator Brand. He was the common tentacle that touched on nearly everyone involved.

"But Coyne is too young to have been on the boat." No one answered him, of course, but he had to talk it out. Say the words aloud.

"What's he got to do with all this, other than working at Mitchell's firm? I guess he was an in-house fixer, but why kill Mitchell?" All of a sudden, he needed to hear Stacey's voice. He sat up and called her. It went straight to voice mail. "Hey Stacey, it'sBobby. Just checking..." There was something wrong with the sound on the call. There was an echo, coming from outside the bedroom. He left the room as he spoke into the phone. "I'm just checking in to see how your flight was." He followed the echo and found himself standing next to Sam, looking down at Coyne's body, where the echo of the call came from. "Give me a call when you get a chance. Miss you."

He disconnected the call but stayed where he was. Sam pulled a set of rubber gloves from his jacket pocket, put them on, knelt down to the body and began searching the dead man's pockets. He quickly found the phone they both knew had to be there. He pulled it partway out of the pocket, stood back up with a wince, took a few pictures to record where he found it, then crouched down and retrieved it. "Bobby, can you step into the kitchen and whisper something into your phone, please. Don't make a call, just speak at your phone."

Bobby did so. "Suzy sells sea shells by the sea shore." His voice emanated from the phone in Sam's hand. He rejoined his friend. "What the hell?"

"He's got an app that's linked to your phone."

"Say again?"

"I've seen this app before. With it he knew exactly where your phone was at all times, could activate your microphone to hear everything in the room around you, and could monitor every text and phone call you made."

"Jesus Chr—no wonder he was here so fast. He knew you had the video, was coming here, and that we'd figured out it was him." He looked at Sam's shirt. "You're wearing a bulletproof vest?"

"More like *still* wearing it. I put it on under my shirt for the raid this morning and was going to take it off when I got home."

"Good thing you didn't mention *that* over the phone or he'd have just shot you in the head."

"Ain't that the truth." He crouched down again and used Coyne's thumb to log on to the device. "Give me a second to turn off the security measures on this baby. I don't want to have to visit the morgue every time I need to log on to the thing. I'm hoping this will give us more than a few answers." He tapped at buttons until he was satisfied. He then slipped the phone into an evidence bag he had in his jacket pocket.

"You come prepared. Would a dead man's thumb even work?"

"Not forever, no. And I always carry a pair of gloves and a few evidence bags."

There was a knock on the propped open front door and they turned to see two members of the forensics team, identifiable by their windbreakers with *Westview PD Forensics* stitched on the left side. Behind the officers a small crowd of condo residents was forming but being kept back by the uniformed officer guarding the scene. Sam waved the forensics pair in and turned to Bobby. "Do you want to go back to your nap, or hang around and watch us work?"

He knew he needed to nap, but now that Sam had put the bug of private investigating in his ear, he found he was morbidly curious about the processes involved. "I'll sit and watch, if that's okay."

Sam looked around and pointed at a corner away from Coyne's body. "Of course. Just grab a chair and sit over there, away from blood and brain splatter. An OIS team will be here any minute to start their investigation, since I discharged my firearm, resulting in a death. Standard procedure." He looked down at the knife in Coyne's throat. "Though I probably just sped up what you started. Nice throw."

"Thanks." Out of the corner of his eye he saw Vinnie stroll out of the bedroom, aiming straight for the puddle of blood congealing around Coyne. He hurriedly scooped up the ginger master of the house, tossed him back on the bed, and closed the bedroom door firmly. "I'm pretty sure a cat walking through the scene won't help the investigation."

Sam chuckled. "Not much, no."

Bobby took a chair from the dining room table and sat where Sam had directed him. For the next hour-and-a-half he observed, fielded questions from the Officer Involved Shooting team, and even served coffee and loaf to them all as the process continued.

o0o

By the time Monday rolled around and Bobby stood at the airport's Domestic Arrivals gate with Vinnie in the carrier on his chest, the condo had been professionally cleaned, the calls and texts from Sam checking on him had settled down to one a day, and he'd even made a visit to Rachel in the hospital, where she was due to be released soon. Not wanting to affect Stacey's business conference, he hadn't said a word about the events of the past three days in their daily calls. Some stories had to be told in person.

When she strolled excitedly through the gate with her carry-on in tow and raised an eyebrow at Vinnie before giving Bobby a solid kiss, he smiled and deflected the unspoken question. "It's a long story. I'll tell you on the way home. Your place or mine?"

"Mine, please, for clean clothes and a quick shower. Do we have dinner plans?"

"That'll be up to you, after you hear the long story."

"I'm almost afraid to ask what might have Chef Odini doubting I'd want to dine with him after being away for three whole days."

"And what a trio of days it has been." He linked his arm in hers and led her off to the carpark.

CHAPTER NINETEEN

Bobby considered taking his mother up the Coast Tower for dinner for her birthday on Monday, but Stacey convinced him to have her to the condo for dinner where the two of them would cook together and catch her up on the events without the public around to eavesdrop. Once Bobby had told her about the app on Coyne's phone violating their privacy, she was a lot less keen on chatting in public. She even had Sam bring over a surveillance bug detector with which he swept the entire condo from top to bottom and declared it "clean".

Stacey topped up their guest's wine glass, then placed the decanter on the table and sat. "Mrs. Odini, Bobby said you were on a cruise, recently." Soft jazz played in the background.

"I was. It was a boatload of cranky geriatrics who loved to do nothing more than complain about the service, get drunk, and attack every buffet like it was their last supper."

Bobby joined them, placing a serving of flan down in front of each place. "Come off it, Mom. You loved every minute of it."

His mother took a sip of the wine and smiled slyly. "Not *every* minute, but most of them. In between their bitching and drinking and gorging, there were some really fascinating people there. I made a few friends and will probably be joining them for a cruise later this year. I'm hoping to take Alex. He needs to get back on the water, and I need to spend time with him away from the home."

Bobby lifted his glass in a toast."Here's to buffets and the open sea."

They gently clinked their glasses together and though she took a small sip, his mother placed the glass firmly to one side. "When are you going to tell me what's been eating you, mister? I know you're not nervous about me meeting Stacey, because she's delightful and funny and is going to get you out of your shell... and your kitchen."

"Hardly that, Mom." Bobby took a fortifying sip. "It's just that the whole Chaz Mitchell thing is over."

"It's about time. What happened?"

They each started in on their desserts, Stacey eating in respectful silence. "Well, he was murdered by one of the young lawyers at his firm, who then came after me and MJ's fellow detective, Sam."

"And now he's going to rot in jail, I hope."

"He's going to rot, but not in jail. He's dead."

"Serves him right. Chaz was an arrogant asshole, but he didn't deserve to be murdered. Oh, wait. He ordered Marion's, Alex's, and Rachel's deaths, so yes, he *did* deserve it."

"Fair enough."

"So, the two threats are gone. Excellent. Alex will be happy about that, too. We can all sleep better. Unless...*you* didn't kill him, did you?"

"Actually... I had a part in it. I got him with a knife and Sam shot him, so it was a team effort, I suppose."

"Good for you. How are you dealing with it?"

"It was a shock at first, but knowing we're safe now makes the weight bearable."

"Yes, that can make all the difference in the world. Taking a life isn't easy, but if it's done to protect the ones you love, you try not to lose much sleep over it. You did what you had to do."

Stacey's spoon stopped between her plate and her mouth, and Bobby placed his carefully down, his hand shaking ever so slightly. "Mom, what do you know about killing?"

His mother took a bite of the dessert, savored it, and swallowed slowly. "I admit to nothing, but *theoretically*, if someone, even an estranged family member, threatened to hunt down my family out of some misguided belief that they had abandoned him as a baby, then I suppose I would do what had to be done. *Theoretically*."

Bobby was so overwhelmed that he had no reply. Had his mother just admitted to killing Franco Vetere, her own son? His *mother*? His half-brother had been shot. Where on earth would his mother get a gun... oh crap. His grandfather's. She'd mentioned it. Stacey, pale, eyes wide, glanced over at Bobby. His eyes moist, Bobby nodded.

The three of them continued to eat in silence broken only by the jazz, Vinnie's purring at their feet, and Sophie Odini's occasional exclamations of how delicious the flan was. Bobby had no idea what to do with the information he was sure he now had. He couldn't turn his mother in, of course. He was pretty sure she'd have known not to keep the gun, so there was no actual evidence. If there'd been any witnesses, Sam would likely have mentioned it. Besides, his mother was eighty-three. Maybe dementia had set in.

Was she literally talking theoretically, or did she know exactly what she was doing and being careful not to admit anything. And if she *had* killed Angelo/Franco in order to stop him from hunting down his family, what had she actually done wrong? If she *had* done it, she'd inadvertently taken the vicious hired killer who had butchered her daughter, off the streets. Having helped kill Coyne for trying to kill him and Sam, Bobby certainly understood the lengths a person could go to, to protect loved ones, but *his mother*? Then again, she's woman who tried to cave in her husband's head with a music box while the drunk bastard was smothering her newborn.

It dawned on him that the same resolute determination that would allow his mother to both attack his murderous father and then to actually pull the trigger and put her broken, poisoned son out of his misery like a rabid but loved dog, was what had made MJ such a force of nature, both with her guitar and with her badge. What would his detective daughter have thought about the grandmother who had helped raise her gunning down her own son and dumping his body in the bay? Would she see the life that had been avenged and the lives that had been saved? Or would she see only the crime, the unlawful killing of another human being? All those things ricocheted around in Bobby's head as he ate the dessert like an automaton.

His mother finished her dessert a mouthful before he finished his, and when her spoon made a tiny 'clink' on the plate, he made his decision. He placed his own spoon down, stood, went to his mother, and hugged her where she sat. He offered no words that could be misinterpreted as criticism or praise, he simply hugged her, accepted her. She leaned into the hug. "Thank you, Bobby. I love you, too."

o0o

Sam placed the box of Marion's keepsakes on Bobby's kitchen counter. "Thank you for letting us look through these things. The Feds had a go at them, too, and probably made copies of the photos, but other than the one incriminating photo from the boat, there's not much to help them with any case against Brand."

"But they'll keep digging, I assume." Bobby handed Sam a mug of coffee he'd poured when the concierge announced the detective's arrival.

"Count on it. You've given them a starting place and Vetere's trophy collection will probably give them some juicy stuff, but it's not like they'll share their findings with the likes of us."

"What about the counterfeit bills?"

"That's a whole different story. Except for the bill that your step-father kept, I can't imagine there being anything left of it. Between them, the Secret Service, and the DEA they've probably seen lumps of the ten million show up over the years, but tracing it back to Brand this late on... I wouldn't bet on them linking any of it to him."

"So, he doesn't get charged and gets away with it."

"Maybe, maybe not. It turns out that he is—*was*—Jackson Coyne's uncle on his mother's side, and your bus driver buddy, Rick Plested, was Coyne's godfather and second cousin."

"A real family affair."

"It appears that way."

"I can't get the idea out of my head that Rick has been watching me all these years. He joined Transit around the time Marion was killed. I remember the young rookie coming to Betty's funeral and extending his condolences."

"It would be one way to keep an eye on you, just in case Marion knew anything and told you or someone else in the family."

"That's a seriously crazy *long* game. It would have been easier to just kill the whole family—though I'm glad they didn't." Vinnie hopped up on the counter and threw himself down in front of Bobby. Bobby petted him while sipping his coffee.

"A scorched earth approach would have attracted far more attention than a dead coed in Canada. And we don't even know who 'they' are. Is it Brand? Was it only Mitchell? Could it have been someone in Santacruz's camp?"

"Santacruz's?"

"It's unlikely, but I'm sure they're exploring that avenue as well. If they're going to take down Brand, they can't leave any rocks unturned."

"I know. I'm still trying to get my head around the idea that my baby brother didn't die in infancy but instead grew up to become a psychopathic killer-for-hire."

"Good luck. If it gets too much to deal with, get some professional help. For sure don't lose any sleep over him."

"Not to worry. I'm too busy losing sleep over how Coyne got into the condo and got my gun out of the safe."

"That spy app on his phone was pretty sophisticated. He may have heard you mention the safe key, and maybe you mumbled the door alarm code while you were entering it. I've caught myself doing that at home a few times."

"It scares the crap out of me that such an app even exists, Sam. I wouldn't even know where to look for such a thing."

"Believe it or not, the app store. $29.99."

"*Seriously?*"

"Seriously. It's sold for parents to keep an eye on their children and employers to keep an eye on their employees, with approval from said employees."

"That's crazy." He sipped. "So, what's next for you?"

"Well, Vetere's murder is still unsolved. I'll keep digging, but it's way down my priority list with four other more recent murders to solve, including a pair of tourists down near the fish market."

"They won't just blame Vetere's on Coyne and close the file?" He tried to make the question sound natural and casual, but he could only think of his mother.

"I like Coyne for it, too, but without strong evidence, the case stays open. The Feds will probably dig into it, too, but only if to see if they can link Vetere's murder to Brand or one of their other cases. Your brother was one nasty piece of work, and while no cop likes to leave a case unsolved, none of us are shedding tears over him. I personally sleep better at night knowing there's one less hired gun on the streets of Westview. I won't waste much time digging into that one unless new evidence pops up." He got quiet and squinted at Bobby, studying him closely. "I know I've encouraged you to maybe get your PI license, Bobby, but the Vetere case is one dragon I don't want you poking. Nothing good can come of you looking into the death of a hit man, even if he was your brother."

Bobby nearly laughed out loud and it took great will to keep his smile small and casual. "Not a problem, Sam. Whatever I decide about detecting, it won't be into that case. My brother is dead. May that dragon sleep forever."

o0o

Bobby felt a tap on his shoulder and looked to his left. Chef Peter's assistant, Skylah, smiled at him and gave him a thumbs up. Out on the completely functional kitchen set Chef leaned back on the counter with a glass of wine in one hand and a whisk in the other. "Folks, I promised you a special guest this week and it's time for me to deliver. Normally I would tell you all about this terrific guest chef before I bring him out, but I don't want his incredible story to distract you from the amazing recipe he's going to teach us. Set your PVR because this is one pasta sauce you don't want to miss. Ladies and gentlemen, connoisseurs of palate-teasing and olfactory amazement, please welcome my friend and a true maestro in the kitchen, Bobby Odini!"

The audience of sixty hammered out a thunderous ovation and Bobby's heart seemed to skip a few beats. Despite the warmth of the studio, he was in a cold sweat and found it hard to breathe. Skylah gave him a little nudge in the small of his back to one side of his wireless microphone power pack, and the retired bus driver swallowed, dried his palms on his apron, ignored the tightness in his chest and nausea caused by nerves, and stepped out from behind the curtain, into the bright lights. That's when his world went black and the last things he heard were gasps and a scream as he stumbled, went down on his knees, and hit the floor.

o0o

Bobby pushed himself a little higher in the hospital bed, trying to get comfortable despite the IV in his arm and the wires taped to his chest. Stacey adjusted the pillow behind his back as Bobby questioned the doctor. "A heart attack?"

The doctor looked down at the open file folder in her hands. "A myocardial infarction, to be precise. And it wasn't your first one. Your bloodwork from last week indicates that you've had one other, a minor one, probably recently. You don't remember anything like what happened this morning happening before?"

Bobby looked out the window at the setting sun, trying to focus and remember. "Not really?" He looked back at the doctor and shrugged. "I mean, I felt some shortness of breath, tightness in my chest, and got a little sweaty while I was hiking in the mountains in Canada a while back, but that was because I'm out of shape and was over a mile up in elevation." His breath caught. "Oh, crap. I had a heart attack, didn't I?"

"It would appear so. There's been a little damage to your heart, but the prognosis is good."

"But there *is* damage."

"Yes. We've got you on clot busters and heparin and I've got you scheduled for an angioplasty first thing in the morning, to open a clogged artery. After the angioplasty we'll chat about cardiac rehabilitation, which will focus on exercise, diet, and stress management, with the goal of gradually getting you back to your regular activities."

"I'm game for whatever works, doctor." He squeezed Stacey's hand. "I still have a few things left on my bucket list."

"Good. Excellent. I have another appointment, but if you need anything, press the alarm button and a nurse will respond immediately. I'd suggest you take it easy and have a nap, but you have a visitor. He's only asked for a minute, and although he's not a member of your family, I'm bending the rules for him because I'm such a big fan."

"Thank you." A fan?

"Of course." The doctor left, holding the dividing curtain back long enough for Chef Peter to step into the small space.

The big man's eyes were moist and his hands shook when he took Bobby's free one in his own. "You scared the hell out of me, my friend. Hi Stacey. Bobby, your diagnosis and treatment and whatever are none of my business, but I wanted to stop in and check on you."

"Thank you, Chef. It was a heart attack. I'll be okay, with time and effort. I'm sorry I ruined the show."

Despite the situation and location, the chef laughed warmly and heartily. "You have a heart attack and collapse while doing me a favor and appearing on my show, and *you're* apologizing? Why am I not surprised? You, my friend, are a good man. We need more of you in the world."

"Hopefully with better tickers than I've got."

"Agreed. Now, anything you need or I can do, let me know. Since you collapsed on our stage, while doing our show, our insurance is taking care of everything. When you're recovered and ready, we can give the show another go, if you still want to."

"I *want* to, of course, but I won't know more about the time frame for a few days at least."

"There is absolutely no rush. It's your call."

"Thanks."

Chef gave Bobby's arm a squeeze. "I'd better go before they kick me out. Anything you need, call. Either of you. Even if you just want to chat."

Stacey stood and gave Chef a hug. "Thank you, Peter." Her voice cracked and Bobby realized she'd been so quiet because she was likely close to tears.

Chef left and Stacey returned to Bobby's side, taking his hands in hers, again. "You're going to be fine. I'm going to make sure of it. That great big heart of yours is strong and it will recover and we'll get you back cooking and walking Vinnie and making me laugh, soon."

"I know. Thank you." He lifted a hand to his lips and kissed her knuckles. "I guess this is the wrong time to ask what you think of me getting my Private Investigator license."

"*Bobby Odini!* Seriously?"

"Seriously."

SPECIAL THANKS

Suzy Vadori

Stacey Kondla

Shannon Allen

Sam Hiyate

Lisa Dutton

Ann Cooney

Deborah Easson

Maria Dueck Warner

Virginia O'Dine

The VanMackelberghs: Darren, Maureen, Jordyn, and Camryn

Detective T. K.

Mavourneen Mooney

The Town of Banff

Amalgamated Transit Union Local 583

Calgary Transit

&

Canadian Snowboard Cross Double-Bronze-Medal Olympian,
Meryeta O'Dine, and the Italian sportscaster who called her
"Marionette Odini" on air and got this whole idea started in my head.

ABOUT THE AUTHOR

According to CBC Radio, Tim Reynolds is
"Canada's modern-day Aesop".
That's great praise he struggles to live up to, but what he will admit to is
being a prize-winning, award-nominated Canadian with stories to tell.

Based out of Calgary, Alberta, Tim grew up in Toronto, earning first a
B.A. and then a B.Ed. from the University of Western Ontario.

He currently remains trapped in his house, a willing indentured servant
to his animals.

Find out what Tim is working on now at:
www.TGMReynolds.com

ALSO BY TIM REYNOLDS

Stand Up & Succeed (self-help)
The Broken Shield (an urban fantasy)
The Death of God & Other (short) *Stories*
Waking Anastasia (a ghostly novel about love)
The Sisterhood of the Black Dragonfly (a YA fantasy)
The Gravity of Guilt (a sci-fi thriller)
She Runs with Wolves, He Sits with Kittens (a romantic comedy)
Solo by Gaslight (a psychological suspense)